$\mathcal{B}$eau

ALISON CHAFFIN HIGSON

Copyright © 2014 Alison Chaffin Higson
HFCA Publishing House
All rights reserved.

This book is a written act of fiction. The names, characters, places, and incidents are products of the writer's imagination or have been used fictitiously and are not to be construed as real. Any resemblance to persons, living or dead, actual events, locales or organizations is entirely coincidental.

All rights reserved. With the exception of quotes used in reviews, this book may not be reproduced or used in whole or in part by any means existing without written permission from the author.

ISBN-13: 978-1499524741

Dedication

In memory of my father-in-law, who had three great loves:

His wife, his family and fishing.

He probably never so much as picked up a romance novel, but would be chuffed to bits to have one dedicated to him.

Ronald James Higson
6 August 1937 To 9 May 2009

Fisherman's Prayer
God grant that I may live to fish
For another shining day
But when my final cast is made
I then most humbly pray
When nestled in your landing net
As I lay peacefully asleep
You'll smile at me and judge
That I'm good enough to keep

Author, Unknown

Chapter 1

"Auntie Mack, are we there yet?" Mack glanced back to her six-year-old nephew, Lucas, through the mirror. "No, we're not there yet. Asking me every two seconds isn't going to get us there any quicker."

Lucas had asked this question every ten minutes or so, since they'd left Boston. The first time had been as soon as she'd turned the corner from her apartment building.

Last night, Lucas' parents had dropped him off at Mack's place, so they could get an early start in the morning, but Lucas had other ideas! They had both fallen asleep on Mack's bed watching a movie with a bowl of popcorn between them. When they'd woken up Mack had been thankful he didn't have an upset stomach.

She'd been driving for just over an hour, traveling up the coast to Rose Cottage. The cottage in Maine she'd rented for the summer so she could get a breather from the craziness she called work, and her matchmaking parents. Despite loving them, she couldn't stand the endless dates they threw at her. She wouldn't mind, but they were all the same age as her parents, and lived in the same retirement village.

It wasn't as though she never dated, because she did. For

some reason, she either ended up going out on a date with someone who didn't know how to have fun, or with someone, like her last date, who spent the whole time eyeing up anyone wearing a skirt! How the hell she managed to pick these kinds of guys, she'd never know. Her mother had then decided to take matters into her own hands, and started to arrange blind dates for her – much to Mack's dismay.

She used to have a great time going out with her sister, Melinda. They used to meet some gorgeous guys, but unfortunately, they were only interested in one thing, and Mack didn't do one-night stands. That, of course, all stopped when Melinda married Daniel, and that's when a girl's night out started to get few and far between. Especially after Lucas came along.

Mack loved Lucas dearly, and spent as much time as possible with him. He could be very mischievous, if he wasn't watched all the time. His parents were flying to Europe later in the day, and Lucas had apparently wanted to spend the time with his Auntie Mack, who could never say no. She always told herself to stop spoiling him, but so far, her little pep talks hadn't worked.

As she drove to Cape Elizabeth, she had a car full of clothes, toys, and books, not to mention food. It was with relief to discover Lucas could do without his pet snake, Archie. Mack didn't do snakes, spiders, or frogs; they just frightened the life out of her.

She wasn't quite sure how she would have handled him wanting to bring Archie, because there was no way a snake was going on vacation with them. In fact, Melinda had given Lucas the option of no snake and Auntie Mack, or snake and grandparents.

"Are you sure we're not nearly there yet?" Lucas asked again, fidgeting in the backseat.

She sighed. "Lucas, we'll be there soon. Why don't you read one of your books?"

"Auntie Mack, my books are boring. Can I read one of yours?" He asked all excitedly.

"My books are for adults, and they have no pictures in them." She was thankful that her books were packed in the trunk so Lucas couldn't go rooting around for them.

"But Daddy told Mommy that she would learn a lot if she read the type of books you read, instead of her boring magazines. I like to learn," Lucas replied with his 'cute' face, knowing his Auntie Mack had never been able to withhold anything from him when he gave her 'that' look. He obviously hoped she would give in and let him have a look through her books.

She started to laugh, as well as blush, and wondered just what type of books Daniel thought she read. "They're still adult-only books, Lucas. If you're bored with yours, why don't I buy you some new ones when we get there?"

"As soon as we get there, do you promise?" Lucas tossed his current books onto the floor.

"We'll check the shops out in a day or two." With a quick glance through the mirror, she saw Lucas' face start to fall. "But if you're good until then, I'll buy you one extra book, maybe an atlas, then you can keep track of where your parents are staying in Europe."

Lucas had a 'thinking face' this time. "That would be cool."

"Okay... now that's the end of that. Why don't you have a nap? I'll wake you when we get there. That way, the time will pass very quickly for you."

Eventually, Mack pulled up outside Rose Cottage and turned the engine off. The quiet and stillness must have woken Lucas, because one minute he was asleep, and the next, he shot up in his seat and banged the side of his head against the window. "You all right, Lucas?"

He rubbed his head. "I think so. Are we there yet?"

"Yes, we are, thank goodness! Let's stretch our legs. In fact, I think I can see Mr. Degan over there, on his way to the cottage." Mack pointed to the left.

She climbed out of the car and opened the back door for Lucas. He jumped out and ran around her excitedly in circles, before he ran to meet Mr. Degan.

As she watched him run towards Mr. Degan, she suddenly thought better of it, as there was no telling what would come out of Lucas' mouth. She jogged over to them. "Mr. Degan," Mack said, holding her hand out. "I'm Mackenzie Harper, and this is my nephew, Lucas Cartwright."

"You like fishing?" Mr. Degan asked as he released her hand.

"Err, not really," she replied, thinking there was no way on earth she was going anywhere near maggots.

"I wasn't talking to you, young woman. I was talking to this here imp." Mr. Degan pointed at Lucas.

Lucas was jumping up and down like an excited puppy.

"I've never been fishing, but Daddy says you have to try everything once."

"Mmm, there are some big suckers in the river. I was thinking I could use you as bait?"

Lucas, looked confused while Mack's eyes nearly popped out of her head. "Mr. Degan, I don't…."

"Calm yourself. I'm only pulling your leg. Please, call me Thomas. I may be eighty, but hearing you say Mr. Degan still has me looking for my father."

Mack smiled and decided it was probably a good idea to change the subject. "Okay. Do you have the keys?"

"No need," Thomas replied. "The door's open." He walked to the cottage with Lucas, who placed his hand into his. Mack didn't really know how to take Mr. Thomas Degan.

Mack caught up to them in the kitchen, which was huge. Not at all like she had imagined when she read the description of the cottage online. But it was a nice, pleasant surprise.

She looked over at Thomas. "Have you always lived around here?"

He scratched his chin, appearing deep in thought. "My parents settled in this country around 1924, sailing from Ireland. They went to New York first, but moved here into Rose Cottage in 1927. Of course back then, and as a child growing up, it was known as 'Degan House'. They gave their place a name, like the houses had back in Ireland."

"Wow! Perhaps you could spare some time and tell me more about your parents? Maybe come over for coffee and homemade cake?" Mack hoped the food offering would tempt Thomas, especially since she saw him frown, and guessed he was about to refuse.

He took his cap off. "Maybe."

Thomas seemed like a nice enough old man, especially since he didn't seem to mind Lucas hovering. In fact, Lucas had made a new friend, by the look of things.

"Thomas, I have pizza in the cooler, and there's plenty, if you'd like to join us?"

As Thomas sat at the kitchen table, Lucas begged him to stay, as he climbed up onto his lap. "Please stay, Mr. Degan."

"Don't mind if I do," Thomas answered, grinning at Mack. "I'll keep this little jumping bean occupied while you unload, if you like."

"That would be great, thanks. We don't have too much with us, really, so it shouldn't take that long."

Outside, she just stood and looked around her, noticing for the first time, the clear view to the ocean and the cliffs with the lighthouse perched on the edge of the headland. The cottage was bordered by exploding colors of beautiful and fragrant plants, some even climbing the gazebo wall, others covering the ground in various displays of summer. It looked very pretty. She hoped there would be a bench inside, so she could sit sheltered from the sun to keep an eye on Lucas while he played and she read or just relaxed with a cup of coffee.

There was also a small cottage sitting alongside their own, but it looked empty. If she remembered correctly, it was also available as a summer rental.

Mack looked up to the crystal blue sky and took a deep breath of fresh salt air. With relief, she didn't inhale a lungful of car fumes in the process, like she did most days in the city. Not only did everything smell fresh, it was so blissfully quiet.

No car horns and no noisy neighbors. It was simply paradise to Mack.

She began emptying the car, taking Lucas' toys, their clothes, books and food into the quaint cottage.

The last trip inside was with the food. It was only after she'd put it away in the cupboards and refrigerator, that it dawned on her how quiet everything was. Lucas was six. He didn't do quiet.

Mack listened and heard voices upstairs. With the lid snapped on the cooler ready to throw back into the car, she collected a box of clothes from the bottom of the stairs and headed up. After quickly placing the box in what she presumed to be the master bedroom, Mack opened one of the doors and found them both sitting down on one of the twin beds in the room, while Thomas read, what looked to be a very old comic, to Lucas.

Thomas caught sight of Mack and waved the comic up in the air. "Lucas found it underneath the closet, along with some spiders." He chuckled.

Mack looked nervously around her. "Spiders?" she questioned a laughing Thomas and Lucas.

"I think I'll leave you two alone for now. I'll give you a shout when dinner's ready." She was still looking for spiders as she shut the door and could hear Thomas and Lucas laughing.

God, she was such a wimp!

"Thomas! Lucas! Dinner is ready. Please wash up," Mack shouted from downstairs.

After fiddling about with the aging, but clean oven, she finally produced a nicely warmed pizza.

Mack sliced the pizza into small, evenly sized triangles, arranging them on a serving plate. She placed the pizza alongside the potato salad and coleslaw on the table, just as Thomas and Lucas appeared.

"Hi, take a seat. What would you like to drink, Thomas?"

"Water's fine," he replied while helping himself to pizza and potato salad.

After she'd poured everyone a glass of water, Mack finally sat down, joining the two obviously hungry men.

"So, you folks always lived in Boston?" Thomas asked with a mouth full of pizza.

"Yes. Born and bred there, Roslindale specifically."

Lucas turned and grinned at his Auntie Mack before he turned back to Thomas. "She's a school teacher and frightens all the kids in the class," he blurted out.

"Lucas, don't talk with your mouth full, please."

"You and Mr. Degan just did," Lucas replied indignantly.

"Well, Mr. Degan and I are very naughty then, so you behave."

"Is she always this bossy?" Thomas asked, grinning back at Mack.

Lucas shoveled more food into his mouth. "You really have no idea. You should be thankful she isn't your auntie."

"Hey, I can always take you back, and you can stay with your grandparents," Mack replied sternly, while trying not to laugh.

"No way. They are old and no fun. All they want to do all day is play cards." When he noticed the look on his Auntie Mack's face, he added, "and strip poker."

Mack choked on her drink. "They do no such thing, young man. Well, maybe cards." She glanced across to Thomas, who was trying to eat without laughing.

Lucas was so funny sometimes with the things he came out with. She could see why Daniel always watched what he said around Lucas. Melinda probably wasn't as careful, and their mother obviously wasn't careful at all. Good grief, strip poker!

The rest of the meal was eaten in comfortable silence, and before she knew it, Thomas had cleared the table and started to fill the sink with water and dishwashing liquid.

"Thomas, you don't need to do that." Mack stood up to help him.

"I know I don't need to do this, but I want to. Why don't you get some coffee going?" He winked at her.

With a laugh, she turned to do his bidding. While Mack waited for the coffee to brew, she followed Lucas into the sitting room and switched the Wii on for him. He was allowed thirty minutes, each evening before bed.

With the dishes all washed and dried, she joined Thomas at the kitchen table to drink coffee. She hoped he would tell her about his past. She really enjoyed hearing about people's lives in the early 1900's and before that. It was why she'd chosen to teach history.

"Thomas, would you mind telling me something about your parents? What were they like? What they did?" She grinned at Thomas, who looked as though he'd never been asked before. "Sorry, I find family history rather interesting."

He frowned, gazing into his mug of coffee. "Okay, my parents, hmm. Well, my mother was named Josephine, and my father was named Thomas. They were both born in Delgany in County Wicklow in 1899, and sailed for America in the early 1920's on the RMS *Mauretania* from Southampton to New York."

"I've always wanted to visit Ireland, but it would mean a rather long flight, and I don't like to fly. Have you ever been, Thomas? You must still have family over there?"

"I think there is family over there, but I wouldn't know them, having never had any contact with them. I don't think my father or mother stayed in touch with family when they moved here."

"What did your parents do for work?" Mack inquired.

"When they arrived, my father was offered a good position with a law firm in Portland. The firm paid well, and in 1927, they moved here. They rented this cottage first, and then bought it a few years later. My mother never worked, even during the Depression, and just enjoyed visiting friends and drinking tea. My father worked all the time. He had one hell of a temper. He used to scare the crap out of me."

They took a sip of their drinks. "Were you their only child?" Mack asked, fascinated.

Thomas appeared lost in thought. "No. I had a brother named Charlie. He died towards the end of the Second World War, and a sister.... she died a few years later. My mother died of a heart condition in 1951, and my father in 1964. I hadn't spoken to my father for years when he died. He left everything to me. That's when I changed the name of the cottage." He sighed and Mack could tell that he'd had enough for one night.

"Thank you for telling me about your family. You have a very good memory for dates."

"I've always been good with figures," he replied.

Not long after, Mack announced that it was time for Lucas to have a bath before bed. Lucas moaned and groaned all the way up the stairs. Mack promised him that Thomas would be there in the morning for breakfast, so Lucas flew into the bathroom at hearing that.

Chapter 2

"Auntie Mack, Auntie Mack, it's time to get up!" Lucas shouted as he ran into Mack's bedroom and dived onto the bed. "Come on, Auntie, you have to wake up. The birds told me it's time for breakfast." He paused for breath. "They want pancakes and ketchup!"

Mack slowly opened her eyes and moved the duvet away from her face, took one look at her very excited nephew and slowly registered hearing pancakes and ketchup in the same sentence.

"Lucas, you don't eat pancakes and ketchup together. That's just yuk." She glanced towards the clock on the side table and rubbed her eyes. She really needed glasses, because she was sure the clock read not much past five. She rubbed her eyes again. "Oh my God, Lucas, it's only ten past five in the morning... nobody gets up at this time." She popped her head back down onto the pillow, took hold of Lucas and helped get him under the covers with her. "Now go back to sleep... please?"

"What time can I get up?" Lucas asked, already half-asleep.

"I'll wake you up in a couple of hours." She turned her head to look at him, only to find he was already fast asleep.

Mack finally woke for the day at eight in the morning, to the sun streaming through the curtains. Lucas was still asleep, curled into her side. She just lay there, listening to the peace and quiet, that would only last as long as Lucas slept.

Sliding quietly out of bed, so as not to wake him, she collected her clothes on the way to the bathroom, placing them on the chair in the corner while she showered. Once finished, she headed back into the bedroom, in time to watch Lucas wake up.

"Is it time to get up now?"

"Yes, it is. Come on, let's get you washed and dressed, then I'll make you pancakes with syrup." Mack grinned, as she caught a leaping Lucas in her arms. She swung him around before carrying him through to his room and the bathroom.

"Are you really, really sure I can't have ketchup with my pancakes?" Lucas had a rather angelic look on his face.

"Lucas, you do not put ketchup on pancakes. It was made to go on fries, which is why they made syrup, to go on pancakes."

While she had a glaring match with him, Mack placed the syrup to the side of his plate, along with a glass of chocolate milk.

"Wow, chocolate milk! Okay, syrup is good."

She had to turn away so Lucas wouldn't see her smiling.

Finally, taking her own seat, she finally found herself

waking up as she drank her first, delicious coffee of the day.

After breakfast, she followed Lucas into the sitting room and switched the Wii on for him to play for a while.

As she thought about the sorts of books she enjoyed reading, a blush warmed her cheeks. Mack wasn't sure what Daniel had been thinking, unless he had spotted Seduce by Lexi Buchanan, which had been sticking out of her purse once, a few weeks before.

Mack heard a brief knock on the door and was just about to answer, when Thomas walked in. "Morning, Miss Mackenzie. Hope you had a good night's rest."

"I did, thank you." She'd just finished speaking, when Lucas ran in from the sitting room, straight to Thomas, who bent down and gave him a big hug.

"I was wondering if I could take the kid for a couple of hours?" Thomas asked and pulled a chair out at the table, before sitting down.

"Would you like coffee?" she asked.

He nodded, removing his cap.

Mack poured a cup of coffee for them both, and joined him at the table. "What do you have planned today?" she asked.

"I was thinking that I have a lot of those comics, like we were reading yesterday, in a box in the garage. I thought maybe Lucas could help bring them into the house so we can have a look through them together."

"What a lovely idea. Thank you for asking him, Thomas. By the look of things, Lucas would love that." She burst out laughing, due to Lucas' rather exuberant reaction.

"I'll just go wash up again. Be back in a minute." Lucas

bounded upstairs to the bathroom.

After watching Lucas retreat, she turned back towards Thomas. "Thank you for telling me about your family last night. I really enjoyed listening. I just hope you didn't think I was being nosy."

"It's okay. I haven't really spoken about them before to be honest, and I quite enjoyed sitting here drinking coffee while I talked about them with you."

"I'm glad. I was slightly worried after you left, in case talking about them had upset you."

He shook his head. "It was a long time ago. I was fine."

"Okay then, now about Lucas. Are you sure you don't mind having him? He can be a handful." Mack frowned. She was a lot younger than Thomas, and Lucas could probably tire an elephant out, with the amount of energy he seemed to have.

"Don't worry yourself. If there's a problem, I have your cell number, and I only live five minutes down the footpath."

When Lucas reappeared, Thomas stood up from the table and took hold of his hand. "Bye, Auntie Mack."

Mack smiled. "Bye, Lucas. You behave yourself if you want any chance of being invited back."

Lucas grinned. "I will."

"See you, Thomas. And thank you again." She watched them walk off down the footpath, hand in hand. They looked good together. She really wished she had her camera nearby, just to capture the image.

"Mr. Degan," Lucas asked. "How old are these comics?

There's a lot of dust?" He started sneezing.

Thomas couldn't help but laugh and cough at the same time. "I've had these since I was a youngster. I started buying them with my allowance in 1942, and bought them for about five years, I think." He frowned. "Call me Thomas, okay?" He didn't understand why parents insisted on children calling adults Mr. and Mrs. It drove him crazy and always had. As a child, he would push his mother's buttons and call one of her friends by their Christian name, and then act shocked, as though it was a slip of the tongue. It used to embarrass his mother something wicked. She eventually stopped taking him with her, which of course was what he'd intended.

"Okay. Can I have a look inside this one, please?" Lucas asked, waving around a rather gruesome covered comic.

"That's the Halloween edition. Take a seat, and I'll bring you some milk and cookies."

"Yummy." Then he remembered his manners. "Thank you."

Thomas headed into the kitchen, trying to remember the last time he'd had so much fun, and couldn't. His wife, Janet, died when they were both fifty-six. That was twenty-four years ago. They hadn't been blessed with children of their own. Janet had been an only child, and both of Thomas' siblings had died years before. So, he had no nieces or nephews, just children of friends, who he'd become an honorary uncle to over the years.

It had really been too long since his house had a child inside.

Mack was back downstairs after she'd finished emptying the boxes of clothes and books. She hadn't realized just how many of her books she'd brought with her. They were now in neat piles on the top shelf of the closet, in the hope that Lucas couldn't reach them.

With the boxes dismantled, she decided to store them up on top of the kitchen cabinets. Dragging a chair over to the kitchen counter, she climbed up, hoping there were no spiders. Reaching up to place the flattened boxes on top, she noticed what looked to be a book at the far end.

Mack made sure the boxes were safely stored before she walked along the counter top and reached for the book, thanking God when no spiders accompanied it.

Her feet were planted firmly back on the kitchen floor as she grabbed a cloth to wipe the thick covering of dust from the book.

Due to her love of all things historic, her skin tingled as she held the long forgotten tome. This one looked really old, especially with all the dust. It must have been up there a long time. Mack stroked the front of the soft, leather bound book, before peeling it open to the first page...

This is the diary of a Rose
March 4, 1947

"Oh, my." Mack lowered herself onto a kitchen chair. Stunned. The diary was...sixty-six years old, and who was Rose? Why was her diary on top of the kitchen cabinets? Mack could hardly contain her curiosity.

"Auntie Mack, I'm home!" Lucas ran into the kitchen.

Mack tried to calm herself. Her heart was beating like a freight train with excitement at what she'd found. She certainly didn't want Lucas getting wind of what she had; otherwise he would be searching high and low for it, to read himself.

Thomas walked into the kitchen, took one look at her, noticed the book in her hand, and looked shocked, as if he recognized the object in her hands.

"Do you know anything about this book, Thomas? It says *'this is the diary of a Rose',* and it's dated 1947." Mack waited for his response. "Thomas, are you feeling all right?" she asked, going over to him.

"Yes, yes, fine. I need to get home." He started to move towards the door.

"But isn't this yours? After all, it's your family's cottage."

Thomas turned back around to look at her. "It's okay, you found it, so read it first, and then pass it on to me to read. Have a good evening."

Thomas was gone, just like that.

Later, after she checked on Lucas to make sure he was asleep, Mack headed downstairs to make a cup of hot chocolate, having already showered and changed into her pajamas.

After an exhausting dinner, and an amusing evening spent entertaining Lucas, all she wanted to do was climb into bed and read the diary she'd found.

Sipping the hot chocolate, she headed back upstairs to the bedroom, and switched on the lamp. She kept her door open slightly to listen for Lucas and then picked up the diary before settling down into bed, turning it to the first page.

Chapter 3

This is the diary of a Rose!

March 4, 1947
My name is Rose and I am 19 years old.

This is my first diary. After the events of yesterday, I have decided I must keep one.

Yesterday was a very exciting day in Cape Elizabeth and in my life, because I met the most handsome man....

I worked in the town library, and today I was in the history section dusting the shelves and the books of all things. It really was the worst job Mr. Young, my boss, could give anyone, and for some reason he seemed to like giving it to me.

At the nine mark, my brother JT nearly knocked me off my ladder, as he came running around the corner. He was so out of breath that I started to panic. "JT, what is it? Is everyone all right?" I asked.

"Sis, will you take me to watch the rescue at sea?"

"What on earth are you talking about?" JT had been

known to spin a yarn now and again.

"Walt said a collier ship has gone aground just past the Cape because of the storm. Please, will you take me?"

I would tell Mr. Young a little white lie, it wasn't as though I was busy, and the dust would still be there tomorrow. That decided, I took JT by the hand and briefly left him with Emma while I went in search of Mr. Young to tell him I was sick with a 'female' problem.

Not long after, I walked out of his office and couldn't help but smile as he reacted as I thought he would. He turned bright red and plopped down onto his chair. He probably hoped I wasn't about to divulge any further detail.

We walked alongside each other as we, like most of the town, headed toward the cliffs.

As we approached, we could hear everyone cheering. It sounded more like a party rather than a rescue.

Sarah was standing not too far away with her older sister, so we walked over to them, which was getting rather difficult with JT trying to pull me in a different direction.

"Sis, I want to go over there to Walt and Levi," JT said, tugging on my hand for the umpteenth time.

"Let me go and talk to Sarah first to find out what's going on. Then I'll take you over there, okay?"

I ignored JT while he moaned and grumbled about why he always had to do what the grownups told him to do.

"Sarah, what's happening here?" I asked after we finished hugging. Sarah was the friendliest of people and always 'hugged'. She used to make me feel uncomfortable, but after a while I enjoyed the familiarity.

"They're rescuing crew members at the moment, and

whenever they bring them safely to shore, everyone cheers."

"I wonder if they need help with anything," I said, only to have Sarah's sister scowl at me. Miss prim-and-proper Matilda.

Finally, after about ten minutes of making polite conversation, I let JT steer me towards Levi and Walt, his two best friends, and on more than one occasion, partners in crime.

There was still a bit of a chill in the air, so I kept moving around to keep the chill at bay while trying to keep my eye on JT. There was enough commotion, without JT and his friends causing any more trouble.

When I looked around, not too far away, in the distance, was a really tall handsome man, who was looking straight at me. I couldn't move, he had me hypnotized. Wow! I had never felt anything like that before. I was frozen to the spot. When he started to walk towards me, my heart started to flutter madly in my chest.

As he stood before me, all tall, dark and mysterious, he reminded me of the actor Gregory Peck, but had a more muscular build, I thought.

"Hello. I haven't seen you before," he said to me.

I was still trying to get my mouth to work and just about managed to croak out, "I've been sick." What an idiot. I had the most handsome man I'd ever seen standing in front of me and all that came out of my mouth was 'I've been sick'!

I came back to my senses, and held my hand out to him. "I'm Rose."

He took hold of my hand, I felt as though I'd been hit by lightning and if the widening of his eyes was anything to go by, he'd felt it too.

He cleared his throat. "Jacob Evans. I only moved to Cape Elizabeth about a month ago. Do you live around here?" he asked, his eyes not leaving mine.

"Not too far away, near the beach. I work in town at the library."

He was still holding my hand when JT came running over. "Sis?" He looked between the two of us. "What's going on? Why are you talking to him?" he asked, pointing at Jacob. "You're supposed to be marrying Richard, you can't talk to him."

I blushed at JT's impetuous remark. He was fourteen, and I really wished I could shut him up. I really hated him right now, especially mentioning Richard. Ugh.

I quickly looked up at Jacob. He looked sad as he released my hand and took a step back from me.

"Rose, come on," JT said, whose impatience was really starting to irritate me.

"I better go with him. I hope to see you again," I said, as JT finally succeeded in dragging me away.

"I hope so." The last words he spoke to me at the time would come true. I was a very determined young woman, so I would make sure to see him again.

Before I lost sight of him completely, I glanced back to look at Jacob, only to find him watching me walk away from him. My heart had yet to stop its rapid beating. Such a feeling was entirely new to me.

"Sis, you shouldn't be talking to strange men when you're marrying Richard."

"JT, I am not marrying Richard now, or ever, and one

day Mother and Father will realize that."

After dinner, my best friend Jayne called around to the house. I dragged her around the side to sit in the garden. I didn't want anyone overhearing what I had to tell her. But by the end of the evening, I wish I'd kept it to myself, as she told me I was being stupid. That no one could be infatuated with someone they had only just met!

March 8, 1947
Richard came calling today....

It had been four days since I'd seen Jacob. Every time I walked through town, I found myself looking for him. Why didn't I ask him where he worked? I told him I worked at the library, but perhaps he didn't want to see me, which distressed me more than it ought.

While I'd been spending my time dreaming about Jacob, my mother had been filling my mind with all things Richard. Richard was the only child of Bernard and Evelyn, who just so happened to own the local newspaper, a hotel in Boston, and a few other local businesses. So, of course he was a great catch. Mother didn't seem to understand. I wanted to marry for love not money.

Richard was a really good-looking man; tall, blonde hair with blue eyes, who had more interest in tinkering with cars than he did me, or anyone else for that matter. I actually found him boring. On the two dates I'd been on with him, I couldn't wait to get back home. I'd only agreed to go on them to stop my parents from bothering me about him.

I was lying in the hammock in the garden trying to hide.

Mother had allergies for about everything you could get an allergy for, so despite her love of the garden, she never actually went into it. She certainly wouldn't risk going all blotchy. At least, I hoped she wouldn't.

"Rose, you in here?"

"Richard." He very nearly had me falling out of the hammock. "What are you doing here?"

"I've come to see you, isn't it obvious?"

Why did that reply make me feel nervous?

He helped me out of the hammock and led me over to the bench inside the newly built gazebo.

"How have you been, Rose?" he asked me rather nervously.

"I'm fine now. Thank you for asking. How are you?" I really hated polite conversation.

"Good, good." He started to pace back and forth in front of me.

"Richard. Please stop. You're making me dizzy. Whatever is the matter?"

He stopped pacing and said one word to me. "Marriage."

When I heard what he said, I shot up off the bench and stood in front of him. "Please do not ask me to marry you! We don't even know each other," I begged.

"It's what our parents want." He moved away from me and was standing, looking out to sea, obviously deep in thought.

"Richard, do you love me?" I stood to the side of him, awaiting his reply.

He looked at me. "No."

I sighed in relief. "I don't love you either, and when I

marry, it will be for love, and not because of our parents. That's what you should want as well. How do you expect to be happy if you're not in love with your wife?"

He took my hand and pulled me down beside him onto the bench. "Oh Rose, thank you for being so frank with me. I agree with you. I'm not interested in settling down in marriage just yet. In fact, perhaps its time I start leading my own life, rather than being dictated to all the time. I would dearly value your friendship though."

I smiled up at him. "Yes, that would be great."

Chapter 4

Walking to the beach the following morning, Lucas had insisted on going via Thomas' cottage, to see if he wanted to go with them. Mack tried to talk him out of it, but Thomas was his new friend, and had to be invited.

Lucas ran off ahead of Mack once Thomas' cottage came in to view. She just hoped Lucas didn't badger him. Once Lucas got a bee in his bonnet, it was difficult to bring him around to something else.

Mack climbed the four steps to the porch where Thomas and Lucas were sitting. "Morning, Thomas. Sorry to barge in on your morning, but I'm afraid Lucas has something to ask you."

He put his head back and laughed. "Oh, I know that." Then he had a twinkle in his eye. "Lucas asked me if I wanted to come to the beach with him to watch you," he coughed, "skinny dipping."

Mack had just taken a sip of her water, which ended up down her top. "He never did?" She looked at Thomas, then at Lucas, who looked rather angelic. "Did he?"

Thomas nodded his head.

She narrowed her eyes. "Lucas Cartwright!"

"Granny goes skinny dipping," Lucas said in his

defense.

Mack quickly glanced at Thomas, who looked ready to burst with laughter. She sighed. "Okay. Lucas, we're leaving to go to the beach. Thomas, would you like to come with us?"

He looked from Mack's blushing face to Lucas' hopeful one. "I think I will." Then he winked at Lucas. "Providing your Auntie keeps her clothes on. Might give me a heart attack at my age."

Lucas fell about laughing. Mack continued to blush. Embarrassed.

Once Thomas appeared in his light-weight jacket, Lucas took hold of both their hands and let them lead him to the beach, where Mack guided them over to a shaded area. "Let's sit here so we don't fry like a lobster. I'll still be able to watch you, Lucas, so don't think you can get away with anything."

Thomas chuckled as he watched Lucas run off to play in the small tidal pool close to where they were sitting.

"He sure is a handful," Thomas commented, sitting beside Mack on the blanket.

Mack laughed. "He sure is. I think he listens to his granny too much." She sat with her legs pulled up, resting her chin on her knees. "It's lovely here, Thomas. I've never been to Cape Elizabeth before, which is unbelievable, considering I've lived all my life in Boston. So quiet and peaceful."

After a few minutes, Thomas glanced at Mack then back to Lucas. "I've never lived anywhere else. When Janet, my wife, was alive, we traveled to Europe, Canada, and Australia over the years we were together, but since she passed away, I haven't been anywhere. I don't need to travel after seeing what I have, and having this in my backyard... why bother?"

"It's paradise, Thomas."

"That it is. Why don't you have a boyfriend?"

Mack quickly looked at Thomas. Wow. That question was unexpected!

He laughed. "You're a pretty young woman, Mack. I might be old, but there's nothing wrong with my eyesight."

"I date, but...."

"No one ever lit the spark?"

"That about sums it up." She sighed.

While she enjoyed the silence, Mack mulled over the last date she had been on, at her mother's insistence. He had been fifty-five and a friend of her parents. In fairness, he was handsome and looked younger than his years, but he had three children, two of whom were older than she was, plus he couldn't stop talking about his wife. Soon to be ex-wife. Mack actually told her parents she gave him five months and he'd be back with his wife.

"Auntie Mack?" Lucas joined them on the blanket and cuddled into Thomas.

"Yeah? Are you tired now, Lucas?" He looked really sleepy.

"I think I'll have a nap as well," Thomas added.

"Well, if you're both napping, I'm going to read." She watched them both settle down, before she retrieved Rose's diary from her purse.

Mack moved back and rested against a small rock. She gazed at a yacht far out at sea, until it disappeared from the horizon, then opened the diary to the bookmarked page.

Chapter 5

March 11, 1947
We meet again…

I'd been busy over the past three days since I last wrote in my diary, thanks to Jayne. One night she took me to a dance at her office to celebrate a big contract they had been awarded. I danced with a few of the single men Jayne worked with, which was nice, but I was still hoping to see Jacob again. I couldn't get him out of my head.

Two nights ago we went to the movie theatre watching *It's a Wonderful Life*. I really liked James Stewart. The movie was long and walking home all I wanted to do was drop into bed, I was so tired. Jayne made me laugh, though. She flirted with the movie attendant and ended up having a date with him last night.

Today was my day off from the library and I was so looking forward to meeting Jayne in town. Ever since meeting Jacob, I'd been spending more time over my appearance, just in case I should see him again. It had been seven days since our first meeting; everywhere I went I looked out for him. I so hoped he hadn't left Cape Elizabeth.

It was thirty minutes past twelve as I approached

'Belle's Tea Rooms' to meet Jayne. Belle was from Cornwall and moved to America after the war to be with her husband, who she married while he was stationed over there. She made the most amazing scones and cream cakes, and I was so looking forward to indulging this afternoon, our monthly treat.

"Rose." Jayne shouted from behind me. I slowed down so she could catch up.

"Jayne. I'm glad you're not late again." Whenever I arranged to meet Jayne, she was always at least ten minutes late and kept me standing around waiting for her like a bump on a log.

"Let's get inside. I haven't had lunch yet." Jayne not eating lunch before coming here was nothing new. She made up for it with the cakes!

I opened the door and walked in to be greeted by the most delicious smell. As I looked around, I froze. Across the room, also frozen, his eyes locked on me, was Jacob. Jayne not realizing I had stopped, walked straight into me, pushing me towards Jacob, who had walked across the room to me and took hold of my hands.

"Rose. I can't believe... Rose, you're here?" he said, not letting go of my hands.

"Rose. Who is this?" Jayne asked.

I'd completely forgotten Jayne was with me. "Jayne, this is Jacob. Jacob, this is my best friend, Jayne."

"Nice to meet you, Jayne," Jacob replied without taking his eyes or hands from me.

"Please join us?" Jacob invited, and before I could reply, he was leading us across the room to his companion. I hesitated slightly when I saw the other woman. "She's my sister," he whispered to me with a twinkle in his eye.

"Eleanor, I would like you to meet Rose," Eleanor raised an eyebrow, "and her friend, Jayne. This is my sister, Eleanor."

After shaking hands, Jacob pulled a chair out for me and then, remembered his manners, for Jayne. If I was to be asked later what I ate, I wouldn't be able to answer. While Jayne and Eleanor chatted away, Jacob and I looked longingly at each other.

"Are you really sitting in front of me?" Jacob asked me.

"I thought I wouldn't see you again. I thought maybe you'd left Cape Elizabeth."

He lifted his hand as though to caress my face, but he remembered we were in public and pulled back. "I couldn't remember where you worked." Then he started to laugh. "I tried so many places in town looking for you."

I took his hand. "I work at the library. I've been looking for you as well."

Before I knew it, we had finished our tea and cake. As we headed for the reception room, Jayne and Eleanor headed towards the powder room, while Jacob took my hand and pulled me into an alcove behind a really large potted plant.

"Please tell me you're not marrying that other fellow?"

"No," I replied, shaking my head. He shocked the life out of me by kissing me on the cheek, tenderly.

"Can I see you again?" he asked, moving closer.

"Yes."

His lips came down onto mine. I was sure I could see stars. I couldn't think, my whole world had tipped on its axis.

He pulled his mouth away from mine, and I finally came back to myself. He just grinned at me.

"Wow... I think we need to practice that."

I reached up and pulled his head down to mine. Fireworks exploded in my head. I wasn't usually so forward, but it was Jacob. Wow.

We both pulled away rather breathless. "Can I see you tonight?"

"Oh, yes," I replied excitedly.

I told him where I lived and we quickly made arrangements to meet at ten tonight on the beach.

All the way out of town, Jayne did nothing but go on and on about Jacob and how much my parents would disapprove. I pointed out to Jayne that it was my life, and I would see Jacob if I wanted to. She walked off in a bit of a huff. So from now on, I was going to keep him my secret. I certainly didn't want to have my parents finding out about him before I knew him better.

My father was a snob, and in his eyes, anyone who wore anything other than a suit to work was not worthy of his only daughter. He actually hated me working at the library, all the more reason to do it!

Later that night I brushed my hair until it shined and put one of my new dresses on, which was pale pink with white piping around the neck and sleeves. I applied my pink lipstick and slipped my feet into my pink shoes.

My stomach was full of butterflies with excitement as I sneaked out of my room and down the stairs, through the kitchen then out the kitchen door.

With a deep breath, I walked around Mother's rose

garden and between the gap in the hedges to be able to walk down the path to the beach.

Five minutes later, I turned the bend in the path and could just make out Jacob and the smile that spread across his face at seeing me.

Jacob started walking towards me as I sped up my walk, and before I knew it we stood facing each other.

He reached up with his hands and caressed my face before touching his lips to mine in the sweetest of kisses. The kiss went on and on, by the time he withdrew his lips from mine, my knees were so weak, I wasn't sure I'd be able to walk.

"I can't believe you're here in front of me. That I have my hands on your face. I feel as though I've known you for years and that it hasn't only been a few days since we met," he confessed.

I had tears in my eyes. "I know what you mean. I feel it too, Jacob."

He seemed to pull himself together and stepped back, taking my hand in his. "Come, Rose. Let's walk along the beach, before it gets too dark."

"I'd like that."

We strolled along the beach wrapped in each other's arms. My arm was around Jacob's waist and his was around my shoulders, holding me tight. He felt delicious against my side, and all I wanted was for him to stop walking and kiss me senseless again.

I had been on dates with other young men in the past and held hands, but no one had ever felt as good beside me or so right.

Was I falling in love with him? I honestly felt so happy with Jacob.

As we walked along the beach he told me all about his sister, Eleanor, and how close he was to her.

She was ten years older than him and had been engaged before the war, her fiancé having been killed in France. Apparently, she hadn't been the same since and still missed him dearly.

It brought it home to me about all the people who had lost loved ones during the war. My family included.

All too soon it was time for me to head home before I was missed.

Jacob walked me part of the way home, along the footpath.

"Rose, I don't want to let go of you. How is that possible after only a couple of meetings?"

"I feel the same," I whispered as I buried my face into his chest.

He put his hand under my chin and lifted my face so he could place a gentle kiss to my lips.

"Will you meet me at lunch tomorrow? Near the rocks."

"Yes." I turned quickly and started running back towards my house, then remembered we hadn't arranged a time, so I turned back and shouted, "One o'clock."

"I'll be there," he shouted back.

March 12, 1947
I can't wait for lunch...

I'd spent all morning watching the clock creep very

slowly to one o'clock. Why did the time always drag when you were looking forward to being somewhere else?

"Rose?" *Mr. Young.*

"Yes?"

"I have been talking to you for the past five minutes, but you appear to be here in body only. Are we keeping you from something?"

"Not really. Is the meeting over?"

I made a quick exit, while Mr. Young got all flustered. I grabbed my jacket and purse from the staff room, before I left the library to go and meet Jacob.

I was so excited as I ran along the sidewalk towards the beach and the few rocks. I still couldn't believe how much he had started to mean to me. I even pinched my arm once or twice to make sure it was real and not a figment of my imagination. Then there he was, pacing back and forth, stopping to look around him, then he would start up again. Was he nervous? Worried that I wouldn't turn-up?

He lifted his head again and spotted me. He stilled and a huge grin started to spread over his face.

I ran towards him, and threw myself into his arms. He hugged me real tight and then sealed his mouth to mine.

Being in Jacob's arms with his lips locked to mine made me tingle all over, even in places that I hadn't tingled before, and it sure felt good.

"Rose, I've been really looking forward to seeing you again. I couldn't concentrate on anything this morning for thinking about you." He caressed my face, down to my neck and shoulders.

"I've been watching the clock all morning," I confessed.

Jacob smiled, took my hand and pulled me down the steps to the beach then over to a large rock. He helped me to get comfortable and then put his arm around me.

"I only have about twenty minutes. We don't get too long for lunch."

"I'd rather have twenty minutes with my Rose, than none at all."

I rested my head against Jacob, as we just sat looking out to sea. My eyes found a trawler out on the horizon which I watched until it disappeared from view.

I could sit with Jacob all day in silence and yet still be more than aware that he was sitting with me. That was how comfortable I felt being with him.

If I was to sit at home with my parents, I'd be twitching and desperate for an escape within five minutes, but not Jacob.

"Rose, will you tell me a bit about yourself? About your family?"

I quickly glanced at my watch and realized fifteen minutes had past while we'd both been lost in our own world. "I'm not sure we have time, but I'll tell you that there is my brother JT and my parents. We also have a housekeeper who tries her best to keep JT in-line, but she tends to fail more often than my parents would like." I grinned. "I think we need to make a move."

"I know. I'm having trouble moving. I just want to stay here all afternoon with you in my arms. I'm really falling for you, Rose," he gulped, looking so vulnerable.

"I'm falling for you too… but I need to get back. I don't particularly enjoy my job, but it annoys my father." I grinned and Jacob laughed.

He stood up first, jumped down from the rock then turned around and put his hands on my hips. With his eyes alight with mischief he lifted me down from the rock, moved his hands to my bottom and pulled me in to his body to claim my lips.

Jacob broke the kiss and rested his forehead against mine, while he wrapped a piece of my hair, which had come loose from my braid, around his fingers.

The way he looked at me, as though he wanted to devour me, had my heart beating rapidly in my chest, with what felt like butterflies, flying around in my stomach, and tingles between my legs.

"I can't see you again until Friday, but I want to take you dancing. Will you come dancing with me, Rose?"

Without thought, I said, "Yes."

Once back on the sidewalk we agreed the time and place to meet on Friday then said our goodbyes. We both left walking in different directions.

I missed him already.

Chapter 6

Mack lay in bed, with her thoughts on Rose and Jacob the following morning, not really wanting to move.

The cottage was known as 'Rose Cottage', so it didn't take a lot of imagination to realize the cottage was named after her. That must mean she was a relative of Thomas', as he said he changed the name when his father died. Was she dead? Was that why the name of the cottage changed from Degan House to what it was today? In her memory. It would certainly explain Thomas' reaction yesterday to seeing the diary.

Mack pushed the duvet to the side and climbed out of bed. After a quick shower, she dressed, then walked across the hall to check on Lucas before heading downstairs to start breakfast.

"Auntie Mack, when will Thomas be here?" Lucas asked, not five minutes later.

Mack turned around and found Lucas standing in the doorway, fully dressed with a wet face. "I didn't know you were awake, and you've dressed as well. Wow!" She hid her smile. "He'll be here later today. Come and eat."

Once Lucas sat down, Mack placed his breakfast in front

of him. "Hot cereal! Are you sure that's what it's supposed to be?" Lucas asked in disgust, as he dipped his spoon into the bowl of white looking substance.

"Yes, it's hot cereal, Lucas. Try some syrup or natural yogurt with it."

"I'm not sure I like hot cereal."

"Just be glad I didn't put prunes and apricots in yours." Mack tried not to laugh at the look of horror on his face, while she placed some yogurt and syrup in her own bowl.

"Ugh, yuk. Can we have proper food, like a burger for lunch?" Lucas whined.

"If you eat your breakfast, we'll find a fast food place for lunch, a treat on the way back from shopping. How's that sound?" She laughed.

He'd started to shovel his breakfast into his mouth rather quickly.

It was another sunny day in Cape Elizabeth. After Mack had strapped Lucas into the car, they headed to the closest supermarket. With hardly any traffic around, it was so peaceful. She drove through tunnels of aging trees, past vast farms, some with the tractors working in the fields. She was even lucky enough to drive through a covered bridge, and all this had made her want to pack up home in Roslindale and move to Cape Elizabeth.

Mack wasn't really unhappy in Boston, she just felt as though something was missing. She hadn't had a boyfriend in a very long time, and although her parents and sister were near, they had their own lives, and after all, Cape Elizabeth was only a couple of hours drive away. She would still be able to see Lucas on the weekends.

Perhaps in the next few weeks, she would check out the local schools to see if they had any positions for the start of the semester. She really would give the idea some serious thought.

Lucas was actually being rather quiet in the back of the car—rather unusual. She didn't know Lucas was capable of sitting quietly, especially after their trip out of Boston.

"You okay back there?"

"Yes. I'm being good so I can have ice cream after my burger and fries." He displayed a huge grin.

"Okay."

She drove into the supermarket parking lot and spotted a book-store across the road. With the car parked, Mack retrieved Lucas from the back, took hold of his hand and walked over to see if they had a children's atlas for Lucas to track his parent's travels on.

Not only did they have an atlas, but they also had a new dragon book as well that Lucas just had to have.

As they walked back across the road to the supermarket, she could now understand why her sister refused to take Lucas shopping with her. She had to use the 'on holiday' talk on him, to make him put the twelve or so books he'd chosen back, telling him there would be no room in the car if they bought them all. After many very sweet looks in his Auntie Mack's direction to try and get her to change her mind, he'd settled on the two.

Mack grabbed a shopping cart and instructed Lucas to stay with her and not to disappear. His own father had lost him in a supermarket on a couple of occasions. The first time, Lucas had been found eating grapes under one of the displays and then another time, he was lying on the floor in the children's section with a coloring book and pencils. He had been coloring away, thinking nothing of the fact that his father was running around looking for him.

The fruit and vegetable aisle held little interest for Lucas, who had spotted two girls shopping with their mother. He decided to try and inch away from his Auntie Mack, who apparently really did have eyes in the back of her head.

"Lucas, where do you think you're going?" she asked just as he was about to sneak behind the bananas, making him jump.

"Looking at bananas."

Mack looked amused while she tried not to laugh, knowing exactly what he was up to. "Lucas, I thought you didn't like bananas. Would you like some?"

He had a look of horror on his face, so Mack took pity on him. "Don't worry, we aren't going to buy any, but you better stay put, young man."

At the chocolate aisle, she suddenly realized she was alone. She took some deep breaths, trying to control the panic welling up inside her, as she looked around and rushed up the middle of the aisles, then moved along, when all of a sudden she heard someone scream.

With her heart in her mouth, she ran towards the sound, only to find Lucas in the middle of a water gun fight with two girls who really did look soaked, while Lucas looked as dry as he could be.

"Lucas Cartwright, what do you think you're doing?"

she demanded, while trying to keep a straight face. The whole scene looked rather comical, but there was no way she was going to laugh just yet, she was supposed to be the grown up.

"They asked me if I wanted to have a water fight with them. I was bored and said yes. They had an extra water pistol. Does this mean there's no burger and fries in my future?" he asked with his hands in his pockets and his head down.

"Lucas, please look at me." He did. "Forget about burger and fries for now. I want to know why they're soaked and you're dry?"

"Because they're girls and they can't shoot for beans."

"I'll have you know that some women can shoot better than men." Mack wondered what on earth his father had been saying to him.

She decided it might be better to make a quick escape. So, after grabbing hold of Lucas, they headed for the checkout, and both were thankful the girls' mother didn't catch up to them.

They pulled into the drive of Rose Cottage and saw Thomas making his way over to them.

Mack opened the car door for Lucas, and he jumped out then ran over to Thomas to tell him all about the water fight in the supermarket and having real food on the way home. By the laughter coming from Thomas, he found it just as amusing as she did.

Although as the adult in charge, she should have added a reprimand in there somewhere. There was no harm done and all parties involved seemed as much to blame, so it was left for now.

"Thomas, would you like to come in for something to drink?" she asked, grabbing hold of the shopping from the trunk of the car.

"Don't mind if I do," he replied, opening the kitchen door for her, then followed them both into the kitchen where he took a seat in what appeared to be his favorite chair in the cottage. He then got comfortable and pulled Lucas onto his lap.

"Can you swim, boy?" he asked Lucas.

"I can swim two hundred meters without stopping, and I have a badge at home to prove it." Lucas was rather proud.

"Good, because I was thinking, if you didn't have anything planned this afternoon, I might take you fishing with me for a couple of hours. If it's okay with your aunt?"

"That's fine. He's actually a very good swimmer and has swim team three nights a week back home."

She wanted a quiet word with Thomas about the diary, so she turned to Lucas. "Why don't you go and play your new Wii game for now, while Thomas finishes his drink."

As soon as Lucas walked into the sitting room, Thomas turned to look at her. "Something on your mind, Miss Mackenzie?" he asked while he took a sip of his coffee.

"First off, why don't you call me Mack?"

"Done! Next."

"You know who Rose is, don't you?"

He abruptly stood up, put his cup down on the table before he walked over to the window and looked out, not really seeing anything, as he remembered Rose, and his love for her. "I haven't talked about her in sixty-five years, and I don't intend to now. It's time to go fishing," he said agitated.

"Thomas, what's in that tub?" Lucas asked, because he could see something moving inside it.

"Bait."

"I thought I was bait." Lucas paused. "What's bait anyway?" he asked baffled.

"Bait is what you attach to the end of the line, something fish like the taste of, and when they try to take a bite, the fish get attached to the hook with the bait on." Thomas laughed when he noticed the horror on Lucas' face.

"You're not really going to use me as bait, are you?" Lucas backed away slightly.

Thomas roared with laughter, so much he had to sit down before he fell down. He had tears running down his face, and every time he glanced at Lucas, he set off again.

"Oh, my dear boy," he just about managed to choke out. Then he took some deep breaths to try and calm down. "I can't remember the last time I laughed so much." Thomas managed to get himself under control. "You're safe, Lucas. Come sit by me and I'll show you how to bait a hook."

Lucas sat down and spent the next ten minutes listening to Thomas explain about fishing and how to bait a hook. Lucas wasn't too impressed that he wasn't allowed to try it by himself, but Thomas didn't want little fingers to become part of the hook!

Thomas offered Lucas a cheese sandwich and a drink of lemonade while they sat back and waited for the fish to catch.

"How long have you been fishing?" Lucas asked between gulps of his lemonade.

Thomas quickly glanced at Lucas, then relaxed back against a tree, thinking back to the summer his father took the effort to purchase him something, instead of sending his mother or the housekeeper to do it. "My father bought me a fishing rod for my eighth birthday. That would be about seventy-two years ago now. I spent all that summer fishing with my two best friends, Levi and Walt."

Lucas carried on munching his cheese sandwich then, obviously having thought about what Thomas just told him, asked, "Are they still your friends, or have you had a fight? I fight with my friends all the time."

Thomas chuckled. "Oh yes, we're still friends, although back then we were more like partners in crime, as we used to get up to all sorts of trouble, that used to get me grounded a lot."

Thomas walked to the edge of the river to check the line, then looked back at Lucas, who still had his attention focused on him. "I remember after one fishing trip, we were walking back to my house, when we spotted my neighbor arranging some shoes on the porch. We hid behind some bushes, and when she went inside, we snuck up to her porch and put fish in three of the shoes. We caught about eight fish that day, don't think we ever got so lucky again. I got grounded for a week, but it's the only time my father ever found one of my antics funny. I heard him laughing as he shut my bedroom door, on his way downstairs after telling me off."

Lucas giggled. "That's funny. I think I need to pee."

Thomas looked rather startled and just hoped he didn't

need help. "Okay, Lucas. Are you all right going behind that bush?"

"You mean I get to pee outside?"

Thomas just nodded his head while he tried not to laugh.

"Yeah!!" Lucas took off behind a bush.

"Don't go too far, Lucas, okay?"

"I won't. I'm peeing now."

"Okay, buddy." Thomas chuckled.

Lucas ran back to Thomas. "I feel better now. Please can I have one of those chocolate bars?"

"Yes, you can. Now come and sit back down beside me. Let's clean your hands first with this wipe, and then I'll pass you some chocolate."

Not long after, Lucas' line started to go crazy, which had both of them jumping up, nearly knocking everything into the river. While Lucas jumped up and down cheering, Thomas managed to reel in a yellow perch on Lucas' line.

"Well done, Lucas. Do you want to try again, see if we can catch enough for dinner?"

"Yes. Auntie Mack can cook them," Lucas laughed. "You might have to get rid of the middle first, though, because she's a girl and would scream and run away. That's what Daddy said, anyway."

"Is that right?" Thomas hid his grin.

Mack had spent part of the afternoon baking. When she'd finished, she decided to go and have a walk to the beach, taking Rose's diary with her. She'd left a message pinned to the back door for Thomas and Lucas, just in case they were back before she was. No need to worry them, unnecessarily.

At the beach, she found a sheltered corner and settled down with the diary.

Chapter 7

March 14, 1947
I put my dancing shoes on...

I was so excited to be seeing Jacob in twenty minutes. He was meeting me at the end of the drive to take me dancing and I could hardly contain my excitement.

Not five minutes before I left the house, Mother walked into my bedroom and wanted to know why I had a huge smile on my face. Of course I fobbed her off and told her I was just thinking about something Jayne said the other day. Not sure she actually believed me though.

As I approached the end of the drive I couldn't see any sign of Jacob, which had me worried.

I walked onto the sidewalk and looked in both directions and there was still no sign of him. I decided it would probably be best to wait back from the road, in case anyone I knew saw me, and started to ask questions or even worse ask my parents what I was doing. Ugh!

Just about to step back, I felt arms go around me and lips on my neck. "Hello, Rose," he whispered into my neck, which sent shivers straight through me.

I sagged against him, and turned my head slightly to

meet his lips. "I've missed you and been so looking forward to this evening," I whispered.

"Me too." He turned me around so we could embrace properly. "We better go or we'll miss the bus."

Jacob held my hand all the way to the stop, all through the journey to the dance hall, and only released me when I handed my jacket over to one of the cloakroom attendants.

"Would you like a drink first, Rose?"

"No. Just hold me in your arms and dance with me."

His eyes bore into mine as he pulled me onto the dance floor to dance to Frankie Laine's, *That's my Desire*. I really loved that song.

We danced and danced for about two hours without even breaking for a drink. Part of me was exhausted, but another part of me felt so alive. Being held in his arms while we danced, feeling his muscles shift under my hands had my body overheated. Every time he caressed down my back, goose bumps followed.

I was in love with Jacob. I'd never been in love before, but I knew I loved him. What I was going to do about it though was another thing. It wouldn't be too long before my parents found out about us. Then all hell would break loose with how my father was. Never mind, I would cross that bridge when it happened.

By the time we arrived back to town it was rather late, so Jacob walked me back to the house, and gave me a quick kiss goodbye, promising to meet me on Tuesday.

March 18, 1947
The day I lose my heart...

I'd spent the past four days pining for Jacob. He had to work nights, and for some reason I hadn't asked him what he did. How I hadn't asked him, I didn't know. He also hadn't volunteered it, either.

Eventually, it was five minutes before ten as I sneaked out of the house through the kitchen, with a flashlight in my hand. I quickly made my way to the beach and Jacob.

As I turned the corner, I just made out Jacob up ahead. He saw me and started walking towards me. I picked up speed and ended up running to him, throwing my arms around his neck as he put his lips to mine, while holding me tight against his body.

"Being in your arms feels so right." I leaned in to kiss him again.

All too soon he released me and took my hand, leading me to a sheltered section of beach. He had already laid a couple of blankets on the ground. Once sitting, he pulled me between his legs and kept one arm around my waist as he passed me a hot chocolate with his other hand.

He turned me inside out. When I was with him I felt as though I'd known him my whole life, and when we were apart, I desperately longed for his company. He made me feel protected and cherished, as though nothing could harm me while I was with him.

I turned my head slightly so I could look at his face. "Will you tell me about Jacob?"

"What do you want to know?" he asked me while caressing my face.

"Everything."

He laughed and pulled me back against his chest, snuggled real tight. "Okay then, here goes. I'm twenty-two years old, born in New York. My parents moved to Boston in 1931. Eleanor still lives in Brookline and runs a respectable boarding house. She visits me often. The only time she couldn't visit me was during the war when I was stationed in England."

I turned around to face him with a look of concern. "Where in England?"

"Leominster in Herefordshire. I was in the 5th Ranger Division towards the end of the war. I remember the local children were great fun. We used to give them chocolate and gum in exchange for them going to buy us fish and chips. The kids were the best."

I leaned forward and kissed him. "Thank you for sharing that with me."

He took hold of my hair, which had come loose from my clip and smoothed it behind my ear, caressing my face at the same time. "Now, please tell me about Rose." As I looked up into his eyes they were sparkling with passion, for me. My heart was pounding so much, I felt as though it was about to jump out from my chest.

He leaned forward and placed such a tender kiss to my lips, then smiled at me. "Sitting there looking gorgeous and ready to be kissed, does not mean I don't want to hear about you, Rose."

I smiled up to him, then leaned back against him again. "I've lived all my life in Cape Elizabeth. I had an older brother, Charlie. He was killed in France during the war." I started to sniffle. Whenever I talked about Charlie, I always ended up in tears.

"Rose, please don't cry." Jacob wiped my tears away with his thumbs.

After a few minutes, I took a deep breath and wrapped my arms around Jacob's waist, snuggling in close to his warmth. "I mentioned my younger brother, JT, the other day. He makes me laugh with the things he gets up to with his friends, Walt and Levi. Father grounds him nearly every other day. It doesn't last long though, as Mother gets frustrated when he's under foot all day long. He'll then go and find his friends, and end up getting grounded again. He can also be very annoying."

Jacob started to laugh. "Isn't that what brothers are supposed to be like?"

I elbowed him gently into his side. "Please tell me you weren't an annoying brother to Eleanor?" I raised my eyebrow in question.

Jacob pulled me closer. "Probably, but not all the time. Eleanor is a great sister. Sometimes, I don't know what I would've done without her."

"I feel like that about JT—well some of the time," I said, just before Jacob leaned forward to give me a sweet kiss. "I don't want tonight to end."

He looked at his watch. "It's getting late, you might be missed." We untangled ourselves and Jacob took my hand, pulling me up from the ground, and straight into his arms for a wonderful kiss.

Breaking the kiss, Jacob threaded his fingers through my hair and pushed it behind my ears. "Will you meet me again, Rose? I'm working for the next few nights, but I can meet you on Friday."

"I'd love to meet you again. I feel as though I've always known you. I don't want to leave."

"I don't want you to. Come on, I'll walk you back."

Jacob wrapped the blankets up in some sort of waterproof sheeting and hid them between some large rocks. He then took my hand and pulled me back into his arms as we started walking to my house. Just before we came into view of Mother's parlor windows, he turned me to him and kissed me with so much passion, he left me breathless. My toes curled, my skin tingled, but before I knew what had really hit me, he pulled away again. "I'll see you, same place, but a bit earlier if you can make it on Friday." He then turned and left me without another word. All I wanted to do was cry.

How could I feel so much for a man I'd only met fourteen days ago?

Chapter 8

Mack checked her watch to see if she had enough time to read some more, but to her surprise, she hadn't realized so much time had lapsed. She closed the diary and sat back, gazing far into the distance, right across the sea.

Her mind was filled with thoughts of Rose and Jacob; she couldn't help but wonder what had become of them. She really wasn't going to jump to the last entry, to hopefully find out. At least she hoped she wouldn't do that. Mack wasn't exactly known for her patience.

She collected her things together and started to walk back to the cottage to see if Thomas and Lucas had returned from fishing.

She stopped dead when she entered the cottage, because she was greeted with the bloody mess of the kitchen.

"Auntie Mack, you're back. I caught a yellow perch and Thomas caught two, so Thomas is gutting them. Will you cook them for dinner?" Lucas asked with a very happy, excited face.

She walked over and placed a kiss on his cheek.

"Yuk, Auntie." He groaned, rubbing his face.

"What about me? I caught two you know." Thomas stated, with a wink at Mack, pointing to his cheek.

She grinned then walked over to Thomas and placed a kiss on his cheek as well. "Thank you for taking him fishing. He obviously had a really good time."

"That he did. I certainly did. Don't think I've ever laughed so much before."

"Yeah, he can have that effect on folk. Come on, Thomas, show me how to cook this fish, because I have no idea."

Mack quickly cleaned the mess up and then turned to find Lucas standing behind her. "Auntie Mack, I want to help. I caught one of them, you know?"

Mack laughed, ruffling his hair. "Okay Lucas. I think we both need an apron on, because fish can be smelly."

"Yeah, it stinks in here." Lucas held his nose.

Mack started opening the windows and the kitchen door to try and get rid of the putrid smell.

"Okay, I think we're ready now, Thomas."

"Well, I have one more to gut," Thomas informed them with a grin.

"You're kidding right, because I can see three fish lined up on the block?"

Thomas and Lucas both started giggling.

"Okay, guys, enough. We're never going to get any dinner at this rate."

Dinner had gone well and the fish had tasted delicious

with the seasoning Thomas had asked Mack to mix together. Lucas had cleaned his plate as well, which had surprised Mack, because in the past he had always turned his nose up at fish.

"Auntie Mack?"

"What's up, Lucas?"

"Will you show me some of the places Mommy and Daddy are visiting?"

Mack glanced at Lucas who stood in the doorway to the kitchen in his favorite Power Ranger pajamas, holding his new children's atlas.

He brought a lump to her throat. "I sure will. Come over here."

Lucas walked over to her as Mack lifted him on to her lap, while he placed the book on to the table.

"Okay. Let's find Italy first, because if I remember rightly they're due to arrive in Nice sometime in the next few hours, and Italy is usually easier to find than France."

"I'll find it."

She sat and watched him flip through the atlas and had to bite her tongue when he went past the page.

"Found it!"

Mack leaned forward and kissed him on the top of his head. "Are you sure that's Italy and not, maybe, South America?"

"Oh, Auntie Mack. Are you sure that's South America?" he whined.

"Well, you tell me what these letters are."

Mack reached around him and pointed out the large letters to mark a country, while Lucas tried to concentrate on them.

"B...R...A...Z...I...L. Brazil. Ugh, yuk. That's where you get bananas from."

Mack burst out laughing. Bananas being the only fruit that Lucas hated. "Okay, champ. Let me help you find Italy, otherwise we might be here all night."

She turned a few pages back and pointed out, boot-shaped Italy to him. Lucas took his first sticker from the back of the atlas and with Mack's direction, found Nice over the border in France, hoping one day she'd get the opportunity to visit, providing she could get her head around a long flight.

"Let's go and tuck you into bed."

Lucas jumped from her lap and ran upstairs as she followed at a slower pace with her usual hot chocolate, and of course, Rose's diary.

Chapter 9

March 19, 1947
I miss Jacob already....

It really hadn't been long since I'd last seen Jacob. Last night actually. I missed him so much. I wanted to talk to him and tell him about my day at work and the funny antics of my boss. I wanted his arms around me, and most of all, I wanted his lips on mine. I'd been kissed before, but I'd never reacted to anyone the way I did with Jacob. Right from our first meeting, I'd felt comfortable with him, with his touch. He listened to me, and didn't talk down to me. When he looked at me, it was as though I was the only woman in the room.

I was in my room after a busy day, unable to think about anything else, except the man who had my emotions tied in knots. Just about to change into something more comfortable, when there was a knock at my door. I opened it and found my mother on the other side, looking rather flustered. "Mother, what's wrong?"

"Oh, I'm fine, but Richard is downstairs and really wants to talk to you," she told me, all excited. That filled me with dread. I really hoped she wasn't excited, because she was thinking of wedding bells. That was not going to happen.

I felt stubborn. "Please tell him I have a headache." I put my hand to my head and swooned onto my bed. Opening one eye, I saw my mother still stood in my room with her hands on her hips, not looking impressed at all.

"Put your shoes on and join us in the parlor. Now." With that, she shut my door. *Oh fiddle sticks.*

With the scruffiest pair of shoes on, I headed downstairs to the *parlor*. Richard saw me immediately and jumped up from his chair, nearly sloshed his tea all over Mother as he went to put it down, and then raced to me. He took hold of my hands. "Rose. I've really missed you. I'm glad you're here."

I wasn't sure where he was coming from with this. I pulled my hands out of his. "Richard, it's nice of you to come calling. Are you well?"

"I'm fine. Thank you for asking." He took my elbow and led me over to the sofa, sitting me down beside him.

He poured me some tea, just as my mother stood and made some excuse to leave. *Great.*

"Thank goodness, I thought she was going to stay with us." I just looked at him and tried not to panic.

Once my mother left, he seemed to sag in relief. "What's gotten into you?" I asked him.

"This is a mess."

"What is?" He really wasn't making any sense to me.

With a quick glance at me, he put his head in his hands and took a deep breath. "My father told me last night that if I didn't ask for your hand in marriage today, he would stop my allowance."

"Oh my God. Please don't tell me that's why you're here? We've discussed this already."

"Then tell me no," he said in desperation.

Stunned, I said, "No."

He sighed. "Rose. I'm sorry about all this. I really am. I don't suppose we can be friends?"

I felt such relief, that was over with. "Yes, I would like that, but no talk about marriage."

"Thank you. Now that we're friends, would you like to go to the movies with me on Saturday?" he asked with a grin, "as friends."

I hoped Jacob wouldn't mind me going to the movies with another man, even though we were only friends. "That would be good."

"Then I'll pick you up at six-thirty. Is that all right?"

"Yes. I'll see you then." I opened the front door for him.

Just about to walk through it, he stopped and grinned slightly. "Err... Rose?"

I looked up at him. "Yes."

"Your shoes have a tear in them."

I put my hand to my mouth to stop the giggle from escaping, and closed the door behind him.

"What did you say?"

I turned around to find Mother standing behind me. "I said no, and not to ask me again," I replied stubbornly.

"Well, really, Rose. What on earth will your father say?"

"He's not the one who would be marrying him." I ran back up stairs to my room, and this time I locked the bedroom door.

March 20*th*, 1947
Only one more day....

It was one more day until I met Jacob again, and I could hardly wait. I'd missed him so much. Thoughts of Jacob had been keeping me going these past couple of days.

Father wouldn't speak to me after turning Richard's proposal down. As far as I was concerned, Father was acting like a child.

"Ashoo." *Damn dust!*

For two hours I'd been dusting the shelves and books in the library. I'd lost count how many times I'd sneezed or how many spiders I'd seen.

The library had been very quiet today, and Mr. Young decided he wasn't going to let us sit around doing nothing. That's why I was full of cobwebs and sneezing.

"Boo."

I jumped a mile and turned around to see Jayne doubled over laughing. "That wasn't nice."

"It was funny. You should see the sight of you. You look a mess...."

"Well, thank you for that, and hush up before Mr. Young finds us. What are you doing here?" She very rarely came into the library. My boss scared her.

"Will you double date with me tomorrow night?"

"Oh." I needed to think quickly. "I'm sorry, Jayne, but I've promised Mother I would keep JT occupied."

"You're seriously going to pass, because of your brother?" she asked me in disbelief.

"I'm trying to keep the peace after rejecting Richard. So

on this occasion, I am." It was close to the truth.

"Heck. Okay. I better get back to work. See you later." She turned and headed out of the library.

After my very boring day at work, I ate dinner at home, then took JT to the beach. We had fun again and hunted around for crabs this time. JT found two and I found none! He gloated the whole way home, like a little brat. I ought to stop using his nickname, and maybe then he'd start acting more grown-up.

JT was otherwise known as Thomas James. He was fourteen years old and regardless of what he may think, I loved him dearly.

March 21st, 1947
Tonight I meet Jacob....

At dinner I told Mother and Father that I was meeting some friends in town. Without giving them time to reply, I ran up to my room, and changed my clothes.

Opening my closet, I retrieved my new yellow dress, which had a low neckline and showed too much of my breasts. Daring, but I didn't care. I knew my mother wouldn't approve, so I placed a white cardigan over the dress and buttoned it up high. I slipped my feet into my yellow pumps and walked to the mirror to see how I looked. I smiled. I looked pretty good.

I opened the door to leave and bumped straight into JT. "What are you doing lurking on the landing?"

"You're going meeting him? That guy from the cliffs."

I was speechless, I didn't know what to say. "Um...

What?" I pulled myself together and opened my purse. "Here." I handed him ten cents to buy a comic. "You have to stay quiet about who I'm meeting."

He grinned from ear to ear. "Thanks, sis."

Brothers!

I sneaked down the backstairs and exited through the kitchen, then ran through Mother's rose garden. I doubled back towards the beach path.

When I rounded the bend, Jacob was waiting for me. He saw me and smiled, then started walking towards me. To be in his arms again felt like coming home. I pulled back slightly, but Jacob kept his arms around my waist. As he looked down into my eyes, there seemed desire burning within them – for me. My skin began to sizzle with awareness. I needed something, but I wasn't quite sure what.

He leaned down and took my mouth with his, sliding his tongue over mine, as we groaned into each other's mouths. He tasted of chocolate and felt so good. I didn't want to let go of him.

All too soon, he broke from the kiss and placed butterfly kisses all over my face. "I've missed you, Rose."

"I've missed you, too."

He let me go and took my hand, then led me to the shelter we shared the other night. Sitting on the blanket, he used the other blanket and wrapped it around us both to keep the evening chill at bay. I managed to unbutton my cardigan without Jacob noticing, although he'd notice soon enough.

"Tell me more about you. I want to know everything," I said, and Jacob laughed.

"I work for the fire department at the moment, but my

dream is to become an engineer. I've applied for an apprenticeship in Boston." He grinned. "I'm a huge baseball fan, and can't wait for the baseball season to start. I support the Boston Braves, and I'm going to the game in Boston on April 18th, against the Philadelphia Phillies. Hey, come with me?"

"Yes. Will you take me with you if you get the job in Boston?" I held my breath waiting for his reply.

He took my face between his hands. "Rose, I'll take you anywhere you ask, within my means." He leaned in and kissed me.

Pulling away, he caught sight of my chest. His eyes nearly popped out of his head. He gulped. I hid a smile. I really wanted to feel his hands on me. Heck. I didn't know what was going on but I was shivering all over. My skin felt alive, and between my legs, it was like I was on fire. The feeling was so new. I wanted more.

"Jacob, please kiss me." I turned into him.

He lifted a shaky hand to my face in a caress. "Rose."

He sealed his lips to mine. He slipped his tongue into my mouth. We both groaned. I climbed into his lap and wrapped my arms around his neck. One of his hands pulled me in tight to him, his other hand traveled up my torso and smoothed along the top of my breasts.

I pulled away from his mouth. The pleasure was so intense. He kissed down my neck. I arched into him, coming into contact with the hardness between us. He kissed across my chest and lifted one of his hands to cup my breast.

The pleasure became unbearable and intense as he held me in his arms while he kissed my lips, and before I knew what was happening the pleasure burst into lightening—more than I'd ever felt before.

Panting, Jacob wrapped me up in his arms. "Hell. Rose. That was not supposed to happen. You turn me upside down."

"Can we do that again?" I laughed. I had no embarrassment, being half dressed with Jacob after doing what we'd done.

He fastened my dress with unsteady hands and lifted me from his lap.

I felt rather languid after the pleasure he'd caused my body to experience for the first time.

Blushing, I glanced to Jacob and noticed the large bulge I'd been rubbing against.

He pulled his legs up with a wince and took some deep breaths. "We can do that again," he whispered. "Are you all right?"

"I'm fine. I loved what you did to me."

He groaned. I blushed.

I never in a million years expected to be so, brazen. He was the one. I had no embarrassment with him when I was half-naked. He felt amazing. Next time, I wanted him half-naked. I looked away so he couldn't see my longing.

After a few minutes, he stood and helped me up from the sand. "I need to get you home. That's not what I want to do with you, but I know it's what I *need* to do. Now. Before I lose further control with you," he said blushing. "I'm working until Wednesday. Do you want to go to the movies?"

When I heard Jacob ask me about the movies, I was reminded that I had arranged to go with Richard.

We walked back to my house, hand in hand. "Jacob. I'm going to the movies tomorrow with a friend, Richard." He stopped walking. "He really is just a friend. You're the one I want to be with."

"Okay, Rose. I trust you."

He placed a goodbye kiss to my lips. We parted with the promise of the movies on Wednesday. In five days. It was difficult to put one step in front of the other after experiencing Jacob's touch.

Chapter 10

A week later, Mack was exhausted. First Lucas had been sick with a bad cold, which had kept her house bound, then Thomas had come down with it. She'd insisted he move into Rose Cottage while he was sick so she could take care of him as well. Then two days ago, she woke in the night feeling yuk and sick, so Thomas had played nursemaid, because he had started to feel better. Of course, Lucas tried to help, but kept getting under foot.

All she wanted was a walk to the beach to try and blow some of the cobwebs away, plus she'd missed seeing the ocean this past week. She'd also missed Rose and Jacob, because while she was playing Florence Nightingale, she'd been too tired, then too sick to pick the diary up and had wanted to enjoy Rose's writing, which she wouldn't have done.

Throwing the cover from the top of her, she climbed out of bed and quickly dressed in a pair of jeans, t-shirt, and sweater. The last thing she needed was to get sick again. Then she followed the sound of voices to the kitchen.

Standing in the doorway she just watched Thomas and Lucas interact, while she was unobserved. They seemed to know what the other wanted without words being spoken. It was sweet.

"Auntie Mack, you're awake. We're making you breakfast... You were supposed to be eating it in bed." Lucas didn't look impressed at all.

"Well, I would love to eat the breakfast you've made me, but I'll sit here with you and Thomas. If that's okay? Then maybe after breakfast we can go for a walk to the beach. I need some fresh air."

"Yeah!" Lucas shouted, running around the kitchen.

Mack had to put her hands to her ears with the racket he was making.

"Lucas, you hush up now. You're giving your auntie a headache." Thomas' words managed to shut him up, much to Mack's relief.

They'd both made pancakes, Mack's favorite, which she ate with a small amount of butter and maple syrup. As she placed the first piece into her mouth she happened to glance up and noticed that both Thomas and Lucas were sitting staring at her.

She paused mid chew.

"I dropped an egg shell in it." Lucas had a huge grin on his face.

"Oh."

Thomas started to laugh, while watching Mack try and eat the pancake without choking on egg shell.

She managed to clear her plate with only eating a couple pieces of the shell. "That was delicious, Lucas. Thank you."

"Yeah, she liked it!"

"Thomas are you going to walk to the beach with us?" she asked while clearing the table of the breakfast dishes.

"No, I don't think I will, Mack. I'll walk with you as far as my cottage."

Lucas' face fell. "I don't want you to leave, Thomas. Can't you stay?"

Thomas pulled Lucas on to his lap. "I'm only five minutes away. The thing is, I need my own space. It's been a long time since I've lived with anyone, and even though it's been nice staying here, I need to go home. I appreciate everything that you and your auntie have done for me. In fact I bet your auntie will invite me for dinner, providing she feels up to it."

"Consider yourself invited. Now Lucas, you go and wash-up and bring a sweater down with you. I don't want you getting sick again."

Mack turned to Thomas and had a good look at him. He still appeared pale, but he certainly seemed better than he had been. "Are you sure you're feeling okay?"

He smiled at Mack. "I really am fine. Just tired. I don't sleep too well unless it's in my own bed."

"I know what you mean. I'm a bit like that, but for some reason I haven't had any trouble here. Perhaps it's the fresh air and being so close to the ocean."

"Auntie Mack, I'm ready."

She turned her head and looked at Lucas, who did look ready with his sweater on and his sneakers on the correct feet.

"Come on then, let's go. And Lucas, no messing in the tidal pools today. You've just been sick."

"This isn't going to be any fun," he grumbled.

Mack just smiled and ushered him outside the cottage, took hold of his hand then started walking with Thomas along the beach path.

When they reached Thomas' cottage, Mack stood on the porch with him while Lucas lay in the lounge chair on the front lawn.

"Thomas, can I ask you something?"

"Go on."

"Are you JT?"

Thomas stopped what he was doing and abruptly sat down on the porch swing. "I haven't used that name in a very long time. It was her nickname for me, switching my initials around so no one would know she was talking about me," he explained, wiping his hand across his face.

"Thomas, if it's too painful to talk about Rose, I guess nobody has ever died of curiosity," Mack said concerned.

"She hated me," Thomas whispered.

Mack was stunned. "Who, Rose?"

He nodded his head. "Yes, I was always trying to get her into trouble." He shook his head.

"Thomas no. You're wrong. In her diary she said that she loved you. Wait a minute." Mack quickly retrieved the diary from her purse and found the relevant part in the diary. "This is dated March 20, 1947. Rose says, *'JT is otherwise known as Thomas James. He is fourteen years old and regardless of what he may think, I love him dearly.'* That was what she wrote in here, Thomas."

"I never knew," he whispered.

After a few minutes of silence he stood up and unlocked his front door. "I'll be fine, Mack. I'm glad you found her diary and told me. It means a lot." He tried to reassure her. "You go and have fun with the boy and I'll see you both for dinner."

Thomas walked inside his cottage as Mack looked towards Lucas, who was waiting patiently in the garden. She just hoped he would be all right.

Mack and Lucas had both taken a nap when they'd returned from the beach, where they'd collected an assortment of clamshells and smooth stones. Mack loved shells and had them all over her apartment. For the past three years on her birthday, Lucas had painted some and stuck them to some sort of clay item that he'd made. She smiled in remembrance of the flower pot, vase and coffee mug he'd made her. All unusable, but they meant more to her because Lucas had taken the time to make them. She knew she'd treasure them always.

After they'd eaten dinner, Thomas decided to stay while Lucas had his bath and then he read him another *Our Gang* story before they both said goodnight.

Sitting with a coffee in the sitting room with Thomas, Mack hoped he had decided to talk about Rose.

"What do you want to know?"

"Tell me about your sister."

"Oh boy, she was amazing, so full of life." He paused and took a deep breath. "I was with her the morning she first met him. Does she say that in her diary?"

"Yes, she does. She says you dragged her away from him."

Thomas laughed as he remembered. "Yes, I did. Our father was a snob. He would have made her life so difficult if he'd any idea she was interested in someone who didn't come from money. He barely allowed Rose to work at the library, but she refused to give the job up and said she wanted to make her own money. I don't think she liked working there much, but it was her bit of freedom, I guess. It probably made her feel good, knowing she was going against Father's wishes."

He took a minute. "I caught her once or twice, sneaking out to meet him, so she would bribe me with ten cents to buy *Our Gang* comics. She actually went out and bought me the April 1st edition to keep me quiet, as Father had told Mother I couldn't have that issue for getting up to no good. I sometimes wonder if I'd told my father about what she was doing, that maybe she would have lived."

Mack just stared at him and wondered if she heard him correctly. "What do you mean?"

With a glance into the darkness, Thomas then turned back to Mack. "She died the night she was running away with him, April 14, 1947. She'd left to meet him, to go away to marry him, I guess. That was the last time I saw her." Thomas wiped his eyes.

"How did she die?" Mack asked.

"That I really don't want to talk about."

"Do you know if she met up with Jacob?" She couldn't stop with the questions.

"No, she never made it. About a month later, I overheard my father talking to my mother. It turned out it was about Jacob. I heard him telling her Jacob had rung the house asking for Rose. He told Jacob she was happily married to Richard. He said Jacob sounded really upset, and then he hung up on him."

"Oh my, so if he's still alive, all this time Jacob thinks Rose changed her mind and didn't love him and used him probably," Mack said with tears in her eyes. "That's so sad, Thomas. I have to see if he's still alive and tell him what happened to Rose."

"If he is, he'll be older than me. When I overheard my parents talking, my father said he was three years older than Rose, so he would be... around eighty-eight, I think."

"I have to try, Thomas. If you read her diary, you can see and feel just how much she loved him, and if his feelings were the same as hers, then he has to know." Mack still had tears running down her face. "If he's still alive and remembers her, I think he will, then he has the right to know the truth, and just how much she loved him."

"I think you're right." He stood up to leave.

"Thank you, Thomas, for sharing that with me. It breaks my heart knowing how their love ended."

"You have a soft heart," Thomas told her, placing a kiss on her cheek.

"Are you okay walking home? It's pitch black out there."

"I've been walking home in the dark since I was five years old," he told Mack with a chuckle on his way out the door.

"Okay, goodnight then. Why don't you join us for breakfast?" Mack couldn't help but notice the look on his face and thought perhaps Lucas had mentioned the hot cereal. "Pancakes, eggs and sausage," she quickly added.

"I'll be here at eight."

"Goodnight."

She stood on the doorstep and watched Thomas head home, thinking about Rose and Jacob. Their story was so sad.

Inside the cottage, she locked up for the night and headed upstairs to shower and change into her pajamas.

Back downstairs, she made her usual hot chocolate and retrieved Rose's diary from her purse, then headed to bed with a heavy heart, knowing how it all ended, but unable to stop reading Rose's story.

Chapter 11

March 22, 1947
Movie night with Richard....

Richard came calling for me, just as he said he would, in his father's car. I was really looking forward to watching the movie, *Road to Utopia*. Dorothy Lamour was one of my favorite actresses. I didn't really have the heart to tell Richard, I'd already seen the movie with Jayne. At least it was a fun movie to watch, so I really didn't mind seeing it twice.

We took our seats and Richard was ever the gentleman, even though I had reminded him that it wasn't a date, and we were just friends.

"Rose, are you comfortable?" he whispered. The movie theatre was really full tonight.

"I'm fine, thank you. Do you like Dorothy Lamour? I think she's great," I asked.

"She's all right, but I prefer Bing Crosby. I think he is very good."

The movie started to get underway and stopped the chit-chat. I was relieved, really. I didn't know what to say to him. During the interval, I visited the restroom, and was just about to open the door when two hands grabbed me, then pulled me into the cloakroom. *Jacob.*

"What...?" He slammed his lips down to mine. His tongue slipped between my lips. We both moaned.

"God, Rose. I can't stop touching you. Wanting you." He kissed me again. My arms were wrapped around his neck. His arms were wrapped around my waist. He held me against him and I felt the hardness between us.

"I wanted to remind you just who your guy is."

"Okay." I pulled his head back to me. I really couldn't get enough of this man.

We were both breathing heavily when the bell sounded to let everyone know the movie was about to start up again.

"I need to get back to work. One of the guys is covering for me." He caressed my face.

"I better get back as well. I'm really going to miss you." I had to fight back my tears.

"I'll miss you as well, Rose. I'll see you soon. Now go."

He placed a quick kiss to my lips and shoved me back through the curtains. I quickly made my way back to Richard, who looked at me with widened eyes. *Oh heck.*

"Are you coming down with something? You look really flushed."

"I think I might be, but I feel okay, really." I took my seat again and avoided looking at him, until I felt his hand creeping across the back of my chair. "What are you doing?"

"Um, stretching." I wasn't sure whether to believe him or not.

"Well, stretch somewhere else."

He huffed and put his arms back down.

The movie seemed to drag after the interval with Jacob. Eventually the lights went up, and everyone stood to stretch their legs, ready to exit.

"Would you like to go and have a slice of pie and chocolate milk?" Just about to refuse, my stomach grumbled. "I take that's a yes, then."

I didn't really have much choice, so I let Richard take me to the diner. On entering, he started to lead me to the front, he then froze and backtracked to the booths at the back of the room.

"Richard, who are they?" It looked like he was trying to avoid the three guys seated by one of the windows.

"I don't know."

He was grumpy now and I hesitated to say that he looked troubled. "Richard...."

"Please don't ask again, Rose."

"*Okay.*" Well, that was odd.

We ate in silence, but by the time we had finished, he seemed to be back to normal.

"Thank you for this evening, Rose. Perhaps we could do this again sometime?"

I tried to hide a yawn. "Maybe."

Richard walked me to the front door, which made me nervous, but luckily, JT opened the door and saved the day.

I quickly said goodnight and dragged JT inside, closing the door behind us.

March 24, 1947
Richard doesn't have to marry me...

It had been two days since I last saw Jacob. I missed him terribly. I was sitting on the porch, day dreaming about the night on the beach, when Richard appeared in his father's car.

He climbed out and came running over to me. "Rose, will you come for a drive with me?" I hesitated. "Please?" he begged.

Oh, what the heck. I wasn't exactly doing anything. "All right. Let me just grab a jacket and my purse."

I ran inside to quickly grab what I needed and ran back outside. Richard opened the door for me. I climbed inside his father's luxurious car and admired the cream leather interior with a dark mahogany wooden dashboard, while Richard shut the door and ran around to the other side.

"Richard, what's going on?" I was both nervous and curious.

"My father has agreed I don't have to marry you. So I thought we could celebrate with pie and chocolate milk," he replied, grinning at me like a little boy.

I laughed. "Well, let's celebrate then."

He drove to town and parked at the crowded diner. We walked inside and I spotted Jayne on her own just finishing eating. I walked over, sitting down beside her. "What are you doing here?"

"Richard wants to celebrate not being forced to marry me."

Her eyes nearly popped out of her head. Which made me laugh.

"Rose, Sandy is going to bring our favorite pie and milk over. Hello, Jayne. Would you like anything?"

"No, I've just finished eating. Thank you, though."

Richard sat opposite me and engaged Jayne in conversation. I so wanted to confess to Jayne about Jacob, but I was afraid she would say something to someone else. She may be my best friend, but she had trouble, big trouble actually, keeping things to herself.

I had just finished my pie when I noticed JT sitting with Levi, Walt, and some girls at the back of the diner.

Excusing myself, I walked over to their table. When he saw me, he went bright red and stood up. He grabbed my arm and pulled me away from his friends so they were out of hearing range.

"What are you doing here, sis?"

"I'm with Jayne and Richard. What about you? You know you're not allowed in here."

"I'm with Walt and Levi." He glanced in their direction.

"I have eyes, JT. I'll walk back with you, so you don't get into any trouble with Father. I also don't want Richard getting any ideas."

He laughed. "Wouldn't want that, sis." He strolled back to his friends and said his goodbyes, then walked back to me.

"Let me just tell Jayne and Richard I'm leaving," I said, quickly walking over to where they were sitting.

"Sorry, but I'm going to walk back to the house with JT, before Father gets home."

"Rose, please don't leave. Can't JT walk back on his own?" Richard asked, frowning at JT, who stuck his tongue out at him.

I gave him a shove. "Stop that." I turned back to Jayne and Richard. "I really need to make sure he gets there without causing any more trouble. I'll see you both later." I turned quickly and grabbed hold of JT's arm, then dragged him out of the diner.

March 26, 1947
The night I became a woman....

    Sneaking out of the house had JT catching me, again. I owed him an *Our Gang* comic. He sure was getting a lot out of me.

    Jacob was waiting for me at the bottom of the drive. I ran straight into his arms, and we kissed and kissed while he spun me around. "I've missed you so much," he caressed my face, "my Rose."

    "Always."

    "Let's go, before we miss the bus." He took my hand as we walked to the bus stop. We should be more careful, because I didn't want Father getting wind of me going out with someone other than Richard. While Jacob was holding on to me, I really didn't care.

    We were going watching *The Shocking Miss Pilgrim* with Betty Grable. I loved her movies, so I was really looking forward to watching it.

    Jacob held my hand all the way there, and during the movie, I cuddled into him, moving slightly to give him a quick kiss.

    After the movie ended, we only had time to catch the bus home, but we jumped off a stop earlier. We walked along the cliffs, Jacob had his arm wrapped around my shoulders with mine holding him tight around his waist. He felt so amazing. I never wanted to let go.

Suddenly stopping, Jacob turned me to face him and held my face in his hands, caressing me with his thumbs. "Rose, I love you," he whispered.

I reached out to him with my hand and tangled my fingers in the hair at the nape of his neck. He shivered. He put his mouth to mine. I moaned, searching out his tongue, sliding mine along his in a dance as old as time. Our breathing started to grow heavy. I moved in closer to him. He put his hands on my hips and brought me in even closer, while he continued his assault on my senses.

"Make love to me, Jacob." He looked startled.

"Are you sure?" he asked me in a whisper as he moved my hair behind my ears with an unsteady hand.

"More than ever." I kissed his palm.

Chapter 12

Mack was in the kitchen cooking breakfast when Thomas arrived bearing a gift of daisies. He shoved the flowers at her with a slight blush. "Picked you these on the way."

Smiling at him, she reached out and took the flowers, then gave him a kiss on his cheek. "Thank you, Thomas. I don't ever remember being given flowers by a gentleman before."

She stretched up to the top shelf of the cupboard for a vase. "That guy in that fancy suit at your apartment gave you flowers," Lucas stated.

"Yes, but he wasn't a gentleman. Now go wash up and stop listening to adult conversations." She tried to hide her embarrassment by setting the table for breakfast.

Sometimes she really wished she could gag Lucas. He was her nephew and she loved him, but sometimes…. Ugh!

She turned back towards Thomas, who appeared to still be chuckling at Lucas' comment. "Are you all right, Thomas?" she asked, having been worried about him after last night.

"I'm fine. Don't be worrying about me."

She gave him a long look. "Okay, I won't for now."

"I was wondering if Lucas would like to come back with me to look through some more comics."

"That would be fine. What comics are they?"

No sooner had he sat at the table, she put his breakfast in front of him. "Thanks, Mack. *Our Gang*. I have every issue as well."

She was sitting at the table, now that Lucas had joined them. "You know I've heard of them. They're the 'Little Rascals characters' right?"

"That's right. I have from the first issue in October 1942, to the last one before they added Tom and Jerry, which would be issue thirty-eight in November 1947. Didn't much care for the *Tom and Jerry* stories," he said, enjoying his breakfast.

"Wow, that's some collection you must have."

"I know."

They finished the rest of their breakfast in silence, apart from Lucas, who kept slurping his milk.

The morning was spent with Lucas and Thomas bent over the atlas, trying to find where his parents were now.

Not long after, the two headed out for some fun, hand in hand. Mack was really surprised with how quickly they had become friends. Lucas was used to spending time with older people, because of his grandparents and where they lived, but it usually took a lot longer for him to warm up to someone new. Then again, Thomas wasn't like the people at her parents' village. He was, different; all grumpy on the outside, and like a mischievous little boy on the inside, so perfect for Lucas.

"Thomas?" Lucas said with a quizzical look on his face. "Why don't you like Tom and Jerry?"

Thomas really hadn't expect that question and burst out laughing. "I preferred the *Our Gang* kids. They used to get into trouble, like I did as a child." He grinned. "Used to give me some good ideas, too!"

As they walked hand in hand to Thomas' cottage, it brought back memories of another time. Except he was the child, and his sister, Rose, was the one holding his hand. She had been taking him to the beach, probably close to seventy-five years ago now.

With his cottage door open, Lucas ran inside, straight to the front room where Thomas kept the comics for him to read. Thomas followed behind him with his mind still on Rose. He hadn't thought about her in a long time. He'd loved his sister, and always thought she'd died hating him, until Mack had started to read the diary.

He'd lived with regret about that final night, and in sixty-five years, he hadn't spoken about it. If only he'd told his father, perhaps Rose would have lived her life with the man she'd obviously loved. It wouldn't have been easy at first, because of their father, but if their love was true, they would have made it work.

An excited Lucas brought him back to the present. "Can I look at this one, Thomas, please?"

He glanced down. "Not that one." He removed it from Lucas' excited fingers at the same time as he offered him the next issue. "Try this one."

Thomas moved away from Lucas and walked the short distance to his bedroom, still holding the comic in his hand as he glanced down at it while he remembered. Sitting on the side of his bed, he placed the comic on his night table to read later, when he was alone.

It was dated April 1, 1947, the comic his sister had bought him as a surprise. She'd left it on his bed the night she died. He'd placed it in to the box with the other issues, having never opened it.

Perhaps it was time to lay old ghosts to rest and read it.

Mack, who had the morning alone, decided to retrieve her laptop and hooked it up to her Internet connection, so she could start doing some very important research. She really needed to try and find Jacob. Hell, she was half in love with him herself.

Okay, she knew his name back then was Jacob Evans, and going with his age, he was born around 1924. She decided to check New York first, and started to get all excited when only one result appeared, who was born around 1924.

As she looked at the information, Mack was delighted there was no death certificate, but there was a marriage license dated April 19, 1947.

After about ten minutes, she found a telephone number and address for him in Brookline, Boston. She wasn't sure whether to get in touch or not, as he seemed to get married just a week after Rose died, although he didn't know that, he thought she hadn't loved him, so perhaps he got married in anger. But a week after - why?

He also phoned Degan House a month later asking for Rose. Surely he wouldn't have done that if he'd married, unless, of course, the wrong year had been entered on the website? She would have to purchase some credits to view the marriage license for a correct date. For now, she would act as though this was the correct Jacob Evans. She had nothing to lose and everything to gain, if he was the correct Jacob.

With a deep breath, Mack picked her cell up and dialed the number, which was answered on the second ring.

"Evans residence."

"Oh, hello. My name is Mackenzie Harper, and I was wondering if Mr. Jacob Evans lived there?"

"What's the reason for the enquiry?"

"Who am I speaking to, please?" Mack asked in reply. She needed to be a bit cautious in case she was talking to his wife.

"I'm Martha, Mr. Evans' housekeeper." Then she was silent, having realized she'd just practically admitted to Mack she'd found the correct person.

"All right, Martha, this is going to sound strange, but I've come across a diary dated March and April 1947, and it contains information about a Jacob Evans. If your employer is the same Jacob Evans who lived in Cape Elizabeth, Maine, during that time, then I really need to speak to him. I'm concerned he's been living all this time thinking something happened that didn't. If that makes any sense?"

"That's some story, Miss Harper. I'll have to find out for you. Can I take your number and your address?"

Mack gave her the phone number and address for Rose Cottage, hoping Martha really would pass the message on. Otherwise she'd have to visit once Lucas had gone home to his parents.

"Okay, I have that. Thank you." Then Martha put the phone down on her.

"Who was that, Martha?"

She was surprised. "Oh, Mr. Dean! I didn't know you were home. It was a young lady asking about your grandfather."

Dean placed his helmet on top of the side table. "What about my grandfather?"

Martha was all flustered. "She said she'd found a diary from 1947, and wanted to know if the Jacob mentioned was your grandfather. It can't be, really, because apart from the war, I don't think he lived anywhere other than here, and certainly not Maine."

"Hmm, did you take her contact details?"

He walked over to Martha and took the information from her. "Please don't mention anything, until I've had time to check this out, okay?"

"If you're sure, Mr. Dean?"

"I am."

Dean had been thinking about escaping for awhile now, to get away from his mother, who kept throwing Cynthia at him and going on and on about getting married. All because she wanted grandchildren. She really was driving him nuts, so he'd just been given the perfect excuse to escape.

Once in his room, he tossed his things on to his bed and walked over to his desk, pulled out the chair and sat down, opening the lid to his laptop. Dean brought up a search engine and had a look at available summer rentals near Cape Elizabeth, and felt his luck was in when the cottage right next door to the mystery caller's address appeared to be available for the next few weeks.

After he debated with himself about whether or not this really was a good idea he picked up his cell and dialed the contact number before he could change his mind.

His last contract had just come to an end, and the new graphic work he had scheduled didn't start for another two months, so it was the perfect time to head on vacation.

He paid the deposit with his credit card and arranged to pay the rest in cash when he collected the keys from his new landlady.

On his way out of the house, Dean left a message with Martha for his mother, saying he had gone away for a few weeks, much to Martha's amusement. She knew he would do anything to avoid his mother and her matchmaking.

Dean climbed on his Harley and headed north up the coast, thinking about Miss Mackenzie Harper.

It was mid-afternoon when Mack heard her cell ring and dashed to answer it, only to find her sister Melinda on the other end.

"Hi sis, how's everything? Is Lucas okay? Any gorgeous guys? Bored yet?"

Mack sighed in relief when Melinda finally shut up, probably to breathe. For some reason, when Melinda was on the phone she could hardly shut her up, but when you talked to her in person, she could hold a perfect conversation.

"Everything's okay. Lucas is great. No gorgeous guys, unless you count a charming eighty-year-old named Thomas, and no, we aren't bored yet."

"Sorry, Mack." Melinda laughed down the phone as she realized she hadn't shut up long enough for Mack to answer her questions.

"All right, I'm used to you by now."

While she was still listening to her sister chat away, Mack heard a motorcycle outside. She plastered her nose up against the kitchen window just in time to see a jean-and-leather clad guy pull up next door. Wow, he looked hot. Tall, dark and mysterious.

She grabbed a magazine off the counter and used it to fan herself, because she'd started to get all hot and bothered. He looked delicious, and Mack really hoped when he removed his helmet, his face matched the rest of him.

"Mack, are you listening to me?" Melinda asked.

"Yes."

"No, you're not. And did I hear a motorcycle?"

"Yes you did, and a very hot guy with a gorgeous butt, which I wouldn't mind getting my hands on, has just pulled up outside next door. Hope he's moving in. He looks sinful… Mmm!" Mack laughed at her sister. For once, she'd managed to shut her up. She turned around to find Lucas stood behind her with a big grin on his face. "Here, talk to your mother." She passed him the phone.

Mack was still gazing at the guy next door and had switched off from the conversation Lucas was having with his mother about Thomas.

The hot guy had removed his helmet. He was tanned,

had plenty of muscle, and cropped dark hair. Mouth watering! Mmm, she wouldn't mind getting to know him. Things were looking up!

After hiding her disappointment from Thomas, because the new neighbor who they'd heard rustling around next door, hadn't stopped by, Mack baked a pound cake. She'd planned on taking it around, once Lucas had left with Thomas to go fishing again before dinner, but the new neighbor had climbed back on to his bike and disappeared.

Sighing, Mack made a cup of coffee, retrieved Rose's diary from her purse, curled up in the sitting room and settled down to read more about Rose and Jacob.

Chapter 13

March 27, 1947
We embrace in the library....

When I woke up this morning, I felt sore and achy between my legs, even after having a bath last night. It was early, so I filled the bath with just enough warm water to cover my hips and soaked for about ten minutes. I felt wonderful after that and so much in love with Jacob. He said he would call into the library to see me. I really hoped he would.

Jacob wanted to become an engineer and there were opportunities in Boston, he told me. I really hoped he would take me with him when he leaves. He said he would take me anywhere, and that he really loved me. He made me feel so special.

I walked to work and bumped into Jayne, who was dashing to the office where she worked. Late again. "Jayne, if you didn't spend so much time getting ready, you wouldn't be late so much." I pointed out to her.

"I have to look perfect, Rose. It takes a while dealing with perfection."

I rolled my eyes and laughed at her.

"Come on. If you're going to walk with me, you need to speed up some."

Well, there went my leisurely walk.

We dashed through town when Jayne started giving me odd looks. I had to know why, so I pulled her to a stop. "What's wrong?" Was she blushing? "Jayne?"

"Richard has asked me out to dinner," she blurted out.

For a second, I just stared at her, then started to laugh in relief. "Thank God for that." She didn't seem too impressed with my giggling. "I'm glad he's moving on. He's a nice guy, but not for me."

She stood with her hands on her hips. "Are you seeing that man from the tea rooms?"

Heck. "You do realize you're close to being very late for work."

"Oh no. I'll see you later."

Lucky escape.

I finally arrived at work and was greeted by Mr. Young, who was in a tizzy because two of the staff hadn't showed up for work, and there were about six people already in the library, which was unusual so early in the morning.

I followed him to the staff room and stashed my jacket and purse, then turned around practically bumping into him. "Mr. Young, please calm down," I told him, safe in the fact that he wouldn't fire me today, because I was the only one there.

"Rose, there are a lot of people out there this morning and only you here to help them. What are we going to do?"

What an idiot. "Mr. Young. I'm quite capable of helping who ever needs help. There aren't that many people in there."

We walked out to the main library floor, and I headed over to the front desk to check some books out for four of the people. "Mr. Young, I'm just going to place these books back on the shelves. Are you capable of looking after the two remaining?" I asked, getting the evil eye from him.

He ushered me away with his hands. I quickly grabbed the books that needed to be returned to the shelves and headed to the geography section first, then with the last remaining book, the history section.

I'd placed the last book on the shelf when I heard a throat being cleared behind me. I turned, and to my delight, I discovered it was Jacob. I quickly glanced around to make sure there was no one close, then took his hand and pulled him into the storage closet next to where he was standing.

"Are you all right?" he asked, caressing my face.

I smiled up at him. "Oh, Jacob. I am more than all right. Please kiss me."

He placed small kisses over my eyes, nose, and cheeks before sealing his mouth to mine in a beautiful kiss.

"I really want to go to Boston with you." He frowned down at me. "I love you and want to be with you all the time."

"Your parents wouldn't let you come away with me, and you know that."

I grinned at him. "I'm not planning on telling them. I'm going to sneak away with you."

"Now, Rose. I really don't think that's a good idea."

"Don't worry, it will be fine, and probably after a week or two, they'll forget all about me." I realized what I'd just said, was more likely the truth.

"I'll try and pop in again one day. I'm on nights for now and won't be able to meet you, but I better go before I get you into trouble. This conversation isn't over." He kissed me quickly, before I could argue with him.

We both slipped out of the closet, and I stood watching Jacob walk away just as Mr. Young walked around the corner heading in my direction.

"Rose, I've been looking for you. Where have you been?" he asked, looking between me and Jacob's departing form.

"I've been placing books back on the shelves, like I said." I walked towards the desk again and tried not to laugh at Mr. Young, who was huffing and puffing behind me.

March 28, 1947
Why me....

I was walking along the cliffs with Richard, who seemed to have developed a nervous twitch. "Richard, is something wrong?"

He took a deep breath. "Rose, I have to ask your father's permission to marry you."

I was stunned and just stared at him. Not this again. I really thought this had all come to an end.

"My father has been talking to yours, which has set this whole thing off again. I'm awfully fond of you and we could grow to love each other." He offered me a wry smile.

I sat down rather heavily on a large rock and just looked at him, not knowing what to say. Richard crouched down in front of me and took my hands into his. I was still in shock and just left them there.

"Richard, I can't marry you. I'm sorry our parents are putting you in this position, but please, don't say anything to my father. My life will be unbearable at home."

He sighed heavily. "I'll tell my father something to put him off for a short while, but Rose, you're actually the only woman I would consider marrying."

I looked quickly into his eyes. "I don't know what to say. I thought you were all right with us just being friends?"

"I am, but for my father pushing me, I wouldn't be here talking to you about this." He let go of my hands and sat beside me. "I will have to ask your father eventually, Rose. I have to."

"I need to go back." I turned and started walking back to the house rather quickly, with tears pouring down my face.

It wasn't as though I could admit that I was in love with Jacob. My father would hit the roof, especially now that he wanted me to marry Richard. What the heck was wrong with Father?

April 1, 1947
I really miss Jacob....

I really missed talking to Jacob and being with him, so imagine my delight when I spotted him walking into the library. I looked around to make sure Mr. Young wasn't present. Then I followed him to the history section, again.

He looked really tired. I took one look at him and held his hand, pulled him to a dark corner, then took his weary face into my hands. I pulled him down to meet my lips. "I love you."

"I've missed you so much." He rested his forehead against mine and just looked into my eyes. "Oh, Rose, I love you."

Still holding his face, I used my fingers to brush the hair out from his eyes. He turned his head and kissed my palm.

"I still don't know when I'm free to meet you, but I'll let you know as soon as I have a free night." He ran his hand over his face. "I'm so tired. I need to catch up on some sleep." He quickly kissed me and with one long, lingering look, walked out of the library.

April 4, 1947
Finally, I get to meet Jacob again....

I'd just had dinner with my parents and was up in my room brushing my hair, ready to go and meet Jacob. He'd come into the library last night, just before it closed, and after a rather hot embrace in the store cupboard, again, he'd asked me to meet him behind the library tonight. My mind was whirring with thoughts of him, thoughts of leaving with Jacob for Boston.

"Rose!" my father shouted from downstairs.

I threw my brush back onto the dressing table and ran out of my room, then hurried down the stairs, wondering what Father wanted. It was very rare for him to call me down, as he didn't really take any interest in me.

When I walked into the front parlor Richard was sitting there with an 'odd' smile on his face.

On seeing me, he stood and walked over to me, taking

my hand in to his. I had a really bad feeling about this. I tried to pull my hand free, but he tightened his hold, so I stamped on his foot.

"Rose," my father roared, "that is not the behavior of a young lady, especially towards her fiancé."

I froze. *What did he say?*

My father saw the shock on my face. "Richard has asked for your hand in marriage, and I have agreed."

I looked at my mother, who refused to meet my gaze. Richard looked as though he wished, to be elsewhere and father looked... relieved.

My tears were ready to fall. "There is no way I am going to marry Richard." I turned to him. "I'm sorry Richard, but I can't." I turned back to look at Father. "I will only marry for love, and Richard is a friend, and that is all he ever will be."

I turned and ran out of the house in tears. Richard called out to me. I ignored him.

With tears running down my face, I ran to the library and hoped Jacob was already waiting for me. I really needed his arms around me.

Jacob saw me come running around the corner and started to walk towards me. I ran straight into his arms and held on tight as I cried all over him.

"Rose. Oh God, what's wrong? What's happened?"

"Richard asked my father if he could marry me, and Father said yes." Jacob stilled at my announcement. "I told Father there was no way I was marrying him or anyone that I don't love. I then had to get away, so I ran here, to you."

Jacob placed a tender kiss to my lips, before he asked, "Do you want to go to my apartment?"

I just nodded my head, and by the time we arrived at his apartment, my tears had dried up, but I was left feeling angry that my parents would do something like they had. Leading the way inside, Jacob glanced around. Probably checking to make sure it was tidy.

The apartment was small, but nice and clean. The sitting room had a kitchen attached with a separate eating area. There were two doors off from the hall, which I presumed led to a bathroom and bedroom.

Jacob led me directly to the bathroom, to wash my face. Afterwards, I felt ten times better and went looking for Jacob.

I found him in the kitchen, boiling a pot of water to make us both a drink. I just stood and watched him, unobserved. He was gorgeous. My heart thumped in my chest. It felt so right being together in his apartment, fixing tea together.

He turned and caught me watching him. His whole face lit up. "Are you feeling better?" He walked over to me and took my face between his hands, then kissed me.

I wrapped myself around him and just held on. After a few minutes, I looked up into his eyes. "Make love to me, Jacob. Show me how much you love me."

He just looked at me for the longest time, then took me by the hand and led me to his bedroom. He stood in front of me and started to unbutton my dress while keeping eye contact with me. I lifted my hands and unbuttoned his shirt, smoothing my hands over his chest. He groaned and leaned down to take my lips in a passionate kiss. Goose bumps erupted all over my skin.

I left his shirt and slid my arms around his neck. My

fingers ran through the hair at the nape of his neck, while we continued to kiss.

Jacob removed my clothes and laid me down on his bed. He stood to the side of me and very slowly removed his own clothes.

After we'd made love, Jacob pulled me back into his arms, then just held me against him.

Making love on the beach had been wonderful, but in Jacob's bed had been beyond wonderful, and without the pain of him breaking through my womanhood.

"Rose?"

I lifted my head from his chest to look at him. "Yes?"

"If I manage to get an apprenticeship in Boston, will you really go with me? And be my wife?"

I burst into tears. "Yes, yes, yes!" I kissed him all over his face as my tears continued to flow. I was so excited that his feelings for me, were the same as mine for him.

Jacob helped me to mop up, laughing at my enthusiasm.

I laughed. "You only want to go to Boston because of the Boston Braves," I teased.

"That does have its advantages."

Chapter 14

After reading about the love between Rose and Jacob last night, Mack woke up feeling refreshed and light-hearted.

If only to have a love like they had, to know once in a lifetime, what it would be like to love someone so much and for it to be returned.

Since Lucas had been spending time with Thomas, he'd been falling asleep pretty soon after going to bed and waking up after Mack, much to her delight.

After her morning shower she dressed in her favorite shorts and headed downstairs, only to find Lucas already sitting at the kitchen table reading.

"How long have you been up, Lucas? I thought you were in bed," she asked, ruffling his hair as she walked past him to start the coffee.

"Just now. Thomas said he's going to come for breakfast again, so I didn't want to miss him."

She laughed. "Oh, Lucas. I can assure you that there is no way you would have missed him."

There was a knock on the back door. Lucas bolted out of his chair and ran to answer it, while Mack rooted around in the bottom of the refrigerator for some eggs.

"Auntie Mack, it's the very hot guy with a gorgeous butt you want to get your hands on," Lucas shouted from the back door, which had Mack banging her head on the refrigerator.

She turned around and met the heated look of the man from last night.

"Oh my God!" Was the first thing that came to mind after what Lucas had just said, with the guy actually being in the kitchen. Mack couldn't remember the last time she was so embarrassed. How the hell was she going to get out of this one? *Pretend Lucas hadn't said anything!*

"Hi. I'm Mackenzie Harper, but everyone calls me Mack." She held out her hand to him.

"Nice to meet you, Mack, I'm Dean Simone. I just rented next door for a few weeks." He tried not to laugh at her embarrassment while he admired her legs, which looked amazing. She was pretty hot as well, especially in very short shorts.

Before anyone could respond, Lucas did. "She already knows. She was hanging out the window telling my mother on the phone when you arrived."

With a shocked intake of breath, Mack slapped her hand over Lucas' mouth. "How many times have I told you not to listen to adult conversations?"

"It's a bit difficult when I'm in the room when you're having the adult conversation," Lucas replied with a huge grin, knowing exactly what he was up to.

At a loss for words, Mack hustled Lucas into the sitting room to play a Wii game and just hoped Thomas arrived very soon.

She turned around and caught Dean looking at her legs,

again. He very slowly moved up her body, his eyes finally meeting hers.

She was flustered, thanks to him. "Dean, what can I do for you? I presume you called around for a reason?" she asked in a husky voice.

Now that he'd seen her, he wasn't too sure of his plan, as she really was pretty, not as tall as he was, slimly built, long dark hair, and lovely clear skin, apart from a sprinkling of freckles over her nose. He would really love to lick each and every one. Not the response he should be having to someone he'd come to investigate, before telling his grandfather about her and her questions.

"Dean?" Mack questioned, all embarrassed, sure he'd just been giving her another once-over.

"Oh, Sorry. I seem to have forgotten things like coffee, milk, and sugar. I was wondering whether you would take pity on your new neighbor and loan me some."

God, he had a killer smile, and she was stuttering in embarrassment. "That's fine. In fact there's some fresh coffee over there, if you want to help yourself to a cup."

"Great, thanks." He walked towards the coffee, and while he poured a cup, he couldn't help but watch her out of the corner of his eye. He'd been stunned when the little kid had answered the door and shouted back to her, probably her words from last night. How the hell he managed not to laugh was beyond him, and then stepping inside to see the most perfect butt he'd ever seen sticking out of the refrigerator. She made his mouth water.

He watched Mack openly as she started to cook breakfast, which reminded him, he really did need to shop for food.

Thomas walked in through the door with a bunch of tulips in his hands just then and went straight over to Mack, not noticing Dean yet. "Well, Mack, you look pretty good this morning. Mavis told me there's a handsome young man moved in next door. Why don't you go and introduce yourself." He winked at her.

Thomas jumped around when he heard a throat being cleared, to come face to face with a grinning Dean.

"Hi. I'm Dean from next door."

He looked between Mack and Dean. "I'm Thomas, and do I need to leave?"

Mack laughed. "Don't be silly. Breakfast won't be long. Lucas is waiting in the sitting room for you." She watched him walk away, and then turned towards Dean. "Would you like to stay for breakfast?"

"Mmm, I'm hungry. What's on offer?" he asked, then laughed out loud when Mack's eyes opened wide.

"Well, it certainly isn't me! How about pancakes and syrup instead?"

"That will do... for now!"

She finished mixing the batter for the pancakes while only half-concentrating, as she was finding Dean's presence overwhelming in the small kitchen. He just seemed to permeate every single space.

"You can go relax in the sitting room and watch them both on the Wii, if you like," she said to try and get him out of the kitchen before she did something stupid.

"No, I'm fine right here... watching you."

Not knowing what to say, she turned her back and

started cooking the pancakes.

Once made, she bent over to place the cooked pancakes in the oven to keep them warm. She turned back around, and with a quick glance at Dean, placed warmed syrup and butter on the table.

"Dean, are you okay?"

He met her eyes. "Those shorts should be illegal," he growled.

"What?"

"Those shorts. On you. Should be illegal. I'm not going to be able to move any time soon." He grinned. She blushed.

She still felt a bit tongue-tied and decided it might be best to ignore him and called Lucas and Thomas in for breakfast.

After Mack had placed the food and drinks on the table, the only seat left was the one next to Dean. With a quick glance at him, their eyes met as he smiled over a forkful of pancakes, but it assured her that his mouth was at least busy, for now.

Eating in silence, Mack felt all hot and bothered, and she kept telling herself it really had nothing whatsoever to do with the really hot guy sitting next to her. Unfortunately, his voice matched the body, and he was no doubt, used to using his voice to get women to drop their panties. Squirming in her seat as Dean kept throwing hot glances her way, she decided a distraction was needed, before she said to hell with it and jumped the guy.

"Auntie Mack?" Lucas said, distracting her.

"Yes, Lucas?"

"Will you make me a cake today, please? If I promise to

be good."

"I baked a pound cake yesterday. You can have a slice of that after dinner," Mack offered, feeling herself blush, and certainly not admitting she'd made it for Dean. "Now eat up, so you can go off with Thomas."

She turned to Thomas, and asked, "What are you up to today?"

He winked at Lucas. "Well, me and my buddy here thought we might dig for worms."

Mack had just taken a sip of coffee, which ended up going down the wrong way and she started to choke. Putting the cup down rather heavily, it sloshed everywhere. She jumped up to grab some paper towels, only to find Dean already on the case.

Actually, he was more interested in drying her legs than anything else.

"Dean, you about finished down there?" She stood with her hands on her hips, trying not to laugh. It had been a long time since a man had been on his knees before her like that.

"Babe, I've not even started!" he whispered.

She opened and closed her mouth, lost for words, with Dean on his knees flirting with her.

He took pity on her when he saw her blush, and quickly stood back up, taking his seat again.

She glanced across the table only to see both Thomas and Lucas watching the show. Thomas looked as though he was about to burst with laughter.

"Now where were we?" Mack asked, once seated again.

"Worms. They're to use as bait, because Thomas dropped the maggots," Lucas announced with glee.

With a glare at both Thomas and Lucas, Mack couldn't decide if they were serious or not and from the look on Dean's face, neither could he.

"Where did you drop them?" Mack asked very slowly.

Both Lucas and Thomas looked rather shifty. "I think it's time to go. Come on, Lucas."

"Okay, bye, Auntie Mack. Bye, Dean," Lucas shouted as he skipped off in front of Thomas.

She leaned forward and put her head in her hands then groaned. "I could kill those two."

Dean laughed. "Are they always like that?"

"Pretty much."

Mack started moving the dishes from the table, while Dean filled the sink with water and started to wash them. She picked up a hand towel and started to dry them, still a bit stunned there was a sexy guy in her kitchen who didn't disappear the minute he'd finished eating. A keeper, as her mother would say.

It had been a really long time since anyone had flirted with her, and it felt really nice. The fact that Dean at least seemed a decent guy added to the pleasure.

"Do you want to go for a ride on my bike?" Dean asked before he could stop himself.

She seemed like a really nice, good-looking woman who he actually wanted to spend time with, but he needed to find out if there was a diary. Why the hell did he use his mother's maiden name when he introduced himself? She would have probably been okay with his real name. Mack certainly didn't seem like an opportunist.

"You mean the Harley?" Mack asked with a huge grin

on her face.

He winked. "Is there any other?"

"Give me five, to put some jeans on."

Dean groaned, wishing she didn't have to cover her amazing legs, with jeans.

As she ran upstairs, she was really excited. Mack had always wanted to go on a Harley, but all the guys she usually attracted had compact cars you couldn't even breathe in!

Chapter 15

Dean, in the meantime, was really hoping she didn't look so hot in jeans, otherwise he'd have a heck of a job keeping his hands to himself. He looked up when she was on her way back into the kitchen, and froze, his mouth going dry. She was wearing the tightest jeans he'd ever seen, that rested very low on her hips. Her top began to ride up as she moved, and he caught glimpses of her stomach.

"Okay, you ready?" she asked, already on her way out through the door.

"Oh, yes," he whispered.

"What?"

With a slight cough, he tried to clear the restriction in his throat. "Yes, let's go." He followed her outside, watching the sway of her delectable butt.

※

She was standing to the side of the bike while Dean fastened her helmet, unable to resist standing in close to him. He was wearing some sort of cologne and smelled delicious.

She climbed on to the bike and didn't know where to put her hands.

"Hold the brackets here and here," Dean told her.

"Okay, thanks."

"Or me!" He grinned just before he put his helmet on.

He sat on the front of the bike and took in some deep breaths to try and calm his raging hormones, which shot straight back up again as soon as he felt her hands sliding around his waist, under his t-shirt, bringing her hands into contact with his skin.

Mack grinned to herself, as she felt his stomach muscles quiver. Two could play at that game.

She felt all hot and bothered, and didn't know why she had to suffer on her own. She moved forward, her legs closing in along his thighs. He clenched his jaw together to stop the groan from escaping.

As he started the bike up, Dean just prayed he would get them to the lighthouse in one piece.

"Thomas, what do you think Auntie Mack and Dean are doing?"

He looked at Lucas, who was sitting in the lounge with cookies and milk, reading yet another *Our Gang* comic. "Erm, talking. They are neighbors, you know," he replied.

"He seems okay. I think he likes Auntie Mack. Do you think he'll marry her and go live with her?"

He didn't really know where Lucas was going with that question. "Would that bother you if he did, Lucas?" he replied, taking a seat beside him.

"I wanted her to marry you!"

He laughed. "Lucas, I'm an eighty-year-old man. Your

aunt is young and needs a younger man, like Dean, or someone like him."

"Have you ever been married, Thomas?" he asked with a frown.

"Yes. I was married for thirty years before she passed away."

"That's sad. What was her name?"

He was deep in thought. "Janet, the love of my life."

"Hmm, well, would you be my granddad then? Scott has two granddads and he says it's really cool."

"We'll have to see, Lucas. Let's get back to reading. Do you want me to read you this one?" he asked, rather amused.

"Yes, please."

Be his granddad. If Lucas only knew how much he would really enjoy that. Hopefully, Mack would stay in touch with him when it was time for her to head back to Boston. He would miss them both terribly.

Dean was at the Portland Head Light watching Mack while she walked along the edge of the cliffs. With the light breeze from the ocean, blowing her hair back from her face, she was stunning.

He'd really enjoyed spending the day with her. They had driven into Portland and browsed around the Old Port shops. Then on their way to the lighthouse, they had stopped for lunch, eating a delicious lobster meal.

Dean, for the first time in a long time felt as though he could breathe. Mack was like a breath of fresh air, so easy to talk to. To laugh with. She listened to what he had to say without interrupting, offering her opinion once he'd finished. She even listened while he went on and on about his work as a graphic novelist. He worked with a couple of authors, who had great ideas, but couldn't put their vision on paper, which is where he came in. He loved his work and the flexibility it gave him.

They had walked around the lighthouse already. He'd taken hold of her hand as they approached the cliffs. She'd kept her hand there, lacing their fingers together.

As Dean walked over to her, she turned and saw him approach, offering him a dazzling smile. Dean missed a step. She was so beautiful, she took his breath away, with all that flowing brunette hair.

He stood in front of her without saying anything and moved his hands to her face in a light caress, lowered his head then placed a light kiss to her lips. "You are so beautiful." He lowered his head again and used more pressure against her mouth. She moved in close and put her arms around his waist as the kiss deepened. Mack opened to him and sucked his tongue into her mouth.

He shivered and groaned. "I think we better stop," he whispered, placing small kisses around her lips.

"Then why aren't we?"

He couldn't stop touching her, and smoothed his hands down her arms. He then moved his hands to caress her waist under her t-shirt. "Because I don't have any will power with you. This top has been driving me crazy all day. Every time you move, I catch a glimpse of your stomach."

"I was so tempted to put my hands elsewhere when I sat behind you on your bike earlier," she said, laughing, then squeezed Dean's butt before she took a step back.

"God, I don't know how I managed to get us anywhere without crashing, with your hands on me. Nothing ever felt so good."

She winked at him. "I know!" Then she sauntered towards his Harley. She knew damn well his eyes were on her butt all the way, which made her feel desirable, for the first time in a long time.

As he walked Lucas back to Rose Cottage, Thomas couldn't help but think about his sister again. In a way, Mack was a bit like Rose, with her spirit and soft heart. Maybe one day soon, he might be ready to talk to Mack about the night Rose died and the regret he'd lived with all these years. If only he'd talked back then, things might have worked out differently.

First though, he had to find the courage to finally read the comic Rose had bought him. Her last gift to him.

"Thomas! Look! Auntie Mack's been on Dean's bike. Come on," Lucas shouted as he ran towards them to watch his aunt climb off the bike.

She removed her helmet, then held her arms out to him. Lucas ran straight into them.

"Auntie Mack, have you really been on Dean's bike?"

"Yes, I have."

"That's not fair. I want to!" Lucas started to get tearful, although Mack knew for a fact Lucas was rather capable of putting on the water works at will.

"Hey, Lucas. You want to sit on the bike and I'll take

you around the yard?" Dean asked him before the water works really started.

Lucas dived out of Mack's arms and ran straight over to Dean, who lifted him aboard.

Dean winked at Mack. "You need your helmet on, young man," Dean said to him, while he placed one on to his head.

She felt a bit unsure with Lucas being on the Harley, and walked closer to Dean, who caught the frown on her face. He took hold of her hand and placed a kiss to her cheek.

"He'll be fine, don't worry." He leaned in to give her another quick kiss, on her lips this time, before he climbed on the back of his bike. Dean surrounded Lucas with his body as he explained to him what the different instruments were for on the panel in front of them.

Mack walked over to the steps leading into the cottage and sat down beside Thomas. She couldn't help but blush slightly when she met his eyes, and the knowing look in them.

"I see you made friends with the neighbor then?" He chuckled.

She grinned. "Oh yeah!"

Dean switched the bike on and very slowly put it into gear and started moving around the yard with an excited Lucas sitting in front of him. With a glance at Mack every time he passed, Dean winked at her, which really amused Thomas.

"Thomas, do you like Dean?" Mack asked just as Dean switched the bike off.

"I don't swing that way!" He tried not to laugh at the

stunned look on Mack's face.

With a laugh, she nudged him with her elbow. "You know exactly what I mean."

"I only met him briefly this morning, but from what I can see, and how he spoke to me, I would say he's one of the good guys."

"Thanks."

"Auntie Mack, Thomas, did you see me?" Lucas just about managed to get out before diving on Mack.

"We certainly did. You were pretty good there."

"Thanks, Auntie Mack."

"He's great." Dean ruffled Lucas' hair. "Listen, I'm going to leave you guys for now. I have some things to take care of. I'll come round tomorrow, if that's okay?"

Mack smiled up at Dean, slightly disappointed that he wasn't staying for dinner. "We'll see you at breakfast, right?"

Grinning, Dean asked, "Was that an invitation?"

"Sure was."

"I'll be there," Dean replied, hesitating. He really didn't want to end his time with Mack.

Mack turned to Thomas. "You going to eat dinner with us?"

"No, thank you. I'm meeting a couple of guys at the Irish Pub tonight, so I'll see you all at breakfast," Thomas told her.

Dean took hold of her hand and pulled her up. "Walk with me a minute?"

Thomas grinned at the two of them and stood up then took hold of Lucas' hand. "Come on, Lucas, show me that game you keep talking about before I leave." They entered the cottage, giving Dean and Mack some privacy.

They walked over to the front door of Dean's cottage holding hands. He didn't know what to say, because all he really wanted to do was drag her inside and never let her go. He wondered where the hell that thought came from. It wasn't one he'd had before.

He turned to Mack, took her face in his hands and brought her in close. She put her hands on his hips and moved in even closer, coming into contact with Dean's erection.

His mouth descended to ravish her with a hot, open-mouthed kiss. Surprising even herself, she wrapped her arms around his neck, raising one leg around his hips.

He pulled away from her mouth to take in some much-needed air, then shuddered as she rubbed herself against him. "Mack, we have to… stop."

She dragged his head back down to meet her lips again, while he put his hands on her hips and brought her into closer contact with him.

He forced himself to move his mouth away from Mack's, when he heard a throat being cleared. "You're both giving me high blood pressure!" Thomas shouted from the kitchen window.

They both started laughing. He put her slowly back down then stepped away from her. "I think you better go, before I drag you inside."

She took a few steps away from him, then on unsteady legs started to walk away to her own cottage. She couldn't help but look back to a very aroused Dean. "Promises, promises." She entered her own cottage laughing.

Dean let out a sigh of relief as he entered his cottage. Heck, he had it really bad for Mack. He'd just come so close to taking her up against the door.

Her hair was so soft and smelled of raspberries, her skin lovely and smooth and those freckles, he thought they were sexy as hell. She'd kept teasing him all day with glimpses of her stomach, every time she moved, he just wanted to reach out and caress her skin. She was basically driving him crazy.

Hopefully, sometime soon, she'd mention the diary, or he could get her to tell him, then perhaps the perfect opportunity would arise for him to tell Mack his real name and about his grandfather.

He really wished he hadn't been an idiot and given his actual surname of Evans instead of Simone.

Mack had a quiet dinner with Lucas, and afterwards she played a new Super Mario Brothers game on the Wii for half an hour with him. He kept winning, telling her she was worse than his friend Scott.

Lucas was in his bed asleep, while she was lying propped up in bed, drinking her hot chocolate, thinking about Dean.

He was really appealing, both in personality and looks. She had never felt so attracted to someone so quickly. He was taller than she was, and his body rippled with muscles, without an ounce of fat on him. With his blue eyes and the tattoo that peeped out from the neck of his t-shirt, he was gorgeous and maybe a bit rough around the edges. But he'd certainly got her motor running.

After being lost in her own thoughts for ten minutes, she reached out and picked up Rose's diary to read some more, thinking she may show Dean in a day or to and get his opinion on what to do if Jacob didn't get back to her.

Chapter 16

April 5, 1947
Breakfast with my parents....

After the upset of yesterday, I really didn't want to get up. I snuggled down for five more minutes, thinking about Jacob and how gentle he was when he'd made love to me in his bed. He made me feel cherished and loved.

I'd promised to marry him and move to Boston. I could hardly wait. I wanted to be with him desperately. My heart was filled with so much love, when I thought about my future with him.

When he walked me home last night, we talked about our plans for Boston. At first we would rent one of the rooms his sister had available in her boarding house. Apparently, she only rented rooms to married couples, so to begin with, until we could marry, we would pretend. Jacob had already spoken to his sister about me, and she had agreed to let us stay together and treat me as his wife.

I finally dragged myself out of bed, rushing to the bathroom, then back to my room to dress for work. I was actually dreading facing Mother and Father at breakfast. If I could avoid doing so, then I would.

I took a few deep breaths for courage, then walked out of my room and down the stairs.

"Morning, Mother, Father," I said, acting as though nothing untold happened last night.

I took my seat, where my breakfast was already waiting for me. While I buttered a piece of toast my father cleared his throat.

"Where did you disappear to last night?"

"Somewhere peaceful," I replied and started to eat.

"Rose, dear, we just thought that it would be a good match between you and Richard. He would be able to look after you," my mother said, patting my arm.

"Richard would be able to look after you well. His family has more money than we'll ever see."

"Father. I'm sorry, but I'm not going to marry Richard. As your only daughter, you should want me to marry for love and to someone who can make me happy just by being with them. Money shouldn't come into it at all."

"You need money to live, Rose," Father said, starting to get irritated with me.

"That's why there are jobs. I intend to marry someone who doesn't mind getting his hands dirty, and who doesn't mind working for his money. I have no intention of marrying someone who just spends all day spending the family inheritance, without working a day in his life."

I stood up from the table and looked at both my parents. "Please don't expect me to marry him, because I will always refuse." I walked out of the room, collected my jacket and purse, then started walking slowly to work.

Unfortunately, my slow walk to work didn't go as

planned. No sooner had I left the front path, Richard pulled up to the side of me. "Rose, let me give you a lift to work."

I ignored him and carried on walking.

"Rose, please talk to me," he begged, running up to me. "I'm really sorry about last night. My father said something that made me do what I did."

I sighed. "Richard, I'm sorry, too. I think it would be for the best if we don't see each other again for a while, that way your father won't get the wrong idea about us."

I walked past him and left him stunned behind me. Not long after, I heard his car screech away from the curb, obviously in a temper.

At the library, Mr. Young put me on the desk, which could be even more boring than dusting shelves. Throughout the day, I helped around ten people.

It had just turned three when I looked up, having heard the door opening. I looked straight into Jacob's eyes. I only just stopped myself from running into his arms.

I stood and asked Mary, who was close by, to watch the desk while I popped to the restroom. I then followed Jacob to the Philosophy section.

Jacob took hold of my face and pulled me into him for a soul-shattering kiss. "I hated sleeping on my own last night, after having you in my bed." He kept kissing all over my face and finally came back to my mouth, slipping his tongue between my lips.

"I can't wait for us to be in Boston, to wake up with you every day, to eat our meals together. Oh, Jacob, I'm so excited."

"My Rose." He couldn't stop kissing me. Not that I was

complaining. "I better go. I'll see you again soon. Remember, I love you," he told me.

I just stood watching him walk away and out through the door.

The rest of the afternoon went really slow. All I wanted was to be with Jacob.

Finally, after a very long day, I left work and walked slowly home, with my thoughts on Jacob and what our life would be like in Boston.

I entered the house and was greeted by both my parents, again. I stopped dead and looked from one to the other. "Rose, please come in here a minute, I have something to say," my father said.

Dreading what my father was going to say, I followed my parents into the front parlor.

"I've spent most of the day thinking about what you said this morning." He looked very ill at ease. "We really don't want you to be unhappy, and I'm sorry if we gave you the impression your happiness doesn't matter, because it does. Richard seems to care for you, and he would be able to make sure you are well looked after. Even if he doesn't do anything." Did my father just smile? "Saying all that, we do want you to marry well, so please don't get it in your head that anyone will do, because they won't."

I wasn't sure what they expected me to say to Father's little speech. "Thank you. May I leave?" Father looked ready to continue speaking, but thought better of it and just nodded his head.

April 7, 1947

Oh my, I was introduced to a wall tonight....

Just checking a book out for Mr. Willis, I looked up and saw Jayne walking into the library. She always made me laugh as she looked around to make sure Mr. Young wasn't lurking about anywhere.

"Jayne, why aren't you at work?" I asked, leaning on the desk towards her.

"I'm on an errand for one of the bosses. What's going on with you? I have hardly seen you. You haven't been to any of the local dances like you usually do. Are you seeing that, what's his name, Jacob?"

I guess I didn't hide my shock very well, my face gave me away. JT always said I made a terrible liar.

"Are you out of your mind? What if your parents find out?"

My face fell. "I know what my parents are like, but I love him, Jayne. I don't want anyone else. I'm going to be with Jacob whether or not they agree. I intend telling them soon, but not yet." I really hoped she wouldn't tell anyone.

Not long after Jayne left a student from the local school came in asking if I would help him with a paper on George Washington. I'd no sooner said goodbye to the grateful student, when Jacob walked in. He came straight over to my desk.

"Are you free to meet me at my apartment tonight?" he whispered.

"Yes." He caressed me with his eyes.

"I'll see you later."

"Who was that?" Mary asked, after he left.

I didn't really like her, because she talked about everyone behind his or her backs and it was very annoying. "He wanted to know if we had a new book he'd heard about. I told him we hadn't had a delivery of books for about four weeks. He said the book was released about two weeks ago." I turned my back to her and started collecting some books that needed to be returned to the shelves.

I spent the rest of the day watching the time to when I could be with Jacob. The day really dragged on, and once or twice, I nearly went to see Mr. Young to tell him I had woman problems. He usually didn't ask questions if one of us told him that, and he couldn't wait to get out of sight. But I didn't. I stayed until closing. Then after brushing my hair and applying more lipstick, I dashed out and quickly walked to Jacob's apartment.

Jacob opened the door, took one look at me, grabbed hold of my arm and pulled me into his apartment, kissing me. He pushed me up against the wall with his body. There wasn't one inch between us as his body was molded to mine while he kissed me until I was breathless.

My arms went around his neck. His hands searched under my skirt, bringing it up around my waist. "I need you, Rose."

"Yes."

And before I knew it, we'd both experienced the brief burst of pleasure that only Jacob could create within me.

"I'm sorry. I shouldn't have taken you like that, up against the wall."

"Jacob, you can take me like that anytime you want, as long as we're not in public. It was amazing."

He laughed, helping me to get my feet back under me. Then he fastened his pants, while I pulled my underwear back on. He took my hand. "I want to show you something."

After we were comfortable in his sitting room, he passed me a letter. "Read it," he said, sitting beside me.

The letter was from an engineering company in Boston, offering him an apprentice position that started on Monday, April 21st.

"Will you still come with me, Rose?" He looked so nervous.

"I love you, Jacob. I have already agreed to be your wife, so yes, I will still come with you. I'll go anywhere with you." He sighed in relief.

"Do you think you could be ready to leave a week today on the 14th? It would be easier for you if we get settled in Boston before I start the job. Eleanor has said you can help her with a few minor things around the house during the day, if you like."

I smiled at him. "I do like, and I can hardly wait."

"The money is pretty good, so we can save up and find ourselves an apartment, or if you want to stay longer at my sister's, then we might be able to save for a deposit on our own home, but I would prefer that we get married fairly soon."

I pulled his head down to mine and kissed him ever so softly. "I would marry you tomorrow if that was possible."

We sat cuddled on the sofa, not talking for the longest of time, and then all too soon, I had to head home.

Jacob walked me part of the way, while we made plans to meet at eleven, the night of the 14th, next Monday.

I planned to take some of my things to Jacobs' apartment on Friday, and then whatever else I wanted, I would have to sneak them out with me on the 14th.

My biggest regret was that I couldn't take JT with me. I would miss him so much. *I love you, brother!*

I will miss Mother and Father, but they have forced me to make this choice. If I thought for one minute they would accept Jacob, I would have told them.

Before going to bed, I needed to find a hiding place for my diary so no one would stumble across it and stop our plans.

I knew the perfect place!

Chapter 17

Mack couldn't get Rose and Jacob out of her thoughts, and thinking about them brought tears to her eyes. She ended up cooking the eggs for breakfast in tears.

"Hey, Mack!" Dean said in greeting as he walked into the kitchen and headed straight to the coffee pot. He pulled up short when he saw the streaks on her face. Changing direction, he went straight up to her, and after looking closely, wiped the tears away with his thumbs.

He removed the pan from the burner and turned it off just as he pulled her into his arms. "Mack, what's wrong? Why are you so upset?"

She couldn't answer and just burrowed her face deeper into Dean's chest, then put her arms around his waist while she sobbed.

A few minutes later, she pulled away and went to the sink to splash cold water on her face, stopping briefly as she heard Thomas outside talking, probably on his cell. "It's something and nothing. Please don't say anything?"

Dean frowned. "Okay, are you all right now?"

"Actually, I think I am, but a good morning kiss might make me feel so much better." She stood right in front of him. He placed his hands on her shoulders and leaned down for a very quick kiss, too quick.

"Auntie Mack, are you really doing kissing things with Dean?"

"Oh my God." She turned crimson, while Dean just grinned and walked over to Lucas doing the high five thing.

"How's it going, champ?"

"Good. I slept in today," Lucas replied, trying to see out of the window, obviously looking for Thomas.

"Thomas will be in soon, Lucas. I think he's on the phone."

"I wish he'd hurry up."

Just then the back door opened and in walked Thomas. "Morning, folks."

He walked over and gave Mack a bunch of peonies.

She leaned over to give Thomas a big hug and a kiss on the cheek. "I think you need to marry me, Thomas." He was so sweet and would make a good grandfather.

"Hey, not funny. He can get his own girl. You're mine." Dean pulled Mack into his arms, laughing.

Suddenly, she was all serious and looked up at Dean. "Am I really?"

Dean stopped laughing and caressed Mack's face. He pushed the hair back from her forehead. "Mack, I've never felt like this before, but, I'm starting to think, that maybe, yes you are." He then placed a lingering kiss to her lips.

"Auntie Mack, are you making breakfast?"

Thomas chuckled. "I think she wants to be making something else, buddy."

All flustered she pulled away from Dean and finished

the breakfast, deep in thought.

Mack wondered what the hell she was doing. How did this happen? Why did this, with Dean, feel so right? Never in her life had she been so attracted to anyone. Dean had popped into her life literally twenty-four hours ago. How the heck had he managed to get under her skin so quickly? When he kissed her, she practically swooned at his feet.

Dean, meanwhile, was thinking about the mess he'd made for himself, and how he really needed to come clean about his name before his relationship could go any further with Mack. When she asked if she was his girl, his heart had flipped. Looking into her eyes, he knew he would do just about anything to make her his.

Mack was finally composed and turned from the stove to place the eggs, bacon, and biscuits onto the table.

"Okay folks. Can we eat without mentioning anything unpleasant?" She caught a smile on Thomas' face as she took her seat and started to load her plate with food.

"This looks good."

"Thank you."

Thomas looked rather tired. "How was your evening?" Perhaps that might explain it.

"Late night, but a good one. I won at poker, fifty bucks," he said rather proudly. "I don't think I've won that big since 1998."

Mack froze with a fork of food halfway to her mouth. "You serious?"

"Sure am. I think Lucas here is my good luck charm."

"My granny and gramps play strip poker. Is that what you played?"

Dean couldn't help but roar with laughter, which in turn had everyone else laughing, except for Lucas.

"What's so funny?" Lucas asked, baffled. He looked at the adults as though they'd lost their minds.

"Your granny and gramps playing strip poker, and no, that wasn't what I played," Thomas managed to reply.

"But why is that funny? Granny says..."

"Lucas, that's enough. Your breakfast will be going cold." Heaven knew what Lucas was about to say. Mack wasn't waiting to find out.

Lucas, not wanting to be hushed, carried on. "Auntie Mack, I was only going to say that Granny said she wasn't embarrassed about her body, or her droopy boobs at her age, but if Mommy didn't stop having her boobs made bigger, they'll pop, and then Daddy won't have anything to hold onto." He paused to catch his breath. "What does that mean, Auntie Mack?"

Both Dean and Thomas made a quick exit outside. She could hear Dean laughing on the other side of the kitchen door.

She giggled herself, and told Lucas to ask his father.

God, she really needed to have a word with her mother, who was the most flamboyant person she had ever known. Her mother still lived in the sixties and wasn't bothered who knew it, getting more outrageous as she grew older. Sometimes she forgot whom she was talking to, as Lucas just proved. No matter how much like their mother Melinda was, she would've hit the roof if she'd heard that comment.

She could remember growing up with Melinda, how proper behavior was expected when they were in school.

Their mother used to threaten to wash their mouths out with soap and water if they said anything untoward. Perhaps she needed to try that same tack with their mother now. Give her a taste of her own medicine.

With breakfast now finished, she stood and walked to the backdoor to find Thomas and Dean sitting on the steps. "Thanks for your help, guys."

Dean grinned. "Is it safe?"

"It is. For abandoning me, you get to wash the dishes!"

He stood up and kissed her, then walked back inside to finish his breakfast along with Thomas.

"Lucas, what would you say if we go fishing this morning and read some comics this afternoon?"

"Sounds cool."

Thomas was holding Lucas' hand as they walked to his cottage to get the rods from the front porch where he'd left them before going for breakfast.

He chuckled to himself about Dean and Mack. He'd noticed them both glancing at each other all through breakfast. Things looked to be heating up there. They'd only met yesterday, but they seemed so in tune with each other. Sometimes a man and woman could spend a lifetime together and never be truly 'together'. His mother and father came to mind. He really hoped everything worked out for Mack and Dean. They made such a promising couple.

"Thomas, do you know how to make a cake?"

Lucas broke his train of thought and he looked down to see him waiting for a response. "What do you want to make a cake for?"

"For Auntie Mack."

Thomas raised his eyebrows. "Why? Is it her birthday?" She hadn't mentioned anything.

"No, but she always makes them for me, so I thought I could make her one this time, with your help."

"Hmm. Well. I think it would be safer if we buy one. It might be more like the blind leading the blind, trying to make a cake." Thomas grinned at Lucas, who looked ready to carry on discussing a cake, then obviously thought better of it.

"Okay, I guess."

They reached his cottage. "Let's try and catch some fish for dinner instead." He collected the rods and his fishing basket, took hold of Lucas' hand again, for the walk to the stream. It was his favorite fishing spot that he'd been coming to for more years than he cared to remember.

Chapter 18

Mack was now alone with Dean, and all she wanted was to feel his lips on hers or even better, his hands on her body. Smiling to herself, she perched on top of the kitchen table, fluffed her hair, stuck her chest out, then smiled in Dean's direction.

"Dean."

He turned to look at her and nearly dropped the plate in his hand. "Mack," he croaked. "What…" He coughed, gulped, put the plate to one side and very slowly walked over to her. "You are playing hell with my intentions, Mack. You know that?" Dean leaned in and placed his hands on Mack's hips. He was a breath away from her lips.

Mack reached up and ran her hands through his hair, then smiled when she felt a shudder work its way through him.

"Mack." He breathed heavily as his lips met hers in a slow seductive kiss. Their tongues met and mated as Dean took hold of Mack's head to hold her in place while he deepened the kiss.

Mack wrapped her legs around Dean, and pulled him closer.

"I'm not doing this." Dean broke from the kiss.

"Doing what?" Mack replied, innocently.

Dean groaned. "You know what. I want you, Mack, but I want to take things slow, spend time with you."

"This is spending time with me," Mack interrupted.

Dean untangled himself and stepped away, resting his back against the kitchen sink then just stared at her.

"You. Are. Lethal. I have no intention of going anywhere, so we are going to spend time together, without sex getting in the way." Dean laughed at the look on Mack's face. "For now, that is."

"You're serious, aren't you?"

"Yep." He crossed his arms over his chest and waited her out.

"Oh, all right then. What do you want to do?" His eyes flared at her question, which Mack caught and snickered. "Just remember whose idea this was."

"I won't forget. Lets grab our jackets and climb on the Harley."

They'd spent the morning driving along the coastal roads, with Dean pulling over now and again for Mack to take some photographs. Although he'd been convinced that she'd only wanted to stop to grope his butt.

Back at the cottage, Dean parked the bike up and waited for Mack to climb off, before joining her. With their helmets removed and placed on the bike he took hold of Mack's hand, pulling her down the path to the beach.

Mack slid her hand out from Dean's and moved in closer, wrapping her arm around his waist, as Dean put his arm around her shoulders.

"You feel good against me, Mack."

"I know," she smirked.

She really was driving him crazy. In fact he considered himself an idiot for refusing her in the kitchen, earlier. *What the hell had he been thinking?* He'd actually been thinking, that he wanted it to last, to hopefully build what had started with Mack, into something more, and he didn't want to screw it all up with sex getting involved, at least until they'd gotten to know each other better.

"Dean!" Lucas shouted, just before the Frisbee clonked him on the back of the head.

Mack burst out laughing as Dean took off running after a Lucas, who ended up falling over, giggling so much.

"Stop. Stop. Stop."

"Are you sorry?" Dean asked him, while they both wrestled in the sand.

"It wasn't me," Lucas just about managed to get out.

Dean froze. "Are you telling me you didn't just throw the Frisbee at my head?"

Lucas just nodded and pointed towards, Thomas.

Dean glanced at Mack who was openly laughing, stood up brushing the sand from his jeans, then started walking towards Thomas with Lucas running behind him screaming for Thomas to run.

Before Dean could get to Thomas, Lucas tackled him from behind which sent them both tumbling back down.

Dean couldn't hold his laughter in anymore and grabbed Lucas, gave him a quick tickle, then got them both upright again.

"Lucas, I wasn't about to tackle Thomas to the sand."

Lucas looked from Dean to Thomas. "You weren't?"

"No, but I did think we could have some fun and maybe get Thomas to sit over there, while you bury his feet in the sand for letting me think it was you with the Frisbee."

"Hmm, I think I like that idea. I need some ants."

Both Mack and Dean started to chuckle at the look that crossed Thomas' face. "The sand will be enough... this time!" Dean told him.

"Oh, all right."

Dean stayed back, pulling Mack into his arms again as they stood and watched Lucas take hold of Thomas' hand, leading him to the place Dean had suggested he get his feet buried.

"They're really going to miss each other when we go back to Boston."

"We're not too far away in Boston. It's only a couple of hours, we can bring him back to visit," Dean replied, grinning when Mack realized he'd said 'we'.

Mack grinned back, buried her head in Dean's chest and kissed him, while holding on tight around his waist.

Chapter 19

The past week had flown by, with Mack and Dean, spending most of their time together, and occasionally taking Thomas and Lucas with them, in Mack's car. Lucas though, preferred to spend his time with Thomas, who sometimes would take him to meet up with Walt and Levi. This had left Mack and Dean alone more often than not, so they would spend their time sitting, cuddled together on the beach, or in the evenings, on the sofa. Dean had spoken about his love of drawing and art, while Mack had spoken about the joys of being a teacher to a mischievous class of seven-year-olds.

She would really miss Thomas when the summer was over, and leaving Thomas, would probably break Lucas' heart. At least with him constantly being entertained he hadn't missed his parents as much as she thought he would. He would talk to them on the phone most nights, and go over his antics of the day.

He'd gone fishing again with Thomas, and they planned on reading some more comics, while Mack hadn't even picked up Rose's diary in a week. She'd been too exhausted and giddy after spending her days with Dean, who had yet to get her naked!

"Spend the day with me?" Dean asked, making her jump, as she'd been lost in thought.

He walked over to her as she glanced up at him. "I'd like that. Do you want to go to the beach and take a picnic? I want to tell you about something."

"That would be great." He really hoped she was going to tell him about the diary. It had nearly killed him, this past week, not saying anything with how close they'd become. He'd tried to tell her on numerous occasions, but he'd always chickened out. Hopefully, the perfect opportunity would arise at the beach. He just hoped she wouldn't be too pissed with him.

She'd put a small picnic together. Dean walked over, took the blanket from the drawer, tucked it under his arm, picked up the picnic basket and finally took hold of Mack's hand as they headed down to the beach. During the walk, Mack couldn't help but wonder whether she was making the wrong decision, trusting a guy she'd only known a short time. He was certainly the first guy to get her libido to sit up and take notice from the get go. That had never happened to her before, perhaps it was an omen.

She led Dean over to the sheltered section of beach she'd come to favor over the past few weeks. He unfolded the blanket as Mack set the beach mats on top with the back supports built in, these were the best purchase she had made in a long time. She loved sitting on the beach, reading. With this support she was rather comfortable and could sit for hours.

Dean sat down and reclined against one of the mats. He held his hand out for her. She reached into her purse for the diary, then snuggled into a comfortable position between his legs, resting against his chest.

He put his arms around her and they just enjoyed the peace and quiet for a few minutes. Dean felt good with her wrapped in his arms. A soft, warm woman with curves. Not only was she hot, she had the biggest heart going. Not many young women would befriend an eighty-year-old man like Thomas.

Mack broke the silence. "The day after we moved into Rose Cottage, I was putting some boxes on top of the cabinets in the kitchen, and found this." She showed him the diary. "When I opened it, the first page says, '*This is the diary of a Rose, March 4, 1947'*."

"Wow, that's sometime ago." This could be his moment. The time to admit whom he was related to.

"I know. I've been reading it, and it's a love story between Rose and a young man by the name of Jacob Evans."

He went still and Mack gave him an odd look. "Carry on, it's interesting," he told her.

"Okay. It's so sad, Dean. They didn't even know each other more than two months, when she died trying to run away with him to Boston."

He didn't know what to say, so stayed silent, lost in his own thoughts. He knew his grandfather had married in 1947. It was also the year his father had been born.

It seemed impossible that his grandfather, who had always seemed so in love with his grandmother, Eliza, could have wanted someone else. Whenever they passed each other, they always touched or shared a loving embrace.

For as long as he could remember, his grandparents

always looked to be in love, always touching and kissing, whenever they passed each other. Whenever his grandfather had gone away on business, his grandmother had always accompanied him. They had five children, his father, James, his uncles Luke, Peter, and Derek, and his Aunt Rosalind. Could Aunt Rosalind have been named after his grandfather's first love 'Rose', without his grandmother's knowledge? It seemed so farfetched.

"Dean?"

"Yeah." He leaned down and placed a kiss to her forehead.

"The part that upsets me the most is that the night Rose died, Jacob had no idea she passed away. All these years, her family has led him to believe she married someone else."

"Seriously?"

"She was on her way to meet him when she died. A month later, apparently Jacob rang to ask about Rose, and her father told Jacob that she had stayed and married this other man, who was interested in her, named Richard, and that she didn't want anything to do with Jacob. So all these years, he's believed she chose someone else."

"That's so sad, Mack."

"Exactly. I found him. Jacob Evans. He's eighty-eight and lives in Brookline, Boston. I left a message with his housekeeper, but he hasn't gotten back to me yet. I know he's married, but I need to tell him, Rose really did love him, but died before meeting him that night."

She lifted her head from Dean's chest. "Thomas is Rose's brother, she referred to him in her diary as JT. He told me what his father said to Jacob on the phone. Do you think that I'm right in wanting to tell Jacob about Rose? It really does break my heart."

He looked down into Mack's eyes, which were full of tears. "Come here." He pulled her even closer and used his thumbs to wipe her tears away.

"Yes I do." He took a deep breath for courage. "I'll help you see Jacob Evans, because I'm…"

"Auntie Mack, look at the size of this fish," Lucas shouted, running towards them on the beach.

Damn, just when he'd worked himself up to tell her the truth, they were interrupted.

Mack stood and started heading towards Lucas. She turned back to Dean. "Thanks, for listening."

She ran over to Lucas. "Wow! That is huge!" Then stopped short. "Is it dead?"

"Don't be silly. Of course it's dead!" Lucas replied, in disgust.

"Do you both want a sandwich?" she asked.

She sat back down on the blanket, as Dean started to wrestle around the sand with Lucas. Mack wished this was her family. She was really falling for Dean.

That was something she had never wished for before, with anyone else, until now. Reading Rose's diary had made her long for that kind of love and commitment.

There was something real happening with Dean, although they didn't know a great deal, if anything, about each other. Over the past week she'd mentioned family, but for some reason he always changed the subject, although, on one or two occasions, Lucas had interrupted.

"No thanks, Mack. We'll leave you two alone. We're

going to put the fish in the fridge, have lunch, then more comic reading!" Taking hold of Lucas, Thomas pulled him along to leave the lovers alone.

"Bye, Auntie Mack. Bye, Dean."

"See you later, rugrat."

"We'll see you both later then," Mack said.

As he watched them walk away, Dean knew he now had the perfect opportunity to come clean and break it to her gently. He was praying he didn't upset her too much.

"Tell me about Mackenzie?" he asked. He took Mack by the hand, and pulled her back down to lie cuddled into his side, with her head resting on his shoulder, and his arm around her.

She smiled and inhaled deeply. "Okay. You already know some of this, but let me refresh your memory. Mackenzie Louise Harper, is twenty-seven years old and a teacher from Roslindale, Boston. Her parents are Louise and Alex Harper, who are fifty-nine and sixty-five years old, respectively. They live in a retirement village on the North Shore, after spending more than thirty-five years teaching high school. My sister, Melinda is four years older than me, and married to a doctor, Daniel. They only have the one son, Lucas. I'm not divorced, married, or in a relationship. I think that about covers it. What about you?"

Now or never. He inhaled. "Mack, my name is Dean James... Evans." He felt her go still next to him. "My mother's maiden name is Simone. I'm a graphic novelist, my sister, Alice is five years older than me, and married to Simon, who's in financing."

He took another deep breath for courage while he

glanced at Mack. "I'm thirty-two, not divorced, married, or in a relationship. My parents are Anne and James, who are sixty-two and sixty-five years old, respectively. They live with my grandparents in Brookline... They are Jacob and Eliza Evans."

She was so still and silent. He felt sick and really hoped he hadn't lost her because he hadn't been totally upfront. "Mack, did you hear me?"

"Yes," she whispered.

"I wanted to tell you the minute the name Simone left my mouth, and I don't know why I didn't, or rather I didn't want to look like an idiot in front of a woman I couldn't take my eyes off. I'm really truly sorry, Mack."

"Why?" She sat up and rested her arms on her raised knees and just gazed out to sea.

"My grandfather made rather a lot of money, so did my father. People get ideas about it, contact us for various reasons, sometimes shady reasons. When I heard Martha on the phone with you, I told her I would check you out first. I knew the minute I saw you that you weren't in that category, but I'm so worked up over you and want you like crazy, that I can't kiss you again, until you know the truth."

Mack was so quiet as Dean continued. "After listening to you earlier, I think my grandfather really is your Jacob Evans. I have an Aunt Rosalind. Could he have named her after Rose?"

"Seriously?" she asked.

"Yes."

After what felt like an hour of silence, but was probably only five minutes, she took hold of his hand and laced her fingers with his. "Thank you for telling me. I'm glad you told me now, rather than later," she said blushing.

Dean moved in close to her. "Am I forgiven?"

"Is that the only untruth you've told me?"

He looked slightly sheepish. "I really am single, unless you're still willing to be my girl, in which case I'm spoken for." He grinned. "But my mother is trying to marry me off to her friend's daughter, Cynthia. That's one of the reasons why I decided to check you out. I needed to get away. I'm sure glad I did."

"So am I. Cynthia?"

He sighed. "Yeah." Not really knowing where to start, he just hoped he didn't blow it. "My mother decided she wanted grandchildren, and my sister refused to cooperate, so she focused on me. Cynthia's mother has been friends with mine since school, and as we're of similar age, backgrounds, they decided to get us together."

He glanced at Mack. "I'm not interested in Cynthia. In fact she's starting to annoy me, always showing up wherever I am. No one but Martha knows I'm here right now, and I plan to keep it that way. You're the only one I want, Mack."

She smiled and brushed the hair from his forehead. "Thank you for telling me. What was the other reason?"

He blinked, having completely forgotten he'd told her Cynthia was one reason. "Curiosity, after your message. I love my grandparents, and I think if my grandfather truly did love Rose, then I'll take you to see him and distract my grandmother while you speak to him."

He noticed the frown on Mack's face. "They go everywhere together, always have and always will, I guess."

He swallowed back the lump in his throat. "When one passes away, the other one will follow, not long after, I'm certain."

She gently used her fingers to swipe the tears away from her eyes. "Oh, Dean!"

She climbed astride him and took hold of his face, then placed a light kiss to his lips. "That is so sweet, and heartbreaking at the same time."

"Yes, it is." He moved in to kiss Mack again and licked along the seal of her lips.

She felt Dean's tongue against her lips, opening her mouth she allowed him entry, hearing him groan as a gentle kiss became heated.

Dean could feel the blood in his ears pound and wondered why, when he was sure all his blood had gone south the minute she opened her mouth to him. She felt totally amazing in his arms.

Mack was desperate for more of him and wriggled further into his lap, where she came into contact with his swollen body part. She ran her hands through his hair, deepened the kiss even further and rubbed herself against him.

Dean pulled away, breathless. "Hell, Mack. We have to stop, because I'm seconds away from taking you here on the beach."

Mack placed a light kiss against his lips. "I want that, too." Dean's eyes darkened. "Lucas could reappear. Heck what am I thinking? We're on an open beach, you made me forget."

He rested his forehead against hers. "I know!"

She climbed off him and avoided looking into his lap.

"Do you want me to read some of the diary to you?"

"That would be great." He pulled Mack in beside him.

"I must warn you, though, there's some racy writing in it." She laughed at the look on Dean's face.

"Can't we miss those bits?"

"No, we cannot," she grinned. "Those are the best bits!!"

As she picked up the diary, Dean hoped there weren't too many explicit tales. He didn't want to imagine his grandparents in that way. Ever. He was having a hard enough time keeping his hands to himself.

Chapter 20

April 9, 1947
Jayne went out with Richard....

Today was a lovely, sunny day, and for the first time, in a long time I was actually looking forward to going to work, or I was, until Jayne called around to the house to walk to work with me.

"Why are you so grumpy this morning?" she asked.

"Work," I replied, and thought I better keep to myself how much I was looking forward to walking to work on my own, so I could get lost in my thoughts.

"I went out with Richard last night."

I raised my eyebrow when she stopped talking, waiting for her to tell me how it went. It wasn't like Jayne to keep anything to herself, especially about her dates.

She sighed. "All he did was talk about you. He is really angry you refused his marriage proposal, and I think he only asked me out to try and make you jealous. When I told him it wouldn't make you jealous, he declared it was time to take me home."

I hadn't been expecting that. I actually thought he only wanted to marry me because of his father, but perhaps that was what he wanted me to believe. I rubbed my temples, feeling really confused. "Jayne, I'm not interested in Richard. In fact, the last time I saw him, I told him I didn't want to see him for a while. I was so angry with him for talking to Mother and Father."

"Are you still seeing Jacob?" My silence spoke a thousand words. "Rose Degan, you have to stop right now. Your father will make your life so difficult if he ever finds out."

"I can't stop seeing him. I love him." I blurted out, close to tears.

"Richard asked me last night if you were seeing someone else. I avoided the question, but it won't be long until he finds out." She saw the look on my face. "It won't be from me, I promise you."

I parted from Jayne outside the library. She worked one block over from me. I really hoped Richard didn't cause any trouble. I only had five days left in Cape Elizabeth, and I really wanted them to go smoothly.

My parents had been leaving me alone, and I really hoped they continued to do so.

April 10, 1947
A strange day....

This morning on waking, I had to run to the bathroom to be sick. *Yuk.* I ate dried toast and sipped some water, which seemed to help some. With my stomach settled, I had a slow walk to work.

As soon as the library doors were unlocked, Richard

walked in. He gave me such a weird look, before he went to find whatever book he'd come in for. He didn't leave with a book though, as he left, he glared at me, then stomped out.

His behavior was odd. After what Jayne had told me yesterday, I still found it hard to believe. He seemed so genuine when he said it was his father making him ask me to marry him. Now I really didn't know what to think.

"Rose, can you come into my office for a minute, please?" Mr. Young asked, taking my mind off Richard.

"Yes." I walked into his office.

After he cleared his throat a few times -- *horrid* -- he looked at me. "Take a seat." I sat down. "Rose, I'm afraid I have to cut your hours. The library isn't as busy, so I can't justify having as many staff."

He just sat staring at me. I wasn't sure what he wanted me to say. "Okay. From when will the new hours start?"

He seemed relieved. "From May 6th."

I would be gone by then. I felt like telling him what to do with his job, but I wouldn't give Father the satisfaction of knowing I'd given my job up.

I have four more days to go. I felt apprehensive, but excited as well, for my new life with Jacob.

Before going to bed, I played cards with JT, who was so infuriating. He cheated -- *all the time.*

I really wished I could take my brother with me. I would miss him more than anyone.

April 11, 1947
A delightful discovery....

I was sick again this morning. Could I possibly be pregnant? I didn't have any experience with this kind of thing, and couldn't exactly ask Mother. *Heaven forbid.* I had some toast for breakfast again, which seemed to help calm my stomach.

I was meeting Jacob this evening with some of my things. I loved him so, and couldn't wait to see him. Before I left for work, I packed as much as I could into my travel bag, then stuffed it to the back of my wardrobe and just prayed it wasn't discovered while I was at work.

How I got through the day, I would never know. Mr. Young had a bee in his bonnet and did nothing but fuss the whole day. I actually felt like a wet lettuce leaf as I walked home. He had us running around, doing this, that and the other. Nothing was right, and as soon it was time to close Mary, Emma, and I stopped what we were doing to retrieve our jackets and purses, and left.

Dinner with my parents was a silent affair. JT had been in trouble again. Not sure why this time, but no one spoke. It was pretty horrid really. Excusing myself, I dashed up to my room and retrieved my travel bag.

Luckily, my bedroom overlooked the back garden and Mother's rose bushes, so I stuck my head out of the window to check that the coast was clear, and dropped my bag and prayed it didn't land in the middle of the roses!

I slipped out of the house, having snuck down the kitchen stairs, and retrieved my bag. The roses were intact. Thank goodness.

I walked to the end of the drive and found Jacob there waiting for me. I dropped my bag and threw myself into his arms. "I've missed you," I whispered.

His lips met mine. The kiss lingered. He tasted divine.

We were breathing heavily when we finally parted, and Jacob took my hand while we walked into town. I should have been bothered about my parents seeing us, but I wasn't. In town Jacob pulled me into a photography studio.

"What are we doing in here?" I asked.

He smiled at me. "I want a photograph of us both. We'll get two copies so you can give one to your brother."

I had tears in my eyes as I followed the photographer through to the back of the shop. Jacob stood behind me with his hands wrapped around my waist. I cuddled into him as the photographer snapped our moment in time. He used one of the new Polaroid Land Cameras, and could produce our photographs in minutes like magic.

With two copies of the photograph safely in his pocket, we continued on to his apartment. Jacob placed my bag down by the side of the chair in the lounge area.

He turned and cupped my face between his palms, then proceeded to kiss me. He pulled away, and placed tender kisses over my eyes, cheeks, to the tip of my nose and then back to my lips again.

"Make love to me." I didn't hesitate as I took him by the hand and led him into his bedroom.

He undressed me in slow, sweeping caresses and lay me on his bed. He started to remove his clothes, which I found delightful, watching his muscular frame appear. He had an amazing body.

He lay down next to me. "I want to touch you," I whispered softly.

He gulped. "I hope I survive." He watched me through heavily lidded eyes.

"I love you so much, Rose," he whispered, as he pulled me into his arms.

"I love you just as much…I have something to tell you, and I hope you'll be as happy as I am."

Jacob turned to me. "You can tell me anything, Rose."

I looked into his eyes, and told him, "I think I'm pregnant."

He froze beside me, then turned away.

I could feel my eyes filling with tears as I watched him shut me out.

"Jacob?"

He sighed, sitting up to the side of the bed with his back to me. I watched him put his head in his hands.

I couldn't stay. I needed to leave. Sitting up, I started to climb from the bed in tears, when Jacob caught hold of my wrist, pulling me back down and into his arms.

"I'm sorry, Rose. I wasn't expecting you to say that. It was a shock." He gradually started to smile which spread across his face. "Rose, not only have you given me your love, but you've given me the most amazing gift… a child. I promise, I will always love, and provide for you and our child or children."

He stroked my stomach tenderly. I watched him with silent tears cascading down my face. I was so happy with Jacob, my Jacob.

"Let's leave tonight," he said so seriously.

"We can't. I'm not ready tonight, but I will be on Monday."

He pulled me into his chest. "I just want you with me."

"I want that as well. It's only three more days." I kissed him.

He made love to me once more, then we dressed and he walked me home. I hated parting from him. I just wanted to stay wrapped in his arms.

April 12, 1947
Richard was sneaking around....

I was so sick this morning. There could be no mistake. I was pregnant. I found myself unable to wipe the smile from my face. I was so happy, and my new life with Jacob was just two days away.

At work, I found myself humming while I placed returned books back onto the shelves. I got some weird looks from my colleagues, but I didn't really care.

Richard walked into the library and just stared at me. Until the other day, I didn't ever remember him coming in before. He actually made me feel uncomfortable. If I didn't know better, I'd say he was up to something. I prayed it didn't involve me. I just had a really bad feeling, though.

Dinner tonight was, yet again, a rather quiet affair, as JT had been grounded again! Pinching an apple pie from Mrs. Jenkins, next door. Apparently she had left the pie by the window to cool, and JT and his friend, Levi, had taken it, hoping she would think it was a dog. Then she had caught them taking the plate back!!!

April 13, 1947
Only one more day!

    I felt a bit better this morning, and my breakfast stayed down, thank goodness. I walked out of the front door and bumped into JT, who was sulking because he wasn't allowed out after yesterday's fiasco with the pie. Father had told him, school and home and nothing in between. I could guarantee that by the time he arrived home this afternoon, he'd be in more trouble.

    At the library, Richard came back and actually walked over to me. "Rose, I want to speak with you."

    Well, nice to see you too!

    He took hold of my elbow and pulled me out of hearing of anyone who might have come along. "What does he have that I don't?"

    "What?" I asked, stunned. Surely he couldn't be referring to Jacob. Could he?

    "I saw you two days ago, wrapped around a tall guy. You were acting like a… like a… hussy."

    The nerve of him. "What I was doing and with whom, is none of your business," I told him, walking away.

    He grabbed my arms and turned me around. "If you continue to see him, I'll tell your parents. I bet they don't know, do they?"

    "You have no right interfering in my life. Who I have a relationship with is my business, not yours or my parents. So please stay out of it."

    He turned away from me and headed towards the exit.

"We'll see, Rose. We'll see."

For the first time since I met Jacob, I felt really shaky, and was afraid all our happiness was about to come tumbling down. I really wished Jacob was with me, to hold me and to tell me everything would be all right.

After lunch, I got my wish. I heard the front door open and glanced up, meeting Jacob's eyes. He took one look at me and obviously knew there was something wrong. I stood and followed him to the back of the library, near the storage closet. I walked past him, took his hand, and pulled him after me into the closet.

"What's wrong? Are you sick?" he asked me with his heart in his eyes.

I just shook my head and burrowed my face into his chest. "Richard came in this morning. He said if I didn't stop seeing you, he would tell my parents." I looked up into his face. "He saw us kissing the other night."

"Nobody threatens you, Rose. Do you hear me? I'm going to go see him."

Oh no! "Jacob, please don't. Knowing Richard, he'll report you to the police, and then you'll get arrested and we won't be able to leave tomorrow."

While I held him tight, I stayed silent. I just wanted him to cool his anger and calm down.

As he pulled away from me, he stroked my stomach then knelt down. He wrapped his arms around my hips and kissed my stomach. He brought tears to my eyes. I didn't know what I'd done to deserve him, but I was so grateful.

He stood and kissed my lips. "I better go, before I get you in trouble."

I grinned.

"Erm... any more trouble." He chuckled mischievously. "Everything is set for tomorrow night, so don't worry, okay?"

"I won't. I'm really excited to finally be with you all the time."

We snuck out from the cupboard and I picked a couple of books up from one of the shelves to make it look as though I was returning them. I watched Jacob leave, then rounding the corner to the next aisle, I bumped into Mary.

"That's the same man as before. Are you sure you don't know him?"

Mind your own business. "No, I don't know him."

Work was over for the day, for which I was grateful. After Jacob's visit, Mary kept watching me. She knew I was lying to her, but her constant gaze was very unnerving.

I took my time walking home, because I knew if I rushed I would be in time to see Mother and Father before they went out. Luckily, I missed them. I really hoped Richard hadn't been to see them. I was leaving tomorrow evening, but I wouldn't put it past him to cause a great deal of trouble.

I entered the house through the kitchen and stopped dead. JT was in the kitchen, stuffing his face with cookies and ice cream. "Haven't you eaten dinner?"

"Yes." He carried on eating.

"You're going to be sick."

He gave me a chocolate-covered grin. "I have an iron stomach."

"Ha, you wish." I made myself a sandwich and sat down with him. Once finished, I helped him eat the cookies, dipping them into a glass of milk.

I really wished JT was a bit older so I could confide in him. I hoped I didn't live to regret not telling him.

Chapter 21

Mack stopped reading and closed the diary. She really wasn't sure if she would be able to continue. There was only the last entry left to read, the one that changed everything.

"Mack, what's wrong?" Dean asked, as he sat up and massaged her shoulders.

She reached back to cover his hands with hers and leaned back into his chest. "I'm nervous to continue, knowing it ends with Rose's death." Mack wiped at a wayward tear with her fingers.

Dean wrapped his arm around her waist and rested his chin on her shoulder. "Don't you want to know what happened on her last day?"

"Yeah," Mack whispered.

"Do you want me to read it?" Dean offered.

She let out a sigh. "No. I'll be okay. Let's eat and then we'll read about the 14th."

"Okay, babe." Dean reached for the picnic hamper. "Cheese or ham?"

"Ham, please."

Mack took the sandwich from Dean and sat resting her chin on her drawn up knees, looking out to sea while she ate.

There was another couple further down the beach who were playing Frisbee with two children, and a dog running circles around them. She could hear the children giggling from where she sat.

Mack turned back to look at the ocean. When her sandwich was finished, she turned and knelt between Dean's legs, looking at him.

She grinned and moved closer. Dean's eyes widened when she reached the bottom of his t-shirt. "I need distracting for a few minutes, and I want to have a closer look at the tattoo I keep catching glimpses of."

He groaned. "Mack, I'm not sure this is a good idea." He sucked in his breath when Mack's hand slid inside his t-shirt, up to his chest. She climbed onto his lap and managed to pull the t-shirt over his head. Dean didn't protest too much.

"Mmm, you look... damn good." Mack licked her lips. Dean's breathing had become more erratic.

Mack kissed him on the lips then moved down to his chest and smoothed her hands over his biceps, crawling from Dean's lap and around to the back of him. Now it was her turn to suck her breath in.

On his back from one shoulder to the other spread an eagle. It was magnificent, like nothing she'd ever seen before. Mack reached out and started to trace the wings with her fingers. Dean broke out in goose bumps as she moved closer and started kissing her way across the wingspan.

"Mack," Dean hissed, "unless you want to put on a display for the family down the beach, I suggest you stop."

Mack smirked. She knew exactly what she did to him. "Spoil sport." She crawled back to the front of him and couldn't help but notice the bulge in his lap. "Your eagle is amazing."

He smiled. "I drew up the design and the tattoo artist did an excellent job of transferring it to my skin."

"That he did," Mack agreed as she straddled Dean's hips.

She sealed her lips to his in a heated kiss, which ended all to quickly for Dean's liking.

"Very nice. Okay, I'm rested and I think, ready to finish the diary."

She climbed off Dean and turned around to scoot back between his legs.

"Thank you for the distraction."

"Yeah, well, if you carry on wiggling that butt where you're wiggling it, you're going to get more of a distraction than I think you'd planned for the beach."

"That really is a tempting offer. I've always wanted to make out on the beach. We'll have to take a rain-check for when it's dark." Mack turned her head and laughed when she looked into Dean's lust-filled expression. "Okay, fun's over, for now." She reached for the diary, laughing to herself at the look on Dean's face, because she was passing him over for a diary dated 1947.

Chapter 22

April 14, 1947
Today's the day....

On my way down the stairs, I felt really well, or at least I did, until Mother asked me to join them for breakfast.

I entered the dining room and could tell straightaway that something was wrong. JT wasn't there, which meant he'd been told to eat in the kitchen.

"Who is this man you've been seen with?" *Heck.* So Richard had been to see them.

I decided to be as honest as I could. "I have fallen in love with a good man, and he's asked me to marry him, and I've agreed. I love him with all my heart."

Father looked ready to burst. "If he's a good man, why hasn't he been to ask me for your hand in marriage?" he roared.

"Because I asked him not to," I said quietly. Father was such a snob.

"Why?"

I took a deep breath. "Because Jacob doesn't have a lot of money. He has an apprenticeship awaiting him in New

York. I love him and want to be with him. I was afraid you wouldn't understand, and that you would prevent me from seeing him." There was no way I was mentioning Boston.

"So you keep saying you love him, yet you're ashamed to bring him to meet your parents?" Father threw his napkin down on the table.

"I'm not ashamed. Frightened, yes, but never ashamed." I was as stubborn as my father when I wanted to be.

"Then prove that to me, bring him for dinner tonight." Both Mother and I sat in shock.

"If you're serious, then I will."

"I'm serious. Seven this evening, we'll meet this young man you say you love." Father sneered.

I turned and stomped out of the house. I was halfway to work before I realized I hadn't eaten breakfast. I felt slightly dizzy so I stopped at Belle's to buy a pastry, which I quickly ate in the restroom so Mr. Young wouldn't catch me. No one was allowed a morning break.

Finished eating, I brushed the crumbs from my blouse and headed onto the library floor, then practically bumped into Richard, who I ignored by walking past him. He came after me.

"Rose, wait. I want to talk to you." He grabbed hold of my arm.

"I have nothing to say to you. Please stop bothering me." I tried to pull my arm free, but he was holding me too tight.

"You're going to regret being with him. He's not worth it. He can't give you what I can."

I started to get really cross with him. "I will say this for the last time. Leave. Me. Alone." I stamped on his foot. He released my arm. I hurried away, back to the desk. Mary gave me a quizzical look, but I ignored her and pretended to be sorting some papers out on the desk. Richard left and I sagged against the desk in relief.

Not long after, Jacob appeared, so once again, I followed him behind the antiquated books.

He pulled me straight into his arms and hugged me really tight. I lifted my face for his kiss; he didn't disappoint me. "I love you. Are you sure about tonight?" he asked.

I took his face in my hands and pulled him down to me. "Yes. I love you, and want to spend the rest of my life with you." I kissed him.

"Transport is arranged for our lift to Boston. Eleanor is really looking forward to having us both living with her."

"I'm so excited, Jacob, but... I need you to come to dinner tonight." He paused with his hand caressing my face. "Richard told my parents about us and what he'd seen. I told my father at breakfast I love you and plan to marry you. So my father told me to bring you to dinner tonight."

"Then I'll be there. What time?"

"Seven sharp."

"Rose, everything will be fine and if it isn't, then we can still slip away tonight, all right?"

"Yes."

We heard voices approach, so he placed a quick peck on my lips and headed out of the library.

How I managed to endure the rest of the day I would never know. It was such a relief to be on my way home.

I'd just left town when I heard someone shouting my name. I looked behind me... *Richard*. "What do you want now?"

"I'm walking you home, and I plan on staying outside your house all evening to make sure you don't go sneaking off with him."

I just glared at him, shocked. "Have you lost your mind?" He really was crazy.

"No, but you have, for dallying with him."

"I'll have you know that Father has invited Jacob to dinner. So you see, I don't need to sneak out, because he will be eating with me and my family tonight." I stomped off and left him as I reached my house.

I ran upstairs and looked out of the window on the landing only to see Richard still sitting at the end of the drive.

I really couldn't believe he was doing this, to what gain, I had no idea. In my room, I quickly changed into a clean dress, rather than one that was rumpled from a day's work. I brushed my hair and applied my lipstick.

As I ran down the stairs, I was just in time to watch Jacob walk up the porch steps. I spotted Mother and Father approaching from the parlor, so I ran and opened the door for him, then barely stopped myself from throwing my arms around his neck.

"Rose." He winked and grinned at me. I felt like melting into a puddle.

"Rose, are you going to invite the young man inside?" my father asked.

"Yes, of course," I replied, grinning at Jacob. I took his hand and pulled him inside, then refused to release him.

"Mother, Father, I would like you to meet Jacob Evans." *Please* let us just get through this meal.

My parents were polite and shook his hand. Mother stared as we held hands. I loosened my hold slightly, but Jacob tightened his fingers and entwined them with mine.

We took our seats in the dining room and all was quiet. Too quiet.

"So Jacob, Rose was telling us you have been offered an apprenticeship in New York."

With a quick glance at me, he looked back at my father. "Yes, sir, I have. It's with an engineering company, they also pay well."

"Hmm, so what do you intend towards my daughter, if you're planning on leaving Cape Elizabeth?"

Jacob placed a hand on my leg underneath the table, knowing I was seconds away from saying something. "Rose has agreed to become my wife, so I'll be taking her with me."

Yes!

"That is enough. You are not going to be marrying my daughter, because she is already spoken for."

I stood up and faced my father. "No, I am not, and if you mean Richard, we have already had this discussion."

"I forbid you to spend any more time with this man."

Jacob stood up and wrapped his arm around my shoulders, which, with my father in the room, wasn't the wisest thing to do. "Don't worry, Rose. I'm going to leave now, but please don't worry," he whispered into my ear. "I'll go now." He turned to me. "Remember, I love you, Rose." He then walked out of the house and I ran upstairs to my room, crying.

Although I knew what my father was like, I'd hoped he would accept Jacob and all would be well. I was stupid to hope.

With my tears dried, I made sure my door was locked and then retrieved another travel bag, before packing my few remaining belongings. I came across the *Our Gang* comic, April 1st edition that I'd bought for JT, because Father had refused to let him have it. I bought it for him to bribe him to keep quiet.

Taking out the photograph of myself and Jacob, I wrote on the back a small message to JT. I told him I loved him and wished I could take him to Boston with me. I also wrote the address of Jacob's sister, in case he ever needed anything, and I begged him not to tell Mother and Father.

I placed the photograph in the middle of the comic, then put it to one side, ready to leave on his bed.

Dressed in slacks and a warm sweater for traveling, I climbed onto my bed to rest before it was time for me to leave. I had started to become nervous about the whole thing. I had no doubt whatsoever that I loved Jacob and wanted this baby, his baby, our baby, but was going to be stressful, doing what I was about to do.

I wondered what to do about my diary. Part of me wanted to take it with me, but another part wanted to leave this part of my life behind. I would have to leave it somewhere safe, where hopefully one day, someone would find it, and know just how much I was in love and maybe even return it to me, if I was alive when it was found.

It was ten-thirty. I climbed from my bed and collected my purse, bag, and JT's comic, then slipped quietly out of my room. I went into my brother's room and watched him sleep for a minute before I had to leave him. I placed the comic on his bed, as my tears started to flow.

As I walked down the stairs to the kitchen, I'd decided to leave my diary on top of the kitchen cupboards. They never got cleaned, so it could be a long time before it was discovered.

Goodbye diary.

This is the end of a Rose!

Chapter 23

Dean had no idea what to say, which was a first. Hearing about the love 'Rose' had for his grandfather, and the love his grandfather had and lost for another woman, totally blew his mind.

Mack started to shake. He realized she was sobbing her heart out, her face buried into his side. He pulled her further into his arms and started to gently stroke her back. "It's okay, Mack, just let go." And let go she did, while he just held her tight.

She pulled slightly away from Dean to search for a tissue, managing to control the water works, while he also felt like bursting into tears. "God, their story is so sad." Mack started to cry again. "She loved him so much, and he obviously loved her. It breaks my heart, knowing that she died that night, and Jacob never knew. He always thought she'd left him."

Dean pulled her close again. "Mack, why did Jacob only make one phone call to find out about her, a month after he left? Why not come to see if she'd been held up that night? Why wait a month to try and contact her? It doesn't make sense."

Still cuddled into his chest, she looked up at him and

gave him a watery smile. "Then let's try and get Thomas to talk."

He leaned in and kissed her forehead. "What does the J in JT stand for?"

"James."

"Now I really am sure, but it doesn't make sense, why if he's with another woman, would my grandfather name his first born after his first lover's brother."

Mack had a quizzical look on her face.

"My father is James Thomas Evans, and remember, James is my middle name."

She sat up suddenly. "Oh my God, and then you said your Aunt Rosalind..."

"When do you want to see my grandfather?"

She looked out to sea and found it hard to get her head around anything. Jacob obviously had loved Rose to have named his first born after Rose's brother, and then his daughter after Rose herself.

If he loved his wife as much as Dean said, then he couldn't have told her about Rose and the names of his children, unless his love for Eliza only grew after the children were born, and he was still missing his Rose all the time. None of this made any sense. She was going to have to ask Jacob, and just hope he could clear everything up.

"I don't know, as I can't really take Lucas, and I don't feel comfortable leaving him all day with Thomas. He can be a real handful."

"Who? Thomas or Lucas?"

"Ha ha... both!!" She turned back to look at Dean. "Soon. Can I meet him soon?"

He reached up and moved a piece of hair behind Mack's ear. "Let me know when you're ready and I'll take you."

Mack took hold of his hand. "Thank you." She placed a kiss gently on his knuckles. "So, am I your girl?" she asked with a large grin on her face.

"Yes," he replied, without any hesitation, leaned closer and nuzzled her neck. "You are!"

"Mmm. Good, because you're my guy!" She reached up and ran her fingers through his hair, sending shivers down his spine. "I think we'd better head back. If there's an opening in conversation, I'll ask Thomas about the April 1st edition of *Our Gang*, see what he did with the photograph. I would love to see a photograph of Rose and Jacob."

"That would be amazing. We would also know for sure if it's my grandfather. There are photographs all over the house in Brookline, so I'll be able to recognize him straightaway."

※❖※

Mack made chicken parmesan with rice and she'd also made two pies, one apple and the other cherry. In fact, she hadn't stopped since getting back from the beach.

Dean was playing one of Lucas' Mario Brothers Wii games in the sitting room, and apart from him coming back and forth for a beer or munches, or even delicious kisses, he'd pretty much stayed out of the way.

When they'd read the diary, it had really upset her. She had cried all over Dean, for heaven's sake. Dean hadn't minded though, he'd just held her and tried to comfort her.

Her thoughts turned back to Rose. She wondered if

Thomas had known about Rose's pregnancy. Did anyone but Jacob? Jacob had known Rose was pregnant, so wouldn't he have wanted to know about the baby? He seemed to be happy at the prospect of becoming a father. She really needed to speak to Jacob.

"Auntie Mack, I'm home. Did you miss me?"

Mack held her arms out and Lucas ran straight into them. "I sure did, buster. Dean's in there, playing Mario."

"Yes!" Lucas darted out of the kitchen to join Dean.

"Hi, Thomas, come sit. Would you like a drink of lemonade?" Mack asked as he took a seat at the table.

"That would be mighty fine, thank you."

She poured him a large glass of homemade lemonade. "Can I ask you something?"

He smiled. "You usually do whether I want you to or not."

She placed his drink in front of him and sat down on the chair beside him. "Thomas, do you have a photograph of Rose and Jacob together?"

He hesitated. "No I haven't. Never saw one either."

Mack was puzzled. "Are you sure? In her diary she says as she was leaving the house, she goes into your room and leaves the April 1st edition of *Our Gang* on your bed, and inside she'd put a photograph of herself and Jacob with a private message on the back for you only."

Thomas looked really shaken. "All this time, I've had a picture of her with him, and I didn't even know?"

Mack was puzzled. "I don't understand, Thomas."

He leaned forward and put his arms on the table with his head in his hands. He sighed. "I knew Rose had bought me the comic, and I found it that night, but I didn't get a chance to read it then. When I finally went back to bed, we had been told that Rose had gone over the cliffs, so getting into bed, I just held the comic and cried, then placed it in the box with the others, and never opened it. I couldn't."

Mack took hold of Thomas' hand. "Do you still have that comic?"

He nodded his head. "I took it away from Lucas, and placed it on my night table, intending to finally read it. Maybe it's time. I'll look through it tonight."

"If you find a photograph, will you bring it tomorrow? I'd love to see what Rose looked like, and the man she loved."

He raised his head. "Okay, Mack. I will."

"Thanks, Thomas. You're staying to eat, right? I've made chicken parmesan and then there's cherry or apple pie with ice cream."

"You do know they say that the way to a man's heart is through his stomach!" He chuckled.

"Really!" She turned away laughing, to check the chicken in the oven, then turned back to Thomas. "Dean's surname isn't Simone, that's his mother's maiden name."

She had his full attention. "His name is Dean James Evans, and the James is after his father who Jacob named James Thomas. Dean is Jacob's grandson."

"What are you saying, Mack?" Thomas whispered.

"I'm not sure yet, but Jacob named his first born James Thomas after you, Rose's brother. He also named his only daughter Rosalind, obviously after Rose. He married after Rose died, so by naming his first born and then his daughter in memory of Rose, he was obviously missing her terribly, and maybe he insisted on those names with his wife, Eliza."

"That is some story," Thomas replied, shaking his head.

"Thomas, did you know Rose was pregnant the night she died?"

He took a deep breath. "Yes. I overheard a conversation between my father and mother after Jacob phoned the house. Apparently my father had known she was pregnant. I don't know how, but he said he told him Rose had lost the baby. He also told my mother that Jacob sounded very shocked. I didn't want you thinking badly of Rose, about her being pregnant, so I didn't tell you when we talked before."

Mack wiped her eyes on the apron she was wearing for cooking. "Thomas, it's okay. It's hard to explain, but somehow I feel as though she's talking to me and wants me to help," she waved her arms around, "I don't know, maybe set Jacob free, as ridiculous as that sounds."

They sat lost in their own thoughts for a few minutes. "I know you said Rose had gone over the cliffs, but how, exactly? What happened?" Mack asked.

"Let me sleep on it, Mack." He shook his head. He looked so sad.

She felt guilty having bombarded him with so many questions, bringing back memories.

Mack stood up with Thomas, giving him a hug, followed by a kiss to his cheek. "Thank you, Thomas. I don't know about you, but I'm starving. Let's eat!"

Chapter 24

Mack was upstairs reading Lucas a bedtime story, and Dean was lying on the sofa thinking about his grandfather. If everything in Rose's diary was true, and it looked like it was, then why had no one in his family ever mentioned a Rose in his grandfather's past, or that his grandfather had lived in Cape Elizabeth for a time?

His grandfather had always said he lived in Boston, apart from the war, when he was in England. Unless, he loved and missed Rose way too much to talk about her.

He had seen wedding photographs of his grandparents, and they'd looked really happy. Dean's father was the eldest, and had once told him that his parents were the most loving couple he had ever seen, and from being a small child, he remembered them always holding hands and kissing. He had a really hard time imagining his grandfather like that with anyone but his wife, Eliza.

"You look deep in thought." Mack moved away from the doorway and leaned over the sofa to get a closer look at him. He looked sexy, lying there in his stocking feet, well-worn jeans, and Rascal Flatts t-shirt.

"I'm really blown away with everything I've learned today, about my grandfather's past. It's unreal."

"I know what you mean. I can't stop now. I need to find out what really happened. It's really important to me."

"Is Lucas asleep?"

"Yeah, he was exhausted."

"Come, lie down with me, Mack." He held his hand out to her, wondering if she had anything on under the robe she was wearing.

She climbed half on top of him, flashing a bit of thigh. Dean caught his breath. He reached out and put his hand on her hips to steady her, only to get one hell of a view of her breasts through the gapping robe.

He inhaled at the sight of her hovering over him, practically naked. "Mack, you're killing me." He gritted his teeth as he closed his eyes from the sight of her.

Dean felt her straddle him. His eyes flew open just in time to watch her lose the robe.

"We wouldn't want that now, would we?"

"Let me stay with you tonight. Just to sleep. I think you've done me in, but I need to hold you in my arms all night."

"Mmm."

Just lying on the sofa, with Mack still cuddled around him made him feel like the luckiest guy alive. He should be running away, but instead, he wanted to stay right where he was.

Over the past week he'd started to fall in love with her. The thought of her with anyone else made him see red. *Hell! He was in love with her.* He just hoped she was in the same place that he was, because he had no intention of letting her go.

Mack slept blissfully in his arms.

Thomas climbed into bed and couldn't help but feel unsettled. Discussing Rose after all these years was rather upsetting, and to discover she had left him a photograph with possibly a note on the back... Ah well.

He picked the comic up from his night table and slowly started to turn the pages, holding his breath each time, until he turned to the middle of the comic. He found what he was supposed to find sixty-five years ago, which brought tears to his eyes.

A Polaroid photograph of his sister Rose, wrapped in the arms of Jacob Evans, looking so much in love.

Mack had said there was a message on the back for him. He just hoped the ink hadn't faded with age. He took a deep breath and turned the picture over to look at the handwriting he never thought he would ever see again.

Dear Thomas,

I want you to know that you are the only one I will miss. I love you so much, brother, please forgive me.

If you ever need anything, go to the address at the bottom and ask for Eleanor, she will know how to find me.

When we have our own place and are settled in Boston, I will be back to see you. It may take a few years, but know that I will always be thinking about you.

All my love, Thomas, my JT,

Rose

He used his fingers to wipe his eyes and with shaking hands, he placed the comic and photograph back on the table to the side of his bed. He needed to tell Mack what actually happened that night, and maybe then he would feel better. After all, he had carried around so much guilt for all these years.

First though, he would show her the photograph and then think about what to say.

At eighty, it was time to be free and have peace of mind at last.

Chapter 25

Mack woke with a smile, snuggled against a hard male chest. Dean was spooned behind her, his arm over her waist with his hand cupping her breast. She was overwhelmed with contentment. He felt totally amazing, and she didn't want to move.

She couldn't believe she had fallen asleep on him last night. She hadn't even woken up when he'd carried her upstairs.

"Morning, babe," Dean whispered into her ear, sending shivers down her spine. He smoothed his hand down the curve of her waist and hip, then over the top of her thighs. She was the most beautiful woman, he'd ever seen, ever known; inside and out.

"Morning… you feel so good." She turned her head for his kiss, moving closer she rubbed against Dean; his hands shook.

Dean turned her to him, and pulled her in to his body, resting his chin on the top of her head.

"I wish we could stay in bed all day," Mack murmured, filled with contentment.

Dean smiled. "I do too. But I guess Lucas is going to be awake soon, so we need to make a move."

Mack was the first to pull away. "I'll shower and dress so at least one of us is decent when he awakes," she said climbing out of bed.

"I'll just admire the view." He grinned, watching her walk buck-naked into the bathroom.

He gave a sigh of relief as she disappeared from sight, but his relief was short lived as the shower went on and he had a front row view of Mack as she took a shower.

Mack towel-dried in the bathroom, then walked back into the bedroom to dress, stopping short when she met Dean's heavy-lidded eyes.

Dean moved from the bed. "I'm going to have a very cold shower. Please be dressed by the time I get out."

"I'll start breakfast." She grinned and watched Dean climb out of bed, so ready for action!

"Even better." He walked past her, with a swat to her butt.

Downstairs Mack was cooking bacon, sausage, eggs, and biscuits for breakfast. She whistled away, feeling her life was perfect, for the first time in a long time. She couldn't remember ever feeling this way before. She knew then, that she had fallen for Dean Evans. He always seemed to know the right thing to say, or what she needed without her having to say anything. He was good on the eyes as well, which was an added bonus, and when naked... *Oh boy*!

Thomas walked through the kitchen door, which brought Mack out of her thoughts of a very naked Dean. "Morning, Mack," he said, but not with his usual flare.

Mack looked more closely at him and noticed how pale he was. "Thomas, are you all right?" She walked over to hug him. "Come, sit down and tell me what's wrong. You don't look well. Do you need to go to the doctor?"

"It's not that, Mack," Thomas explained, just as Dean came down the stairs.

"Morning, Thomas." Then he saw Mack's concerned expression. "What's wrong?"

"It's been a very long time since anyone was worried about me. But I'm not ill, just a bit in shock, I guess."

Thomas looked at Mack. "I found this last night, right where you said it would be." He took the photograph of Rose and Jacob out of his pocket. He handed it to Mack with shaking hands. She took hold of the photograph and placed it face down on the table, sitting down next to him, took hold of his hands and just held them.

"Thank you, Thomas."

"Look at it, Mack, and read what she wrote to me." He had tears in his eyes.

"Auntie Mack, I'm up," Lucas shouted as he came bouncing into the kitchen. "Thomas... Dean... you're both here, really early." He pulled up short.

Not knowing what to say, Dean placed one of his hands on Mack's shoulder. He just needed to touch her. "I'll go distract him while you talk to Thomas," he whispered. He was curious about the photograph, but right now, distracting Lucas was the priority.

Mack turned to look up at Dean, took hold of his hand and pressed a quick kiss to his palm before letting go. "Thank you."

She watched Dean and Lucas retreat to the sitting room, no doubt to play some more Super Mario Brothers, which they were both addicted to.

She turned her attention back to Thomas and reached out to pick the photograph up, turning it over to take her first look at Rose.

The photograph showed a young couple who were obviously in love with each other. Jacob was taller than Rose, she came to around his shoulders. They were both slim built, although Jacob looked to have some muscle on him, with broad shoulders. Rose just looked slim and delicate, with a ribbon tied around her long blonde hair. At least it looked blonde.

Mack had to fight back tears as she looked at the photograph. These two were so much in love, and the relationship ended so tragically. It broke her heart.

She didn't feel ready to read what Rose had written, but knew she must, for Thomas, and because it would only play on her mind if she didn't. She turned the photograph over and finally read what Rose had written to her brother all those years ago.

"Oh, Thomas." She placed her hand over her mouth. Tears rolled down her face.

"I know, Mack. She really did love me, and if she had made it to Boston, she said she would have come back to see me eventually. Probably when she could stand up to Mother and Father."

Mack dried her eyes. "Thomas, would you mind if I just take a picture with my cell of this photograph?"

"No, that's fine. We'll have to get you a proper copy

made."

"That would be great."

Just as Mack was about to snap a copy of the picture, Lucas came running into the room. Thomas quickly picked the photograph up off the table and put it back into his pocket.

She pulled herself together. "Come on, time for breakfast," Mack announced, just as Dean walked into the kitchen.

He walked over to her and couldn't help but run his hand down her back in a loving caress. "Are you okay?" he whispered in her ear. Dean bent down and placed a sweet kiss to her lips.

"I am now," she replied, grinning. "Come on, Dean. Let's eat."

Breakfast was a silent affair, and all Dean wanted to do was pick Mack up and hold her until all her troubles were gone. She'd been crying when he'd walked into the kitchen, probably looking at the photograph Thomas had quickly hidden when Lucas appeared. This whole thing with Rose and his grandfather had really gotten to her. He hated how much it upset her.

It also shocked him just how much he was feeling for Mack. She'd gotten under his skin and he was sure she was there to stay. He just hoped she felt the same, because he had no intention of letting her walk away.

"You're looking mighty happy with yourself, young man," Thomas said, pointing his fork at Dean.

"Um, yes I am," he replied, while eating his breakfast.

"Are you going to share?" Thomas looked between Dean

and Mack.

"I might share my thoughts, but I'm not sharing my woman," Dean said, to a laughing Thomas across the table.

"Who's your woman?" Lucas piped up.

Dean paused with the last of his breakfast about to disappear into his mouth. "Your Auntie Mack. Is that all right with you, Lucas?"

"If you make her cry, I'm going to beat you up," Lucas growled.

Dean about managed to swallow a mouth full of food without laughing. "If I make her cry, I'll let you beat me up. Is that a deal?" He held out his hand to Lucas, who looked at it then shook it with sticky fingers.

"Deal."

"Don't I get a say in any of this?" Mack asked.

Lucas and Dean both looked at her. "No!" they said together.

She laughed. "Okay, if all the macho stuff is out of the way, what's everyone doing today?"

"I'm going with Thomas to the Irish Pub," Lucas informed them, rather proudly.

"Oh, you are, are you?" She raised an eyebrow in Thomas' direction and waited for an explanation, which wasn't long in coming.

"Well now, I usually meet a couple of old guys every week, and today is the day. We play cards, and just people watch. They want me to bring Lucas, as I mentioned him the other night, a time or two."

Mack still frowned. She wasn't too sure about the pub idea. "Are you sure Lucas will be okay there?"

"Don't be worrying. You have enough on your plate right now. Lucas will be fine. If I didn't think he would be, I wouldn't take him."

"Okay, but I'll pick him up just after lunch."

Lucas started to jump up and down. "Yes, yes, yes, I'm going to the pub, I'm going to the pub." He started to sing around the kitchen.

Mack put her head in her hands. Dean and Thomas roared with laughter.

"Oh my God, Lucas. Do not, under any condition, tell your father."

"Why, Auntie Mack? Daddy always says you have to at least do everything once."

Mack glanced at Thomas and Dean then gave them a dirty look because they were still laughing. "Lucas, I don't think your Daddy meant for you to do it all while you're still six!"

"Okay, scouts honor, this is our secret. I'm going up to wash my hands. Back in a minute, Thomas." Lucas rushed off.

"You do realize as soon as he sees his father, that's going to be the first thing he tells him?" Mack picked up her coffee and took a sip, while thinking about Lucas' trip to the 'Irish pub' with Thomas. Hopefully he wouldn't get into too much trouble.

"Spend today with me again?" Dean asked, breaking into her thoughts.

"I'd love to."

"Well, who do we have here, Thomas?"

"This is my good friend, Lucas Cartwright. Lucas, meet a couple of friends of mine, Levi and Walt. We've been friends for seventy-five years."

Lucas' jaw dropped and Levi smiled. "Well, come on over here and tell us some gossip, kid."

He took a seat between Levi and Thomas. "What do you want to know?"

"Well now, let me think. What's going on up at that cottage of Thomas' that you're staying in?"

"Oh, that's easy. My Auntie has a secret about something she found about someone named Rose, and Dean slept in her bed last night, but she doesn't know I know that. Is that what you mean?" Lucas looked at the stunned faces looking back at him. "What did I say?"

Thomas came back to his wits first. "You did fine, Lucas. Why don't I teach you how to play poker, so you can fleece your father," he replied, trying to change the subject.

"That would be cool." Lucas grinned.

Thomas hadn't expect that kind of gossip to come out of Lucas' mouth. He was a handful all right. He chuckled to himself.

Tomorrow. Tomorrow he would talk to Mack about the night Rose died. Maybe. Maybe not.

Thomas glanced quickly over at Levi and Walt, who still seemed a little bit preoccupied. He was guessing they were thinking back to the time Rose died.

"Okay, let's shuffle the cards."

Chapter 26

"Dean, do you think the library here in town will have newspaper archives from 1947?" Mack moved to sit beside him on the sofa.

He reached out to her and pulled her in towards him for a hug. "Probably, why? What are you thinking?"

"I'm thinking that if Thomas can't talk, then surely there would have been something about a young woman going off the cliffs written up in the newspaper. If there was, why didn't Jacob read about it? Most people read newspapers."

"You've got a point. Do you want to go?"

She sat up to look more closely at him. "Are you sure you don't mind spending time at the library?"

"As long as I'm with you, I don't mind." He caressed her face then leaned in to kiss her.

As he started to pull away, she took hold of his face and sealed her lips to his for another quick kiss. "Mmm." She licked her lips. "Thank you for being understanding. I really appreciate it. We could go somewhere after the library if you like."

"I'd like."

"Oh, I almost forgot. I took a picture of the photograph Thomas found. Let me show you."

She stood up, reached for her cell and searched through her pictures to find the one she wanted. Unfortunately, it was a really bad picture and didn't really show the faces. She must have taken the picture just as Thomas removed it from the table when Lucas appeared.

"Damn, this is totally crap. Look." She passed her cell to Dean.

"You can take another one again, Mack. In fact, when we go to visit my grandfather, I'll bring my laptop and portable scanner over, and we can get a better copy for you." Dean stood up and grabbed his jacket from the back of the kitchen chair.

Mack followed him out of the cottage. "That would be great. Thanks."

He put his arm around Mack's neck and brought her in close to him, then placed a soft kiss to the top of her head. "Come on, the library awaits," he said, not wanting to let her go.

As Dean pulled his bike into a parking space outside of the Thomas Memorial Library, Mack wondered if it was the same library where Rose worked all those years ago. Parts of it certainly looked old enough, although it looked like new sections had been added over time.

They climbed off Dean's bike and removed their helmets. Mack reached up to him and pulled his head down to hers for a sizzling kiss, then pulling away she gave him a saucy grin.

"What was that for?" He wrapped his arms around her

and pulled her even closer to nuzzle her neck.

"I can't resist you." She groaned.

A car suddenly backfired, which brought them back to their senses. Dean took a deep breath and moved her a bit away from him. "We better head inside, before I put you over the bike, and take you back to the cottage."

She giggled when she caught the look on Dean's face. They were acting like lovesick teenagers. Mack opened the door to the library and stood with her hands on her hips, waiting for him to catch up.

Inside the library he leaned against one of the pillars in the middle and just watched his woman walk over to one of the library assistants. She'd put more of a sway into her step, which she'd done deliberately to get a reaction out of him... *Hot damn*!

Last night when Mack took matters into her own hands, literally, it was a very nice, pleasurable surprise. He hadn't been expecting that, although he'd hoped. What guy wouldn't?

Yesterday, when he'd listened to Mack read about his grandfather's love life, he'd found it kind of creepy and hard to imagine the Jacob from the diary, who was in love with Rose, to be his grandfather who was in love with his wife, Eliza.

Mack waved him over to follow her. He straightened from his slouched position and followed her to an archive room. She seemed to be in deep discussion with the male library assistant, who was ogling her. Dean's woman.

Dean placed their helmets on top of the large table in the center of the room, and his leather jacket over the back of one of the chairs. He walked over to Mack, wrapped one of his arms around her waist, and pulled her in close, laying his claim. She didn't let him down either. She placed one of her arms around his waist with her hand going in to his back pocket to squeeze his butt. The little minx! Dean leaned over and placed a kiss on top of her head as he pulled her in tight to his chest.

The assistant seemed to get the message, because after he'd finished telling her to come get him if she needed anything else, he dashed from the room.

She grinned, reached up and pulled his head down to hers for a quick kiss, as she walked off towards the shelves where a lot of rather large books were stored.

"The newspapers we want are over here. Apparently, each page is laminated for protection, so he didn't have any problem leaving us alone in here." Mack looked back to Dean.

"Alone? For how long?"

She laughed. "Get your mind off body parts and come over here and help. You're taller than me."

"Yes, ma'am!" He sauntered over, laughing.

He lifted the volume down that covered the week of April 14, 1947, and set it down on the table, while Mack took her denim jacket off and placed it on top of his on the chair.

She was really excited, hoping there was something in these papers about what happened to Rose. It appeared to have been awhile since anyone had looked through them, because they were caked in a few layers of dust. She blew it off the best she could, then turned the page to April 15th. They both eagerly scanned each page closely to try and find something.

As they carefully looked through the 19th, Mack started to lose hope of finding anything. It was five days after the event, and surely it would have been covered before then.

Just as she started to turn the page, something caught Dean's eye. He put his hand out and stopped the page from turning. "Mack, look. Read this."

April 19, 1947

Today the Coast Guard has called off the search for the missing girl, who fell to her death, over the cliffs on the evening of the 14th. Clothes have come ashore on the beach, but as yet, there is still no sign of a body.

If anyone has any information about the identity of the missing girl, please contact...

"Could this be Rose?" She lifted her face up to look at Dean, excitement filling her eyes.

He pulled her out of the chair and onto his lap. "I don't know. It sounds like it. But why isn't her name in the article? It's as though no one knows it's Rose."

She snuggled more into him. "I'm going to have to ask Thomas. It just doesn't make sense. Her family obviously had money. If her father was trying to marry her off to a wealthy guy, her drowning should have been bigger news."

"Come on, let's go and get something to eat, then head back and see if there's anything out there on the Internet about Rose. There should at least be a death certificate we can view."

Chapter 27

"Are you enjoying your lunch?" Thomas wiped his mouth with a napkin and smiled at Lucas, who was arranging his remaining fries into a row of soldiers on his plate.

"Yeah, that was really awesome." He shoveled more ketchup-covered fries into his mouth. "Hey, look! It's Auntie Mack and Dean," Lucas shouted, then shot up out of his chair, ran out of the door and into Mack's arms.

"Are you okay, Lucas?" she asked as Dean walked around his bike and started to ruffle his hair.

"Great, I can play poker," Lucas added with great pride.

"Oh, you can, can you?" She grinned at Dean.

Dean took Mack by the hand and led the way inside to be introduced to Levi, Walt having already left.

Mack looked stunned. "You're Levi. I mean, *Levi*?" She laughed. "Sorry, I'm not usually an idiot. I mean Levi, as in childhood friend of Thomas?" She found it unbelievable that Levi and Thomas were still best friends after all these years.

Dean handed her an ice cold Pepsi and put his down on the table, then carried a couple of chairs over for himself and Mack. He put both chairs close together, and then eased Mack down into hers. He needed to touch her, and put his arm around her, gave her shoulder a squeeze, and whispered in her ear. "What's wrong?"

Mack turned to reply and stopped when she realized just how close to Dean's face she was. Looking into his eyes, she leaned forward slightly. "It's okay." Then she kissed him. "Just making sure the ladies over there know you're mine. Plus, I couldn't resist."

She moved slightly away and noticed a twinkle in Thomas' eye. *He probably had us married already, she thought.* After she took a long drink of her Pepsi, she looked over at Thomas. "How long have you known Levi?"

"Seventy-five years, or there abouts."

Dean put his drink down rather abruptly. "Damn, that's a hell of a long time."

Mack looked just as shocked. "In Rose's diary, she mentioned you a couple of times. In fact, the description that really made me laugh was about you and Thomas absconding with an apple pie, and that you both got caught returning the plate."

"I remember as though it was yesterday," Levi replied, laughing.

Dean could see the wheels turning in Mack's head and wondered how long it would take for her to start questioning Levi.

He was seated close with his hand caressing her thigh, her hip, or anywhere else he could reach. Right now, his hand was caressing the back of her neck. Mack had her hand on his thigh and was sliding it up and down. He wasn't sure she knew what she was doing. Boy, another couple of inches, and she would know just how much she affected him.

"Levi, can I ask you something?"

He paused and took a drink, then he quickly glanced at Thomas. "Yes, I guess. As long as it isn't going to get me into trouble."

Dean reached down and removed her hand from his thigh. She was playing hell with his libido. He laced their fingers together while she decided what to ask Levi.

"Do you remember Rose? What she was like?"

"I do." He had a slight blush. "She was the most beautiful girl I've ever seen, and I had one hell of a crush on her."

"What's a crush?" Lucas asked, having just finished his huge ice cream sundae.

"A crush is when you really like someone, and you can't think about anyone else," Mack replied to Lucas, who still looked confused.

"So you mean like you and Dean?"

With everyone laughing, Dean let go of her hand, took hold of her face and kissed her, very slow and very soft.

"Yes, like me and your Auntie Mack," Dean answered grinning, at Mack's dazed look.

Just then, Dean's cell started to ring. "Excuse me a minute. It's my mother." He stood up, and before he walked outside to answer his cell, placed a quick kiss to the top of Mack's head.

Her sandwich arrived and she started to eat it, but kept glancing outside to catch a glimpse of Dean on the phone. She liked to look at him. Wherever he was, her eyes were always drawn to him. Was this how Rose felt when she was with Jacob?

Dean came back inside and appeared rather distracted as he sat back down next to her. "Is everything okay? You look bothered."

He sighed in frustration after he'd talked to his mother. "I'm fine." Then he looked directly at Mack. "I have to go to Boston tomorrow, for a garden party at my folks' place. Do you and Lucas want to go with me? We would, of course, have to go in your car, but we could share the driving. We could also bring my laptop and scanner back as well."

She stayed silent, not sure whether it was a good idea to meet his family after only knowing each other for a short time.

"Mack?" he asked nervously.

"Are you sure you want me to meet your family?" she whispered.

Dean took hold of Mack's hands. "Yes, I do. I need to warn you though, Cynthia, who I mentioned before, will be there trying to get her claws into me... you know... maybe this isn't a good idea after all."

She heard Dean say Cynthia was going to be there, so Mack decided there was no way her man was going to a party without her, when another woman wanted him. No way in hell.

"Yes, we would love to go," she replied. She noticed part relief, then fright, cross Dean's face. She giggled. "I'll sharpen my knives, right? No one messes with my guy, so don't be surprised if I can't stop touching you all the time, laying claim to you!"

"Christ, you're hot when you get pissed, and babe, you can touch me as much as you want. I'm all yours!" Dean whispered into her ear, feeling relieved and happy that she obviously felt something strong for him.

Thomas stood up and took hold of Lucas' hand, with a cough trying to smother his laughter at Mack and Dean, said, "We're going to the beach for the afternoon, so I'll have the boy back home for dinner."

"Are you sure, Thomas?" She was worried about leaving Lucas all day with him.

"Of course I'm sure. I'm not about to miss dinner!"

They finished their lunch in silence, as they watched Thomas and Levi take Lucas across the road to the shady part of the beach. Mack, for the second time, wondered what it would be like to live in Cape Elizabeth instead of the city.

"You finished?" Dean asked her rather abruptly.

"I am, thanks. That was really good." Mack wiped her mouth on her napkin.

She watched Dean place the dishes onto the bar and let her mind wander back to last night, how he looked naked and aroused.

Dean started to walk back to Mack, noticing the steamy look in her eyes and hesitated. "What do you want to do now?"

She licked her luscious lips and stood. "Mmm, how about going back to my place and getting naked?" she whispered.

Dean tightened his hold on his jacket, picked the helmets up, then practically dragged Mack out of the door and onto his bike.

Come dinnertime, Mack was once again in the kitchen, while Dean was trying to beat his score on the Super Mario Brothers game. All she could really think about was the gloriously sexy afternoon she'd just spent with him, in fact she was lucky she didn't burn herself while cooking the dinner.

After being ravished on the kitchen table, Dean had carried her and all their clothes upstairs, where he'd proceeded to make love to her again, in the shower, then when they came out, on the bed.

She was sure that he would have made love to her again, if Lucas hadn't been due back with Thomas.

Dean came up behind her, and put his arms around her waist to place open-mouth kisses along her neck. "Mmm, you taste good. I can't get enough of you."

She smiled up at him, quickly kissed him then pushed him slightly away. "Thomas and Lucas are here!"

Dean watched Mack hug Lucas and wished for things he had never wanted before... until now. She was an amazing woman, and the more time he spent with her, the more he was falling in love with her. She'd said she loved him, but he hadn't spoken the words to her. Was she disappointed? He didn't want them to follow her declaration. He wanted to say them when she least expected them.

Thomas seemed to have fallen for her as well, in a different kind of way. He also seemed to be pushing them both together, which was probably his way of saying 'I approve'.

"What have you been doing while we were at the beach?" Lucas asked, which made Mack blush and Dean smile.

"I've been cooking and Dean has been trying to beat his score on that Wii game you both seem to like."

"Cool!" Lucas headed into the sitting room to check out Dean's latest score.

"Thomas, can I ask you something about Rose, please?" Dean asked, which drew both Mack and Thomas' attention.

"I guess." Sitting down, Thomas looked apprehensive.

"Why isn't Rose's name in the newspapers about her disappearance?" Thomas raised his head. "It says in the paper 'missing girl' and they also ask for anyone to come forward if they know her identity. We visited the library archives this morning."

Thomas let out a long slow sigh. "It was Rose. Richard, who wanted to marry her, was the son of the paper's owner at the time. My father had a word with him, and although something had to be printed, they made sure it was very small and with no names."

Mack and Dean shot each other a quick glance.

"Looking back now, I guess they could have done that so Jacob, if reading a paper, wouldn't have a clue it was Rose. Why, I don't know. Perhaps they blamed him and thought he would suffer more anguish thinking she didn't love him and had chosen Richard instead of letting him know that she'd died," Thomas said.

"That is sad. Did they ever find her?" Mack asked.

Tears stung Thomas' eyes. "No."

Mack took hold of Thomas' hands, while Dean put his arm around Mack's shoulders. "I'm so sorry, Thomas," she said, crying with him and for him.

"Don't worry, it was a long time ago. Reliving it is hard." He patted Mack's hand.

"I'm not helping, am I?" She wiped her tears away.

"It's time I got everything off my chest. I'm feeling weary tonight, but maybe tomorrow."

She squeezed Dean's hand in thanks and stood up, then started to put the dinner out on the table.

While she was lost in her own thoughts, Dean was inviting Thomas to go with them to the garden party tomorrow, much to Lucas' delight.

Chapter 28

Dean was driving into the city with the most beautiful woman he had ever seen sitting beside him. He felt so much for her. She was amazing, and all his. Since he wasn't sure what kind of reception they would get from his mother, he hoped and prayed Mack would still be his at the end of the day.

Before he went up to Cape Elizabeth, Cynthia, her mother, Gladys, and his mother were all hinting it was time to 'pop the question', even after only one date. The rest of the time, he was with Cynthia, she just kept showing up wherever he just happened to be. In the end, he'd stopped telling anyone at home where he was going and just said to use his cell phone if they needed him. He'd escaped to Cape Elizabeth and met Mackenzie. His Mack.

He was smiling as he started to daydream about Mack. He'd been shocked when she appeared downstairs this morning in the soft pale pink dress that fell like silk against her curves and gorgeous legs, especially showcased in the strappy sandals.

"Lucas, stop fidgeting." Mack twisted around to look at him in the back. He was in neatly pressed jeans and a striped polo shirt, which she'd insisted be tucked in, much to Lucas' disgust.

Thomas started a game of eye-spy, to try and occupy him.

"It isn't too far now," Dean announced, hoping his body didn't misbehave with her so close, smelling delicious.

Mack was sitting in the front seat and starting to get more nervous than she was before leaving Maine. She'd never been in the position of 'meeting parents' before. For the first time in her life, she was with a guy she had fallen in love with, so getting approval from his folks would mean a lot. Then there was Cynthia, who Dean had told her didn't mean anything to him, or did she? Mack had spent practically all her time with Dean since he'd arrived in Cape Elizabeth, so there hadn't really been time for him to spend it with anyone else, or for him to sneak back to Boston. Ugh. She was driving herself crazy with all these thoughts.

Dean quickly glanced at Mack and took hold of one of her hands. "Mack, it'll be okay, I promise. Don't be nervous."

"I can't help it. I've never met a guy's parents before, and knowing there's going to be a woman there who thinks she's yours, is making me a nervous wreck." Mack tried to smile, but failed miserably.

Dean pulled over to the side of the road, climbed out of the vehicle and walked around to the other side. He opened Mack's door, unclipped her seatbelt, and then looked into the back at Thomas and Lucas. "Just give us a minute, guys."

She climbed out of the car to join Dean. He took hold of her hand, pulled her around the back of the car, then into his arms and held her tight. "Just remember that you're the one I want, for always Mack. No matter what anyone says or does, it's you and only you making my heart pound and my blood roar. No one has ever made me feel like this before. Just remember that, okay?" He tilted Mack's face up to his and placed a very gentle, sweet kiss on her lips. "All right, Mack?"

"Okay, Dean. Just try and stay close," she asked, still feeling nervous about meeting his parents, but more sure of herself with Dean.

He grinned. "Wasn't thinking of doing anything else."

She'd just climbed back into the car, when Lucas tapped her on the shoulder. "Auntie Mack?"

She turned around to face him. "Are you, okay?"

With his face all scrunched up in a frown, he asked, "Do you love, Dean?"

Mack felt a blush start to creep up her neck to her face, with Lucas putting her right on the spot. "Yes. I do, Lucas." She looked at Dean.

Thomas just smirked while sitting back in his seat, enjoying the discussion.

Dean grinned, leaned forward, and placed a slow kiss to her lips. "I love your Auntie Mack as well, Lucas. Is that okay?

Mack was mesmerized, while Dean smirked, feeling rather pleased with himself.

After some thought, Lucas said, "Yeah, that's cool.... I guess."

"Thomas, will you be all right meeting Jacob?" Mack asked with some concern, trying to change the subject.

"I think so, Mack. I never actually met him, but he may remember my name, unless we just forget about my surname for today?"

"Okay, that might be for the best, at least at first," Mack replied.

Dean pulled into his parents' drive, only to find there were already a lot of cars parked up. He felt nervous and wondered just what kind of garden party was taking place this afternoon. When he'd spoken to his mother yesterday, she'd said it was 'just family', and the last time Dean counted, it didn't include this many people.

As Dean switched the engine off, he ran around to help Mack out of the car, not wanting her to break her neck in the sexy-as-hell heels.

As he was standing there admiring her legs, she grinned up at him, knowing how she aroused him. "You enjoying the view?"

"You have no idea how much." He smoothed his hand over her hip and pulled her close while his hand traveled south to caress her butt.

They heard some chuckling from the back of the car, which reminded Dean to step back and open the door, so that Thomas and Lucas could climb out.

Lucas was still looking as neat as a pin, and Thomas looked as though he was really enjoying himself at Dean and Mack's expense.

"Dean. You're finally here. Cynthia has been asking for you!" Mack froze at this comment from Dean's mother.

"Mack, remember what I said on the road, okay?" he whispered to her, trying not to panic himself.

Dean took a tight hold of her hand, to reassure her that he was totally hers. He then led the way to introduce her to his mother. "Mother, I'm sure Cynthia can manage on her own. I want you to meet the woman who has stolen my heart, Mackenzie Harper. Mack, this is my mother, Anne."

"Nice to meet you." Mack held her hand out in greeting, only to be ignored.

"Who are they?" Anne asked Dean. She tried to drag him away from Mack, but he was having none of it and stayed attached to her.

"This is Lucas. He's Mack's nephew, and this devil is Thomas. He's a good friend to us both. Actually, I think he's trying to steal Mack away from me!"

"If I was a hell of a lot younger, I would give you a run for your money, young man!"

"Wouldn't I get a say in any of this?" Mack asked, as she raised one of her eyebrows at Dean and Thomas.

"No, babe. I'd just carry you away and tie you up until you agree to be mine," Dean announced, laughing.

"Mmm, would you now?"

"This is ridiculous. What am I going to tell Cynthia and her parents, now you've turned up with this..." Anne trailed off, waving her arms towards Mack, Thomas, and Lucas.

Dean tightened his hold on Mack's hand, as she tried to break free. He wasn't sure if it was to go back to her car or to hit his mother. She would be within her rights to do both. Dean was getting really pissed now.

"Okay, Mother. I will say this for the last time. Please do not mention Cynthia or her parents to me again. This is Mack, and she is my woman. The woman I'm in love with. You will treat her with respect as well as Thomas and Lucas." He paused. "Do I make myself clear?"

She stiffened her spine. "Very."

"Father, this is Mackenzie, otherwise known as Mack." Dean had spotted his father coming towards them.

He held his hand out to Mack. "It's nice to meet you, Mack. Please call me James."

"Nice to meet you too, James." Mack released his hand. She was still upset over the reaction from Dean's mother.

"Dad, this is Thomas, a good friend, and this is Lucas, Mack's six year old nephew."

"Nice to meet you both, glad you could all come today."

James watched his wife disappear into the house. "Sorry about your mother, son. You know what she's like with Cynthia and her folks."

"Hopefully, this is the end of it." Dean felt Mack start to withdraw from him. He turned to look at her and saw that she was holding back tears.

She took a deep breath. "I don't think I can do this, Dean." She started to back away slightly.

"Mack, please don't go. I promise to stay by your side. Ten minutes, then we'll go the minute you say." He took hold of her face and placed a gentle kiss to her forehead, before pulling her into his arms for a brief hug.

James realized, on hearing his son talk to Mack and seeing his show of affection towards her, that she meant a great deal to him. "Mack, please join us. I suspect Anne may already have learned her lesson."

"Ten minutes." Mack took hold of Dean's hand. Lucas slipped his small hand into her other one.

"Dean, your grandparents aren't here. Some friends of theirs are going on vacation tomorrow, so they wanted to have a quiet afternoon with them."

He looked towards Mack.

"Don't worry, Dean." She squeezed his hand, hiding her disappointment. "Let's do this."

They walked around the side of the house, which was huge. Mack very nearly walked into Dean, as he stopped, rather abruptly.

"Dean, what's wrong?"

Too stunned to answer, he looked at his father. "Dad, we don't have this much family!"

"I think your mother got carried away."

"Auntie Mack, I need the potty," Lucas announced, as he tugged on her hand.

"I'll take you, Lucas. I could do with a bathroom break myself," Thomas added, taking hold of Lucas' hand.

"Follow me. I'll show you where they are," James said.

Mack watched Thomas and Lucas walk off towards the bathroom, and wished she could go with them. With a quick glance over Dean's shoulder, Mack could see rather a lot of people, some of who were watching her and Dean together. She felt so nervous.

"Babe, come here," Dean pulled her into his arms. "Don't worry, I'll look after you."

She breathed his scent into her lungs and raised her head up to meet his eyes.

He lowered his mouth to kiss her. "Open for me, Mack," he whispered against her lips.

She did as he asked, then all her worries just fell away.

She reached up to take hold of his face and deepened the kiss even more. One of Dean's hands traveled south and landed on Mack's butt, which he squeezed, then pulled her even closer to him.

James appeared behind Mack and cleared his throat, which broke them apart, although Dean refused to let go of Mack. "Dad."

"I think everyone gets the idea about the two of you now! Why don't you go and introduce Mack?" James smiled and walked off to join the party.

"You okay?" Dean placed a quick kiss to Mack's nose.

"No, I think you should show me your room." Mack offered him one hell of a sexy grin.

"Christ, woman. Come on, let's go and join everyone. I need a drink!"

They both laughed as Dean led Mack down to his 'family' and collected two glasses of orange juice on the way.

He introduced her to so many people, she couldn't remember who was who. Up to now, she hadn't met any of Dean's family members, other than his parents. None of his uncles, aunts, or cousins were present. Apparently they were spread right across the United States, with a couple in Canada.

While Dean talked briefly with everyone, Mack kept looking around to try and spot Cynthia. She was really curious as to what she looked like, and wondered why Dean wasn't interested in the woman.

Mack turned back to Dean and found a woman in a pink 'something' standing in front of her. She had no idea what to say, as anything she would have normally said flew out of her head. She'd never seen anything like it before, and had no idea what the woman was wearing. It looked to be a dress covered with feathers in different shades of pink.

"Hello. I'm Mack." she held her hand out, trying not to be too rude and stare.

"Beryl. So you're the woman who has my godson in such a spin, and his mother in such a bad mood."

Stunned, Mack felt tongue tied, but Dean, thankfully, came to her rescue. "Aunt Beryl. I thought you were in England?" He leaned forward and placed a kiss to either side of her face.

"I arrived back two days ago to find your mother with her panties in a twist looking for you. Wanting to know the best time of year for you to get married." When she saw the look on Dean's face, she giggled like a fifteen-year-old school-girl. "Don't worry. I told her you'd get married when you were good and ready, and not before, and definitely not because she wanted you to."

Dean grinned and then sighed in relief that he had someone else in his corner. "Thank you for that. This is Mack. The woman I'm in love with."

Beryl chuckled. "She introduced herself, although she left the love bit out of the introduction."

Mack decided she liked Beryl, once she got over the shock of seeing her dressed in feathers. "I can assure you, the feeling's mutual," Mack added, taking hold of Dean's hand.

"Well, it's been interesting. Now if you'll excuse me." Beryl walked off towards another couple who had just arrived.

"Dean. I haven't seen you for a while. How are you?"

While Dean had a conversation with a guy named Adam, Mack noticed two blonde women talking and looking in their direction, their faces covered with fierce expressions. Was it Cynthia and her mother?

Mack thought it best to look away so they didn't come over. She looked back to Dean, who let go of her hand and put his arm around her waist instead. He just wanted her as close as he could get her and wanted her to know he was there for her.

She snuggled into Dean while she carried on looking around at the lovely tables covered with pale lilac tablecloths, vases overflowing with calla lilies along with an assortment of drinks and food. Even the trees around the garden had been decorated with lilac-colored ribbons.

She felt so out of place at Dean's family home, and really wished she'd refused when he'd asked her to come with him. She'd only agreed so Cynthia couldn't get her claws into him. But realistically, she trusted Dean to be true to her.

"I don't believe we've met." Mack turned slightly as Dean sighed at the inevitable.

"Cynthia, Gladys, I'd like you to meet my girlfriend, Mackenzie Harper... Mack, this is Cynthia Brandon and her mother, Gladys."

"Hello." Mack held her hand out in greeting, only to be ignored, once again. Dean tightened his hold on her and stiffened.

"Auntie Mack!" Lucas shouted. A hush fell over the gathering.

Lucas saw he had Mack's attention across the garden. "I

need help. I can't find my weenie!!" he shouted.

"Hell," Mack whispered under her breath, she didn't know whether to laugh or cry.

"I'm coming, Lucas," she shouted back as she pulled away from Dean, ignoring Cynthia and her mother, who'd turned their back on them.

"Mack, I'll come with you. Sounds like a guy thing." Dean followed her, trying not to laugh.

Usually, Lucas never wore anything tucked into his jeans, in order to make it easier for him to go to the bathroom. When she'd gotten him dressed, she'd forgotten, and she'd put a shirt on him then tucked it into his jeans and made him wear a belt. She'd wanted him to look smart.

They finally reached Lucas and each took hold of one of his hands to lead him back to the bathroom. Once there, both Dean and Lucas stood their ground and refused to let her inside, making her wait outside by the door.

Mack giggled once they had both disappeared.

"Hey, what's so funny?"

"Oh, Thomas. Lucas and his mouth again." Thomas raised an eyebrow in question. "He just came out into the garden and shouted to me across the lawn 'I can't find my weenie'."

Thomas was silent for a moment, then he roared with laughter, causing a few people to turn in their direction.

Lucas walked out of the bathroom and looked between the two of them. "What's so funny?"

"Err, Thomas just told me a grown up joke!" Mack replied quickly.

Dean lifted his hand to caress the side of Mack's face.

"It's the first time you've laughed today. Let's go home. We can eat on the way back."

"Yeah! Does that mean I don't have to tuck my shirt in anymore?"

She didn't know whether to leave or stay. "Thomas, would you mind taking Lucas over to get a drink for a minute please?"

Thomas and Lucas headed over to the refreshments, as she turned to Dean. "These are your family and friends, and I don't want you rushing away because I'm uncomfortable. If this is going to work between us, then I have to get used to them."

"Babe, the only family here right now are my folks and none of these people are my friends. Hell, my sister isn't even here. I know most of them, yes, but my friends help me relax, and I'm not relaxed here. All this isn't me. I'm more comfortable shooting pool or in a cottage in Cape Elizabeth with the woman I'm in love with."

He lifted his hands to Mack's face and used his thumbs to wipe her tears away. "Come on, we're leaving. I'll talk to my grandfather and arrange a time to visit them." He smiled. "I'll tell him I want to bring someone special to meet him and my grandmother, which will guarantee they won't go anywhere else."

"Let me just wash my face in here." Mack dragged Dean into the bathroom with her.

She walked over to the sink and washed her tears away, then used the towel Dean passed to her to dry her face. She opened her purse and applied some more mascara and lipstick, while Dean lounged against the door with his ankles crossed.

He suddenly realized Mack was up to something and straightened slightly, while keeping eye contact as she sauntered towards him.

She stood in front of him, moving in very close, and placed her hands on his chest, moving them upwards in a caress, "So you love me, huh?" she asked huskily, taking his face between her hands, bringing his head down to hers.

First she nibbled on his bottom lip, then moved up to the top one. She continued her assault on his senses and used her tongue to trace the seam of his lips. He opened his mouth and she sealed hers to his in an explosive kiss. Dean was lost. He took over the kiss and lifted her right up, towards him, then turned around to pin her to the door with his hips.

Mack wrapped her legs around his waist. He deepened the kiss even more, only to be abruptly brought back down to earth with someone banging on the door.

Breathing heavily, he rested his head against the door, his mouth attached to Mack's neck, which made her shiver. "Yeah?"

"Are you about done in there?"

"No!" he whispered into Mack's neck.

"Give me five," Dean shouted to his father on the other side of the door.

"Okay, son, take your time. Tell Mack, Thomas and Lucas are sitting in the car."

Mack began to unwrap her legs from around Dean's waist, embarrassed James had caught them, very nearly going at it.

Dean laughed, placing a tender kiss on her nose. He

edged Mack away from him, helped to straighten her clothes, then opened the door.

He took Mack's hand and walked her over to say goodbye to his parents, then practically dragged her to the car, laughing.

"I'm sorry about my mother."

She frowned and looked across at Dean. "Why are you laughing?"

"My father was embarrassed at catching us in the bathroom together. He doesn't embarrass easily, so I can't help but find it funny." Dean helped Mack into the car.

"Auntie Mack, why did you pull Dean into the bathroom with you?" Lucas asked from the backseat.

"You saw that, huh?" Mack asked, glancing at Dean.

"Oh yes. We saw that." Thomas replied.

Chapter 29

They made a quick exit from Dean's parents' house and headed back up the coast. Dean pulled off the interstate into the McDonald's in Biddeford, at Lucas' request, of course.

"What's your pleasure, Lucas?" Dean pulled into a free parking space and turned to him.

"Mmm, can I please have chicken nuggets, fries and chocolate shake?"

"You certainly can, Lucas. Mack, Thomas, do you both want something from here?"

"I think I'll have the same as Lucas, please." Mack did the high-five with Lucas.

Dean turned to look at Thomas. "Now you're not going to let me down, are you, Thomas?"

Mack rolled her eyes. "Men!"

He rubbed his stomach. "No, sir, I'm not. I'll have a burger, fries, and coke, please. This is my first trip to a McDonald's, you know."

"Wow! You've never been to a McDonald's before? But what do you eat, if you don't go to McDonald's?" Lucas asked, totally amazed.

"Real food."

Dean laughed at Lucas' expression. "Okay, you guys, want to eat here or drive a bit further to Fortune's Rock where we can see the ocean? Maybe we'll get lucky and find a parking place."

All three replied, "The Ocean."

Dean grabbed the blanket from the trunk of the car, then headed over to the beach with a rather excited Lucas in tow.

Mack removed her sandals, then took hold of Dean's hand as they carried on walking to find a perfect spot on the beach to watch the ocean, and some yachts that were further out at sea.

With the blanket placed on the sand, they all sat down and ate their McDonalds food. Mack had no idea she was so hungry, until she started to eat. She watched Thomas, who consumed his meal nearly as fast as Lucas.

"Well, Thomas, what did you think of your first McDonalds burger?"

"I enjoyed it, thank you, Dean. Not as good as the burgers I make, but good enough." He ended on a burp, that sent Lucas into a fit of giggles.

"Auntie Mack, please can I go and play in the waves?"

"Give me a couple of minutes, okay? Then I'll take you."

Thomas stood up and looked between Mack and Dean. "I'll take you, buddy. I could do with some exercise after eating all that."

"Are you sure, Thomas?" Mack motioned for Lucas to come and stand in front of her.

"Of course I am."

"Let me roll your trouser legs up, okay. Don't get your jeans wet, as you have nothing to change into."

"I won't."

"Are you going to roll my trouser legs up, too?" Thomas gave her a cheeky grin.

Not being one to back down from a challenge, she grinned, "Come here then."

After rolling both sets of trousers up, Mack lay between Dean's legs, resting against his chest.

"You smell delicious, Mack." Dean started to caress her arms. "So soft."

"Mmm."

She moved in closer to Dean and could feel what she did to him. Loving his reaction, she wriggled slightly, then laughed when she heard him groan.

"You're playing with fire, you know that?" He put his arms around her waist and pulled her in tight. "You feel so right, Mack, in my arms and in my life."

"That's the nicest thing anyone has ever said to me."

With one of her arms wrapped around Dean's waist, she snuggled in tight and started to drift off to sleep. She was snuggled against the man she loved.

Thomas splashed in the chilly surf with Lucas and realized it was a lot of fun. Fun, something Thomas had only started having again, since he'd met Mack, Lucas, and Dean. When he was a boy, he used to spend all his free time either at the beach or fishing with Levi and Walt. What fun they used to have.

Thomas spotted some small pebbles as he looked down at the water around his ankles. He bent down to pick them up.

"What have you found?" Lucas questioned.

"Just some small pebbles. When I was a kid, Levi, Walt, and I used to spend a lot of time skimming pebbles across the water."

"What does that mean?"

"I'll show you." Thomas stood to the side, moved his arm back, and then brought his arm and whole body forward and released the pebble, which bounced a few times across the water before sinking. He glanced at Lucas and started to laugh. He was just standing there with his mouth wide open. "I take it you liked that then?"

"Wow! Yeah! Will you teach me?"

"I will, but it takes a lot of practice, so don't be too disappointed if you don't get the hang of it today, okay?"

"I won't."

After about half an hour of practice, Lucas finally managed to get the stone to bounce twice before sinking, much to his delight and Thomas' relief. He had visions of still being there at midnight with one very determined young man.

Chapter 30

Yesterday had been a tiring day, and Mack had been as tired as Lucas by the time they arrived home. Strangely, she hadn't been ensconced in Rose Cottage all that long, but she was already calling it home.

Thomas had gone back to his cottage, and Dean had carried Lucas up to bed.

Dean and Mack showered together, before heading to bed, where Dean made love to her before they both fell asleep, entwined together, exhausted.

In the morning, Dean had gone home to shower and change, saying he would be back shortly. So, as she was standing in the kitchen waiting for him, she heard rustling at the back door. Mack turned in time to watch Thomas walk in with another bunch of flowers.

"For a beautiful woman!" Thomas held out a lovely bunch of carnations he'd brought for her.

She took the flowers from him. "They're lovely. You're already in my heart, you know, and I'll still feed you, even if you run out of flowers."

He winked at Mack. "I'll never run out of flowers for you!"

"Are you trying to pinch my woman again?" Dean asked

as he entered the kitchen, going straight over to Mack laughing. He planted a very possessive kiss to her lips, then asked, "Where's Lucas?"

"Sitting room."

Dean disappeared into the sitting room, no doubt to play on the Wii with him for a short while, letting Mack finish breakfast.

She started to stack the pancakes, letting Thomas sit and get lost in his own thoughts.

"After breakfast, Mack, do you think, Dean would look after Lucas for a time, so we can talk? I need to tell you what happened that night."

Thomas had taken Mack by surprise. She'd hoped that Thomas would talk to her about the night Rose died, but she wasn't expecting him to do that today. It hadn't even entered her head this morning.

"I'm sure he would. Thank you, Thomas."

With a nod of his head, he took his seat at the kitchen table.

She shouted Dean and Lucas through for breakfast. After everyone had washed up, they sat down to eat the feast she'd made.

"Dean, would you mind keeping Lucas occupied this morning, maybe on the Wii, while I go out for a short while with Thomas? That's if you don't have anything planned?"

Dean grinned across to Lucas. "I was only planning on hanging around here today anyway, so that's fine."

"Thanks."

"Dean."

"Yes, Lucas." Dean wondered what was on his young mind.

"Are you going to marry Auntie Mack? Because that will make you my uncle."

Dean didn't really know how to answer. "Would it bother you if I did?"

"No. I like you and wouldn't mind having an uncle. Thomas has already said he will be my other granddad."

He laughed. "It doesn't always work like that Lucas, but I'll tell you a secret." Lucas moved closer to Dean, as he whispered into Lucas ear. "I love your Auntie Mack, and I hope to be around her a very, very long time. Will that do for now?"

"Yes. Just as long as you remember it's my birthday soon, and there's a new Mario Brothers game coming out, so if you are my uncle, you have to buy me a present."

He ruffled Lucas' hair. "I'll remember that. Now, are you going to let me win this one?"

"No way!"

When they arrived at Thomas' cottage, Mack looked across at him and noticed he looked really frail, and for maybe the first time, he looked his age.

"Thomas, are you sure you're okay doing this? You look awfully pale," she asked, concerned.

"I'm fine, Mack, just trying to collect my thoughts, so they don't come out all jumbled."

They entered through the porch and Mack couldn't help

but notice how neat and tidy everywhere was. Nothing like her apartment.

"Let's go in the sitting room, Mack. It's comfortable in there."

"Okay, lead the way."

She took a seat in the sitting room and looked around, spotting all the photographs on the sideboard. Thomas noticed her looking. "Those are pictures of my wife and various friends over the years."

She stood and walked over to take a closer look at the photographs of Thomas' life, and picked up the photograph of Rose and Jacob, which he had already framed and placed in the center of the pictures. There was a wedding photograph, which was obviously Thomas on his wedding day.

He saw the photograph that had grabbed Mack's interest. "That's Janet and me on our wedding day in 1958. She was the most beautiful woman I'd ever seen. Couldn't believe it when she showed interest in me." He laughed. "After our first date, we were pretty much inseparable and married three months later."

"These are amazing, Thomas. Wow, is that you?" Mack picked up a photograph of what looked to be a younger Thomas in uniform.

"That's me. I joined the army as soon as I was old enough. Against my father's wishes, I might add. He never spoke to me again after I became a soldier."

She was angry on Thomas' behalf. "I wish he was here now, so I could give him a piece of my mind."

"Don't worry, Mack. It was a hell of a long time ago. In

fact, that picture was taken just before I shipped out to Korea in 1951."

"Wow."

"Come sit next to me, Mack. Let me tell you a story."

"I'm all yours, Thomas."

"It might disappoint you some, as my reluctance to talk is more about guilt, than anything else."

"It's okay, Thomas. Don't worry. Just tell me what you remember."

"I remember that last night as though it happened yesterday. It was just after ten thirty when I woke up, having heard my bedroom door shut. Turning over, I heard a thump, so, climbing out of bed and turning up the lamp in my room, I discovered the *Our Gang*, April 1st edition on the floor. I realized it must have been Rose who had just been in my room."

He sighed. "I then put the comic back down on my bed and put on my slippers and a sweater before creeping down the stairs. Spotting a light in the kitchen, I slipped inside quietly, just in time to see her going out the door with her purse."

He took a sip of water. "I knew she was going meeting, Jacob, but I had no idea she had planned to run away with him. At least not then. It must have been about five minutes later, when Richard came banging on the back door. He had seen Rose sneak out and wanted to know where she was going. I told him I had no idea. He frightened me. I ended up blurting out, that I thought she'd snuck out to meet Jacob and she would probably take the cliff path towards town."

Both Mack and Thomas had tears in their eyes. "Are you

sure you're okay to continue?" Mack asked.

"I haven't spoken about that night before now. I need to tell you."

"All right, go on."

"Richard seemed to go wild when I explained. He said 'I will find her and bring her back where she belongs; and that is as my wife'. I have never forgotten those words. Richard then took off towards the cliffs and that was the last I saw of him, until he returned just over an hour later, when Mother and Father were home, and told them he saw her go over the cliffs. I remember Richard looking really upset and as he was telling us, he just crumbled, breaking down, sobbing."

"Oh, Thomas." She knelt at his feet, taking his hands into hers. "Did you believe Richard when he said she'd 'fallen' off the cliff, or did you consider Richard might have pushed her off?"

"I don't know, Mack. That was a possibility, and I guess that night Richard looked wild enough to do anything, but he never, in all the years before that night or following showed any sign of being dangerous. Plus, I think he really did love her. He seemed a gentle kind of guy before then, I thought."

Mack sat bolt upright. "Thomas. Is Richard still alive?"

"He is, Mack. He lives in a nursing home now, because he needs round the clock care."

Mack sat back down across from Thomas. "Do you think they would let me talk to him?"

"He has a daughter, Sally, I think. She works in town at the coffee shop with the yellow paint. You could go see her and maybe she'll phone the home to give permission for you to visit."

"Over the years, have you ever asked Richard what happened that night?" Mack asked him tentatively.

"I tried, when I was older, maybe ten years later. He said that he lost the only woman he has ever loved that night, and didn't want to remember. Then he walked away from me."

"I don't know what to say. But I do know more happened that night than what you were told, I'm sure of it. I'm going to find out what. Perhaps now that Richard isn't doing so well, he may be more open to talking about what happened that night, providing he remembers."

Thomas finally pulled himself together and looked across to Mack. "Thank you. This is the first time I've ever forced myself to remember that night, and I feel as though a weight has been lifted from my shoulders. I've always blamed myself, you see, for not telling my father. If I had, he'd probably have done his best to split them up, but at least she would've lived. It was my fault Richard went after her on the cliff path."

"You don't know that. She could've still run away with him. Please don't blame yourself anymore. It wasn't your fault. I'm glad you told me, and I'll let you know how my visit to see Richard goes," Mack explained.

"Take Dean with you when you go, okay, Mack? He might need round the clock care, but I don't want you alone with him."

She glanced at Thomas. "Okay. Do you want to come back with me for some lunch?"

"No, thank you. I think I just need some peace for a short time. I'll see you for dinner though."

When Mack left Thomas, she realized that she still had

many unanswered questions.

Chapter 31

Mack walked into Rose Cottage and was met by cheers and shouts coming from the sitting room. Lucas and Dean were obviously enjoying the Wii game.

Feeling rather cold, she made herself a cup of coffee and took a seat at the kitchen table, mulling over everything Thomas had just told her.

There were many 'what if's' about that night, and she just couldn't stop obsessing about them. She needed to call for coffee in town and ask Sally if she would let her visit her father, or beg if needed.

If Richard found Rose that night, which he obviously had in order to have seen her go over the cliffs, then he must remember something, and perhaps, she was hoping, he would decide it was time to tell someone what really happened.

"Hey, Mack. I didn't know you were back." Dean walked over to pour himself some coffee. Not getting an answer from Mack he stopped mid-pour and turned back around to take a look at her, noticing she was miles away. "Mack. What happened?" Dean asked, going over to sit beside her, pulling her onto his lap.

Mack turned to Dean and wrapped her arms around his neck, hugging him close, breathing in his scent. All man. She felt soothed sitting with Dean, as though all was okay with the world.

With Dean holding her tight, caressing her back, Mack finally felt herself warming up. "I'm okay, Dean. Just upset, and I guess frustrated. I still don't know what happened the night Rose died." She sighed. "Thomas told me he'd watched Rose sneak out, and that shortly after he told Richard, who then followed her. A short while later, Richard returned to tell them she had gone over the cliffs."

"Mack, I'm sorry you still don't have closure."

"I won't have, until I know what actually happened, and I've told your grandfather."

"I'll arrange that soon, okay?" Dean continued stroking Mack's back, not wanting to let her go.

"Thanks, Dean. There is one more thing. Richard is still alive."

"What?"

"Apparently he's in a nursing home and needs round the-clock-care, but he has a daughter who works at the yellow coffee shop in town. So, I was thinking, maybe after lunch we could take a trip down there, and with luck get her permission to talk to him."

"Okay. I'll make us some sandwiches, we'll go drink coffee, then hit the supermarket, where you can load the cart to your heart's content and I'll pay." Dean planted a kiss on her lips to stop her protesting. "I've eaten here practically every mealtime since I've been in Cape Elizabeth, so I'm paying. If it bothers you that much, you pay next time."

With her forehead resting against his, she looked into his eyes. "I love you. It's never happened to me before, and I've only known you a short time, it's kind of frightening."

"What I feel for you, Mack, frightens me as well, but instead of running, I'm not going anywhere, because you belong to me. Is that okay?"

"Most definitely!"

"Now that's settled, lunchtime, I think." Dean walked over to the refrigerator to retrieve some cold meats and salad vegetables.

Watching him work, Mack found it a real turn on. She watched the rippling muscles across his back when he moved. *Oh boy,* what a view she had when he dropped a tomato and bent down to pick it up.

"Yummy!"

Dean turned to look at Mack, raising an eyebrow in question, wondering what she was up to. When he saw the direction she was looking, laughed out loud. "You like what you see, babe?"

"Mmm, I certainly do."

He pointed the butter knife at her. "Control yourself, lunch is ready in a minute. You can nibble on that for now."

"Spoil sport!"

"Who's a spoil sport?" Lucas asked, running into the kitchen and sitting on Mack's lap.

"Dean is. He won't play," she pouted.

"You're no good on the Wii, so that's probably why he won't play with you."

She tried not to laugh. "Dean's making lunch, then we're going to head into town for a short while. After that, we're going to the supermarket, where under no circumstances do you get involved in a water fight again."

"Water fight?" Dean queried.

"Please, don't ask."

The coffee shop in town was a small wooden structure, painted in yellow with white trim, with a large corner window facing towards the ocean. They had tables and chairs outside on the sidewalk, underneath white canopies, with an amazing view of the ocean.

Inside, there were a few people already drinking and busy chatting away. Lucas had chosen his seat, in the corner where there were toys to play with, so Mack and Dean joined him.

"Mack, Lucas, what would you both like to drink?"

"Vanilla Latte for me, please. Lucas, would you like a chocolate milk?"

"Yes, please."

"Okay, back in a few minutes."

Mack looked around and could see a couple of girls who worked there and they both looked to be in their early twenties. Neither of the girls could possibly be Richard's daughter. They were far too young.

The girls seemed friendly enough, so as one of the girls walked past, Mack got her attention. "Hi, I was wondering if Sally is around?"

"She's in the back. Does she know you?"

"My name is Mackenzie Harper, and I would really appreciate five minutes of her time."

"Okay, give me a minute." She dashed off, doing a double-take when she caught sight of Dean, who had no idea he'd just been eyed up.

She smiled to herself as Dean sat back down and placed the drinks on the table. "What?"

"You were just being ogled, and I was kind of having a happy dance in my head, because you're all mine!"

"Who by?" he teased, as Mack smacked him on the shoulder.

"Behave."

"Hi, I'm Sally. Did you want to talk to me?"

"I do. Do you have time to join us?"

Sally had to be in her late fifties or early sixties, but didn't look that old. She was of average height, with a slim build and light brown hair. She took the seat next to Mack. "Okay, I only have a minute though."

Dean was holding her hand underneath the table, offering his support. "Sally, would it be possible for you to let me talk to your father?"

Sally's eyes opened wide as she obviously hadn't expected that. "Why my father? Do you know him?"

"No, I don't know him. I'm staying at Rose Cottage and I've found a diary that was written by Rose Degan in 1947, and she mentions your father. He was the last one to see her alive, I just want to ask him what happened."

"I'm not sure it would be worth your while," Sally said.

"Please, Sally," Mack begged.

"He loved Rose. I once asked my mother why Dad was the way he was to her. Oh, he loved her, but not how a man and woman should love each other. She told me that he had been in love with another woman, who went over the cliffs one night. He never spoke about her or could abide to hear her name spoken." Sally looked towards the window. "I'm not sure after all these years if he'll be much help to you, and how he will be, hearing Rose's name. I just don't know." Sally chewed on her bottom lip.

"Please, Sally. At least let me try."

"Perhaps it's time to lay old ghosts to rest before he dies. He hasn't got long left. I'll make the call for you. When do you want to go?"

"Tomorrow, if possible."

She pushed the chair back to stand up. "Give me a minute and I'll get you the address."

Mack watched Sally retreat to the back of the shop again and turned to look at Dean. "Will you come with me?"

Dean placed a quick kiss to Mack's lips. "Yes," he whispered.

Mack realized Lucas had hardly drunk any of his chocolate. "Lucas come, finish your drink. We're going soon."

He stood from the floor where he was sitting playing with some wooden blocks. "What are we doing later?"

"Shopping!"

"Here you go." Sally handed Mack a card with the address of the nursing home written on it. "If you go in the morning, he's more responsive."

"Thank you, Sally. This means a lot."

Chapter 32

Climbing out of the car at the supermarket, Mack turned to Lucas, only to watch him slip his hand into Dean's. Dean looked pleasantly surprised, but recovered quickly and gave his little hand a squeeze.

With a bit of luck, Dean would keep him out of trouble. "Lucas, you behave this time, okay?"

"Auntie Mack, can Dean take me to the book shop instead?"

Mack glanced at Dean, then back at Lucas. "If Dean says it's okay, then its fine by me."

"That is the best idea I've heard in a long time. Come on, champ. Mack, I'll be back before you pay," Dean said confidently.

"We'll see!" Mack muttered as she walked inside the supermarket, relieved at not having Lucas with her, to cause trouble.

"Dean, look at this book. It has pirates in it."

"Do you like pirate stories?" Dean asked as he pulled Lucas onto his lap in the reading corner.

"Oh yes, and dinosaurs and dragons. I like those comics that Thomas reads me as well."

"Which comics are those?" Dean didn't remember any comics being mentioned.

"*Our Gang.*"

Ah those; the ones that Rose and Jacobs picture had been hidden in for all those years. "Okay, well you have a pirate book here, so what do you say about finding two more books, one about a dragon and the other about a dinosaur, then we'll go and find your Auntie Mack?"

Forty-five dollars later, they crossed the road back to the supermarket to look for Mack.

"Hey, wait up, Lucas. Let's go in here and buy your Auntie Mack a present." Dean opened the door to the jewelers. "Don't touch anything in here, okay, Lucas?"

"Okay."

Not really finding anything he liked in the bracelet section, Dean moved on and found a pair of small gold shell earrings. "Lucas, what about these shell earrings?"

"Oh yes. Auntie Mack likes shells. She has them all over her apartment."

Before Dean had a chance to change his mind, the shop assistant had them wrapped and charged to his credit card.

They exited the shop looking shell-shocked. "That was quick, are you sure you paid for them?"

Dean laughed and ruffled Lucas' hair. "Oh, I paid. That was the first thing I did. Come on. Let's go find Auntie Mack, and remember, don't say anything about her present, okay?"

"I won't."

Mack arrived at the checkout at the same time Dean and Lucas reappeared. "Hi, guys." Then she turned to Lucas. "I see Dean's been buying you another book."

Lucas had a cheeky grin on his face. "He bought me four. We couldn't decide between two dragon books."

"Oh, really." Mack cocked an eyebrow at Dean.

"Yeah, I liked the green dragon, but Dean wanted the red dragon, so he bought both books because we couldn't agree."

She laughed and started to load the shopping onto the checkout with Dean helping her. "Just who's the child here?"

He grinned. "That wasn't what you said last night."

She threw the burger buns at him. "I can't believe you said that."

They finished unloading the shopping cart and heard a throat being cleared, only to discover the cashier had been listening to everything they'd been saying. Mack blushed and Dean laughed as he paid before leaving to go load the car with the groceries.

Dean had waited until after dinner before retrieving the earrings that he'd bought for Mack. Taking them out of the box and putting them into his pocket, he went in search of Mack. Finding her sitting outside on the step with two glasses of wine, Dean sat down behind her, with a leg on either side, and wrapped his arms around her.

"Hey, you okay?"

She snuggled deeply into Dean. "Oh, yeah."

Dean placed a kiss to the side of Mack's head. "I bought you a present today."

She moved slightly away from him, so she could see him. "What?"

He felt nervous when he pulled the earrings out of his pocket and held his hand out to Mack. She studied them intensely, close to tears.

"Oh, Dean, they're gorgeous." She took them from his palm. "I love shells."

"Hmm, a little bird might have told me that."

She smiled and removed her current earrings to replace them with the shells. "How do they look?"

"Amazing." Smoothing his hands down the side of Mack's face, he gently pulled her forward and placed a kiss to each earring. "I love you, Mack."

Mack shivered. "I love you, too… Take me to bed."

"My pleasure!"

Chapter 33

En route to Richard's nursing home, Mack watched the countryside flying past, while she nervously pondered what Richard might tell them.

Yesterday, when they got back from the supermarket, Dean had taken them to the beach where they'd had fun in the sand and sea with Lucas.

Dean had sat and watched them wading in the ocean, and when they returned, he had produced a sketch of them. The image had brought tears to Mack's eyes, he'd captured the love between aunt and nephew.

Mack had spoken to her sister last night and both Melinda and Daniel were missing Lucas something fierce. Melinda had told Mack they were going to try and get a flight home and then take Lucas down to Florida for a week.

Thomas would miss him when he went home to Boston, and Dean would have no one to beat him playing on the Wii. At least Mack got to see him all the time. She'd already planned to stay in touch with Thomas when the summer was over and perhaps bring Lucas to visit every few weeks. They would both like that. Mack would enjoy visiting with Thomas, also, she'd started to look on Thomas as a part of her family.

Mack was so in love with Dean, she had no idea what was going to happen at the end of the summer. However, she had a gut feeling Dean was with her for much longer than the summer.

Lucas was staying with Thomas and Levi in the bar until after lunch, so they had a couple of hours to spare. Mack just hoped Lucas behaved himself, and with a bit of luck, kept his thoughts to himself for a change.

"We're here, Mack." Dean pulled into a parking space at the home.

She stared out of the window and surveyed the scene as Dean walked around to open her door.

Still sitting in the car while Dean rested his arms on the side of the car, he asked, "You ready to do this?"

"No, not really. Do you think I'm doing the right thing?" She was terrified of what Richard might reveal.

"You have to do this. If you don't, you'll always regret it."

She let Dean pull her out of the car and took hold of his hand as they walked towards the entrance.

Inside they were greeted by a nurse who asked them the name of the person they were there to visit.

Mack replied, 'Richard', then it suddenly dawned on her that she didn't know his surname, but when she mentioned Sally, they were pointed to the correct room.

On entering Richard's room, they found it rather dark, with only having small lamps switched on offering a soft, orange glow.

"I can't see you over there," a rather rough voice grumbled.

She moved forward, her hand still held tightly by Dean, and took a seat to the side of the bed.

"Hello, Richard. My name is Mackenzie Harper, and this is a good friend of mine, Dean... Simone. We're sorry to disturb you, but we were wondering if you would be willing to talk to us about something that happened a long time ago?" Mack held her breath while she waited anxiously for Richard's reply. He took a while to answer that she started to fidget, so Dean tightened his hold on her hand in reassurance.

"Do I make you nervous, young lady?"

She hesitated. "Actually, yes, you do. I'm nervous about asking you what it is I need to know."

"So, ask me and get it out of the way."

She inhaled deeply. "I found a diary dated 1947, it belonged to Rose Degan."

Richard inadvertently froze. His eyes narrowed.

"You remember Rose, don't you, Richard?"

After a few moments, he focused on Mack. "Rose was the first woman I ever loved, and I never loved anyone else like I did her. She was everything to me."

"Will you tell us what happened the night she died? Please, Richard?"

"I've never spoken about that night since it happened, and then I only said I saw her go over the cliffs from a distance."

"So what really happened?"

He sighed heavily as he shut his eyes, Mack actually thought he had fallen asleep, until he started to talk, slowly, but directly.

"I stayed outside that night after she got home from

work, to make sure she didn't sneak out to meet him. I'd taken sandwiches to eat for dinner, and a thermos of coffee. Unbeknown to me, Jacob had been invited to dinner by her father. Don't know what happened, but he left soon after arriving. So I stayed, knowing deep down she would try to sneak out to see him. Later, I don't know what time it was, I saw a figure moving quickly away from the house. I knew instinctively it was Rose, so I ran in the same direction and then she disappeared from sight."

Richard opened his eyes and looked longingly at Mack. "I'm not proud of what I did next, but I loved her and I panicked."

"We're not here to judge you, Richard. We just want to know what happened to Rose."

He realized Mack was serious. Richard took a deep breath. "I went running to the backdoor and started banging on it, only to have it opened by Thomas, who looked upset himself. I threatened him, so that he would tell me where she had gone." He paused and shook his head. "He told me he thought she had gone to meet Jacob, and that she normally took the footpath over the cliffs."

Richard looked distressed, so Mack stood up and moved to help him take a few sips of water.

"Thank you."

He didn't look too good. "Richard, do you want to continue?"

"Yes. It's about time I admitted the truth."

"Okay." Mack took her seat next to Dean again.

"I caught up to Rose on the cliffs. She was just standing there, near the edge, lost in her own thoughts. I made her jump in surprise." He coughed. "She turned around to look at me and wanted to know what I was doing there. I told her I loved her and wanted her to stay with me and marry me. She laughed in my face. Rose told me that she was in love with Jacob, and only him, and that she was..." he wiped tears from his eyes, "pregnant, with Jacob's child and that she was running away to marry him. I begged her not to. I told her I would still marry her and we could raise the child as mine. She told me no, and as I started very slowly walking towards her, she took a couple of steps back, and went off the cliffs."

Richard stopped and gulped in some much needed air. "After that, I went back to Degan House, by which time her parents had arrived back home. I told them I saw her go over the cliffs from a distance and that I never had chance to talk to her." He paused. "About a week later, her father came to see me and asked what really happened. I told him about the baby. He was angry as hell and ended up punching me. He told me never to talk about Rose ever again. I really did love her, Mackenzie."

As Richard finished talking, Mack handed him a tissue. She took one for herself and looked at Dean, who also had tears in his eyes. She turned and hugged him tightly.

Mack looked at Richard. "Thank you for telling us. It means a lot."

"Tell Thomas I'm sorry for not saying any of this way back then. I was in shock, and a coward. I'm not proud of my actions. I thought everyone would think I'd pushed her off, because she was going to him instead of choosing me."

"Oh, boy." Mack had to take some deep breaths to stop from crying.

"I need to rest now." Richard became agitated. He dismissed them with one sweep of his old, wrinkled hand.

Dean took hold of Mack's hand and led her back to the car and helped her inside before he ran around the front to climb in himself. "Where do you want to go from here, Mack?"

She offered him a sad smile. "Just take me home."

"Okay, babe. Anything you say."

Chapter 34

Back at Rose Cottage, Dean ushered Mack inside and into a chair at the kitchen table. "Your hands are freezing." He turned to warm some water for a hot drink, trying to bring some life back to her.

With a drink made, he passed it to Mack and wrapped her fingers gently around the cup. "Thank you, Dean, for being there with me."

He moved his chair closer to Mack's as he put an arm around her and rubbed her shoulder with his hand. "I'm here for you... now and always. I love you and I'm not going anywhere." He put his hand underneath her chin and brought her face up to his for a sweet, slow kiss.

"Are you really, Dean?"

Dean smiled. "Yes, Mack. I am. If that's okay with you?"

"Mmm. That's more than okay."

The next minute Lucas barged right through the kitchen door. "Auntie Mack, you're back!" Not realizing he'd interrupted anything, Lucas carried on walking straight through to the sitting room. "You coming, Dean?" he shouted.

Dean glanced at Mack. "In a minute, champ." She

seemed to be pulling herself together, so standing, he took hold of her hand, urging her up and into his arms.

With her arms wrapped around his waist, she snuggled into his chest, slid her hands further down Dean's back. She pulled his hips into contact with hers, then lifted her face up to look at him. He sealed his lips to hers.

He was breathing heavily as he pulled his lips away from hers. "You're asking for trouble doing that!"

"Promises, promises." She gave him a saucy grin.

About to grab her again, Dean stopped himself as Thomas walked through the back door.

"Are you feeling better, Mack?" Dean asked. "We'll finish what you started later," he whispered. He gave Mack a quick kiss before he joined Lucas on the Wii in the sitting room.

Mack felt all hot and bothered after having Dean's hands and mouth on her, as she watched Thomas walk cautiously into the room, making eye contact with her. "You look like a flushed ghost," he observed. Mack raised an eyebrow. "You're white as a ghost and obviously flushed with whatever that young man was doing to you."

She blushed even more. "Thomas, we spoke to Richard this morning." She took a seat at the table and waited for Thomas to join her. "He told me what happened that night, and he also told me how your father knew Rose was pregnant."

Thomas silently rubbed his face with his hands. "I did wonder if Richard had spoken to her before she died, because I could never figure out how Father knew she was pregnant."

"Apparently, he found her at the cliffs and begged her to

stay and marry him. He said she's the only woman he has ever loved, and I believe him. Richard told Rose he would even bring her child up as his own."

He shook his head. "He was married and has a daughter. Are you saying he admitted to only loving my sister, Rose?"

"No. He said she was the first woman he had ever loved and he never loved anyone else as much, so I guess he did love his wife, just in a different way."

"Then I feel sorry for him. His wife was a lovely woman, in fact, she was best friends with my wife, and when Janet died, she would bring meals to me three times a week."

Mack just sat quietly for a short time, lost for words. "Richard said to tell you that he was sorry he never told you anything about that night. He presumed everyone would think that he'd pushed her off, because she'd chosen Jacob instead of him."

Mack glanced into the sitting room to make sure Lucas was still being entertained by Dean and the Wii game they were playing. She caught Dean's eye. He winked at her and blew her a kiss, making her smile.

She turned back to Thomas. "Your father visited Richard about a week after Rose died, wanting to know what had happened. He hadn't believed Richard's account of that night. He told your father everything, including about her pregnancy. Your father punched him."

He sniggered. "Yeah, I can believe that. My father didn't lose his temper often, but when he did, you didn't want to be anywhere near him."

Thomas took hold of Mack's hand and squeezed. "Thank you. I guess at the back of my mind I have always wondered whether or not he had anything to do with her death. I can't imagine what he must have felt like, watching the woman he loved going over the cliffs."

"It's all so sad. Dean is going to arrange for me to meet his grandfather soon. I'm not looking forward to telling him, but he needs to know and I really need to be the one to tell him. I feel so connected to Rose. Their story breaks my heart."

Dean was standing in the doorway watching Mack and Thomas talking. He was falling more in love with her. She was the most compassionate woman he had ever met, and hopefully, she would be all his for a long time to come.

"Dean, you okay?" Mack asked, bringing him back to the present.

He walked over to her and placed a tender kiss to the top of her head. "When you look at me like that, I'm more than okay."

"Auntie Mack, after dinner, can I go and have a sleepover at Thomas' cottage... please?"

Mack glanced at Thomas who was nodding his head. "Are you sure, Thomas?"

Thomas looked choked up. "I'd love that, I really would."

Mack looked back to an excited Lucas. "Well then, I guess we better pack you a bag, then I'll get dinner ready," she said smiling, and looked forward to having the evening alone with Dean.

Chapter 35

Mack was sitting outside with a cup of coffee, waiting for Thomas to bring Lucas home, and for Dean to shave and change clothes.

Seeing a car pull into the drive, Mack put her cup down on the step. She didn't recognize the vehicle, but no sooner had she stood up to check it out, her sister was running towards her for a hug.

"Mack!" Melinda threw her arms around Mack's neck.

Mack hugged her back. "What are you doing here? You said you would text me if you got an earlier flight."

"Sorry, Mack, but it was a standby flight, and we just had time to get on board. Where's my little Lucas?"

Mack was still a bit stunned. "He's with Thomas, but he'll be back soon. Wow, I can't believe you're here."

Melinda held Mack at arm's length. "You're at home here," she stated.

Mack grinned at her sister. "Yes, I am… Wait until you meet Dean later. He's the hot guy who's renting next door." She laughed and headed inside, leaving her sister to follow.

As Melinda followed Mack inside, she couldn't work out whether Mack was teasing, or being truthful. "Are you sure there's a hot guy named Dean living next door?"

"Positive. You'll like him, but he's mine, so no flirting, sis!" Mack pointed a finger towards Melinda.

Melinda was the biggest flirt going, and Mack always wondered how Daniel managed to get her to behave. They'd been married seven years, and still seemed to be in love. Daniel was older than her sister by five years, but acted much older, which was probably what Melinda needed to calm her down.

"Sis, where's Daniel?" Mack asked as she suddenly realized her brother-in-law was missing.

"Finishing a call on his cell, in the hire car," Melinda replied, going to have a look around the cottage.

Mack headed towards the backdoor. "I'll be back in a minute, Mel."

"Okay."

Mack walked out into the yard and spotted Daniel still sitting in the car.

As he climbed out, Daniel spotted Mack walking in his direction. "Hey, sis!"

"Hey, Dr Daniel!" Mack laughed and ran around to the driver's side of the car to give him a big hug and a quick kiss on the lips.

As far as Mack was concerned Daniel wasn't her brother-in-law, but her brother, the one she had always wanted. He also treated her like his sister.

Unbeknown to Mack, Dean had seen their little interlude at the car and was pissed, wondering what the hell she was playing at, because an hour ago, she'd been naked in bed with him. *So who the hell was that guy?*

Trying to decide whether to go around to Mack's, or stay there and fume, he picked up his keys and stormed next door to make a claim on his woman, because she belonged to him.

Dean walked straight into Rose Cottage without even knocking. He spotted Mack standing near the coffee pot, walked straight over to her, took her face in his hands and kissed the very life out of her. He lifted his head, grinning down at Mack, who appeared to be having a little trouble focusing.

"Wow, do you greet everyone like that?" Melinda asked, wiggling her eyebrows.

Dean had just noticed the woman in the kitchen, starting to realize perhaps he'd misunderstood the hug and kiss outside.

"Err..." He looked slightly sheepish.

"I think someone saw something outside and got the wrong idea!" Daniel stated, trying not to laugh.

Mack put her arm around his waist. "Dean, I'd like you to meet my sister, Melinda, and her husband, Daniel."

Dean leaned in to shake their hands. "I think I did get the wrong idea."

"Thought so."

"Guys, this is Dean," she looked at her sister, "he's the guy I'm in love with."

Well, that was probably the first time ever Melinda had been left speechless.

Dean noticed Daniel looking oddly at him. "Is anything wrong?"

Daniel sat down beside his wife. "What are your

intentions towards Mack?"

Melinda looked towards her husband in surprise. "Daniel, you're not her father." Melinda swatted him on the shoulder.

"Her father isn't here right now, so as her brother I think I should act in his place."

Mack tried not to laugh at the look on Daniel's face. Dean put a hand on her arm. "I'm in love with Mack, and my intentions are no one's business but ours, but I'll tell you that I don't plan on letting her go."

"Okay, now that's settled, let's have coffee and cake and wait for Thomas and Lucas to appear," Mack said, relieved. Least said, soonest mended, she thought to herself.

Thomas entered the kitchen first, with a bunch of carnations in his hand for Mack. "To the lady of my heart," he said with a wink.

"Mommy!" Lucas shouted as he walked in behind Thomas. "I didn't know you were coming. Where's Daddy? I need to tell him I went playing poker in the Irish Pub in town." He launched himself into his mother's arms for a big hug and kiss.

"Daddy is out with Dean, but he'll be back soon." She put him down and Lucas ran into the sitting room, shouting for his mother to join him. "Calm down, Lucas. I'll be there shortly."

Melinda walked over to Mack, laughing. "Wow, it seems like you have been busy, Mackenzie Louise Harper. Just how many more guys are going to be coming knocking on the door, proclaiming their love for you?"

She nudged her sister with her hip. "That would be telling!" Mack teased.

Mack walked over to Thomas and took the flowers from him, giving him a hug and a kiss on the cheek. Thomas blushed.

She suddenly remembered it was the first time Thomas and Melinda had met. "Thomas, this is my sister, Melinda."

"I gathered that, Mack." Then he moved over towards Melinda and held his hand out to her. "Nice to meet you. You have a good boy there. I'm going to miss him." Thomas turned away and walked into the front room to join Lucas on the Wii, wiping his eyes secretly as he went.

Mack followed Thomas with her eyes and turned to her sister. "I think they'll both really miss each other, Melinda."

"Perhaps he could come and visit us in Boston, it isn't too far away." Melinda suggested.

"I've thought about that, and was wondering if perhaps I could have Lucas every, maybe, third weekend, and bring him up here? I think they would both love that. Plus, it will give you and Daniel some free time."

"Mack, that would be great. But what about Dean?"

"I love him, Mel, and he says he loves me and I believe him. I don't know what's going to happen, but we both live in Boston, and I believe we'll be together, so we both can bring him up here."

"Just be careful, Mack, you haven't known him for long, and I don't want to see you get hurt."

"Says she, who met, fell in love, and married Daniel, all within ten days. Without telling anyone until the deed was done, I might add."

"Okay, okay, not the best person to give advice, but... that was seven years ago, and I still love him, Mack." Melinda took hold of Mack's hand.

"I know, Mel, thank you. Let Thomas take Lucas fishing this afternoon before he leaves, if he'll go that is, now that you guys are here, he may not want to. We can hang out at the beach with the guys. Besides, I want to tell you a love story."

"Oh, this sounds... interesting."

Mack was walking hand in hand with Dean to the beach behind her sister and brother-in-law, and it filled Mack with so much love that she stopped walking and looked into Dean's eyes. "Kiss me, Dean."

"Anytime, babe." Then his lips came down onto hers with a possessiveness she'd only ever experienced with him.

She moved in close to him, put her hands into his hair and massaged his scalp as the kiss deepened. Dean growled and grabbed hold of Mack's hips, pulling her in close enough to feel what she did to him.

Melinda and Daniel turned around. "Get a room!" Melinda shouted.

Out of the blue, Melinda suddenly turned and engaged her husband in a very hot lip lock.

Mack and Dean pulled apart, laughing, and when they saw Melinda and Daniel, Dean let out a wolf whistle. Dean took hold of Mack's hand pulling her forward. "Come on, let's go down to the beach and make out."

"Oh my God, please tell me you aren't going to be.... well, you know." Melinda trailed off, waving her arms around.

Dean replied, laughing, "We just might!"

As they carried on walking to the beach, they were still holding hands. Mack was excited being here with Dean, along with her sister and Daniel. She certainly couldn't wait to see how Dean reacted, once she removed her shorts and top.

She watched her sister and husband as they stopped a bit in front of them. They seemed to be having a 'discussion', but about what, Mack couldn't make out, as they were whispering.

Sometimes she found it hard to believe Melinda and Daniel were a couple. Her sister was the flighty one, and Daniel the straitlaced doctor.

Once, when both Mack and Melinda were having a night on the town, they'd gotten rather drunk and Mack had asked her sister what Daniel was like in the sack. Instead of censoring her reply, she had given Mack more details than she actually needed, or wanted to know. Luckily her sister hadn't remembered, but unfortunately Mack had.

Dean let go of Mack's hand, having arrived at the beach. He then started to strip, first his t-shirt came off, showing his tight abs, then his jeans, to reveal a pair of swimming shorts, which he wore low on his hips. Both Mack and Melinda stood frozen to the spot.

Mack came back to her senses, licked her lips, then nudged her sister. "Hey, he's mine. Eyes off, Mel." Just as she said that, Daniel also started to strip. Mack was dazzled.

"Wow, Daniel, when did you get that body and tattoo? You do realize I won't be able to look at you as a conservative doctor anymore."

Dean laughed and walked over to put his arm around Mack's neck. "Stop ogling your brother-in-law."

"Jealous?"

He gave Mack a hard kiss. "Yes!"

"Then I don't suppose you want to know that I was ogling you first as you stripped."

"I can carry on if you like?" Dean teased.

"Don't you dare. Later, in private. I'll take you up on the offer."

"You want to go for a swim?"

"Maybe later. I've told Melinda I want to tell her a love story, so I'm going to tell her about Rose and Jacob."

"Okay. I spoke to my grandfather before I came back to the cottage this morning, and he'll make sure they're both home tomorrow morning. He said that they both can't wait to meet the woman who has finally won my heart."

She reached up and kissed him briefly on the lips. "That is so sweet."

As she finished talking, she unbuttoned her shorts, slid them down her legs and kicked them to one side. Seeing the look on Dean's face, she slowly continued to take her t-shirt off and tossed it over to him. He was standing in front of her, looking at her from the tips of her toes to the top of her head, then he met her eyes.

"You like?" Mack asked with a saucy grin and hands on her hips.

He groaned. "You little minx. I'm going for a swim to

cool off." Then he ran to the ocean, with Daniel following.

Mack lay down next to her sister, while Melinda watched the retreating backs of both guys. "He is one hot guy, Mack. God, when he took his shirt off, I nearly fainted."

"Melinda!"

"What!"

"You're drooling over my guy. Stop it, anyway what about Dr Daniel? You've been hiding the real guy from me."

Melinda changed the subject. "Tell me this love story? I'm intrigued."

"Hmm, I know what you're doing and I'll let you off the hook for now." She took a deep breath. "It all started when I found a diary written in 1947 by Rose, Thomas' sister. It's her love for a man named Jacob Evans, who just happens to be Dean's grandfather."

Mack then spent over an hour telling her sister all about Rose and Jacob, and that she'd hopefully be able to rest, once Jacob knew the whole story, even though it was heart breaking.

Chapter 36

Mack was all worked up while she waited for Thomas and Lucas to appear. She was really worried about Thomas. She knew he would be upset with Lucas leaving after dinner with his parents.

Just as she decided to keep busy and clean the kitchen, Dean walked in wearing a pair of well-worn jeans and pale blue shirt. Wow! What a distraction.

He noticed Mack looking upset and walked around the table taking her face in his hands. "You want to get naked?" He kissed her.

"What is it with you two? Two seconds later and you would have had her on the table," Melinda interrupted, walking into the kitchen.

She winked at Dean. "No, we already did that," Mack told her sister, laughing.

"Oh my God, did I need to know that?"

"Need to know what?" Daniel came up to his wife, putting his arms around her.

"Nothing. Let's set the table, the food will be here soon, hopefully at the same time as Thomas and Lucas."

Mack whispered. "You look hot. I'm going to show you later just how hot!" Mack walked past Dean and rubbed against the straining erection he was trying his best to hide.

He shuddered. All he wanted to do was grab hold of her and go some place quiet. She drove him crazy with her sassy mouth and sexy body.

Not long after, both Thomas and Lucas arrived, and shortly afterwards, the food finally arrived as well.

Dinner was eaten with everyone slightly squashed up. The table was made for four people, but had six seated around. It was cozy.

"Lucas, did you catch anything this afternoon?" Daniel asked his son.

Lucas had a mouth full of food and grinned. "We caught three more yellow perch. Thomas is going to clean them, and freeze them, to eat when I come to visit."

Everyone went quiet. "That's great, Lucas, and I hope I get to eat some with you when I bring you to visit." Mack wanted to reassure Thomas that Lucas would be back.

"Of course you can. Will you make a cake for us? Thomas said it would be the blind something, when I asked him to bake you a cake."

Thomas laughed. "I said it would be a bit like the blind leading the blind, if Lucas and I baked a cake."

"Oh, Lucas, leave the cake baking to Auntie Mack, okay?"

"Okay, Mommy." Then he grinned. "Granny said..." before he could finish Mack shoved the ice cream in front of him and his mother shoved a piece of chocolate in to his mouth. Mack glanced at Dean, his face alight with mirth, trying not to laugh aloud.

Lucas not wanting to be outdone, swallowed the

chocolate, grinned at Thomas, then said, "Mommy, all Granny said, was that she gets some herbs from the Jamaicans at the market, and puts them in her cakes. Mrs Green was there one day and she said they were the best cakes this side of Boston, but grandma never lets me eat them. I don't know why, but she said I'm not old enough to take an aphrodizzyache, no that's not right. It sounded something like that though," he finished with a puzzled expression.

"Aphrodisiac," Daniel supplied, which broke the silence that had followed Lucas' little speech.

Once all the dishes were clean, Melinda, Daniel, and Lucas were ready to leave. Mack walked over to stand beside Thomas and leaned in close to him. "You'll see him again real soon, Thomas. That I can promise you."

He took hold of Mack's hand. "Thank you. You're a kind young woman, and if you were my daughter, I would be proud with how you turned out."

Mack had watery eyes. "Thomas, that is so sweet. Thank you. You've brought tears to my eyes, again." She tried to wipe them away before anyone else noticed.

"Auntie Mack." Lucas threw himself into her open arms.

"Bye, Lucas. I'll see you soon, okay? Will you say hello to Mickey Mouse for me?" Mack didn't want to let him go.

"Will do," he replied, and moved onto Thomas. Lucas wrapped his little arms around his waist as Thomas bent to hold him, kissing him on the head. "I'll miss you."

"I'll miss you too, kid," Thomas replied in a rough

voice.

Dean walked over to Mack and wrapped her up tight in his embrace. "You okay?"

Mack just nodded her head, moving out of Dean's embrace, but still felt him close, as she hugged her sister and brother-in-law. Then she watched them leave with Lucas.

Chapter 37

Mack and Dean called to check on Thomas first thing the following morning, before driving into Boston. Thomas hadn't showed up for breakfast, but they discovered he was well, although a bit down, with Lucas having departed last night.

Once again, Mack was left in her own thoughts, wondering how Jacob would react to what she had to say. It had been a long time since his love affair with Rose, but Mack would bet anything that he remembered Rose as though it was yesterday. You don't forget a love like they obviously had, especially with it ending like it did, and no matter what Jacob believed, it was still tragic.

With everything going on, she'd forgotten to get another copy of the photograph of Rose and Jacob, which was unbelievable, considering how obsessed she was with them.

Mack was praying she didn't meet Dean's mother again. God, what a shark.

Dean brought the car to a stop in front of his family's home and turned to look at Mack. "Are you ready to do this? I have to admit, I'm kind of nervous."

"I'm really nervous, and excited to be finally meeting him. Not just because of Rose, but because he's your grandfather."

Dean climbed out of the car and walked around to help Mack out with a kiss to her lips. "Thanks, come on."

They entered the house and were met by Martha, his grandparents' housekeeper, who looked down at their joined hands and back up to their faces. "Mr. Dean, I didn't know you were coming home."

"I'm not, Martha. This is Mack, and we're here to visit my grandparents. Where are they?"

"Your grandfather is in the study, and your grandmother just went to the... powder room."

"Okay, thanks." He turned to Mack and pulled her towards his grandfather's study. "I'll go in with you and introduce you, then I'll go and distract my grandmother."

"Okay."

"It'll be all right." Dean gave her a quick kiss.

He knocked on the study door, and then walked in, dragging a partly-reluctant Mack behind him.

"Dean, my boy, where have you been?" his grandfather asked while he hugged Dean with obvious affection.

Mack got a better look at him. She saw a distinguished older man with gray hair, who was still well built, with a very slight paunch. He looked to be in his sixties, not eighty-eight.

"Grandfather, I want you to meet my girlfriend, Mackenzie Harper, otherwise known as Mack."

His grandfather moved slowly forward to meet Mack. "Well now, you are mighty pretty," he said, taking Mack's hand.

She had to swallow the lump in her throat to try and not burst into tears, Mack felt Dean's hand on her back as she looked at his grandfather. "Thank you. Flattery will get you everywhere!"

"Oh, I like you. Can we keep her?"

"I'm working on that, grandfather."

Jacob sat down and pulled Mack down beside him. "So, tell me… What brought tears to your eyes when you saw me?"

Mack looked at Dean, wondering where to begin. "I'm going to find Grandmother, while you two chat." Dean quickly kissed Mack on the forehead as he left the room.

"Now I'm more curious than before." Jacob gave her a quizzical look.

"May I call you, Jacob?"

He smiled and patted her hand. "Seeing as you're practically family, that would be fine. Although, I hope you will call me grandfather, eventually."

"I just might." Mack took a deep breath and started her story, "If I told you that Dean and I met in Cape Elizabeth at 'Degan House', what would that mean to you?" She watched him carefully, saw him pale slightly, and his hands started to tremble. "Jacob, I found a diary dated 1947, written by a Rose Degan. She was in love with you, wasn't she?"

Jacob nodded. "Yes," he whispered. He looked away from Mack and appeared to be lost in his own thoughts.

"She never married Richard," Mack announced.

He turned back towards Mack. "Pardon?"

"This isn't easy, Jacob, but Rose was running away to be with you, when she…" Mack took a deep breath, "she lost her footing and fell over the cliffs. Jacob, she did love you so very much, she didn't leave you for Richard like her father told you. She just didn't get the chance to leave with you."

Jacob was agitated. "I don't know what to say."

"Jacob, why did you wait a month to call Degan House to speak to Rose? Why not look for her that night? You knew she was pregnant, I guess it just doesn't make any sense to me."

"I don't remember," he said abruptly.

Mack was a bit surprised at Jacob's response.

Dean came back into the room, looked first to Mack, who was upset, then his grandfather. "Is everyone okay?" he asked as he approached Mack, wiping her tears away.

"I think so," Mack replied.

"Sorry for cutting this short, but Grandmother is waiting in the parlor and was about to head this way, as she's getting rather impatient. I've been sent to get you both." He grinned. "She's keen to meet you, Mack."

He was leading Mack out of the room, followed by his grandfather, when Mack noticed a photograph sitting in a lovely frame on the bookcase. She walked over to have a closer look. "Who's that?" Mack asked, pointing at the woman in the photograph.

Jacob replied, "Eliza, my wife."

"Mack, what is it?" Dean asked.

"The woman in this picture. It's Rose."

"Mack, that's my grandmother."

Mack heard Dean, but she was not able to think properly, because all the blood seemed to be running through her head and ears. Why was that picture framed? What did it mean? *It couldn't be. Could it?*

"This is the same picture Thomas has that Rose left for

him. That's Rose, not Eliza," Mack whispered.

"What? Mack, that's impossible." Dean searched her face and realized she was serious. He looked towards his grandfather, then his grandmother walked in and Mack took one look at her. Dean watched while Mack lost all color and dropped like a ton of bricks in a dead faint. He just managed to catch her.

Chapter 38

"Mack, come on, babe. Please wake up." He sat on the sofa in his grandfathers study. Mack was cradled in his arms. "Why does Mack think the picture is of Rose?" he asked his grandparents.

"Dean, what are you talking about?" his grandmother asked.

"The photograph of the two of you taken just before you got married, when you were pregnant with my father. Why does Mack think it's Rose?"

"Because she is Rose. Rose Elizabeth Degan, Eliza," Mack answered Dean's question. She'd woken up and heard the end of Dean's question. "Am I right?"

"There were only two pictures taken, we have one...." Eliza said quietly. Her voice trailed off.

"You gave the other one to Thomas, which is how I saw it."

Sitting down, Eliza looked at Mack. "How do you know this?"

"You're Rose?" He saw his grandmother slowly nod her head. "She found the diary that you wrote when you met my grandfather. Also, Thomas and Richard helped fill in the blanks."

"Thomas?" Eliza whispered.

"Your brother," Mack told Eliza.

"No... no, no, you're wrong. Thomas died in 1951 in Korea... didn't he?" Eliza asked, barely able to finish. Jacob was now sitting next to her, his arms around her.

Mack asked them the one question that she needed to know the answer to. "Why? Why pretend you were dead? And what do we call you now?"

"I've been Eliza longer than I was Rose. Please use Eliza...Can you tell us about Thomas? Then we'll tell you our story."

She was clinging to Dean. "Thomas is the owner of Rose Cottage, which I rented for the summer. It used to be known as Degan House. I found your diary and started reading it. All this time, Thomas had no idea about the photograph and message you wrote to him. After your death, he couldn't bring himself to read the comic, until I read about it in the diary. It was only then, did he find the photograph and message."

"But he's dead. How, I don't understand," Eliza said.

"Why do you think he's dead?"

"Mack, I took Eliza back to see Thomas in 1952. She missed him terribly, only to be told by her father he'd been killed six months earlier in Korea," Jacob answered.

Mack wasn't sure she'd heard right. "Your parents knew?"

"Yes, or rather, my father did," Eliza whispered, with tears in her eyes, "Please tell me about Thomas."

"He did serve in Korea, but he didn't die. In fact, he has become a good friend to Dean and me. He loves to fish and taught my six-year-old nephew. I would say he still gets up to trouble with Levi, who I've met briefly."

"All this time wasted," Eliza cried.

"Will you tell us your story now?"

Eliza wiped her eyes. "I will. You already know about everything up to that night, yes?"

"Yes," Mack replied.

As Eliza collected her thoughts together, Mack took a good look at her. She still looked beautiful at eighty-five, wearing her silver hair pulled back into a bun. She had high cheek bones, small button nose, and her skin looked to have aged well. She wore a deep purple dress on her slim figure with low-heeled black and purple ballerina pumps. Very stylish, and both Rose and Jacob still looked so much in love after all these years together.

Dean pulled Mack closer into his arms and sat back further into the cushions. "We might as well get comfortable. Are you okay, Mack?" he asked, kissing her briefly, but tenderly.

"Yes. Are you?"

"Everything always is with you in my arms."

"Good answer," she whispered, snuggling more into him. He always made her feel loved and cherished with his concern for her wellbeing.

"Okay." Eliza sighed. "I was on my way to meet Jacob. I'd taken the path along the cliffs, when Richard came running up to me. He wouldn't let me go and kept grabbing me, begging me to stay and marry him. I told him about the baby, thinking he would let me go then, but no such luck. I started getting worried, because I didn't want Jacob thinking

I'd changed my mind if I wasn't there by eleven."

Eliza couldn't continue, so Jacob carried on from where she left off. "I knew Rose was going to take the cliff path to meet me. I walked along it from town to meet her, and that's when I heard her arguing with Richard. I went running up and pried his fingers off Rose and took her into my arms, before putting her behind me. Richard made a grab for her again and ended up knocking Rose's bag over the cliffs into the ocean."

"So that's how the clothes washed ashore," Dean stated.

Eliza nodded her head.

"Yes. After that he seemed to calm down and I begged him to tell everyone Rose had gone over the cliffs. He refused at first, but Rose knew something about him, so he agreed in return for her silence," Jacob said.

Mack was too stunned to speak, but Dean wasn't. "So, you faked your own death?"

"It wasn't planned that way. Rose really was just going to run away with me to be my wife, but pretending she died seemed the safest option. That night, I met her parents for the first time and her father made it more than clear he didn't want us anywhere near each other. Her father had a lot of influential friends, and was a very hard man. He would have come after us both with everything he had, and all we wanted was to be left alone to get on with our lives, together."

"But what about the phone call to Degan House a month later. Thomas heard your father telling your mother about Jacob calling and telling him you had married Richard. You said your father knew you were alive?" Mack asked, needing answers.

"We left that night to go to Boston and stayed with

Eleanor, Jacob's sister. After about a week of living there, Jacob arranged for us to be married. We knew I was really pregnant by then, and he didn't want me showing without having the paper to prove we were actually married. He also wanted assurance that if my father discovered the truth, it would be harder for him to take me away from him, as I would be his wife." Eliza paused. "After a few weeks, Jacob thought perhaps he should ring to ask to speak to me and see what my father or mother had to say. I didn't like the idea, but went along with it. My father was just awful to Jacob and told him that I had married Richard and miscarried his child. I cried for the rest of the day."

Jacob wiped the tears from Eliza's eyes. "Then it was maybe three weeks later that I opened the door and my father was standing there. Jacob was at work and I didn't know what to do, so I stepped outside with him. My father was so angry and said I really was dead to him, and I better not let my mother know I was alive and obviously well. I asked my father how he knew, and he told me Richard had told him a week after the accident, that I was with child. But it was only the week before, that he'd discovered I was actually alive. Apparently, a friend of his who he hadn't seen for awhile, saw me in Boston and asked my father about me. My father then went to see Richard again, and he told my father it was true and I was still alive."

Dean and Mack were sitting on the sofa in silence. You could have heard a pin drop. Mack felt overwhelmed with the turn of events. Rose was alive. She had known there was something wrong with the information they'd uncovered. Although she'd hoped for a happy ending for Rose, she certainly hadn't expected one. "So, you eventually went back to see Thomas?" Mack asked, finding her voice.

"Yes. It was 1952. Rose had missed Thomas so much. Her mother had died the year before, so there was no fear of her finding out about Rose. We had a car by then, so I drove up to Cape Elizabeth. Her father was home. I asked him about Thomas, and he told us he had died in Korea. It broke Rose's heart, she cried for weeks. I can't believe that bastard lied to us. I guess we should have expected it, but we didn't," Jacob replied.

"We have to see Thomas." Eliza wiped her eyes.

"Grandmother, I think this is going to be one hell of a shock for him. Let Mack and me break it to him and then we'll arrange a get together or something. But we need to go easy. Up until Mack read your diary, he actually thought you died hating him!"

Eliza brought her hand up to her mouth. "I loved him, and he has always been in my heart."

"He has always loved you, Eliza. He told me that himself. What did you know about Richard?" Mack asked, as she tried to mop her face up a bit.

Eliza and Jacob exchanged a look. "He loved Rose a lot, we really believed that, but Rose had discovered he preferred... men," Jacob said.

"Oh." Mack hadn't been expecting that at all, but all of a sudden she remembered about Rose's friend, Jayne. "What about Jayne? Did she know you were still alive?"

Eliza smiled. "I got in touch with Jayne about two weeks after we left Cape Elizabeth, and I knew for once, she would keep my secret, because she has, all these years. Jayne was, and still is, my dearest friend. She's gone away with her husband now, it was her house we went to the day of your mother's garden party. Would you believe, she actually married Jacob's best friend from the engineering company he started to work for all those years ago."

"Thank you for telling us your story. I can't tell you how much it means to me, knowing you're alive and lived all these years, happily married to Jacob. It broke my heart when I thought you'd died, and that Jacob had been told you'd left him for another man," Mack said, close to tears again.

Dean stood up and moved over to the desk to retrieve a box of tissues, offering some to Mack and his grandmother. He knelt in front of Mack and pulled her close so he could wipe her tears away, then kissed her. "Babe, come here." He took her into his arms for a much needed hug.

"Dean, may I have a word with you, please?" his grandmother asked. She started to leave via a door on the opposite side to where everyone had entered.

"Will you be okay?"

"Dean, go. I'll be fine."

He still looked apprehensive. "I won't be long."

She smiled back. "Don't worry about me."

Mack sat quietly with Jacob as Dean and his grandmother disappeared through the other door. Jacob looked at Mack and smiled slightly.

"So what did Eliza write?" He roared with laughter when he saw the look on Mack's face. "That good, huh! Might give me a heart attack now."

Mack started to giggle. "It's pretty hot stuff, I can tell you."

"Mmm, hot stuff. That's what she was back then, she still is. She's the only woman I've ever loved. I can still remember the first day I saw her, thought I was dreaming. It was a rescue at sea, and I was helping out on land. Heading back to get a warm drink, I just happened to look up and glance over to the crowd, and there she was." He was lost in his thoughts. "She was the most beautiful woman I'd ever seen, and I felt my heart summersault in my chest. It was love at first sight for me, and before I knew it, my legs were carrying me over to where she was standing."

Jacob wiped his eyes, setting Mack off again with the water works. "We introduced ourselves and I just didn't want to ever leave her. I wanted to carry her away with me and keep her forever."

"Which you did, but a month later." Mack smiled.

"Yes, I did. The only thing I regret about what happened back then, is that we didn't just go and get married before going to see her father, and just telling him. Rather than pretending she died. He probably would have acted the same, but at least there might have been a chance of Thomas being in our lives as he got older."

Eliza came back into the room. "Jacob, what have you been saying to upset Dean's girl again?"

Mack smiled. "He was telling me how it was love at first sight, when he saw you. A bit like Dean and me, really."

Eliza sat down next to her husband. Dean moved to sit back down next to Mack and took her hand in his, lacing their fingers together. "Just like us, Mack."

"If you want the truth, Mack, neither his grandmother nor I thought we would see the day when he would fall in love, so not only have you made our day telling us about Thomas, but you have made our day by loving our grandson. So, thank you."

She smiled at both of Dean's grandparents. "I want you to know I love Dean so much. He has become part of me in such a short time." She turned to Dean and placed a tender kiss to his lips.

"Now you've made me cry," Eliza said, wiping at her eyes again.

Dean stood, pulling Mack up from the sofa. "We're going to go and rest for a while, before heading out. We'll see you before we leave."

"Make sure you do," Eliza said.

Mack hugged Eliza and Jacob.

"You take good care of her, you hear?"

Dean looked at Mack. "Yes, sir," he replied, looking at his grandfather.

Chapter 39

They walked out of the study. Dean escorted Mack through to the back stairs to his room, so that Martha wouldn't see them and engage them in conversation, because all he wanted was to be alone with Mack, who looked exhausted.

Mack was still really pale after discovering Rose was still alive, having been living all these years as Eliza. God, Dean hadn't seen that one coming, although he should have realized something wasn't right with the marriage license and the name of his father and aunt.

"Mack, come and lie down. You look drained."

She moved over to Dean and wrapped her arms around his waist. "Don't let go."

He picked her up into his arms and carried her to his bed. "I don't intend to."

He lay down on the bed with Mack cradled in his arms. "You're the first woman, apart from my grandmother, to come into my room, Mack." He hadn't realized until then, with Mack in his arms, in his room, how sacrosanct his room, and possibly his heart had become. He hadn't realized that his grandmother was so worried about his heart. He was glad that he had Mack though. She was his Rose, the only woman he'd given his heart to.

"I love you, Dean," Mack whispered, then fell asleep.

As Mack started to wake up, she'd forgotten where she was and why, but she certainly recognized the body holding her.

She smiled, feeling so full of joy, knowing Rose hadn't died and had lived a long life. Sixty-five years with the love of her life, Jacob. She didn't know how to break the news to Thomas, but hopefully, he wouldn't be too upset, now he had the family he'd always wanted.

She wrapped her arms around a sleeping Dean, and kissed his chest. "I'm so thankful that you took the trip to meet me in Cape Elizabeth the day that I spoke with Martha, rather than ignoring the call," she whispered.

"So am I."

She lifted her head and met Dean's eyes. "I didn't know you were awake."

"Been lying here awhile, thinking about everything that's happened today, and since I met you. I wouldn't change any of it." He gently squeezed her.

He slid slightly down so his face was level with Mack's, then smoothed her hair back from her eyes, and used his finger to trace her eyebrows, and down her lightly freckled nose, to her lips, caressing them. She opened her mouth slightly.

"Marry me, Mack."

She froze.

"God, I didn't mean to just blurt that out. I love you.

Right from the first time, Mack. That's never happened to me before. I don't want to lose you." He saw the tears in her eyes. "I know we haven't known each other long. Hell, we can even have a long engagement. I just want to know you're mine."

Mack laughed and cried. "Yes."

He smiled at her, as his nerves from a few minutes ago started to dwindle. He reached into his pocket and produced a ring, then took hold of her left hand, slid the ring slowly on her finger, as he looked into her eyes. "My grandmother took me out of the room to give me this ring. She said it was the ring my grandfather gave her sixty-five years ago. It had belonged to my great-grandmother."

He had to take a couple of deep breaths, because he was getting all choked up. "She took it off her finger, Mack, to give it to me. She said it had never once left her finger, and that she wanted me to give it to you, because she could see the love we have for each other, and who better to have it, but the woman who returned her brother to her." He leaned in and kissed her lips, ever so gently.

Mack had no idea what to say. She was touched beyond words that Eliza would give her engagement ring to Dean for her. No wonder Dean had been all choked up telling her what his grandmother had said.

"Let me look at your finger." He raised her hand so they both could admire his grandmother's ring. He kissed her finger. "It looks amazing, and it's a perfect fit."

"Yes, it does, and I think it's a good omen that it fits perfectly. Hopefully, we'll have sixty-five plus years together as well."

"I hope so. I think we need to celebrate!"

She felt much better, so she stood up at the side of the bed and smiled at a surprised Dean. Mack started to unfasten her blouse and placed it on the chair to the side, then she removed her skirt, all the time keeping eye contact with him.

She turned her back to him and slid her panties down her legs, kicking them towards the chair, followed by her bra. She could hear Dean's breathing change, as the bed moved slightly, she turned back around to face him, only to discover Dean yanking his clothes off, letting them fly any which way.

Mack laughed and gave him a wicked grin. "Mmm, you look good enough to eat!"

He groaned with laughter. "You're going to kill me, Mack."

"Oh, I don't think so." She replied, and crawled over the bed on her hands and knees, towards a very aroused Dean.

Chapter 40

They took a shower, which usually only lasted about five minutes, but with Dean 'helping', more time was needed. Mack was standing at Dean's bedroom window, looking out over the gardens to the back of the house, while Dean had a rather heated conversation with his mother on his cell phone, in the bathroom. He obviously thought Mack wouldn't be able to hear, but she could, crystal clear!

She was dreading having to meet his mother again, who apparently was downstairs, entertaining Cynthia and her mother. His mother, once she discovered Dean was home, had phoned him on his cell, asking him to join them for coffee in the conservatory. Dean had declined and hung up on her.

Not five minutes had passed when she was on the phone again, basically telling him to get himself downstairs. He'd told his mother that he was busy, not wanting his mother knowing he had a woman in his room. Announcing he'd been having sex all afternoon to his mother, should not happen.

God knows how she would react when she discovered they were engaged. At least they had the blessing of his grandparents, which was lovely, and for Eliza to give up her ring for Mack, was a wonderful gesture.

The bathroom door opened and Dean walked out, frowning. His hair was all ruffled, because he'd more than likely been running his fingers through it.

Mack walked over to him and placed her hands on his chest. "Dean, I know your mother is giving you a hard time about Cynthia." He looked into her eyes. "The bathroom isn't sound proof."

"Hell. Sorry," Dean replied and sat down on the bed. "My mother wants me to go have coffee with her, Cynthia, and her mother. If you heard the conversation, then you know I told her I'm in love with someone else, and it wasn't going to change. God, she's a total pain in the ass."

"I didn't hear you say I was here, so don't you think it's the perfect time to tell your mother you're off the market, as we're engaged, and I'll make it clear you're my guy, mine alone?"

He smiled at Mack. "I love it when you get all huffy!"

"I do not get huffy…. I get pissed!"

"Christ, come on. You better hold my hand for courage."

"Dean, I'm fine. I don't need courage if I believe in what I'm fighting for."

He grimaced. "I'm the one who needs the courage, after all its my mother we're talking about."

"Oh!" Mack said, just as Dean pulled her out of the bedroom.

Dean stopped Mack just before going into the conservatory and pulled her into his arms for a soul-shattering kiss. He took her hand in his and opened the door. Three stunned faces greeted them when they saw the two together.

"Dean, what is the meaning of this? You said you were in your room, and I thought you said nobody but you were allowed in there?"

"Mother, Cynthia, Gladys, you remember Mack. I'm sure you do. She was with me in my room because she's my fiancée. We're going to be married as soon as Mack will have me."

Mack was stunned. Dean had told her it could be a long engagement. She started to smile and looked at Dean. "How's next weekend sound, at Rose Cottage?"

"Dean, slow down. You're not getting married next weekend, that's impossible. There would be too many details to arrange in such a short time."

"Mother, the only people we want at the wedding are Mack's immediate family and mine. And if it can be arranged in time, this weekend, in Cape Elizabeth, at the house where Grandmother grew up."

"What on earth are you talking about?" his mother asked, having completely forgotten about Cynthia and her mother.

"The grandparents will tell you about it later." Dean explained. "Mother, don't worry, everything will work out fine."

"Yes, but what about..." Anne trailed off and waved her arms in Cynthia and Gladys' direction.

Dean took a deep breath. "Cynthia, I'm sorry, but it was love at first sight for me when I met Mack. There's a guy out there for you, but I'm afraid it's not me."

"Bravo, Grandson!" Jacob was grinning from ear to ear.

Both Mack and Dean turned around to find Eliza, Jacob and Dean's father, James, standing behind them, smiling.

Eliza moved over to Mack, taking her face into her hands. "Thank you for making our grandson so happy." With both Mack and Eliza close to tears, Dean wrapped an arm around Mack's waist. "Let me see," Eliza asked, as she lifted Mack's left hand. "Oh my. Perfect fit. It looks lovely."

Mack wiped her eyes and took hold of Eliza's hand. "Thank you for giving this ring to Dean. You have no idea how much it means to me."

"Oh, I think I do," Eliza added.

While everyone seemed to be talking at once, Mack noticed Cynthia and Gladys leaving. Although Mack was really looking forward to putting them in their place, she couldn't help but feel sorry for them. Cynthia would never have stalked Dean, but for the interference and cajoling from both mothers.

She had a wedding to plan for the weekend! How the hell did that happen? She didn't even have a dress, then there's flowers, food, cake. No, the calm of earlier had gone, and panic was setting in. "Dean, can we go outside for a minute?"

He looked at Mack, frowning. "You okay?"

Mack just laughed and walked Dean outside on to the back patio.

"Dean, you do realize I don't even have a dress. I'm only going to do this once, so I want all the trimmings, cake, flowers, family, and bridesmaids."

"I'll help with everything, I promise. I'm not going to leave it all to you. It would be too much, especially with us wanting it all done for the weekend."

"Thank goodness for that." Mack admired her engagement ring again.

"Come on, babe. Let's go say our goodbyes." Dean took hold of her hand and pulled her in for a quick kiss. "We have a wedding to arrange!"

Chapter 41

In the morning, Mack was sitting on Dean's lap in the kitchen sharing a cup of coffee, while they made a list of what they needed to organize for their wedding. Mack wasn't quite sure how she ended up announcing this weekend was fine for a wedding. *A moment of insanity?*

Yesterday had been an amazing day. Not only had Mack discovered Rose and Jacob had been together all these years, Rose as Eliza, but she was now wearing Eliza's engagement ring as her very own.

They were going to tell Thomas about Rose, and prayed it wouldn't be too big a shock for him. What Rose and Thomas' father had done to them, lying about his son's death, was disgusting and unforgiveable. All this time wasted. All these years Thomas had been alone with no family after his wife died. It was so terribly sad, to think he had a niece and nephews out there, not to mention great-nephews and nieces, that he had no knowledge of. Hopefully it would go smoothly, as Mack wasn't too sure how she would handle Thomas, if it didn't.

"Dean? Do you think your mother would like to come looking at wedding dresses with me and mine?" She saw the shock on Dean's face. "She's going to be my mother-in-law, so the least I can do is try and get along with her. But if she's rude again, all bets are off, okay?"

"Okay. Just tell me when and where and I'll let my mother know."

"Thomas is here."

"Mack, he'll probably be shocked at first, but he has a family now. He's no longer alone. He's stronger than you think."

"Am I interrupting something?" Thomas asked, coming into the kitchen.

She stood up, laughing, and walked over to Thomas. "We got engaged yesterday, Thomas. We want to be married here, at Rose Cottage, this weekend."

"Oh, my." He cleared his throat. "Congratulations to you both." Thomas hugged Mack, then shook Dean's hand.

"Sit down, Thomas. That's not all our news."

He sat down and glanced from Mack to Dean. "Well, you can't be pregnant yet. Can you?"

"No, I'm not pregnant, Thomas. This is my engagement ring." Mack lifted her hand up so Thomas could see the ring.

"That's lovely, Mack." Then he turned to Dean. "Is it a family heirloom?"

"Yes, it is."

"Thomas, there's no easy way to say this." She took a deep breath. "Yesterday, when we went to visit Dean's grandparents, we discovered that Eliza, Jacob's wife, Dean's grandmother, is actually Rose, your sister." Thomas' eyes focused completely on Mack. "Rose didn't die that night, Thomas. Rose and Jacob blackmailed Richard into telling your parents he saw her go over the cliffs."

Dean passed Thomas and Mack a glass of water and continued the story. "Rose came back to see you and tell you the truth in 1952, only to be told by your father that you'd died in Korea. All these years, Thomas, she thought that you were dead."

Thomas leaned forward in his chair, putting his face in his hands. Mack went over to him and put her arm around him, feeling him shake while his tears fell silently.

He lifted his head. "After all these years. Because of the both of you." He shook his head. "I can't take it all in. I never expected you both to come back from Boston telling me my sister's alive." He looked at Mack then Dean. "You're my great-nephew?"

Dean smiled. "I certainly am... Uncle Thomas."

Mack wiped her eyes. "Eliza and Jacob will be here this weekend for our wedding. She's waiting for your call, Thomas."

"I can talk to her, after all these years? What's she like?"

"She looks about twenty years younger than she is. In fact, Jacob certainly doesn't look his age, either. Thomas, she was just as shaken as you are, when she learned you were alive. She said she has missed you so much over the years. She still wishes to go by Eliza, though."

"I can understand that, after all that's what she's used for a very long time... So she gave you her engagement ring," Thomas said, looking at Dean.

"She did. She said she wanted the woman of my heart, who returned her brother to her, to have her ring."

"Then I guess if you want a wedding here this weekend, you better get a move on." Thomas laughed.

She felt relief that Thomas was taking the news about Eliza so well. In a way, it was a dream come true for her, because not only had she fallen in love with Dean, but Thomas as well, and after she married Dean they'd all be family. She also knew one little lad, who would be thrilled to bits to discover Thomas was going to be part of the family.

He stood up. "I'll take her number, if you will, then leave you to it."

Mack handed him the number she had already written down for him. "Here you go. Are you okay?"

He pulled Mack into his arms and just held her close. "I'm more than okay. Thank you so much. You're the daughter I never had," he whispered, close to tears.

Epilogue

It was three hours before the wedding, and regardless of how many people had told Mack that it was bad luck to see the groom before the wedding, she insisted she was going to be there to see Thomas and Eliza meet for the first time in sixty-five years.

She hadn't dressed in her wedding finery just yet, so she headed downstairs in search of Dean, to watch the reunion, still in her shirt and jeans.

When they'd told Thomas, Rose had been happily married to Jacob for all these years, it was harder than they both had thought it would be, even Dean was all choked up.

Brother and sister had talked on the phone daily since the news had broken, and there had been a lot of tears, as well as laughter.

As she entered the kitchen, Mack found a very nervous Thomas, and a very hot-looking Dean sitting at the table, trying to wait patiently for Eliza and Jacob, who were being driven to the cottage by Dean's parents.

"Hey, beautiful. What are you doing down here, in jeans? There's a wedding happening in a few hours."

She walked over to Dean and wrapped her arms around him from behind. "I have it on good authority the gorgeous bride has it all under control!"

She kissed Dean on the top of his head and walked around the table to Thomas and gave him a hug as well.

"What if she doesn't like me?" Thomas asked in a worried voice.

"Oh, Thomas, Eliza said you have always been in her heart. You could have two heads, and she will still love you. Please don't worry. In fact, I bet Eliza is probably thinking the same as you. Sixty-five years is a long time."

She walked back to Dean and sat on his lap, feeling awfully nervous for the reunion.

Thomas pulled himself together, sat up in his chair, reached inside his jacket and took out an envelope. "This here is your wedding present." He tapped it on the table top. "I want you both to know that up until last week, I didn't have any family. Now I have, and it includes you both. I certainly don't have anyone to pass anything on to, although Lucas has spoken up for the *Our Gang* comics." He took a breath. "Having said all that, because of you both, I have my sister back, and that's worth more than what's in here."

He handed the envelope to Dean.

Mack's hands were shaking far too much. Dean opened it and couldn't believe what he was looking at.

"Dean, what is it?" Mack asked.

He had to swallow around the lump in his throat. "It's the deed to Rose Cottage, in both our names."

Mack and Dean just looked at Thomas. "You're both at home here at Rose Cottage, and I'm getting too old to look after it. I want you both to have it, and to live here and raise a family. Besides, I happen to know the local school needs a teacher, and I have it on good authority that Auntie Mack is a very good one, although a bit bossy."

Mack was stunned, she certainly hadn't expected the cottage as a wedding present, but she should have known Thomas would do something like he had. Rose Cottage was where it all started. Not just for herself and Dean, but for Rose and Jacob all those years ago.

Standing up she met Thomas, who was walking towards them for a very big hug. "I don't know what to say, Thomas," she told him, unable to hold the tears back.

"Thank you, will suffice."

She pulled back and took hold of Dean's hand. "Thank you, I do love it here." She looked at Dean. "If it's okay with Dean, then we'll live here. Besides, someone has to make sure you don't get into any trouble."

Thomas chuckled. "Just make sure those babies appear sooner rather than later. I'm not a spring chicken anymore."

"I'm sure we'll get started on that pretty soon." Mack blushed.

"With plenty of practice, I'm sure we'll get it right." Dean chuckled.

They heard a car pull up outside, which stopped the laughter, and panic flickered across Thomas' face.

Mack took Thomas' hand. "Come on, Thomas, you can do this. Just remember Eliza and Jacob are going to be just as nervous as you are."

Dean opened the back door and held it open as Thomas stepped out, holding Mack's hand really tight, as though he expected her to bolt. Dean followed them outside and ran over to open the car door for his grandparents.

His grandfather stepped out first, then turned back towards the car to help Eliza out.

With Dean on one side and Jacob on the other, they made their way to Mack and Thomas who were waiting not too far away.

Mack could feel Thomas shaking, and from the look of things, so were Eliza and Jacob. Meeting Dean's eyes, Mack nudged Thomas forward, at the same time Eliza let go of both Dean and Jacob, to put her arms around Thomas. They were both sobbing as though their hearts would burst.

Mack took two steps straight into Dean's arms and cried all over him. He ran his hands up and down her back in a soothing motion.

Mack finally managed to get herself under control and wiped her face on the handkerchief Dean's father passed her. "Thank you."

Eliza took hold of Jacob's hand and pulled him slightly forward to meet her brother. She had written in her diary how much she wished that Thomas and Jacob could get to know each other. Although it was a long time ago when she had expressed that wish, it was now coming true.

Eliza turned towards Mack and walked over to her. Mack let go of Dean and walked straight into Eliza's embrace. "Thank you, Mack. You have no idea just how much everything you have done means to Jacob and me," she whispered.

Mack pulled away and wiped her eyes giving both Thomas and Jacob a hug before she returned to Dean's waiting arms.

Mack's one wish was that she could get through the

wedding without shedding any tears. No doubt she would start up again when she caught sight of Dean standing in the Gazebo, waiting for her to become his wife.

Mack turned around to take the first look in the full-length mirror.

She didn't think she was particularly unattractive, but had never been one to pay a lot of attention to preening. After all, she was a school teacher of small children, and classes tended to be messy. But when she turned and saw herself in the mirror, she was stunned. Staring back at her was... "A princess," Melinda said, as she saw Mack in her wedding gown.

"Is this really me?" she whispered.

"Mack, you are so beautiful today, as you are always. Today though, you are simply radiant. Are you really happy, Mack?" Melinda asked, taking hold of Mack's hand.

"Sis, I've never been as happy. I love Dean so much, I can't imagine my life without him." She paused. "I also can't imagine living anywhere other than here."

"What are you trying to tell me?"

Mack smiled. "Thomas has given Rose Cottage to Dean and me as a wedding present. Apparently, Lucas has claimed all the *Our Gang* comics, and he doesn't have anyone else to leave this to. He said that we're his family, and he wants us to have it and raise a family here."

"So, you're going to move here?" Mack nodded. "This is what you've always wanted, Mack. A house out of the city near the beach, with a good loving man and lots of kids. Part of your dream has come true, and I'm really happy for you," Melinda said.

"Thank you."

"You do realize that Lucas will always want to come and stay with you?"

"As long as there's no school, he's always welcome, you all are."

They both turned on hearing the door open. "What are you girls doing in here? You're supposed to be downstairs."

"Mom," Melinda winked at Mack, then turned back to their mother, "I was giving Mack the birds and the bees talk."

Louise walked further into the room, walking around Mack with tears coming to her eyes. "You look stunning... Your father is going to cry like a baby." She then turned her attention to Melinda. "And I'm sure she doesn't need the bird and the bees talk considering the very hot groom downstairs," she commented, fanning herself.

"Mom! You're not supposed to notice things like that," Melinda said in fake shock.

"I have eyes... and a sex drive."

"Eww, Mom," Melinda said with a shudder.

"Come on, there's a hot as hell guy downstairs wanting to make you his wife, and your very nervous father."

Mack took another look at herself in the mirror and allowed her Mom and Melinda to escort her out of her room and down the stairs to her father, then her groom.

Dean was standing in the gazebo while he waited for Mack to appear. He'd started to feel nervous. There wasn't a huge amount of family present, but only just meeting Mack's parents, with her father giving him the third degree, hadn't helped any. All he wanted was his Mack.

Thomas was sitting close by, waiting to act as best man. He was still a bit shaky after his meeting with Rose. A very emotional time.

It took Mack about half an hour to calm down. Then she was mortified to realize both her eyes were puffy, so after cutting chunks of cucumber, had disappeared back upstairs saying she would see them all at the wedding.

Thomas came to stand beside him. "You're one lucky man."

"Don't I know…" Dean trailed off when he caught sight of Mack in her long, fitted, white, strapless dress, covered in lace. She started walking towards him. He couldn't take his eyes from her. She truly was the most beautiful woman he had ever seen, but most importantly, beautiful on the inside too. He swallowed around the lump in his throat and tried to take hold of his emotions. As he did so, Dean glanced at his grandmother and noticed her crying softly into his grandfather's arm.

He looked back to Mack and spotted his mother with her handkerchief guarding her eyes as well. She had apologized to Mack for being so rude, and had welcomed her into the family. Mack had accepted the olive branch, and even asked Dean's mother to accompany her when she went looking for a wedding dress, along with her own mother.

Lucas came to a stop just over to Dean's side, with a huge grin on his face. Dressed in a pale grey suit, dark grey shirt and silver tie, he looked so handsome. He leaned towards Dean. "Don't forget, when you're my uncle, you have to buy me a present and my birthday's next week. And seeing you don't know how to play, maybe you can ask my grandma how to play strip poker. She says it's very easy and stimulatering, or something like that."

Dean laughed and turned back to Mack, who was about to reach his side. He was thankful she'd decided to rent Rose Cottage for the summer, where she'd discovered 'the diary', which had brought Dean to the Cottage, and eventually brought his grandmother back together with her brother, after all those years apart. They'd come full circle, and he couldn't be happier.

Mack passed her flowers to Melinda and turned to look at Dean. When their eyes met, they realized this was where they belonged, with each other, at 'Rose Cottage'.

THE END

About the Author

I was born in Bolton, Lancashire within the United Kingdom, where I lived, and worked at the University of Bolton. In 2010, I moved to Ireland with my husband, four kids and pack of animals.

I'm a NY Times and USA Today Bestselling Author of Devour, and International Bestselling Author of Seduce and Sizzle under my pen name Lexi Buchanan.

My time is spent writing when I can get away from Facebook, and chasing after the kids and animals.

One of my all time ambitions is to visit Mount Everest base camp in the Himalayas.

Thank you to each and every one of you for your continued support.

http://www.lexibuchanan.net
@AuthorLexi
authorlexibuchanan@gmail.com

Made in the USA
Charleston, SC
28 June 2014

Bodies Under the Pier

By Tod Mottram

dedicated to
Ikpomwosa *aka* **Adam**

original cover photograph by
Dave Sloan

the stuff of nightmares

Nathan Hart is a complex, burnt-out, ex-serving police officer. Having retired sick in his thirties, Nathan reinvents himself as a self-employed, civilian, data analyst support worker.

Bodies of two young men wash up under Portsmouth's Southsea Pier, reminiscent of the body in the Thames case, exactly ten years earlier.

Battling his own ill health and poor lifestyle choices, Nathan picks through the mess of information to find leads to this serial killer - putting himself, his family, and associates in increasing danger.

Nothing in Nathan's home life and work life is simple, and then child-in-care, vulnerable teenager Polly joins the fray.

Bodies Under the Pier is a gritty, procedural, police crime-thriller set in Portsmouth, England, and includes snippets of true crime.

Contents

Chapter One 1
Chapter Two 6
Chapter Three 18
Chapter Four 48
Chapter Five 74
Chapter Six 92
Chapter Seven 107
Chapter Eight 135
Chapter Nine 163
Chapter Ten 175
Chapter Eleven 189
Chapter Twelve 211
Chapter Thirteen 223
Chapter Fourteen 242
Chapter Fifteen 261
Chapter Sixteen 273
Chapter Seventeen 282

Chapter One

Nathan swiped open his personal iPhone to read the message from his wife.

'How's your first day going? I bet you nailed it, clever boy. We have a guest staying. With history. Forewarned is forearmed'.

He tapped his response.

'Allegations?'

'Yep. She's sweet, but a bit hard work. You'll love her.'

'Sorry Bernie. Am I keeping you from your game of Candy Crush?'

Nathan took a moment to process his nickname. Looking up, he responded.

'You are, sir. But it can wait.'

A wave of giggles rippled around the room.

'As I have your attention, Bernie, do you want to add anything?'

Nathan stood and turned to face the room, from where he had sat on the spare chair at the sergeant's desk. He perched on the end of her desk.

'I know some of you from before.' There were a few nods from the audience. 'I am Nathan Hart. I started back today as a civilian number-cruncher. I will start, well, crunching numbers and hopefully feedback to you, presently. Have a nice day.'

Nathan took his seat again, squeezing shut his eyes against the pain in the back of his head and a sudden overpowering smell of acetone nail polish remover. The inspector's voice droned in his periphery.

'… and that is why we now pay Bernie so much public money; use him. Remember, he is a two-way street.'

The audience left the room or returned to their workstations. The inspector returned to his glass panelled office, slamming shut the door. Nathan watched the aluminium doorframe shudder.

'Management by isolation?'

'He's on borrowed time, Nath.'

'Aren't we all, Vicky?'

'Shouldn't you call me serg, Nath?'

'Shouldn't you call me Mr Hart, Vicky?'

'Up your arse, Nath. At least I don't call you Bernie. Why are your eye's red? You better not be pissed on your first day back.'

'Not yet. A bit of a headache. Anyway, I am not *back*. You fired me.'

'You retired.'

'Ok, you *retired* me.'

'You were lucky we didn't prosecute you. How's Amy?'

'I didn't feel very lucky. I'll tell her you are asking after her.'

'Probably best not. And I suppose that was all my fault, as well.'

'You shagged her husband.'

'You told her that I shagged her husband.'

'Why is this investigation not run like a murder enquiry? No wonder the guv is on borrowed time.'

'It is a murder enquiry. But we think it relates to people-smuggling or modern-day slavery.'

'Because they are black? If this was two headless white girls, with arms and legs hacked off, instead of two black boys, we wouldn't be looking for border infringements.'

'That is a little unfair, Nath. We think they were trafficked …'

'Because of their skin colour?'

'… and we are concentrating on that line of enquiry as likely to be the most productive.'

'Perhaps I'm just being Devil's Advocate.'

'Perhaps you are just the Devil. We need results, Nath. Like yesterday.'

'I wasn't here yesterday. Even you will struggle to blame me for that one.'

Nathan returned to his own desk. He spent the morning setting up spreadsheets, databases, and links. Most of the software, which he brought with him, he had stolen from the force during his time serving. He had already tweaked and improved it in his previous position, and now splashed over his company logo, added his electronic signature, and sold it back to the force along with his own time.

Relevant information downloaded from the local server and the U.K. Police Database into his system.

Unsurprisingly, the U.K. Police Computer security team cleared and approved his system in record time – it being largely their own. Nathan imported the contact details of the investigating team.

'Nath.'

'Serg.'

'Look up when I'm talking to you. A spinning egg timer doesn't require your supervision.'

Nathan stood to face Vicky. She stood with two young women.

'Your team.'

'I am a lone consultant. I don't have a team.'

'I apologise for your colleague's rudeness. It is not his fault; he is just rude.

The uniformed officer extended her arm. 'PC Gill Walker.'

Nathan held her eye but did not take her hand until the moment she moved to retract it. Flustered, she took his hand, blushing deeply. Nathan shook hands, before offering to shake the second woman's hand.

'Anneika Maneet. Mr?'

'Nathan Hart. And you must be the token black person to reflect the victim's heritage.'

'I was just born black, Mr Hart.'

Another bolt of pain shot across his head. Concentrating hard not to flinch, the vision in one eye blurred a little, and he felt his eyes cross.

'Are you ok, sir?'

'Sure Walker. I just stood up too quick. Look, can we make a start, please? Settle-in and log-in. Constable, I realise you are here to spy on us two civilians, but I hope you are not above a little data inputting and processing.'

'No sir, of course …' The officer blushed again.

'And let's start off on first-name terms, please. Life is too short.'

'Is that Nathan, Nathan? Or Bernie, Nathan?'

'Nath will do, Anneika.'

'Make that Ann, Nath.'

'Start by populating the blank reports in order. Except, do the DVLA inputting first. I want all the numberplate recognition data from all the Portsmouth and Hampshire traffic cameras referenced against all the people of interest and known associates. Let's see if we can't see a pattern. Start from two weeks prior to the estimated time of death until one day afterwards.'

'Yes sir. Which one of us …'

'Sort it out amongst yourselves. Don't call me sir. And don't ask me any more questions.'

'Sorry, sir.'

Ann guided a scarlet Gill towards their workstations as Vicky rolled her eyes.

'I can't believe I got you this job; you arrogant git. And let Amy know she can sleep easy – I can't remember why I shagged you before, and I certainly have no intention of doing it again!'

Chapter Two

Nathan pulled his BMW 3 series into the drive. He checked the mirrors and scanned the surrounding area on autopilot. Dropping his door keys onto the table, he raised his left hand towards the gun safe as his right hand slid under his jacket.

'Goodness. Is it called a Freudian slip if you do an actual action?'

Nathan turned to his wife. 'I haven't had a firearm for over three years. It must be an association with going into the office.'

'How was your first day?'

'Absolutely fine. There is a lot …'

'Did you see her?'

'See who? I …'

Amy stepped forward, forcing three fingers into Nathan's mouth to silence him. She gestured towards the living room with a backwards nod.

'I haven't got time for your shit. Did you see her?' She pushed her fingers further back into his mouth for emphasis.

Nathan took her wrist and gently pulled away her hand.

'She is my boss.'

'Fucking great!'

'Look, if it makes you feel better, she said …'

'Shut up Nath. Just shut up.'

'Who have we got?'

'A seventeen-year-old. Police protected. Her name is Polly.'

'Pretty Polly. I had better say hello. My smile is fixed and ready.'

'You know her?'

'No. Should I?'

Amy led the way into the sitting room.

'Polly, this is my husband, Nathan.'

'Hey, Polly. Nice to meet you.'

'Are you a paedophile, Nathan?'

'No. Of course I'm not.'

'Why *of course*? Am I stupid? Are there no such things as paedophiles?'

'No. I am not saying that.'

'So, what are you?'

'I am an emergency foster carer.'

'That's the same as a paedophile, innit.'

'No, not exactly. They check us carefully.'

'I bet you think I have lost my V-card.'

'What's a V-card?'

Polly laughed, throwing back her head. Nathan smiled, always amazed at the robustness of these children.

'V-card! V-card, innit.'

'Go on.'

'Do you think I'm a virgin?'

'No! Well, yes or no. I have no idea. Look, we absolutely can talk about this.'

'Talk about my virginity? Pervert.'

'No. I mean, we can talk about sexual activity. Yours specifically if you like. Or in general terms. Amy is great at these subjects. We should ask Amy.'

Polly laughed again, pulling her legs onto the sofa, which swamped her tiny frame.

'You are so square! How old are you? Like one hundred?'

'Thirty-five. I am …'

Polly's renewed laughter silenced Nathan.

'I am not talking about my virginity to you and the bitch.'

'Please don't …'

'But as you ask. I still have my V-card.'

'I didn't ask.'

'So, you can put that in your report, innit.'

'I'm not putting it into any report!'

'And I will put it in my report that you asked about my V-card, innit.'

'I didn't ask!'

'Us kids have what we call a honeymoon period, where the foster carers are like, you know, ok.'

'Us foster carers say the same about the kids.'

'After that, the foster carers are, you know? Like mostly … sort of. Like, just a bunch of cunts.'

Nathan laughed this time. For the first time in weeks, his headache left him.

'But I don't dislike you.'

'I don't dislike you either, Polly.'

'I'm putting that in my report, paedo!'

'I need a coffee. Follow me and I'll show you where we keep the snacks.'

As Nathan walked into the hall, Amy stepped back from the door.

'Well, level-two, emergency, out-of-hours foster carer of the year, that went well.'

Nathan kissed the top of her head.

Alcohol was an emotional trigger and beverage of choice for many of the children emergency fostered. Nathan poured a healthy portion of red wine into a plastic squash beaker. Hiding the bottle at the back of the top shelf, he purposely left a Ribena bottle on the counter, in plain sight.

'Is that wine?'

'Ribena. Help yourself from the kitchen.'

'It looks like wine, innit. Can I have some?'

'What are you watching?'

The television blared with adverts, the compressed noise rattling inside his head.

'*Mafs*.'

'Maths? What, like a school-science programme?'

'You are weird. *Mafs* – Married at First Sight. Do you watch Love Island? This is the Australian *Mafs*, innit. Better than the English one.'

'Perhaps that counts as geography.' Nathan closed his eyes against the sound of a young woman screeching in an Australian country drawl.

'Is it too loud?'

'You're ok.'

'I was going to watch You Tube in my room. But the bitch won't let me have the Wi-Fi code.'

'If you stop calling Amy a bitch, I might talk to her about Wi-Fi access. But not in your room. Perhaps in here with earphones. Or in the kitchen. I mean it Polly, show some respect.'

'Earphones? You are so ancient!' Polly laughed again. Nathan smiled to himself. 'What's your job?'

'I am an emergency out of hours foster carer.'

'Your day job.'

'Computers and stuff.'

'What are you hiding, innit?'

'*Nuffin. Innit.*'

Polly smiled, the mental cogs turning. 'Are you the filth?'

'No.'

'Are you a pig?'

'I just said no.'

'Do you work for the *feds*?' The split-second delay in his answering was sufficient. 'You are! I knew it. I can smell you lot a mile off.'

'I am a civilian. I work in admin. I only started today, so I doubt I smell of pork already.'

Amy walked into the room, brushing her drying hair.

'Nathan said I could have Wi-Fi and a sip of his wine. You didn't tell me he is a pig.'

'He isn't a police officer anymore. Why did you say she could have Wi-Fi without speaking to me first? And none of his wine, not even a sip.'

Polly stared at the couple, a huge smug grin stretching across her face.

'I didn't say she could have Wi-Fi or any of my Ribena. And I didn't tell her I used to be an officer either, but you just did.'

Nathan's grin stretched almost as wide as Polly's. Amy rolled her eyes.

'Great. Two *mind-gamers* in my house. Are you hungry?'

'No.'

'Tired?'

'No. Are you sending me to bed?'

'You should get some sleep. You have had a busy couple of days.'

'What? You two want time alone? Is that what you do? Have sex on the sofa with a vulnerable child upstairs.'

'No! Of course not. Look, stay up if you like. I just thought …'

'I know what you were thinking, dirty … missus. Ok, I will leave you to it. But it is going in my report.'

'We aren't …' Amy tailed off as Polly left the room. 'What report?'

'She thinks we will write a report to her social worker.'

'Well, we do. At her age she can ask to read her notes, so she will see what we say.'

'So, she says she will write a report about us.' Amy shrugged at Nathan's reply. 'We have had our first breakthrough.'

'And how do you make that out?'

'She called you missus, instead of bitch.'

'Whoopty-do. Are you ok with me going to the meeting tonight? Should I leave you alone with our new friend?'

'What meeting?'

'PCiCN.'

'No. You go. I don't do two hours of navel gazing and slagging off social services. That's your department.'

'Ah yes – everyman is an island.'

'I think the term is: no man is an island. John Donne, I believe.'

'Yes, I know! But thanks for mansplaining.'

'That wasn't mansplaining. Mansplaining is when a man …'

Amy shot round to confront her husband. Seeing him unable to keep a straight face, she pounced on him, tickling his ribs. She squealed as he returned the tickle. Polly stamped on her bedroom floor in protest.

Nathan poured the rest of the bottle of wine into the beaker and settled in front of his laptop. Much of his work was only accessible from his works laptop, tethered in the office. But he could access some emails and press releases from home. He spent an hour reading-up what he could on the case, much of which was in the public domain.

Two dismembered and mutilated bodies were found under Southsea pier by jet skiers. Weaving between the Victorian ironwork to impress his female passenger, the rider ran the jet ski over the bodies, sending a spray of putrefied flesh over the couple. They beached the jet ski and phoned the hire company, who dialled 999 and informed the police, giving the What3Words location of the couple.

The find was of two bodies chained together. A second chain had fastened around the leg stump of one body and presumably connected onto a weight or structure, yet to be identified and recovered. With decomposition, the weighted chain loosened through the mush of flesh, until the bodies floated to the surface and tangled amongst the pier ironwork.

Vicky sent one report to Nathan by email, which summarised the initial Scenes of Crime findings. The first officers at the scene reported the remains of two white adults. SoC quickly established the bodies were of two young men or boys. Both black, their remains a bloated, pasty-white *grave wax,* tinted blue in streaks. Vicky added that the autopsy had revealed they were of Northeast African heritage, post pubescent, probably teenagers. Head, lower legs, and lower arms missing – sawn and cleaved off.

Nathan jumped to his feet on hearing the scream, sending his beaker of wine spilling across the sofa. He knocked on Polly's door, opening it an inch to talk through the gap, before a second scream made him burst in. Polly stood on the pillow at the head of the bed wearing a Tesco's nightshirt of the type Amy kept as spare.

'Spider! There, look!'

'Right. You get out and wait in the hall. I will catch the little chap. He is more scared of you.'

Nathan caught the grass spider as it tried to scurry under the pillow. Polly now stood behind him, looking over his shoulder and gripping the biceps of his free arm.

'I said wait in the hall. Out. Out!'

Not releasing his arm, the couple walked together into the hall, Nathan releasing the spider through the window. Polly screamed again.

'Ok. Calm down. He has gone.'

'He? How do you know it was a *he*?'

'I don't. Go back to bed.'

'I can't go back in there.'

'Don't be silly. It's gone.'

'But it might have family!'

'Get back to bed.'

'I will sleep in your bed. Unlock the door.'

'No, you won't! And how do you know our door is locked?'

Polly shrugged.

'Go back to bed.'

'No!'

'Ok, sleep here on the floor. I'm going downstairs.'

'To finish your Ribena?'

'What time did you get home?'

'Good morning, darling.'

'Where were you?'

'Did you watch the news? Those two bodies are boys.'

'Yes, I know. That is the case I am working.'

'Why didn't you say?'

'You didn't ask.'

'They didn't offer many details. But said it is being treated as murder.'

'We don't know many details. The bodies are decomposed.'

'Oh, my God. I thought salty seawater would help to preserve them.'

'They were weighted and lying on the seabed, where every passing crustation had a munch. I'm not eating local seafood for a couple of weeks.'

'They had an e-fit of the boys showing height and body measurements.'

'An e-fit? I am surprised. I'll have a look when I get into the office. Where were you last night?'

'The facial features were completely blank and the heads bald. I thought that was a little disrespectful. They could have shown some features and hair length, surely.'

'There are no features remaining. I don't remember you coming to bed last night.'

'Oh no! That is awful. Their poor parents. Hang on. Absolutely no features? Like poor Eve?'

'Exactly like Eve.'

'No! Nath, it is the same time of year.'

'Pretty much to the day. Exactly 10 years.'

Polly burst into the kitchen. 'I'm hungry.'

'Good morning, Polly. How did you sleep?' asked Amy.

'I'm hungry. What are you eating, Nath?'

'Weetabix. I can make you something hot if you fancy.'

'Nah. Weetabix is ok.'

'Amy, this milk is blue.'

Amy took the bowl from her husband and tilted it into the light. 'It looks ok to me.'

Polly took the bowl from Amy, sniffed at the remains of Nathan's breakfast, and shrugged. Using Nathan's used spoon, she shovelled the remains into her mouth.

'What's happening to me today, Nath?' Polly pointedly asked Nathan, blanking Amy.

'Amy knows better than me. I am off to work in a minute.'

Polly continued to stare expectantly at Nathan. Amy spoke.

'You are on police protection for seventy-two hours. We only do emergency foster caring, so I will call the duty social worker at 09:30. Normally, your children's social worker will see you are here; they will have a meeting and visit you during the day. But try not to worry, you can stay here until we know. Have you any questions? Shall we write a list of things to ask your social worker?'

Polly concentrated hard on catching the last dribbles of milk onto her spoon. Eventually, she spoke. 'Nah, I'm ok.'

'Polly love, there are a million rules which us foster carers must follow. One is, we dress modestly and don't walk around in nightclothes. Why don't you get dressed or at least put on a dressing gown? There's a good girl.' Amy spoke softly, but firmly.

Amy walked Nathan to the door.

'Did you use my car last night? What is up with yours?'

'Nothing Nath. I knew you wouldn't be driving after a pint of *Ribena*.'

'If I was called-in, I'd have looked bloody stupid parking next to the Inspector in your deckchair striped beach-buggy, wouldn't I?'

'You'd have got a cab. Nath, please don't tell Vicky I asked about her. Also, you had better tell the bitch about Eve.'

Nathan nodded and took his wife's chin in his fingers, to kiss her on the lips.

'God, you two. Aren't there rules about necking in front of children in care? Innit.'

Chapter Three

'Nath. We are ready for you.'
Nathan followed Vicky into the inspector's office.
'Bernie, sit down please.'
'Thank you, Teddy.'
'Teddy! Dunbar, Inspector, or Ted in the pub. But not bloody Teddy!'
'Hart, Nathan, or Nath in the pub. But not bloody Bernie!'
Nathan took his seat.
'Nathan, how are things looking? Any analysis for me to pin an arrest on?'
'Hardly. The two inputters you gave me are effective, thanks. But we need time, and intel.'
'You have three days of information. That's all we have. You have no time, none of us have. We need pointers Bernie. Currently we are, seemingly, knocking randomly on doors and chasing every scrote in town.'
'Seemingly so, sir. You and Vicky will receive reports from me every morning. Today, I draw your attention to three reports on your desk. The longer report shows all the people you have identified as wishing to speak with, but who remain outstanding. The second, shorter report, shows those on the first list who you have tried to speak with already, but failed for whatever reason. The third report, however, is the

one to concentrate on today. It shows a small list of people you wish to speak with, or wish to revisit, and whose name has cropped up with at least one other officer during interviews and door-to-doors. Not necessarily suspects, it is way too early for that, but just people who others think may help. I also wanted to talk about something else, please inspector.'

'Go on Bernie but keep it short.'

'Ten years ago, almost to the day, a black child was found floating in the Thames, minus a head and limbs. The case remains unsolved.'

'Yes, we know. We were straight onto the Met. Unusually, they are being most cooperative. They have already reopened the cold case. We sent a sergeant and two DCs to London to liaise closely with the Met team. Expect some incoming intel to plough through by Monday.'

'Something else, guv. I need to declare an interest. I lived in London then. I was walking my date over Blackfriars bridge to her tube station. My date spotted the body of the child, Eve, floating in the river. I was, literally, the first officer on the scene. My date was Amy, now my wife.'

'Yes, we know. Welcome to the team. You have spent ten years prattling on about Eve. Now is your chance to put all that angst to good use.'

'Good work ladies. Thank you. Please take a moment, every so often, to sit back and look at what you are doing. We sometimes need a human eye to see a pattern. The intel is of poor quality for now, and we need to drill down to find the nuggets. Which one of you printed the blue reports for the guv?'

The colleagues looked at each other and back to Nathan. Anneika spoke. 'Blue reports, Nath?'

'The lists of people to be chased down.'

Gill raised her hand. 'I did Nathan. We send the reports electronically, but the inspector prefers a paper copy of anything urgent.'

'Good work. Have you imported the DVLA and traffic camera data? Run a report against the shortlist of names, please. Also, you need to enter my personal contact information and that of my wife, Amy. We have some history on a potentially related case. Who wants coffee?'

'I will fetch the coffees, Nath, if you take a moment to tell Gill and I why the inspector and some others call you Bernie.'

The two women sat back in their chairs in unison. Nathan shook his head.

'The inspector needs to get out more.' The two women remained defiantly motionless, waiting for an answer. 'I used to serve. Towards the end of my serving career, I gained the nickname Bernie. That was all a longtime ago. Now, back to work.'

Anneika fetched the coffees, taking Nathan's to where he now stood in front of Vicky's desk. To one side stood a detective constable. Vicky spoke as Nathan took his coffee.

'You know DC Neil Morton?'

Nathan and the DC shook hands. Nathan spoke.

'Only through Hampshire's Willow Team, serg. The DC has been around our house a few times with county partners. Many of our young people are at risk of exploitation. Willow is the mob-hand-multidiscipline team, which tries to capture all angles of risk. All very joined up.'

The DC spoke. 'I hadn't realised you were an ex-officer. Good job I am not a detective or anything.'

'He never acted much like a police officer when he was in the mob. I excuse you for missing the signs.' The two men smiled at Vicky's sarcasm. 'Neil tells me you have experience with the Northeastern African community.'

Nathan shrugged. 'Many of our kids are at risk, none more so than *UASC*. Mostly young men, we take *Unaccompanied Asylum-Seeking Children* when they first come into care. Willow attends the following day, before we move the kids on for processing. We have had around twenty such kids over the past three years of emergency fostering. Mostly out the back of lorries here in Portsmouth, but we have had a couple who rolled in at Dover and jumped out when the lorry stopped at Fleet Services on the M3 motorway. We have had Afghans running from the Taliban and a Syrian refugee. But most have been African – Sudanese and Eritrean.'

'How are they at risk?'

'Your DC here will have a better idea of the big picture. In my experience, our young men pretty much walked from Sudan, say, through the desert. They are raped, beaten, and tortured in Libya, forced down gold mines or into the sex industry to pay the gangs and people smugglers, before being deposited by a small boat in Italy. They then go by foot, train, and bus through Europe, pushed along a conduit of charities and criminals, until they find themselves in my front room being fed Amy's Sudanese sweet potato stew. The risk is the people smugglers come looking for more money, or to use their new commodity in the sex trade, carwashes, nail bars, or cannabis farms.'

'Wow Nath! And you do this for fun?'

'They are among the most rewarding placements we have. Scared, hungry, stinking of oil and poverty, they are rabbits in the headlights. By the time they leave us on the following working day, they are laughing, joking, and dancing to Amazon's Africa Radio Station on Alexa.'

'Have you made contacts in the African communities here in Portsmouth?'

'As emergency out of hours carers, we move the kids on after a day or two. But I know there is a Sudanese community here. Amy networks better than I do …'

'Really? There's a surprise.'

'… and her church is African evangelical Baptist based in Eastney, and she is involved in a Facebook group called *PCiCN* – Portsmouth Children in Care Network. They have face-to-face meetings every Thursday and support foster carers, including *UASC* carers.'

'And that is below you to attend as well, I suppose? And God? He is below you, no doubt.'

'We're a team. We can't both do the fuzzy stuff.'

'Have you any at the moment?'

'A white kid. Amy took the shout, and we still haven't caught up properly. I understand she is in and out of care. Her foster placement broke down. She accused her female PE teacher of watching the girls in the shower and giving her detention because she fancies her. Something kicked off and the connected foster carer called the filth. The filth didn't exactly believe the allegations, but took her into protection and over to us, until social can unravel the mess. Looks like she may have discovered boys.'

'Going back to the African kids, can you, or Amy, call in some favours from the community? Someone must be missing two teenagers. Or heard some rumour or think someone's eyes are too close together.'

'No! I am not a detective and Amy isn't either. You do your job, I'll do mine.'

The DC cleared his throat and studied his steel toe capped brogues.

'These boys might have been two of yours, Nath.'

'And you think we haven't thought of that?' shouted Nathan.

'Hey! Enough.' The DC straightened to his full height. Vicky raised a calming hand.

'Sorry. I didn't mean to raise my voice,' Nathan mumbled. 'We have both thought the worst. We can't keep track once our kids leave us. We worry about every one of them, every day.' Nathan looked around the silenced open plan office. 'Sorry. I didn't mean to shout. I need to get back to work.'

'Nathan.'
'Gill?'
'The boss is hoping you will join us for a drink on the way home, as it's Friday.'
'Some things never change.'
'Three-line whip Nathan.'
Nathan looked up from his laptop. 'Whatever.'
'He said in the …'
'Portsbridge?'
'Yeah, sir. I guess some things do never change.'
'I will be twenty minutes. I will drive and leave the car at the pub. I can walk home from there. See if Ann wants a lift down, please.'

The Portsbridge was already half full, the clientele mostly a mix of police officers from Cosham police station and members of the British National Party, who adopted the pub as their primary meeting place when one of their own became landlord. Vicky and the inspector were already sitting at a small round table in the window bay as Nathan and his team entered together.

'Goblin for you, Nath. The boss's shout.'
'Cheers … Ted. Thanks.' Nathan raised the glass of Hobgoblin real ale, but rested it back on the table without drinking, and taking the stool opposite. Gill

and Anneika were about to make their excuses and head for the bar when the inspector waved his expenses credit card and made a circular motion around the table and the adjacent table.

'Be a love, Gill.'

Gill took the card and moved to the bar with Anneika to fetch another round, returning with beers and piles of snacks. The inspector sighed, firing Gill a sideways glance, causing her to blush. She flicked a look at the grinning Anneika; it was obvious who was trying to max out the boss's card on carbs.

'You had better have the receipt.'

Nathan picked up his first glass again and silently drank three quarters of the contents in one go.

Anneika spoke, punctuating her sentence with a long draught of her own pint. 'We were interrupted earlier, but Nathan was explaining why you call him Bernie, sir.'

'No, I wasn't explaining myself to you, Ann. Good try.'

Anneika shrugged and gestured towards the pool table, as the current player lined up the black. Gill nodded, and the two moved off.

'I have asked your girls to work the weekend, inputting intel from London, Bernie.'

'Not mine, and not girls, Ted. But thanks anyway. They mentioned it. They are each working one day. I will be in as well.'

'I can't sign-off overtime for you Bernie, as you are a limited company, sorry.'

'Don't worry, inspector. I will lose the invoice, nobody need know.'

The inspector's phone pinged and, as he tapped replies to a series of incoming messages, Vicky gestured to the bar.

'By *losing the invoice*, you mean you will work for free?'

Nathan shrugged, signing to the landlord for three more pints, despite still cradling his own full second glass.

'Nice arse. She looks good out of uniform. Your type, Nath.'

Nathan watched Gill take a shot, stretched over the pool table, low slung linen jeans stretching against her hips.

'My wife is *my type*. And Gill is only a kid.'

'Wow! None so righteous as a converted whore. Anyway, half your age plus seven.'

'Meaning?' Nathan looked back at the bar as Gill turned, making eye contact.

'Meaning, in our patriarchal, misogynistic society, it is socially acceptable for a man to lech after a girl half his age, plus seven years. It is a known fact. A 90-year-old man can shack up with a woman in her early fifties. A twenty-year-old lad shouldn't date a girl under seventeen. You are 35, she is 25.'

'I thought it was I who justifies everything through numbers and algorithms.'

'Why are you pushing them away? They are obviously fond of you, despite your arrogance. Bring them in Nath. You are not popular and need good people around you.'

Nathan turned his head to watch the women laughing at a shared joke.

'You give them your version of why you are a narcissistic messed up tosser, or office rumour control will fill in the gaps for them.'

Anneika raised a pool cue in Nathan's direction. Nathan turned around to see Vicky sitting back down with the inspector, carrying their two drinks. Nathan ordered another two beers and joined the women at the pool table. He looked at the blue baize under the bright overhead lights. The blue shimmered and pulsated. He closed his eyes against the glare. The smell of both women's perfumes mixed in his nostrils to form an intense acidic lemon smell, reminiscent of a crammed and cramped traditional sweetshop. Gill lay her hand on his forearm.

'You ok boss?'

'Fine. I necked my second pint too quick. You two play, I'll watch. I would only show you up if I played.'

The women smiled as Anneika placed the white ball on the spot.

'Burnt-out.'

'Sorry Nathan?'

'Bernie is short for burnt-out.'

Gill did not take her shot. 'Go on.'

'I was a bit of a highflyer, believe it or not. I was on a fast-track scheme to make inspector.'

'Not that highflying if you only made it to PC.'

'Thanks, Ann, that was less than helpful. Life conspired to thwart my efforts. I was first on the scene at the murder of a little girl. I dragged what was left of her out of the river Thames.'

'Oh my God!' Ann spoke. 'The girl with the limbs and head missing – like our two boys! That was you?'

'I took it personally and struggled to concentrate on life. I wasn't on the Eve case but took an interest. I tried to distract myself by volunteering for ever more bizarre work.' Nathan looked around at the BNP drinking customers and lowered his voice further. 'I went undercover a few times, without proper support, and lost my way a bit. So, Bernie by name, burnt-out by nature. They retired me, sick.'

Gill put her hand flat on Nathan's chest and pushed him backward until the three colleagues stood together, squashed into the corner. She whispered.

'It was you? You are the copper who shot those three men?'

Nathan shrugged. 'There, I've bonded with the team. Tomorrow, we get back to work solving Eve's case.'

'We aren't on Eve's case, boss.'

As Nathan sat back at the inspector's bar table with Vicky, his phone rang. He pressed *end call*, but the ringing repeated immediately.

'Sorry, I need to get this. Amy. What's up?'

'Where are you?'

'At work.'

'In the pub?'

'Yes, working. What's up?'
'Vicky there?'
'What's up, Amy?'
'That's a yes, then. Just the two of you?'
'Last chance. What do you want?'
'She's gone. Absconded.'
'Who, Polly?'
'Yes Polly, not my bloody mother.'
'Calm down.'
'Don't tell me to calm down. I'm sick of doing this alone. I'm dialling 999.'

'Just wait. I will be home in fifteen minutes. I'll have to walk from the Portsbridge.'

'You've been drinking?'

'Yes. I am in the pub.'

'With Vicky?'

Nathan ended the call, standing to leave. 'Sorry boss. Got to go. It looks like we have an absconder.'

Amy stood looking out of the sitting room window as Nathan walked up the drive.

'Did you get her number?'

'No. The little cow rang my phone like I asked, so she had my number, and I had hers. But she had blocked her number.'

Nathan scoffed. 'Smart kid. And she isn't a cow.'

'Yeah, this is so funny after a gallon of beer with your girlfriend.'

'Did you ring Amanda?'

'Amanda is our supervising social worker. Nothing to do with Polly.'

Nathan was already dialling Amanda's personal mobile. 'Hi Amanda, sorry to trouble you at home. PC Hart speaking. I mean Nathan Hart, sorry.

Their supervising social worker laughed at the end of the line. 'No worries, Nath. Is there a problem?'

'Do you know our young lady, Polly?'

'Not really. I knew we placed her with you. Quite a vulnerable young lady from what I saw. What has happened?'

'You couldn't be a darling and get me her mobile number? I have misplaced it.'

'You have lost her number? Just ask her for it again.'

'No, I have misplaced the child.'

'If she has absconded, Nath, you need to call it in. You don't want her wandering around Portsmouth alone; it will be dark soon. Or worse, wandering around with the wrong people.'

'She isn't missing yet. Amanda, I am just asking for a mobile number.' Amy held out an open notebook for Nathan to read. 'Polly Preti, 4th December 2005. She will be eighteen in a couple of weeks. Her ICS is 246135789.'

'I will call duty and text you back.'

Nathan called from his own mobile, so she would not recognise Amy's number.

'Alright?'

'Polly, Nath here.' The Phone died. Nathan text a message. *'You are not in trouble, Polly. Call me back or I will have to go to the police. Not my decision. You will be eighteen soon. You can cut us all loose in a few weeks and enjoy your life. Don't mess-up now.'*

'Amy, can you drive?'

'Where to?'

'I could hear the Isle of Wight hovercraft in the background. She is on Southsea beach or Ryde beach.'

Amy crawled the beach-buggy along Clarance Esplanade, stopping occasionally at groups of teenagers, for Nathan to jump out and investigate.

'Ok. Back to the hovercraft. If they don't remember Polly boarding, we will go to the fairground. If there is no sign, I will call it in. No, wait. Go to the pier first.'

Amy saw Polly first, sat under the pier on the pebbles, with a young man. They had a disposable barbeque lit, with the remains of sausages, buns, and an empty bottle of cider – all items Amy recognised from her own kitchen. Amy jumped on the brakes, but before she could leave the car, Nathan grabbed her arm.

'Leave her. Let them finish their barbeque.'

'You are joking! She is feral and vulnerable. She comes home with us now, or social can come and get her. I have been worried sick. There were two bodies found just yards away, only a few days ago!'

'Yes, I heard.'

They stopped arguing to watch the couple douse the barbeque with seawater, leaving their rubbish where it lay. Polly walked slowly, alone, to the edge of the sea and reached up to tie a bunch of wildflowers to the ironwork pier legs. She then trailed behind the man as they walked towards the road and the parked beach-buggy, sparkling in red, white, and blue stripes. By the time Polly recognised the car, her young man was only a couple of feet away. Nathan stood leaning against the bonnet.

'Hey.'

The young man looked up at Nathan.

Polly spoke. 'That's them. My foster carers, innit.'

The young man hopped from foot to foot, agitated. 'She ain't done nothing wrong. You can't make her go back with you. It's a free country.'

'That is very true.' Nathan took his phone from his pocket and took a photograph of the young man and of Polly.

'Hey delete that! You can't just take photos of me.'

'Actually, I can. This is a public space and, as you say, a free country. If Polly goes missing again, before her 18th birthday, the police will know where to come looking.'

'I have done nothing wrong! The police can't do me.'

'They could start with *taking away a minor* or *taking away a child in care.*'

'Who are you, a policeman or something?'

Polly cleared her throat. 'Yeah. I think he is, actually. I am not coming back with you, Nath. My life isn't much, but I only have this one. I am staying with Ryan.'

Amy stepped forward. 'Get in the fucking car, Polly! Or I am dialling 999, he's going to prison, and you are going into residential care in the middle of Wales!'

'Calm …'

'Don't you dare, Nath! Get her in the car!'

'She is right, Amy. Who are we to say Polly and Ryan mustn't get all cuddly? We did at their age.'

'What, don't you anymore? Innit.'

'You are not helping, Polly.'

'I am not here to help you, Nath.'

'Where do you live, Ryan?'

'He don't live nowhere.'

'So, it isn't going to happen. I'll tell you what. Why not come home with us now, Polly? In the morning, I will drop you back to Southsea to hang out with Ryan and I will pick you up again early evening.'

'Or what? More threats?'

'I am not threatening you, Polly. I am offering you an option, you decide.'

The young couple looked at each other. Ryan shrugged. Without making eye contact, Polly nodded.

Nathan spoke. 'Can I drop you anywhere, Ryan?'

Polly spoke for Ryan again. 'Eastney, at the black's church.'

Ryan found his voice. Pointing at Amy, he added, 'She knows where I live. I've seen you around the church.'

Amy studied the young man for a moment and shrugged. 'If you say so.'

'No worries. Hop in,' offered Nathan.

'Cool car, for a bitch, innit.'

Around half the detectives and civilian staff were in the office when Nathan arrived on the Saturday morning. Gill and Anneika shared a workstation, agreeing on a strategy to process the London intel, which now poured into the portal. Gill then planned to take the afternoon off and cover the Sunday. Vicky signalled for Nathan to meet in the inspector's empty office.

'All ok?'

'Yep.'

'The urchin?'

'Yep. All good.'

'The wife?'

'Yep. All good.'

'You?'

'Yep. All good.'

'Third world debt?'

'Yep. All good.'

Vicky stared at Nathan across the desk. Saturday morning dress down comprised a knitted crop-tank over three-quarter length red skinny jeans. She wore polished Dr Martin boots with stripy socks pulled halfway up her calves. Nathan raised his look to keep eye contact and to avoid staring at Vicky's figure.

'It must be hard to stare at my eyes without blinking. Are your eyeballs drying out?'

'I have made my decision.'

'Seriously. Are you back too soon?'

'Seriously, all is good.'

'There is nothing wrong with continuing to ask for support. This is early days. No man is an island.'

'John Donne.'

'Who?'

'Who is our guy looking at the autopsies?'

'You are much greyer than a couple of years ago.'

'Three years ago. Who is processing the autopsies?'

'Why, what have you got?'

'You believe the corpses have only been in the U.K. for the maximum of a couple of days before death, based on food traces found in the stomach and gut.'

'Yes. Traces of river clay and vegetation are consistent with having foraged for food along a fast-flowing river located in the Northeast of Africa. Also, traces of DNA and bone residue consistent with bush food found in that area, probably from the guinea-fowl family and a type of rare, or at least shy, deer.'

'And then they were flown to the U.K. and dumped in the Solent before that food and stomach contents were processed – digested or excreted?'

'We are not extrapolating that, no. They were malnourished. We do not yet know how they journeyed here. The remains …'

'Vicky. We need to give these humans a name. They are people.'

'What are you thinking?'

'Above my pay grade, Vicky. Something from the Old Testament, perhaps – appropriate for all Abrahamics. I don't know – Aaron and Asher. Cain and Abel. But not, corpse and remains.'

'Sodom and Gomorrah?'

Nathan dropped his chin to his chest.

'Nathan, I am sorry. Gallows humour. Your little girl in London was Eve. How about Levi and Luke?'

Nathan nodded. 'Yeah, whatever.'

'Did you talk to Amy?'

'About?'

'You were going to come up with a list of elders and contacts from the Eastern African community here in Portsmouth.'

'No, I wasn't.'

'You should include some families containing young men. What about some of your UASC fostered kids?'

'They have been through enough already.'

'The golden hour has long gone. The golden week is fast ending. You are on this team for a reason, Nath. We really need your help. We need your local knowledge of Africans here in Portsmouth. We need your forensic knowledge of the Eve case. We need your powers of intel analysis. No pressure. You will have surmised, being a detective and all that, that you only got this opportunity because of Ted and me. I mean, you are toxic, after all.'

'That is very kind of you to say. I have had a couple of dozen UASC young men showering, eating, and sleeping in my house for a couple of days each. I was never on the Eve case – on Eve's case. You are providing no robust intel worthy of analysis. Think on.

'As I am apparently not allowed full access to your team, then please ask your autopsy lead to request further tests on the stomach contents. Get them to run a sample through a radio spectrometer. And tell them to talk to the Met.'

'What are we looking for?'

'Anything worth looking at. I am not trying to make evidence fit – go where the evidence takes you, serg.'

'Thank you for the lesson in basic policing, Police Constable retired. Don't turn Levi and Luke into Eve, Nath.'

'Thank you for the lesson in basic policing, sergeant.'

'Would it help if Ted and I spoke to your Amy directly about doing some work around her contacts with the community?'

Nathan scoffed. 'You had better take a taser, if you intend turning up at our door.'

Anneika and Gill sat in a huddle around a single screen. Neither looking at the image, but instead staring at each other as they whispered.

'During training, fast tracks like me have in-depth ethics training. We had a lesson called *Officer H.*'

'Based on Nathan?'

'Just listen, Ann. Obviously, we are not told names. *Officer H* was a total clusterfuck. He was also a fast track; destined for CID, promotion, and greatness. He was inexperienced, from the provinces, dead keen. Later, the Met seconded him for undercover work because he was from out of town. *Officer H* had fished a child's body from the Thames.'

'Eve.'

'I am telling you what we were told. Yes, obviously it was Eve, but we weren't told that. *Officer H* was with a young woman who helped to pull the body to the edge. One detail stuck in my mind: *Officer H*'s hand squished into the putrefying flesh under the child's arm. It messed up the copper, more than it did the girlfriend.

'We were told this story by an inspector involved in the fallout. He used no notes, like he was telling a class of tots a story. He was self-critical. The met used *H*, because the experience with the little body had numbed him, seemingly.'

'What fallout?'

'The Met were close to closing down a seriously big Romanian crime syndicate. They had fingers in every pie – trafficking, sex, drugs, rock 'n roll. *Officer H* was only a spotter, ready on the inside for when the swoop happened. The day before the planned operation, *Officer H* would not have known the exact timing, he was drinking Tuica with three top gangsters. They had two young Romanian women, who thought they had been trafficked to work in the beauty industry, starting off in nail bars. However, they were destined for the sex trade. As part of the induction to their new life, the three men gang raped the girls. One girl fought back so bravely, she later died of the injuries inflicted by the men.

'*Officer H* had no comms. No radio and no phone. Later, under caution, he said he was scared to intervene should it jeopardise the operation. He also feared for his own safety. He witnessed the girl's rape and violent attack. A gangster told *Officer H* he was to take part. *Officer H* agreed, saying he needed cocaine first from his car. He returned with his Glock 26 personal protection firearm, with ten rounds in the magazine. He shot each gangster once in the chest, and once in the head.'

'Oh my God!'

'With no robust witness statements, *Officer H* pleaded the self-defence of himself and the girls. When the armed unit arrived, following reports of the gunshots, they found *Officer H* calmly sat in the middle of the floor, cradling the dying girl and holding a T-shirt against her broken head. He had made his firearm safe and left it, slide back and magazine out, on a table.'

'The inspector taking the lesson talked much about the lack of support and checks the Met gave *H,* following Eve and his work undercover. He was also critical of the Met failing to bring charges against *H*. The Met investigated and found he acted lawfully. They referred themselves to the Independent Police

Complaints Commission, who found no evidence of misconduct. A file was prepared, but the Crown Prosecution Service agreed there was no evidence to prosecute.

'The lecturing inspector had another angle of interest regarding ethics. *H* had formed a relationship with a woman associated with the gang. Her trial fell apart when she argued their sex could not be consensual, because she did not know who she was really consenting to have sex with. She claimed *H* groomed and entrapped her. They deported her back to Romania to face other lesser charges at home.'

'Surely they wouldn't have Nathan back as a civilian; is it definitely him?'

'When I sat the lesson *Officer H*, the inspector said *H* remained in service back on his own patch, away from London. The inspector knew *H* had moved to Intel and a desk job and had long periods of time away sick. If the target is non-cooperative and plays the system, it can take a long time to forcefully retire them – especially as he had the Met, the IPCC, and the CPS saying he was not guilty of a crime or misconduct. You and I might not be guilty of a crime, but Nathan Hart has three of the largest prosecuting agencies in the world saying *he* is not guilty. I haven't been in Portsmouth long enough, but I bet one of the old plods in the team will confirm it. We might have to buy a round in the Portsbridge and laugh at their sick, sexist jokes, but I am sure they will confirm it. And he didn't deny it yesterday when I confronted him in the pub.'

'Confronted who?'

Both women jumped at Nathan's voice behind them.

'A boy Nath. Poor Gill here always has boys sniffing around. Not surprising with those eyes the size of a Disney princess's.'

'If you need more work, just shout. In the meantime, get on with it, or stop taking the overtime payments.'

'Bully.' Anneika mumbled as she moved back to her desk.

'What did you say?'

'You heard Nath. Don't take it out on Gill, just because you roll in with a hangover, again.'

Nathan fell back into his chair, closing his eyes. 'I am not hungover. You two just give me migraine.'

Nathan still had his eyes closed when he heard a gentle tap on his desk. He watched Gill place a glass of water and a strip of extra-strength Ibuprofen in front of him. He took her wrist.

'Sorry Gill. I've a bit on. I will be fine once I see results.'

'Once *we* see results, boss.'

Nathan nodded. Gill brought her hand, still held around the wrist, to his shoulder.

'They are 400mg, only take one. You shouldn't have a headache for three days solid. See the doctor.'

'Yeah, maybe. Thanks.' Nathan released her wrist, popped four tablets from the foil and swallowed without water. 'Anyone look at the traffic data?'

'Nothing yet, boss.' Gill turned her chair, so she sat at the end of Nathan's desk. 'Portsmouth is a very dense city. All the camera reports show the cars overlapping, especially around Southsea seafront. But it would be stranger if they didn't. Is the guv thinking the deaths actually happened at the pier? Surely it happened elsewhere, and the bodies just washed up at the pier.'

'If I was a detective, and I am no longer, I would want to see who turned up at the pier shortly after we found the boys. But I am not a detective and anyway, the *perp* probably caught the bus.'

'Where's madam?'

'Out with Loverboy, Nath. I gave her money for the bus. She probably spent it on fags for Ryan.'

'Good girl.'

'What? Necking in public, absconding, and lying!'

'I meant you are a good girl, Amy. Trusting Polly with the bus fare, and to behave herself, will be a big thing for her.'

'Even though I don't trust her, and she thinks I'm a bitch?'

'Especially because you don't trust her, and you *are* a bitch.'

Amy slapped his chest with the flat of her hand, followed up with a hug. Nathan lent back against the kitchen counter, cradling his wife against his chest, rocking slowly from side to side.

'Talking of bitches, was Vicky in the office today?'

'Are you going to ask me the same question every day?'

'Yes. Just the two of you?'

'No, of course not. Half the team was in. It isn't like *Morse* where people disappear to the theatre or the pub halfway through a murder investigation.'

'The Portsbridge doesn't count?'

'That was work. We all get drunk, form two teams with the local BNP chapter and vote on who to arrest next.'

'Any closer?'

'Nothing, absolutely nothing. Pathetic.'

'Have they made a connection to Eve?'

'Yes. But they need to get closer to the Met. We haven't got time to invent the wheel again, from scratch. Hopefully, by Monday we will have something to look at.'

'They have you, Nath. A walking Eve encyclopaedia.'

'They have asked me to do something. Actually, they want our help. Yours and mine.'

'*They* being Vicky? Well, you normally do exactly what she tells you to do. What instructions have you for me today? Make-up her bed?'

'I don't suppose you will meet with Vicky and Ted Dunbar?'

'No! Why should I? Bloody nerve!'

'Because of Luke and Levi. I can't let this go the way of Eve.'

'Luke and Levi? You have given the boys a name? Come here.' Amy pulled herself into a hug again.

'Vicky never loved you as much as I do.'

'I know all that, Amy.'

'And I am a better shag.'

Nathan gave his wife a reassuring squeeze.

'This is where you say *yes*, Nathan!'

'Yes, Nathan.'

Amy slapped her husband's chest again, harder.

Amy rolled over and snuggled against her husband's bare chest.

'See. There is nothing wrong with your performance. Last night *and* this morning – you stallion. The problem is you are worrying about a problem which doesn't exist. And then you talk yourself into that problem; psychosomatic.'

'Not now Amy. This is not the best time to discuss my disfunctions.'

'Apparently, it never is a good time.'

'I'll get the coffee.'

'I will get up with you. I heard Polly padding around.'

'Padding like a baby elephant. How does eight-stone of skin and bones make so much noise?'

'And she didn't wash her hands between flushing and leaving the bathroom.'

'Let it go Amy. She will accuse you of harassment in her report, especially as you've been squealing all night and all morning.'

'I have not! I was as quiet as a mouse. I even bit down hard to keep silent.'

'Yes, I noticed.' Nathan rubbed a bite on his shoulder. 'A *were-mouse* howling at a cheesy moon, perhaps. Pull you bottoms on, don't forget it was a female teacher she reported.'

Dressed in black jeans and a faded blue crewneck sweatshirt, Nathan leant back against the kitchen counter opposite his wife, a favourite spot of Nathan's close to the coffee machine. Polly walked into the room, barely acknowledging them. She pushed against Amy to make room to open the fridge door. Amy went to move out of her way, but Nathan gestured for Amy to hold her ground, squashed into the counter. Polly took a plastic bottle of milk from the fridge, discarded the top onto the counter, and turned to face Nathan. Leaving the fridge door open, she took a noisy slurp of milk directly from the bottle.

'I like our family breakfast times together, innit.'

'So do we, Polly. How are you doing remembering to wear your dressing gown downstairs?'

Polly shrugged. 'What are we all doing today? Going tats? Church?'

'I am going to work,' answered Nathan.

'On a Sunday?'

'I am going to church, Polly. If you would like to come with me,' offered Amy.

Amy and Nathan waited for a scoff of derision. Instead, Polly squashed further against Amy's side before answering.

'Which church?'

'The Sudanese Interior Baptist Church in Eastney, near where we dropped Ryan on Friday. It is great fun. Happy-clappy as Nath calls it. You up for it?'

Polly shrugged. 'Might as well. I want to sing a song for the two black kids.'

'The lads found under the pier?' Nathan tried to ask casually, without seeming to show too much interest.

'They didn't have heads, innit.'

'What makes you say that?'

'Everyone knows, Nath. You are so out of touch.'

'What else do you know?'

Polly shrugged. 'It will be gangs. Drugs and knives. You think I am naïve and vulnerable. You have no idea how difficult it is for kids like me and Ryan to stay away from the gangs. If it wasn't for guys like you two and Dakari Demarcus, we could be the ones feeding fish in canoe lake, with our heads cut off.'

For the first time since arriving on Friday, Polly blushed deeply. She squashed even closer to Amy. Looking at the floor, she continued.

'Why do you only do emergency caring, Nath? Why not have a kid stay for like ten weeks or something?'

'It is what we do, Polly. Other carers do other things, we do emergency out of hours. That is how the police could bring you to us.'

'It's not just because you don't like me?'

'No!' Amy and Nathan answered together.

Amy continued. 'Of course not, Polly, you are lovely. We aren't allowed to have favourites, but if we were allowed, you would be our most favourite young person, ever.'

Amy pulled Polly into an *approved* side hug, but Polly turned to return a full-frontal hug. Nathan smiled at Amy's use of one of his catch-all phrases; allowing the young person to feel loved without putting them on the spot.

As usual, Amy walked Nathan to his car. They were enjoying an unseasonably warm spell; a warm early autumn day greeted the couple. She pushed him back against his car.

'Thanks again tiger, you can come again.'

'Have a nice girlie day. Say hi to God,' Nathan responded.

'Is that why you told me not to move out of Polly's way?'

'Yeah, her jostling you by the fridge was probably the closest thing to a parental cuddle she has had in …, well, ever.'

'I know what you are thinking, Nath. We need to talk about it first. Alone.'

'No, I am thinking nothing. We do emergency out of hours, that is what we do. There is one thing though: I made an appointment to see Rachel tomorrow. Nothing to worry about.

'Why? You wouldn't go to the doctor with a severed head! Sorry. I didn't mean …'

'It's nothing. Honest.'

Chapter Four

Monday morning briefings were longer than other weekday briefings; with the detectives catching up and sharing any progress made over the weekend. The detective chief inspector sat in the meeting to help focus the team. The inspector wrapped up as Nathan raised his hand.

'May I ask about the autopsy and the postmortem journey of Levi and Luke, guv?'

The inspector glanced nervously at his sergeant, not wanting the maverick civilian disrespecting him in front of the DCI.

'Ok Bernie, if your contribution is relative to your civilian role as intel analyst.'

'It is relevant to the investigation of the murder of two children, sir.'

'I said yes, Bernie, now get on with it. We are all busy, not just you.'

Nathan spun around to face the room, his back turned towards Vicky, the inspector, and the DCI.

'Who is the lead liaison officer for the autopsy and coroner, sir?' Although seemingly addressing the inspector, Nathan was obviously directing the question directly to the team.

A young detective constable raised his hand and stood. 'DC Steve Mallick, Mr Hart. I have updated the system with all the details.'

'You have done a good job, Steve. You set a good example for some of these old plods.' A few of the older detectives shot glances between each other and the listening DCI. 'I need some follow-up from these guys around you. Would you be able to summarise, please?'

The young DC glanced towards the inspector, who nodded in response.

'Ok. Yes Mr Hart. We found the two bodies chained together and caught in the ironwork of Southsea Pier. We have had two reports from the pathologist. The second report has only just arrived on my desk and includes the results of a radio spectrometer scan.' The DC looked a little nervous, with the entire room staring back at him. 'Um, inspector, I visited the oceanography faculty at Solent University on Friday afternoon. May I include the results of that discussion? I think the information will be useful for the entire team. I was going to brief skip, first.' The inspector nodded again. Vicky raised a reassuring hand to show she was not offended by him reporting to the team directly, before to herself.

'Ok. Yes Mr Hart. As I was saying. We now believe the two boys are post-pubescent. The pathologist has put a nominal age of seventeen, on both boys, maybe six months younger, or up to a year older. Not directly related. Both boys are male.' The audience laughed, and the DC blushed deeply. 'Obviously. DNA confirms the boys are of Northeastern African heritage, with traces of Arab genetics, which is common in that region. The pathologist states there is an 80 per cent likelihood the boys, or at least their parents, are from Sudan or an adjoining country.

'We discovered the bodies on this previous Sunday, 17th September. The boys likely died within a day or so before being dumped in the sea. The bodies were in the water for around ten days before being discovered. This would suggest the boys died on or around Tuesday 5th September, and dumped in the Solent around Thursday 7th. The pathologist believes both boys died of a single cut to the throat. Each throat, obviously.' His blush deepened. 'The hands, feet, and heads were removed postmortem.'

'How was the cut applied to the throats?'

'That section of throat is missing, Mr Hart. The pathologist has identified the cause of death by how the lungs filled with arterial blood. It would suggest the murderer had some knowledge, like a surgeon or butcher, as asphyxiation did not cause death - had the trachea been crudely severed, which would have likely filled the lungs with a bloody froth. Looking at the toxicology report, the boys were likely conscious during their ordeal.'

'The spectrometer results?'

'The initial autopsy report suggested the boys had digested river clay, consistent with foraging along the banks of a river. Particles from bush food, small deer and game birds, are present. Silicate contents and other elements present would suggest the river ran through land in the Northeast of Africa, away from the coast where soils contain prehistoric particles of sea animals, from when the seas were higher than they are today. But, and this is a big and important *but*, the spectrometer reveals significant levels of gold, silver, and platinum – which are not found naturally in those concentrations.' The audience had long since fallen silent, concentrating on the DC's impromptu presentation.

Nathan spoke again. 'Anything else in the stomach to suggest how long they have been in this country, or since leaving Africa?'

'Yes and no, Mr Hart. The boys were malnourished, and no other *foods* were present. However, the wall of the intestine, specifically the colon, and also the rectum, showed Pollyps and other attributes which might suggest the boys normally ate quantities of processed meats. The pathologist was at pains to clarify processed meat is only one possible factor, or contributing factor, but it would be quite a coincidence for two unrelated young men to show similar signs of having had the same diet. In my report, sir,' the DC glanced towards the inspector and back to Nathan, 'I am suggesting they have been enjoying a western, possibly fast food, diet for one year or more.'

'You said they were dumped in the Solent. They were *found* in the Solent, but presumably they could have been dumped in a river or out at sea?'

'Unlikely, Mr Hart. The Solent used to be a river valley before my time.' The meeting laughed again. Even the DCI managed a thin smile. 'Originally the

Solent was a stretch of the river Frome, a river valley. As the weighted bodies bounced along the seabed, they collected traces of minerals, including Purbeck Ball Clay containing kaolinite found in the Solent from its previous river incarnation. This is not found in the English Channel - nor in freshwater rivers, or Southampton Water. Annelida, or sea worms, moved into the opened cavity of the boys, of the sub-species found in inshore waters, not the English Channel.

'Speaking with a lovely oceanographer from the university on Friday, I gave her the dates, locations, and sample information the pathologist had reported. She believes, with a certainty slightly better than fifty per cent, that the boys were dropped into the sea east of the pier, but not further east than Hayling Island. Apparently, we have more than our fair share of tides in the Solent – four daily tides instead of two, as any angler here might know. Not because the Isle of Wight creates two openings, as you may have heard rumoured, but because the Solent essentially runs downhill, west to east. This creates relatively small tides along the south coast of Portsea Island – compared with Hayling Island, Isle of Wight, and New Forest coasts. My new friend at Solent Uni suggests the bodies would have caught in a lazy series of vortex, or mini doldrums, offshore from Portsea Island, which would prevent the boys washing into the English Channel with the tide. The pier acted as a strainer, snagging the boys before they would have eventually continued west and then out to sea past the Needles.

Nathan stood. 'You are the detectives, not me. So, you don't need me to explain what you just heard. Levi and Luke were in this country or Europe for over a year. They were murdered a week last Tuesday and dumped in the sea a week last Thursday between Southsea and Hayling Island. Thank you, Steve.'

The audience clapped as the young DC took a bow and sat, his blush now crimson.

'Rachel, thank you for seeing me at such short notice. I only have a few minutes; I have shed loads on at work.'

'No Nathan. This is where I tell you how I flipped my diary upside down to fit you in, and that you must now accommodate my limited availability.'

Nathan laughed and shrugged. 'Whatever.'

'You are back at work?'

'Consulting at Cosham nick.'

'Really? I am surprised they will have you back.'

Nathan laughed again. 'Thank you for the vote of confidence.'

'Working with your ... previous contact?'

'Yes.'

'Ah, right. I suppose that makes more sense. And Amy happy with that?'

'Not especially. Look, there is something specific I want to put past you, doctor.'

53

'Doctor now, is it? This is obviously bigger than your schoolboy smirk suggests. Go on.' Rachel Warr leant forward and began tapping on her computer.

'I have a headache.'

'So do I. Go on.'

'Solid. For three weeks.'

'Stress about starting the new job?'

'It started before I knew about the new job.'

'Describe it.'

'It goes from a dull thud all over to a sharp pain here.' Nathan stroked a line from the crown of his head to his nape, and again from ear to ear across the back of his head.

'Perhaps you just have a sore finger. Does paracetamol help?'

'Not really. Then I have migraines. I have never had those before.'

Rachel continued to tap her keyboard. 'That it?'

'Yep. Head related.'

'Go on.'

'I can't get it up.'

'You! You can't get an erection? Blimey. When you have a headache?'

'Not up at all. Not without Viagra. And then not always.'

'Eating, sleeping, ok? Exercise?'

'Yeah. My stools are a little ... loose.'

'Drinking?'

'Yeah.'

'I meant are you drinking alcohol?'

'Yes. Ten to fifteen units.'

'Well, that is better than when we met last.'

'Met in the pub?'

'No, I meant when I last saw you here.'

'Um, that is fifteen units - per day.'

'Ah. Overuse of prescription drugs?'

'A little. But much more under control. Having a headache doesn't help.'

'Cocaine?'

'No. It was down to nearly nothing. Now it is nothing – we have random tests at work.'

'Still smell hallucinations?'

'Worse than before. I smell things all the time. I can smell incredibly concentrated fly spray at this moment. Sometimes other smells start them off, sometimes they are random. I can't wear aftershave or deodorant. It is like a trigger.'

'Yeah, I noticed.' Rachel smiled. She looked up as he spoke.

'One other thing. I am having problems with vision. Whites go blue sometimes. Your skirt looks blue.'

'It is blue. Go on.'

'Colours are vivid, sometimes pulsing. Seemingly unrelated to the headache timings.'

'Ok. Probably nothing. Let's start some tests.'

'What does your computer say?'

'It is only a tool. I went to medical school, you know.'

'And what does it say to a medical doctor, doctor?'

Rachel let out a long sigh. 'Ok. Pregnant – unlikely. Liver disease – more likely. Sycosis – almost certain. Let's run some tests.'

'Is that it, Rachel?'

'Have you been going to Doctor Google behind my back? Ok, also brain tumour. But not many people have brain tumours. Don't fret.'

'Not many people with my symptoms?'

'Let's run those tests. I should really feel your nuts, and stick a finger up your bum, but I could never look Amy in the eye again. I'll make a note for the hospital to do all that. I believe they have a new student nurse. Apparently, he plays rugby, has poor personal hygiene and thick fingers. Look Nathan, well done for coming in. You really mustn't worry.'

'Rugby league? Or rugby union?'

'Amy. Good to see you. Thank you for seeing me. We really appreciate this.'

'*We* as in you and my husband?'

'I meant *we* as in the force. Ted and me.'

'Where is Ted?'

'He's a busy man, Amy.'

Vicky continued to stand; arm outstretched for a handshake. Amy took a long slug of pinot from a large glass. Eventually, she reluctantly returned the handshake. Vicky sat in the adjacent chair, still holding her hand.

'Nath, grab me a coke and another drink for Amy.'

'Yes, Nath, give us both what we want.'

Amy accidentally sent spittle over Vicky's hand. Vicky pretended not to notice.

'Sorry about the venue. I know you and my husband normally drink in the Portsbridge. I would just prefer we meet on neutral ground.'

'Understood Amy. I like the Manor House Pub. Thanks again for meeting.'

Nathan returned with the drinks and sat next to Vicky, facing his wife as he would normally sit in an interview. A moment later, he moved to sit next to Amy, before changing to a neutral stool.

'Oh, for God's sake, sit still, Nath. How can I help, Vicky?'

'Nathan has told me about the amazing work you do with the Unaccompanied Asylum-Seeking Children.'

'I am pleased to hear he is keeping you updated about our private family life.'

'You may have seen the news about the two children washed up on Southsea beach.'

'Levi and Luke. Yes, Nath tells me everything that you both are up to.'

'They are probably Northeastern African, maybe Sudanese, where some of your foster kids are from.'

'Really? I am glad you explained all that to me, but I probably know more about my foster kids than you do.'

'Nath, Nathan, says you both network with people from the African community in Portsmouth and with professionals working with the children. He said you probably do most of the networking.'

'Yes, I try to be a good wife and take my share of the load; there is more to a loving relationship than just sex. I also chase vulnerable kids around our city whilst he buys your beer in the Portsbridge. Are you still fond of Goblin?'

'Bear with me, Amy. I would be so grateful if you could come up with a few names of people, within the professional or African communities, who may have any background information to give us, or any pointers of whom to talk with. I am not suggesting they may have been involved with, or even know, these two victims …'

'Levi and Luke, you mean?'

'Yes. Just anyone who can help us piece together any background to the puzzle. More than that, we hope you will inch-open the door, so we have an introduction and maybe a little background to the contacts. You won't have to see me again; I really understand. Nathan has a young officer working for him. We could make her your contact.'

'Has he really? A young policewoman working for him. Well, that is something he forgot to mention.'

Vicky drove her unmarked Mazda Six back to Cosham police station, where a floor was turned over to the incident room.

'She looked hot.'

'She always looks hot. Although that may have been partly for your benefit, today.'

'I am a detective, a woman, and an ex-mistress of her husband's. But thanks for explaining that to me. I bet she is all over you at the moment. Marking her territory. I saw the hicky under your crewneck yesterday.'

'Yeah, something like that.'

'No need to thank me. You are welcome. Where did you disappear to after the briefing?'

'Private.'

'You are taking time off already? You just had three years off. You've only been back five days.'

'I had a doctor's appointment.'

Waiting to turn right into the police station, Vicky took a long moment to study her colleague before a car flashed her across the road.

'I have never really understood you, Nath, and I am not looking to now. But do me a favour, please. Stop delaying, grab Gill, and get her over to Amy. I want to dig around in the community, but all we are doing now is being blanked by the African bookshop and totally blanked by the illegal immigrants working in that African restaurant on Albert Road. The *community* is not being very forthcoming.'

'The *African Bookshop* is Namibian, the *African Restaurant* is Jamaican, and the *community* is probably feeling a little let down by Portsmouth's finest.'

'Exactly Nath. Have Amy get us in.'

'Amy, this is PC Gill Walker.'

Gill flashed her badge as Amy nodded without looking at it.

'Come in, officer.'

'Please call me Gill, Mrs Hart.'

'Is that what my husband calls you?'

'Um, well, yes. It is my name.'

Amy scoffed. 'Sorry. I am just feeling grumpy. Come on through. Your detective sergeant threatened to have me arrested if I didn't squeal on all my black friends. You must be the good-cop half of the team.'

Gill laughed. 'Damn! You have us sussed.'

Nathan made coffee as the women sat next to each other at the dining table. Gill opened her iPad.

'When you are ready, Mrs Hart, we can fill in these contacts forms together.'

'Please, call me Amy. I can complete the forms with you, but I have already done this in preparation.'

Amy opened a spreadsheet on her laptop. Gill flicked down the document.

'This is absolutely perfect, Amy. If you email me this - job done!'

'I am afraid most of the names are not African. There is a significant proportion of black kids fostered, but very few black foster carers.'

'Sounds like the police world, Amy.'

'I have included names of carers I believe have or had Unaccompanied Asylum-Seeking Children from Sudan. I have included a couple of social workers with Northeastern African heritage, but I think all second generation. Look, I have done my best, but I really don't think this will help much.'

'Would you mind if we mention you when making contact?'

'No problem.'

'It is a bit like selling double glazing. A recommendation makes such a tremendous difference.'

Nathan placed the coffees on the table and ran down the list from over the women's shoulders.

'May I add a couple?'

'*Sure.*' Both women answered together.

'That Jesus botherer of yours. He is an absolute definite.'

'I am not sure …'

'And your mate from *PCiCN*.'

'Obviously, if I thought they were relevant …'

'Sorry,' interrupted Gill, 'are you two talking in code?'

'Amy's church is an African Baptist Church. And she is chummy with the chattering classes of the Portsmouth Children in Care Network. A Facebook group which covers all foster carers, including those with UASC kids. The busybody who runs it is everybody's friend. I don't know if he has ever taken Unaccompanied Asylum-Seeking Children himself, but he will certainly know everyone who ever has. And he'll probably know if any of them have ever sneezed in Tesco.'

'Amy?'

'I don't know why you just didn't do the list yourself, Nath. Obviously, my efforts are not good enough.'

Amy tapped on the laptop, adding contact details and notes for two additional names, Robert Kitty PCiCN and Rev Daniel Abimbola.

'Do you ever read your own reports, Nath?'

'I have been known to, Vicky.'

'Ann has had the shortlist of repeat referrals highlighted against Amy's list of contacts.'

'Yes, I know. And?'

'Two names cross reference. Robert Kitty and Daniel Abimbola. Let's go say hello.'

'I am not surprised. Robert is a charismatic self-appointed leader of the fostering network, and Dan is our righteous conduit directly to the Sudanese God who sits in the clouds above Africa, presiding over war and famine. Good luck.'

'You are coming with me. Grab your jacket.'

'No Vicky. I am a civilian bean counter. Take a DC.'

'I want you along to collate any intel and throw it straight into the pot.'

'Take Gill.'

'No, Nath, I am taking you. You know these guys.'

'That doesn't mean they like me.'

'Nobody likes you, Nath. I'll drive. We can park at the church and take the Hayling ferry to Mr Kitty's. I also want to visit the local Iman, as we are having a *God Day*.'

Nathan trotted next to Vicky as she powered down the stairs to the carpark.

'Not a problem seeing the Imam, serg. But unlikely to be of much help.'

'How so?'

'The boys are not Muslim, as I am sure you realised. I believe all three of Portsmouth's imams are Bangladeshi. I think there might still be an African Arab Imam at the madrasa and spiritual centre near Titchfield; possibly Egyptian.'

Vicky stayed silent until they both sat in her parked car, seatbelts on.

'Ok, Sherlock, how do I realise Luke and Levi are not Muslim?'

'Lemon-entry, dear Watson.' Nathan gestured to a bright yellow fire exit across the carpark.

Vicky laughed, squeezing Nathan's thigh.

'Oh dear, don't make me remember why I fell for you. Not Muslim?'

'Not circumcised. And a diet of processed meats, presumably hams and bacon. You'd struggle to find halal bacon, even in Portsmouth.'

'Damn! You are good.'

'That's what Amy said yesterday morning.'

'Before or after she scratched your back and bit your shoulder – for *everyone* to see? Can you add the *probable non-Muslim* to the boy's profiles, please?'

'Already done, serg.'

'Damn! You are good.'

The colleagues made eye contact, both laughed.

Vicky introduced herself and Nathan to the Reverend Abimbola. He checked Vicky's badge and noted down her warrant card number, gesturing to chairs facing his desk.

'Thank you for seeing us …'

'You should call me Reverend, or Minister.'

'Thank you, Minister. I believe you know Nathan Hart.'

Nathan sat in silence as the minister studied him.

'Yes. But I am sorry Mr Hart.'

'My wife is one of your flock, Mr Abimbola. Unless it's raining, then she visits the God around the corner in Drayton Baptist church. We have met.'

The minister gave a genuine laugh. 'There is only one God, Mr Hart.'

'I think the United Nations recognise over 18000 Gods, over which people around the world persecute each other. I think 80 per cent of believers believe in one or more of fifteen of those gods. However you count them, there appears to be more than just your one.'

The minister stopped laughing, his smile now fixed and false.

'You must come to a few services with your wife, Mr Hart. I have found it impossible for people to remain sceptical of the Almighty God once exposed to his love and the love of his church.'

'His church? I thought the Jews were his chosen people. If Judaism was good enough for Jesus, I am surprised it is not good enough for you, Mr Abimbola.'

'We must talk some more on this subject, Mr Hart. You may not have seen the light yet, but I cannot believe you will turn your face from our Lord forever. Tell me something, Mr Hart, when you are gripping that cliff by your fingertips, about to crash to your death, will you accept God Almighty and cry out for his love and forgiveness? Will you realise your sinful life has been empty and wasted?'

'Probably, yes. And you Mr Abimbola? As you hit the ground, will you despair when you realise there is no God? Will you see your pious work as a waste?'

'Perhaps we will not agree today, Mr Hart. For myself, I cannot imagine how you cannot believe in … something.'

'You believe in one God and denounce the other 17999 gods. I just don't believe in all 18000 gods. Perhaps we are more similar than you realise, Mr Abimbola. I just believe in one God less than you.'

Vicky let the silence hang between the men for a long moment before clearing her throat.

'Interesting as this is, gentlemen, may I focus us on the reason we have asked to see you, Minister? You will have heard that the two bodies found on Southsea beach are those of young men of African descent, probably Sudanese. We are looking to fully engage the African community here in Portsmouth to help identify these victims. And so, Minister,' Vicky shrugged, 'here we are.'

'We are hearing the poor boys were mutilated.'

'We are planning to hold a press conference later today, Minister, to share what we know.'

The minister slowly nodded. 'Yesterday we held a special service to pray for the souls of these poor children and to pray for any perpetrator of such an awful crime, to find the strength to make themselves known to the police and beg the Lord for forgiveness.

'The congregation and we at the church spoke extensively about this appalling situation yesterday. I do not believe any of the congregation knows any details of the crime, nor the identity of the poor children. If anyone reveals anything, I will, of course, urge them to contact the authorities.'

'You have a young man called Ryan staying here with you, Mr Abimbola?'

'Ryan? Yes, we do. Ah yes, Mr Hart, you must be related to Amy Hart, who brought young Ryan's sweetheart to church yesterday.'

'Amy is my wife.'

'Your wife? But …,' the minister trailed off.

'Do you provide accommodation and support to Ryan, and presumably other young people?'

'We do Mr Hart.'

'Can we speak with the group of young people? Perhaps they will have heard something, anything.'

'Again, Mr Hart, I have already spoken with our youth minister about this very topic. To answer your question though, yes, I can ask the minister to invite any young people staying to meet you.

Vicky and Nathan left the car at the church, walking the short distance to the Hayling Island ferry slipway.
'Have you been on one of those people-management courses? *We are almost the same, vicar. I just believe in one less God than you do.* That was going to get him on board, wasn't it?'
'Whatever.'
'I really don't know why I brought you along.'
'Me neither, serg.'
Vicky took a couple of steps along the slipway, keeping her back turned towards Nathan. He watched as her shoulders heaved silently in suppressed laughter.
'Perhaps it is because I still make you laugh, serg.'
Vicky laughed out loud, causing smiling ferry passengers to turn and watch the couple.

Robert Kitty's house stood a short walk along the shoreline from the Hayling Island ferry dock.
'We should search the whole coastline serg, from Hayling, along Eastney, to Southsea.'
'Looking for what exactly, Nath?'
'How Luke and Levi got themselves into the sea, for a start.'
Vicky stopped to scan the miles of coast. 'Yeah. I will talk to Ted. Here we are.'

Robert Kitty's house stood on a large, well-kept plot backing on to where Langston Harbour opens onto the Eastern edge of the Solent. The garden reminded Nathan of his own, with a similar mix of standard specimens, punctuated by clumps of bright annuals and perennials. The house itself looked bright and well maintained.

'Odd looking house.'

'It is a prefab bungalow. Postwar to house the masses of families blitzed out of Portsmouth and the boom of babies who followed. These old temporaries are way past their best before date, the plot is worth a lot more than the house.'

The door opened by a man in his mid-fifties. He stood lean and tall, weathered, and outdoorsy. Vicky held up her badge.

'Mr Kitty?'

'Hello, yes.' Kitty smiled at Vicky, barely acknowledging her warrant card.'

'And my colleague Nathan Hart.'

The smile dropped from Kitty's face as he recoiled.

'Yes. Nathan! How are you keeping? We have met. You are a PCiCN member and your wife …'

'Amy.'

'Of course, Amy. I have a terrible memory for names, Nathan. Come in, come in. Is everything ok? Amy ok?'

'As far as I know, Mr Kitty.'

'Bert, please Nathan. We are like old friends.'

'Yeah.' Nathan scoffed.

Nathan and Vicky glanced at each other and back at Kitty.

'We wanted a quick word about your connections with foster children and carers, Mr Kitty.'

'Ah yes, officer. Of course. Who has been up to what this time? I am afraid I am not permitted to discuss individuals in any detail. I am sure you will understand.'

Nathan replied. 'In your capacity as a Facebook page administrator, Bert?'

Kitty swallowed hard. 'Well, you know. How can I help?'

Kitty led the way to a narrow cedar conservatory, facing west over his back garden and Langston Harbour, towards Portsea Island and the island city of Portsmouth. Nathan picked up a plaster letter *L* from the word *Love* rested against the conservatory window.

'You can paint these letters. My wife has filled our house with them, painted from blood red to baby blue.'

'Yes. I must. They are a present from my niece.'

'*Love* from your niece? Affectionate girl?'

'Yeah Nath. You know better than most how affectionate kids can be. Bless them.'

Vicky began her spiel about engaging with the African community and any local families who may have contact with UASC Sudanese children. Kitty nodded eagerly. Nathan's eyes roamed around the room, settling on a smiling emoji greeting card. He walked to the card, as Kitty's voice rose suggesting some organisations and charities or special interest groups who may help. As Nathan picked up the card, Kitty stood to take it from him, slipping it into a drawer and sliding it shut. Kitty retook his seat opposite Vicky.

Standing behind Kitty, Nathan slid a steel saucer containing garden shed keys off the table and onto the slate floor tiles with a clatter. Kitty yelped and jumped to his feet.

'Sorry. Sorry Bert. Sorry serg. Clumsy me.'

Nathan and Kitty bent to collect the items from the floor, bumping heads.

'Look guys, officer. I absolutely will follow-up on this, I promise. Give me a moment to think and I will put out feelers and get back to you. I am good at that sort of thing. I run a Facebook ... Sorry, I really must press on, but I won't forget. My group has a face-to-face meeting this Thursday, the third Thursday of every month. I will raise this under any-other-business. It will spread through my network like a, you know, like a spider in a ... I will get back to you. Oh, I know, talk to Dakari Demarcus at the Sudanese Interior Baptist Church in Eastney. Oh, and the Reverend Dan.'

Vicky and Nathan took a slow walk back towards the ferry, heading for a pub bathed in autumn sunshine to the side of the slipway.

'Well, he's guilty.'

'Agreed serg. But guilty of what?'

'No idea, Nath. But he's guilty as hell.'

Nathan sat in the dappled shade of a pergola as Vicky returned from the bar with a tray of two cold lagers in one hand and an ice-cream in the other.

'Ice cream from a pub!'

'I know!' Vicky's eyes sparkled with delight. 'How decadent is that? We must go drinking on Hayling Island more often. I can't believe we are just a five-minute ferry ride from the most densely populated city in the U.K. We could be anywhere. Shall I get you one?'

Nathan shook his head. 'But lager?'

'Live a little. We never have a heatwave this late. Enjoy this start and end of the English summer with a cold lager. Anyway, after Amy's comment, I can never give you a Goblin again. Did you tell her, like, everything we did?'

Nathan scoffed. 'She was talking about our shared passion for drinking too much Hobgoblin real ale.'

'I know exactly which shared passion she was talking about.'

Nathan took Vicky's hand holding the ice-cream cone, licked around the edge where it had melted, and sucked ice-cream from her knuckle before releasing her hand.

'Ow!' Nathan held his temples between the heel of both hands. 'Shit!'

'Nath?'

'Nothing. A shot of neuralgia from the ice-cream and cold beer. It will go in a sec.' He screwed shut his eyes against the sun.

'Does a follow-up meeting with your friend, Bert Kitty, fall within your demarcation for intel processing?'

'Not really, serg. You need to be very careful of contaminating admissible evidence.'

'He isn't a suspect, Nath. Chill. You obviously rattled his cage; I would like you to keep on the pressure. Even if he only has an unfounded, biased opinion or suspicion, I want to know.'

'I suppose I could visit again with Gill. As I am a member of his precious Facebook group, I suppose I could pop along to this Thursday's meeting – if we don't have any kiddies to supervise.'

'Or have Amy stay home with the kids? It might make him think if he suddenly sees your face staring up at him.'

'Yeah. I guess. I'm not sure the meetings are that well attended. Just a handful of do-gooders patting each other on the back and slagging off the social workers.'

'Is Amy just a do-gooder?

'No, of course not. I am not saying that. Our kids don't know how fortunate they are to have Amy on their team. Not that they are especially fortunate in most other ways.'

'You still have that young absconder with you?'

'She will be gone by the time I get home. Hopefully, with a local foster carer who can keep her safe until she is eighteen. She really needs a *Staying Put* placement to help prepare her for the big bad world. Amy will be on the blower today advocating for a *PA* Personal Advisor worker, to help arrange benefits and housing for when she leaves care in a few weeks. Talking of which, you need to follow-up with the youth minister from the Church of Our Fallen Madonna with the big boobies. Get a touchy-feely PC on the case, you never know. I will add him to the shortlist.'

'You care so much about the victims of society and of life, Nath. Why are you such a grumpy tosser all the time?'

Nathan scoffed again. He enjoyed being in Vicky's company and regretted having taken the relationship further, to destruction. She made him laugh.

'Can you smell gas, Vicky?'

Chapter Five

'They are sending her to a *residential* near London.'

'What? A kid's home, no way! Have you told her yet, Amy?'

'She is still out with her chap.'

'Christ Amy.'

'Don't blaspheme, Nath.'

'I will talk with the social worker's manager. She needs to be with a family, close to Portsmouth. We were just getting a toe in the door. I am not having it, Amy. London? No way.'

'Not sure it is our decision, love.'

'Who is the manager?'

'Sarah.' Amy held up her mobile to show Nathan the contact screen. Nathan snatched away the phone.

'Wait Nathan. We need to talk this through.'

Nathan pushed *dial*.

'Sarah, Nathan Hart here. We have one of your young ladies.'

'Hi Nathan. Yes, I have been in meetings all day about PP. We have found her somewhere from tonight.'

'I don't think you have, actually.'

'We have Nathan. I thought we told Amy ...'

'Coming up with something inappropriate is not the same as finding her somewhere suitable. Sarah, she is this close,' Nathan gestured with his forefinger and thumb, 'to spiralling into a *problem child*! No Sarah, you have not found her a *suitable* placement where you can keep her safe and encourage her to prosper.'

'Nathan, I am sure you mean well ...'

'The taxpayer will fund her for a lifetime in the justice system ...'

'Thank you for your opinion, Nathan. We have a place at a residential home, where we can keep her safe until ... keep her safe.'

'Keep her safe until when? Until you chuck her onto the streets on her birthday, in less than a dozen weeks?'

'We don't do that, Nathan. We explained to Amy ...'

'You're not having her.'

'Sorry?'

'You are not having her. I am keeping her here.'

'It doesn't work like that, Nathan. These placements are like rocking horse shit. My team worked all day finding her this place. We will pick her up presently. When is the best time?'

'You are not having her. She is in my care. She stays with me until you do your job properly.'

'She is in our care. Hampshire's care.'

'Tell that to the judge, Sarah.'

'Don't be silly Nathan.'

'She is staying with me, Sarah. I mean it.' Nathan ended the call.

'Well, that went well, Nath. And thanks for talking to me first.'

'What went well, innit?'

'How did you get in Polly? You nearly gave me a heart attack!'

'Nath gave me a key.'

'Nath!'

'Hang on, slow down you both. Polly, by *I gave you a key*, you mean?'

'I thought you left it out for me. Sorry. Christ!'

'And by *left it out*, you mean?'

'Like you left it out for me in the hall, innit. Like in the little wooden box, at the back of the secret drawer in the hall cabinet.'

'Which was locked.'

Polly shrugged. 'You call that *locked*? Where am I sleeping tonight?'

Amy looked at Nathan for an explanation.

'Bad news Polly, sorry. They haven't found you anywhere. Looks like you are stuck with us for at least one more night.'

Polly's shoulders dropped in relief as she jigged around in a circle to a tune in her head. 'Can I have a bath tonight?'

'Of course you can, love.' Amy squeezed Polly's hand. 'But only if you wear your dressing gown.'

'Polly, before you go. You mentioned Dakari Demarcus last night.'

Polly shrugged.

'From the church?'

Polly shrugged again. 'Nah, there must be two Dakari Demarcus in Pompey.' She snorted a laugh. 'Yeah, from the church, duh!'

'How do you know him, Polly?'

'How do you know him, Nath?' Polly mimicked.

'Through fostering and Amy knows Rev Dan, of course. I'm just curious. You mentioned him, that's all.'

'He is a friend of Ryan's, innit. They've got short-term rooms for homeless kids. But Ryan's been there for like ever.'

'His own room?'

'They have a dormitory for boys and one for girls. But I have never seen girls there, except I stayed there one night when I argued with my auntie. They don't do kids under eighteen or kids in care, normally. Like only older homeless kids. Like Ryan, yeah? Not *children* kids like me. Ryan helps around the church, so he got his own room, innit.'

'Dakari Demarcus?'

'He runs it all, innit. The decision maker. Tough as an old shoe; the kids don't mess him. But a sweet guy. I like him. Am I leaving tomorrow, Nath?'

'Polly, that is so difficult to answer. We don't know. We only do emergency.' Amy cleared her throat. Nathan continued. 'You are stuck with us until social find you something better.'

'I'm ok here. I don't want *better*.'

'They will find somewhere more supportive. Amy has been on the phone asking for a dedicated PA worker to settle you into your own place when you are eighteen. Help with training for a job, benefits, and all that.'

'I could live with Ryan.'

'My guess is, you can't live in a homeless shelter for boys with a boy. But we can ask your social worker if you want us to.'

Polly looked at her feet. 'Whatever, innit.'

'Do black kids stay with Dakari Demarcus at the hostel?'

'Obviously. It's a black's church. I'm getting a bath. Can I have a glass of your Ribena?'

Polly looked at Amy for an answer. Amy stared daggers at Nathan, sick and tired of always being the *bad cop*.

Nathan answered. 'I drank it all, Polly.'

'There's two bottles in that top cupboard, behind the slow cooker.'

Nathan laughed. 'Maybe when you are eighteen, Polly.'

'So, I am staying here until I am eighteen?'

'Come on, it is getting late. Bath and bed.'

Nathan and Amy watched Polly trudge out of the kitchen.

'Amy, what was the young lad from Sudan called ....'

'Don't Nathan. Fuck!'

'I am not saying one of the boys is that lad, obviously. It's just he was a similar build and ...'

'I know!'

'Don't worry ...'

'Don't bloody worry? Christ, Nathan!'

'Don't blaspheme.'

Amy relaxed a little and smiled. 'Neuro went to Jacquie Jade's from here, remember? I spoke with Jax today. He was going to stay with her until he was eighteen. She was helping him prepare his asylum application. But there are inconsistencies in his story; he was nervous about being deported. Jax woke one morning to a box of chocolates and Neuro - gone.'

'Is Jax on your list of contacts you gave Gill?'

'Yeah.'

'Honestly Amy, it is nothing to worry about. But can you dig out Neuro's details from your notes? I'll just see if we can't put that demon to bed.'

Amy pulled a folded sheet of paper from her back pocket and handed it to Nathan.

'What are you doing, Gill?'

'Tidying up the London intel. Your Eve, from the Thames, also had gold and ground game bones in her gut, Nath.'

'Yeah, I know.'

'It's a shame you aren't running this investigation – we'd already have made arrests for all three murders by now.'

'Take in the governor's reports and point out the cross reference to bone and metals, please. Then have a look for this missing young man on the Police Database, and fish about online. Be careful of him using different names – some of these lads have a dozen different *AKAs*, and family names. Good luck.

Add him on the system, but also let me know what you find. Ask Ann to help as well; two eyes are better than one.'

Four hours later, Nathan watched Gill take sheets of paper from the printer and knock on the inspector's door. Nathan buried his face in the palms of his hands, rubbing his temples with his thumbs. He caught a whiff of printer ink when Gill had walked past with the late reports, and now his nose and throat stung with a bitter chemical smell and taste. The pain in his skull reminded him of the hospital appointment for tests, booked for later that day.

The inspector's office door opened and, as Gill walked towards Vicky's desk, the inspector screamed over Gill's shoulder to summon Vicky. Both women walked together, back into the office; the inspector slamming closed the door behind them.

Nathan watched Gill's face blush deeper as Vicky stood to attention, nodding. The inspector continued to scream – Nathan catching his own name, twice. He closed his eyes again. The door opened and, without waiting for Vicky to call him, Nathan stood and trudged to the office.

The inspector appeared in a no better mood, continuing to shriek at his office guests. Nathan fought to keep his eyes open and impassive, as the fluorescent office lights throbbed an intense violet.

'I understand your frustration, Ted. You have two dead bodies; the DCI and Chief Super must feel disappointed with your progress so far.'

The inspector sprang to his feet, seemingly preparing to throw a punch at Nathan. Vicky stepped forward, pulling Nathan further from the desk.

'Look Nathan, that is not the point. You can't just …,' Vicky started.

The inspector shouted over his sergeant, 'This is my investigation Bernie, not yours! Gill and Ann are not here to run around doing your private snooping. This investigation is for the death of two young men in Portsmouth nine-days ago – not a young girl in London ten-years ago. We have a team of detectives liaising with the Met concerning superficial similarities …'

'Ah come on Ted! Superficial?'

'I spent a gruelling twenty minutes at a hostile press conference yesterday afternoon refuting the idea of a ten-year long spree of serial killings, only for you to steer *my* investigation towards exactly that! How will this look in the Investigation Log? I am making managerial decisions in the log, and you are directing my resource in the opposite direction!'

'Press conferences aren't hostile and gruelling Ted. Having your head and limbs hacked off is hostile and gruelling.'

'You are on borrowed time, Bernie, and that is a threat.'

'You and me both, Ted. At least I haven't got a pension to lose.'

'Enough!' Vicky stepped forward again. 'Nathan, show some respect. You are totally out of order. This isn't an episode of *Frost*. If you want to go off on a tangent, you check with me first and I, or the inspector, will allocate resource, not you.' The inspector went to shout again, but Vicky raised a hand for silence and continued in a calmer, more conciliatory tone. 'Please, sir, one moment. Nathan, what is the story behind this young man?'

Nathan took a deep breath. 'Neuro was one of our UASC foster kids. He has slipped under the radar. He is the same age and similar build to Levi, and from the same region as the boys.'

'When did he go missing?'

'Two years ago, Vicky.'

'And he still lives in Portsmouth?'

Nathan lowered his gaze. 'Probably not. Who knows?'

'So, you can see why it is inappropriate to allocate your entire department to chase this extremely spurious lead without permission.'

'A bit of an exaggeration …'

'Nathan?'

'Yes, understood, serg.'

'We are monitoring any similarities with the Eve case, Nathan, and that is partly why you are here. But we have not yet made a direct connection. This is a stand-alone investigation and if we try to make it fit in with Eve, without supporting evidence, we are doing Eve, Luke, and Levi an injustice.'

'Serg.'

'PC Walker, I am your boss. We work in the direction instructed by the inspector, understood? Nathan Hart handles the day-to-day application of your time, but he does not line manage you. You should already know this.'

'Yes, serg, sorry. Sorry, sir.'

The inspector growled. 'Bloody fast tracks! A disgrace. A disgrace to policing.' The three stood silently for a long moment before the inspector spoke again. 'Get out!'

The three returned to their desks. Gill spoke to Nathan as she looked towards her screen.

'Sorry Nath. I only mentioned your lead to the boss because I was … proud of you. I didn't think.' She wiped tears away with the palms of her hand.

Anneika glared at Nathan.

Nathan replied, 'No worries. Not your fault Gill; all my fault. It's me who needs to apologise.'

Anneika softened and offered Nathan a thin smile, before resting a hand on Gill's back, leading her towards the washroom. Nathan buried his head back into his hands.

Anneika packed up, ready to go home for the day, bringing Nathan a last coffee before heading off. Gill joined them, gesturing towards Nathan's tethered laptop.

'Look at this, guys.'

Gill tapped on the keyboard. A map of Portsmouth flashed onto the screen with clusters of dots around pins showing speed, traffic control, parking, and council CCTV cameras. She tapped a few more keys as most dots disappeared, leaving smaller clusters around two areas.

'Hayling ferry, Eastney's Sudanese Interior Baptist Church and Eastney Marina, Eastney's Hayling ferry dock, and the Ferry dock across the water on Hayling Island. Although the ferry docks are both sides of Langston Harbour, and the ferry is for foot passengers only, the system recognises them as geographically adjacent.' Gill waited for Nathan and Anneika to absorb the information before continuing. 'And here around Southsea Pier and Clarance Esplanade, close to the pier.' She pointed to the second area.

'We have *persons of interest* meeting up?'

'Looks like it, Ann. These are from four vehicles. Once I saw the pattern, I requested information from two months before the murders until yesterday on those cameras.'

'You've looked at the association between the parties?'

'Yes Nathan.'

'And?'

'Guess.'

Nathan and Anneika studied the screen in silence. They glanced at each other, and both shrugged.

Nathan replied. 'No Gill, you are going to have to tell us.'

'All four vehicles are connected to Amy's list of contacts who may know something about

Portsmouth's African community, or UASC foster placements.'

'Go on.'

'A foster carer named Jacquie Jade is showing her registered vehicle being at the Eastney Marina/Baptist Church location, with two of the other three vehicles. This only happened on two occasions - Thursday 20th July, and Thursday 17th August. All other *meetings* are between two of the remaining three cars, but never all three. Most meetings are on a Thursday, the majority in the evening or overnight. Any thoughts yet?'

Anneika spoke. 'Sorry Gill, you have lost me completely.'

'Ok. One of the cars is registered with Robert Kitty. It is repeatedly recorded on traffic cameras around the Hayling Island side ferry dock, close to the vehicle's registered owner's address. Kitty's home address. Concentrate, I will say this slowly.

'We see car-Jade in Eastney on two Thursdays with car-two. On those two occasions, we record car-Kitty as being close to Kitty's registered home address. We see car-three near Kitty's address frequently, with car-Kitty. We see car-three at the Pier/Esplanade locations with car-Kitty on all the other Thursday evenings, except 20th July and 17th August. We see car-two at the Baptist Church/Marina location on every Sunday, whilst car-Kitty is showing at Kitty's home location.'

'Good spot Gill. But I am not sure this is a lead.'

'Thank you, Nathan. Do you still not have an opinion? Just to clarify, the two Baptist minister's cars are often at the church, obviously, but not the pier. I have taken them out of this exercise to reduce background noise. Still nothing Nath?'

Nathan brought a hand to the crown of his head to soothe a dull throb. 'What is the identity of car-two and car-three?'

'Car-two is Amy's. Car-three is yours, Nath.'

Gill studied Nathan's reactions throughout the exchange. She registered concentration, and then surprise at her last comment, but no obvious shock or concern.

'Have you told Vicky?'

'No Nathan. Is there any point? It is obviously coincidence and doesn't involve any suspects – not that we have any suspects yet.'

'Tell her anyway. If we use any future intel in court and the defence can show we cherry-picked information to suit, it could weaken a case. And you don't want to be seen bypassing her twice in one day.'

Gill shot a glance at Anneika.

Anneika spoke, her voice lowered in the open plan office. 'Nathan, I have emailed your personal address. Gill and I found some time to search for your missing UASC lad, Neuro. We couldn't find much, but I sent you the timeline, which goes nowhere, and a few names of professionals from the Home Office, Portsmouth, Hampshire, and Croydon children's services and police. I think you know one name personally; the copper you were talking to with Vicky, from the Hampshire Willow Child Exploitation Team, DC Neil Morton.'

Amy opened the front door as Nathan walked towards it. She held him on the step, resting her forearms on his shoulders.

'Good day? Behave?'

'Yes, a good day. You? Where is madam?'

'I'm going to collect her. Can I take your car, please? Come on, I'll pour you some wine.'

'Where is she?'

'I am collecting her from the church hostel. She's probably been staring into Ryan's eyes all day.'

'What time?'

'Not sure, I will get going in a minute as it is getting dark. But I will wait until she is ready. I won't rush her, boss.'

'Take your own car.'

'Why? You can't drive after your wine.'

'I think it might be low on petrol.'

'I will fill-up for you.'

'Take your own car.'

'It hasn't even got windows, Nath.'

'It has a roof. Take your own car.'

'Grumpy! Ok, I will take mine, Christ!'

'Can you supervise Polly this Thursday? I want to attend the PCiCN meeting.'

'No, Nath, you never go. That is my thing. The PCiCN admin guy has asked the police officer from the Willow Team to talk to us. He also wants to discuss

Luke and Levi. I was going to tell him about the list of contacts I gave Gill.'

'Bert?'

'Yes Nath, Robert Kitty.'

'You normally call him Bert.'

'Do I? Yes, I guess so. I suppose I could come with you. The meeting is in the Marina Lounge. We can collect Polly from the church next door afterwards.'

'You have already been to two Thursday meetings this month. I will go to this one – the third Thursday of the month.'

'Sure.' Amy blushed a little. 'I am just surprised you have time, with work and everything. Just see how late you are from work tonight.'

'I had to pop into the hospital on the way home.'

'Hospital! Why?'

'Rachel wanted me to have some tests.'

'Nath! What is going on?'

'Nothing. I have been having those smell hallucinations for a while now. She wants to check out my liver function. We all know they will just tell me to cut back on the pop. I'd rather smell nail varnish all the time, than cut back.'

Nathan spent all Wednesday daytime, and late into the evening, in the office. He raised a hand at the morning debrief, asking why every contact with the public had not included a routine question regarding their whereabouts on the likely days of the murders and on the likely day the boys were dropped into the sea. Alibi information should have been gathered and verified if appropriate. The inspector turned crimson at having his tactics challenged by Nathan, but there were consenting murmurs from the more experienced detectives in the room. Nathan suggested he should run a report of all statements taken where this had not happened. They should revisit these people – starting with those also on the shortlist of names who had more than one mention, which now included his own and Amy's names. Vicky closed him down, saying they would speak out of the meeting, before the inspector blew a fuse in front of the team.

Towards the end of the day, Vicky sat on the edge of Nathan's desk. Kicking off her shoe, she rested her foot on his knee as he swivelled in his chair. With no apparent inhibition, she listened in on the conversation Nathan was having on his personal mobile phone.

'Go on Rachel. Good news first.'

'The good news is all the tests came back negative. By the way, I heard the rugby playing nurse forgot to snap on a pair of gloves.'

'You are a sick puppy, Rachel; you really are. How can you being no closer to resolving this be the good news?'

'Better than having results suggesting you only have a week to live.'

'I love your bedside manner, Rae. I can't wait to hear the bad news.'

'More tests, I am afraid. I'm booking you in for a day of scans, ultrasounds, and x-rays. I will ring dyno-rod

to see if they have an extra-large cavity camera, which they can clean-up and lend us.'

'I can't spare a day at the moment, Rae.'

'Just find a way. This is non-negotiable.'

'My boss is listening-in. I will break the news.'

'Who? Vicky? Having another go at wrecking your marriage, is she?

Vicky scoffed,shaking her head.

'She heard your question, Rae. I'll let you know her response, later. Bye for now.'

Nathan disconnected.

'Who was that, Nath?'

'Private.'

'Not that private, is it? She seems to know who I shag!' Vicky kicked Nathan away, so that he spun in his chair.

'Rachel Warr, my doctor.'

'You tell your doctor who you sleep with?'

Nathan shrugged. 'She is a school friend of Amy's; they talk.'

'Why are you having tests?'

'This and that. What do you want serg? I am busy.'

'For a start, Nath, stop goading the inspector.'

'Even when I am right?'

'Especially when you are right. And never, ever, in front of the team. The team are already looking for …'

'Competence?'

'… leadership. Run the report you suggested regarding alibis, and I will take a look. But that is a lot of shadow chasing – none of these people are suspects.'

'Already done. You can see the report on your dashboard, and I have included them in the inspector's morning bundle.'

'Have you followed-up on Robert *Guilty* Kitty, yet Nath?'

'Tomorrow evening. Did you follow up with the Right Reverend Dakari Demarcus and his band of merry kids?'

'Yes. We sent two Police Community Support Officers. The minister was most helpful. He had no kids to introduce except for one Ryan Piper – who mentioned you and Amy. I might have to allocate resource to monitor you two, you keep cropping up.'

Chapter Six

Nathan walked in from the carpark with Gill. They both felt the atmosphere of nervous anticipation in the incident room as the full team waited for the inspector to leave his office with Vicky and take the meeting.

'We are keeping to the meeting agenda. This is a professional murder investigation, not a game of schoolboy football. I will, however, lead the meeting by bringing forward one item from any-other-business. I will keep you informed of developments at these morning sessions, otherwise you stay focused on your allotted tasks unless I have reallocated you. Understood?' A wave of nods and agreements spread around the room. 'Sergeant?'

Vicky cleared her throat. 'Ok. Most of you have heard the rumour already. More body parts have washed up in our patch. Following this meeting, I will allocate a team of detectives to relocate to Newport, Isle of Wight. DC Steve Mallick, you will accompany me to the island today and bring back any information you need before visiting that university oceanographer you fancy. Newport nick has started preliminaries. The remains were discovered by, wait for it, not a dog walker, but a llama walker, just after 0500 hours this morning.'

A chuckle spread around the office. A gruff sounding older detective stage whispered, 'Obviously guilty, arrest them.' The giggling increased. A young female answered with 'Don't be a-llama-ist, Ken!'

The inspector shouted over the laughter. 'How would one of you like to accompany me when I break the news to family? Eh?' The room fell silent. 'See if you can't just cheer them up with your adult wit! I am postponing the rest of this meeting for ten minutes, then we will go through the agenda with your full concentration. Someone fetch me a coffee!'

More sombre and chastened, the meeting temporarily broke up as the team headed back to workstations. The female voice raised again, above the now muted background-shuffling. 'Steve, it might rain on the island. You had better al-paka-mac.' The whole team, including Vicky, stifled laughter as they avoided eye contact with each other.

Nathan allocated Anneika to process information as it arrived from Newport and from the liaising Portsmouth detectives.

'Ann, please run the same contact's vehicle lists through cameras at the Wightlink Car Ferry from Portsmouth to the Isle of Wight. Also, the carpark for the foot passenger hovercraft. Start with the same date Gill used for the Hayling Ferry search. Extend it once we have timings for these new human remains. Follow-up Red Funnel in Southampton and Lymington ferry in the New Forest.'

'You mean just the four cars including …'

'No! The whole shortlist of recurring names. Christ!' Nathan sighed. 'Sorry, I didn't mean to shout. Yes, including ours, obviously. We can't be seen to pick.'

'Southampton and Lymington? Is that not schoolboy football, Nath? Let's all run over there, let's all run over here.'

Nathan glared at Anneika for a moment. 'Ok. Start with Portsmouth and let me think.'

As Nathan headed for the door and his meeting with the Willow detective at the PCiCN meeting, Anneika called after him. They stood in the stairwell outside the secure incident room.

'Nothing much to report on the Portsmouth cameras for the ferry crossings, Nath. Talk to Vicky before asking me to spread the net further, please. Gill and I are stretched now, with three sources of intel.'

'Nothing *much* to report?'

Gill looked to her left, towards the landing window and the dipping sun outside. 'Nope. Statistically insignificant.'

'Expand.'

'Well, as you would expect, there is some data. You know.'

'One off the shortlist?'

'Well, yes. We see a car registered in Portsmouth in a carpark in Portsmouth. You know, not that special or anything.'

'Just one car? Or a meeting?'

'Just one.'

'And?'

'And what, Nath?'

'Ann! Get on with it!'

'It was six weeks ago. Nothing to do with anything.'

'Which car?'

'I checked the Eastney and pier locations. They parked the car in the church carpark, before going on to the hovercraft carpark.'

'Which car?'

'Yours Nath.'

'It can't be.'

Anneika shrugged. 'Perhaps you had a daytrip to the Isle of Wight. It happens. Check your diary. Perhaps you and Amy went shopping or boozing in Ryde.'

'Via Eastney? Ann, have Gill apply for CCTV footage of the passengers boarding the hovercraft.'

'No Nath. That is not data gathering. That is you navel gazing. If you want to spy on yourself, or Amy, you talk to Vicky first. If you bully Gill into doing it, I will report you.'

Nathan parked in the Sudanese Interior Baptist Church carpark Eastney, just a short walk from Marina Lounge bar, where the PCiCN meeting was being held. He exchanged texts with Amy about the social services inaction and how Polly might have to stay for the weekend. He watched Robert Kitty step over the low wall, walking in his direction from the Hayling ferry. His face lit up on seeing Nathan's car, offering a big overhead wave. As he drew closer, his expression clouded, and he detoured directly towards the Marina Lounge. Nathan watched him complete the journey and trot up the external steel staircase to the bar.

Three men stood at the rear corner of the church. Rev Dan lent back against the bricks. The second man was taller, leaner, and also black. He wore a tonic black and red jacket over black trousers. Rev Dan nodded towards Nathan and the other men turned around to look. The third man was also tall, but white. He bounced from foot to foot with nervous energy. Nathan wondered if he was Ryan, from the back, but could now see he was older, perhaps early forties. The three then walked together towards the front of the church.

Finishing his texts, Nathan followed Robert Kitty, meeting the Willow DC at the foot of the stairs.

'Hey Nathan! Twice in less than a week. Are you here as a foster carer or as Portsmouth's very own spook?'

Nathan chuckled. 'Hardly a spook, Neil, more a paper-pusher. Amy is on home duties, so I came to the meeting in her place. But to be honest, I was hoping to have a chat before you go.'

The pair entered the lounge together. Both sat with the group of a dozen people, congregated in an empty section of the bar lounge behind an opened sliding wall. Neither ordered drinks. Nathan half listened as the group discussed problems they were having with their foster children, or with social workers, the police, courts, the new failing Mosaic payment system, and the care system generally. Robert Kitty updated the meeting on the status of the PCiCN and a forthcoming Christmas Party he was arranging for foster children and carers own birth children living in Portsmouth. DC Neil Morton explained the role of Willow, for those who had not yet dealt with the group. They discussed a list of telltale signs of exploitation for the carers to be aware of, both for their foster placements and their own children and their wider network of children and young adults. As the meeting ended and attendees stood to leave, Nathan spoke.

'Sorry to spring this on you folks and sorry to hijack your event, Bert, but could I have a quick chat with Ms Jade, Bert, DC Neil Morton, anyone who does or has taken UASC kids, anyone who wants to listen in, Uncle Tom Cobley and all, please?'

Two of the group made excuses and left; the rest remained. Nathan took a moment to introduce himself and run through the case of the murdered boys he was working on. He dispelled a few myths and rumours before handing out his own business card and PC Gill Walker's card, which also had the Crime Stopper number printed on the back.

'One last thing in my capacity as an Emergency Out of Hours foster carer, then I will let you go. I bet you are all busy with the little cherubs we work with.' The group gave a united chuckle. 'A couple of years ago, I took a young African boy called Neuro. He moved on to Jaquie Jade here,' Nathan gestured towards Jax, 'and then slipped off-grid. I'm just wondering if you could ask around your own UASC kids and see if anyone knows anything, please? I promise, hand on heart, I am asking as a carer, not in my role with the police. He is not in trouble. I am not interested in his asylum status. I don't care how he is making a living. I don't even need to speak with him directly. Just an update on how he is doing. I won't even pass any information to my friends in Willow.' Nathan gestured to DC Neil Morton.

Jax raised her hand to speak. 'Just a little thing, Nathan. Neuro is long gone, and I don't think it will help. But he came from you with the name Neuro Kole, but I saw him write his name as Bankole. Just saying.'

DC Neil Morton spoke as he flicked through notes on his phone. 'I remember this young man very well. He gave me, and is still giving me, the runaround. I can't go into detail about an individual case, but I think I can tell you the name, or *a* name I was given. I have Baneuro Yoruba Bankole.'

Following a few more general suggestions and observations, the meeting broke up, leaving just Robert Kitty, DC Neil Morton, and Nathan. Nathan and Neil shot each other the briefest of glances and back at Robert Kitty. With the others gone, he was acting evermore skittish.

'I really haven't anything to add about Baneuro, Nathan, which isn't already on file. But if I hear anything …' Neil trailed off.

'May I say something off the record? If this information goes public, I will know where it came from.' Nathan addressed that comment to Robert and then back to both men. 'Why would children be given, or forced, to eat gold and bones?' Both men shrugged.

'I honestly have never heard of anything like that.' Robert stared at his feet, avoiding eye contact. 'But look, I can't be absolutely certain about this, but I have a geeky memory for names. I am not a churchgoer, but one of my own foster placements and a couple of the groups',' he gestured to the now empty circle of chairs, 'have had older *ex-placements* stay at the church next door, whilst *settling-in* to life outside of care. Once, I was waiting to talk with the youth minister Dakari Demarcus while he was speaking with Rev Dan. They were talking about a lad called, or from, Yoruba. Probably nothing.'

'An impressive memory, Bert. Thank you.'

Robert shrugged and smiled nervously. 'It's a shame I can't retain more useful information, Nathan.'

'Yeah, I know what you mean. But then I'd forget my own wife's name if I didn't write it down.'

Robert faked a laugh before leaving the two men alone. They watched him leave the room before Neil spoke.

'What's his problem?'

'He's an odd one, Neil, that's for sure.'

Neil left Nathan ordering two John Smith's bitters at the bar. He drank the first before the second finished pouring, taking the second to a table near the window. He drank the second pint slower, texting Amy to make sure Polly still needed collecting, before heading for the foyer of the church to find her. There was a small room off the foyer, where Rev Dan allowed youngsters to meet and socialise in the evenings – the door chained open so they could not enjoy intimate privacy. Leaving the bar and making his way down the steel staircase, he watched a group of half a dozen teenagers or young men, possibly including Ryan, step back into the shadows. He walked towards the group; they moved along the side of the church, ahead of Nathan. He rounded the rear corner of the church and was smashed in the face with a bat or lump of wood.

The impact and momentum knocked Nathan off his feet, cracking his head against the stone footpath. Winded and injured, he could not fight off his attacker as a series of kicks to his torso and head forced him against the church wall. He brought his free right hand over his head for protection and his trapped left arm around his back to cover his kidneys. He fought to stay conscious, blood now spurting into his mouth with each kick to his back and sides. Time stopped and then lurched forward. Hands dragged him away from the wall. As his arm flopped over his eyes, he glimpsed Ryan's face looming over him, with Polly stood a few feet behind. Her white shirt glowed blue in the near darkness. The world went blank.

Nathan slowly opened his eyes. The room lights turned low. Struggling to focus past the blurred outline of people, he closed his eyes and spoke.

'Am I in heaven?'

Nathan recognised Vicky's voice from her nonchalant response. 'If you were dead, it wouldn't be heaven you'd be sent to.'

'What happened?'

'I was going to ask you that question, Nath.'

'Does Amy know I'm here, chatting with you in bed?'

'Amy is sat right here, tosser.'

Nathan opened his eyes again to follow the voice of his wife to the chair pulled up to his bedside.

'Sorry love. Just messing.' Nathan extended a bandaged hand and arm to take his wife's hand. She ignored it. 'How am I?'

Vicky spoke again. 'You look ok to me, Nath. But I am not a doctor.'

'Perhaps you lovebirds could enjoy your banter later.' Amy's voice sounded flat. 'Mild concussion, cracked rib, bruised organs, broken finger, hairline fracture to your wrist.'

'How long have I been unconscious?'

Amy continued. 'You were unconscious on arrival. They kept you sedated.'

'Any arrests?'

Vicky spoke. 'No love. Sorry, I mean no Nathan. Uniform will pop-in and take a statement. Obviously, our team is not involved in investigating this incident. Out of interest, though, do you know who did this?'

Nathan snorted. 'I think I might have mentioned that, if I knew.'

'No glimpse of your attackers?'

'I saw a group of teenagers. I walked towards them to ask if they had heard about the murders, but they moved away.'

'You were going to question them in your capacity as *not* a police officer?'

'I was just going to ask if they had heard about the murders and hand out some cards.'

'And you think it was them, Nath?'

'No. I didn't say that, Vicky. I do not know who attacked me or why. Perhaps I was mugged.'

Vicky produced an open evidence bag. Nathan checked his phone, now with a cracked screen, his full wallet, and watch, now smashed.

'Yeah. All there.'

'Any other theories? Who knew you would be there tonight?'

Nathan shrugged. 'Did you tell Robert Kitty I was going in your place, Amy? Or did you tell Jax?'

'Um yes. I think I text Bert just as the meeting started. No one else.'

'Why?'

'Because you were going in my place, Nath.'

'I know that! Why did you feel the need to warn your Bertie?'

Amy blushed and studied Nathan's hand, resting on the sheet, which she had still not taken in hers. 'Just out of politeness. He always asks for numbers. I was just keeping him updated.'

'Nobody else, Amy?' Vicky added the question.

'No! And don't interrogate me, Vicky. I am talking to my husband.'

'You were lucky, Nathan. Someone called the ambulance. The crew were passing the end of your road, returning to the Eastern Road Ambulance Station, following a false shout. They diverted and got to you quickly.' Vicky let the comment hang for a moment. When Nathan failed to speak, she continued. 'You haven't asked who called it in?'

'Um, who called it in?'

'An anonymous member of the public.'

'Not a llama walker?'

'No Nath. A frightened sounding young woman. She called from the landline in the church foyer.'

'Ok.'

'The ambulance reported finding a frightened young woman with you when they first arrived. Any thoughts? And a young man looking distressed and agitated. They left the scene before the police attended. You haven't asked for a description, but I will tell you, anyway. She was small framed, maybe five-feet two-inches tall. Shoulder-length blond hair. Eighteen years old at most. White crop-top, with a white tracksuit jacket over black jeans. He was nearer six feet tall, early twenties, short dark hair, West Ham football shirt and denim jacket. Tracksuit bottoms. No idea, Nath?'

Nathan shook his head.

'Interested in their colour? Both IC1.'

'Still no, Vicky. Sorry.'

'Who else did you see there before the attack?'

'There was a handful of customers in the bar, and bar staff. Maybe twelve foster carers, including the woman I have met before, Jax. DC Neil Morton from Willow. I also saw Rev Dan and another IC3, talking in the carpark with an IC1. They saw me, I think, or at least Rev Dan nodded in my direction. Will you or Ted sack me again?'

'Why should we? Unless you tell me something different, we are not aware this attack is related to the murder investigation, Nath. Can Ann and Gill manage your intel processing alone?

'Yeah. Maybe for a day or two. What is the Isle of Wight body story?'

'Body parts, you mean. Not much to report yet. Hopefully Monday. I need to get back. Get well soon.'

Vicky hesitated at the foot of the bed. Nathan tensed, sensing she intended to hug him. Instead, she offered Amy a thin smile and left.

'Nath, what is IC1?'

'White North European looking; British, if you like. IC3 is Black. African type black, you know, Jamaican etc., with African heritage. Where is Polly?'

'Absconded last night.'

'*Last night*?'

'Yes Nath. It is nearly noon now, Friday.'

'Shit. Did you look for her?'

'To be honest, Nath, I couldn't be bothered chasing after her. I was concentrating on you. I have reported her missing and ended the placement. When the police find her, they can take her elsewhere. I have had enough.'

'We abandon her like everyone else in her life. Great!'

'Yeah. All my fault, Nath.'

'That is not what I said. Have you been here all night?'

Amy nodded.

Nathan continued. 'Look, love, thanks for looking after me. The doctors will start prodding me once they realise I am awake. And the plods will want a statement soon. Why don't you shoot off and get some sleep? Have you any paracetamol, please?'

Amy scoffed. 'You can't just take painkillers; you don't know what else they pumped into you already.'

'How long was Vicky here?'

'Quite a while. I almost felt sorry for her; she looked anxious. The smart talk didn't start until after you woke.'

'Amy love. If Polly finds her way home, please smooth it with social. Don't reject her.'

Amy took a deep sigh and nodded. 'Was it Polly and Ryan who attacked you?'

'No, of course not.'

'Descriptions sound similar.'

'Similar to half the street urchins wandering Pompey.'

Amy nodded. Standing to go, she gently kissed the side of Nathan's mouth with the least stitches.

'And you are happy for me to be alone with Polly?'

'Of course. She's a sweetheart Amy. Just avoid winding her up'

Chapter Seven

Alone in the hospital room, Nathan retrieved his iPhone from under the pillow, where he had hidden it whilst inspecting his belongings. He opened a new yahoo email account using the pseudonym *African King* and opened a Facebook account in the same name, *screenshotting* a family wedding photograph off the internet, as a profile picture. Using various combinations and components of Baneuro Yoruba Bankole, including Kole and Neuro, he searched the web and social media platforms for his missing previous foster child. As he scrolled through names, most without genuine profile photographs, he noticed a Facebook friend crop up a few times against different names. She had used an actual photograph of herself, presumably, and it was her good looks that first attracted Nathan's attention.

The young woman used the mononym Nyekachi. Her Facebook account was mostly public, and Nathan could scroll through her photographs and friends. She was glamorous and popular, her many friends comprised family, influences, and digital music creators. Nathan clicked through her friends and saw patterns of mutual friends. He wished he could sit in the office and import the information into his cross-reference and search software. Nathan followed links to repeating mutual friends.

Four hours after Nathan began the search, interrupted by doctor's rounds, police interviews and a cold, slimy chicken curry with hard rice, Nathan opened a digital music creator's Facebook page to see three familiar faces staring back at him from the friends list – the pretty Nigerian girl Nyekachi, a white boy monikered Ham West, and a white girl called Pretty Polly, with a profile photo of Polly Preti. Ham West used a profile photograph of Ryan Piper – Polly's boyfriend, who was involved, in some capacity, in the attack on Nathan. Ryan's *Ham West* page was secure, as was Polly's. As Nathan clicked on the other friends on the creator's list, and their friends, so another name repeated - Ollie Hart Kole. Ollie's page was also secure. Nathan worked backwards, inviting previous friends, including Polly's *Pretty Polly,* Ryan's *Ham West*, Nyekachi, and her friends, to connect with Nathan's *African King*. Some were obviously digital creators and influencers, who automatically accepted Nathan's friend requests. Others accepted, ignored, or rejected his requests. As the scales fell, so Nathan received friend requests from friends of those who had accepted his requests.

Seven and a half hours after starting the search, Nathan's *African King* Facebook page had just under 250 friends and followers, which he hoped contained a healthy percentage known to Ollie Hart Kole's Facebook page and his friends. He commented, liked and shared content, downloaded reels and shared websites he thought might interest his new social media friends. Armed with this small army of mutual virtual friends, Nathan sent a request to Ollie Hart Kole.

Nathan switched back to his own *Nathan Hart* Facebook account and searched messages for *Pretty Polly*. He tapped a message.

'Hey Polly. Are you ok and safe? I am a bit sore, but on the mend. I prefer Amy's cooking to hospital food. Call me or Amy as soon as you are ready, please. We can collect you or just chat. We can smooth it with Social and the feds. No harm done. Don't forget, if you need, dial 999. Please get back to us soon.'

Nathan closed his eyes for a moment, waiting and hoping for a reply. He fell asleep, still clutching the phone.

'How's Mr Hart feeling this morning?'

'Mr Hart is feeling just dandy, doctor. How is doctor feeling this morning, doctor?'

'You had a few bumps, Mr Hart.' The junior doctor looked tired. She continued. 'But nothing too serious. Nothing some convalescence won't resolve. Nothing life changing.'

'That's a shame doctor. There are a few things in my life I should like to change.'

'I had a chat with your GP this morning, Mr Hart.'

'Really doctor? How is doctor, doctor?'

'You are due some tests, Mr Hart.'

'I am, doctor. Please call me Nathan, or Nath. What shall I call you, doctor?'

'Yes. Are you suffering headaches at this moment … Nath?'

'Yes, doctor.'

'Mm, not surprised. Your usual headaches? Or battered around your skull with a pickaxe handle type headache?'

'Difficult to say. Similar.'

'Smell hallucinations?'

'I can smell antiseptic, alcohol rub, and hand cleaner.'

'Yes. So can I.'

'Nothing out-of-place then, but it can change in the blink of an eye.'

'Visual colour changes?'

'No, not at this moment. I can see your blue scrubs normally.'

'They are green, Nath.'

'I am colour blind, doc.'

The doctor scoffed. She shone a light into Nathan's eyes and then asked him to open his mouth wide. The doctor asked a long list of questions about his general health, life traumas, lifestyle choices, medication, exercise, and relationships. Vicky knocked and entered.

'I can ask the officer to leave, Nath. If you'd rather.'

'It's fine. She already knows me too well, according to my wife.'

The doctor glanced between the two.

'I want our dentistry bod to examine you, Nath. Before we discharge you. Can you slip down the bed, please? How do you sit on the floor to get comfortable?'

'I … I don't sit on the floor, much.'

'When you play with kiddies, or watch telly?'

'I really don't know. On my bum, I guess.'

Vicky cleared her throat. 'After rolling around on the rug in front of a log fire, he sits cross-legged to finish his wine.'

'There you go Nath. Sit cross-legged on the bed. Lean forward slightly.'

The doctor climbed on the bed behind him. Checking her watch and sighing, she firmly massaged his back, using her forearms. Vicky caught Nathan's eye and furrowed her forehead. The doctor moved to his neck, using her palms to continue massaging.

'Any pain or twinges, tell me immediately, Nath.'

The doctor worked gently on Nathan's neck. She hummed and sang softly. Nathan released a satisfied groan, followed by an even snoring.

'Exactly like he does after rolling around by the fire, doctor.'

The doctor scoffed again. She climbed from the bed, pulled a sleeping Nathan to her chest and onto his side. Making a few notes on the chart, she checked her watch and sleepily shook her head.

'I will get dentistry over, then have him discharged. You may talk to him once he wakes naturally. Don't wake him.'

Vicky nodded.

'Nath, wake up. She's gone.'

Nathan woke and sat in bed. 'Who?'

'That doctor. God, she wants to get in your pants.'

'I am married. And I am not wearing any pants. I must have dozed.'

'Are you back in on Monday, Nath?'

'Yes, sure. What day is it?'

'Saturday. I thought I'd pop in and have a chat – away from prying ears.'

'She is my wife, Vicky.'

Vicky shrugged. 'Does plod think it attempted murder? What do you think?'

'What? The attack on me! No, of course it isn't. If it was, they'd have continued to use the bat.'

'Agreed, Nath. Random violence, or related to the Luke and Levi case? Or your dodgy past? Or some of the unsavoury types associated with your foster kids? Or the fact nobody, like nobody, likes you? Did the plods ask if you know anyone who would have a motive? I bet that was a long answer, including your own wife!' Vicky chuckled.

'Hilarious. Anyway, you are the one with a history of married men.'

'Cheeky. I used to think married guys were less complicated. Less demanding. Then I met you and Amy.'

'Did Gill show you something?'

'Your bloody car keeps popping up? Is that such a big thing? One car is going to show the most. One car will show the least. And the rest will be in the middle. Do you really not remember being in those locations?'

Nathan shrugged.

'Apart from Amy, who else uses your car?'

'Nobody.'

'Except Amy.'

'Don't be silly, Vicky.'

This time, Vicky shrugged. 'Has she still got her own car?'

'Yes.'

'The beach-buggy?'

'Yes. Loves it.'

'I remember she drove it round to have a word with me after she found out about … well, you know, us. I thought it was Barbie I had dissed.'

'Don't take the piss, Vicky. We broke her heart.'

'*We*? Anyway, you wouldn't miss that car, would you?'

'Meaning?'

'Meaning nothing. Just saying.'

'Go on.'

'Nothing. Just saying. Are you asking me as a detective, a woman, or an ex-mistress?'

'You've lost me Vicky.'

'I have said enough.'

The pair stayed silent for a couple of minutes. Vicky moved to sit on the bed, holding Nathan's bandaged hand.

'Where is the investigation going, Vicky?'

'I sat down with the inspector and the investigation log. We are keeping open lines of enquiry to the Eve case in London – but we have no firm evidence to connect the two. We are snuffling around Amy's list and looking for leads from the African community in Portsmouth; not discounting the boys could be recently arrived asylum seekers or illegal immigrants. We now have the third body from the Isle of Wight.

'We cannot scour the entire coast, as you suggest. But we have made an appeal for members of the public to come forward with suspicions.'

Nathan sighed. 'Great. No names?'

'We have your shortlist of leads that keep popping up during enquiries, including you, but absolutely nobody suspicious. Except for you.'

'How about Dakari Demarcus? He said he had no kids staying in the hostel, apart from Ryan. But I definitely saw lads loitering.'

'Loitering? Have you been watching Dixon of Dock Green? DC Neil Morton said you were asking about your missing lad. Nothing there?'

'No. Nothing. Neuro is probably living it large in Croydon. Apparently, immigrants get free housing, jobs, benefits, our women, and a unicorn. What about that strange Robert Kitty? He keeps cropping up.'

'Bertie Bassett? Are you asking me as a detective, a woman, or an ex-mistress?'

Nathan spent Sunday at home. He kept up with African King's Facebook chit-chat, sharing and loving posts. Ollie Hart Kole eventually accepted Nathan's friend's request as African King. Nathan returned a waving hand.

'I'll cook dinner.'

'I am going to church. But a late lunch would be cool, Nath. Thanks. Are you definitely up for cooking, all bandaged up?'

'Taking your car, or mine?'

'Mine.'

'Keep an eye out for Polly.'

'Yes, sir.'

'Will your Bertie be there?'

'Robert Kitty? No. He is not a churchgoer. Why do you ask?'

'Dakari Demarcus?'

'The youth minister? Yes, I expect so.'

'Invite him over?'

'Over where? Here? Don't be silly, Nath.'

'Seriously. Invite him for dinner.'

'No!'

'They beat me on church property. The minister might want to see how I am. Rev Dan sent me a card.'

'Why do you want to meet Dakari Demarcus?'

'Why not?'

'Hey Mr H! Good to meet you, at last. I've known your dear wife for some time, of course. Rev Dan felt most enlightened by your views the other day. And now Ryan's girl is talking about you.'

'Minister Demarcus …'

'Please, Mr Hart, let me stop you there. Please call me Dakari.'

'Thank you. Likewise, call me Nath, please. Have you seen anything of young Polly? We are getting worried.'

'I understand Nathan. But sadly not. I do not discuss the youngsters who stay in our hostel, but I will say Ryan is also *awol*.'

'I have added wine to the gravy. Is that ok? Or do you abstain?'

'Abstain? I am a bit of a pisshead, to be honest!' Dakari laughed at his own inappropriateness, slapped Nathan gently on the shoulder, and apologised to Amy for his language.

The three enjoyed dinner together, Amy pleasantly surprised at how well the two men got on. Nathan mentioned Polly several times. Dakari explained he would not feel able to contact him and Amy if Polly turned up at the church, but he would do everything he could. Amy offered to drive Dakari back to the semi-detached manse he shared with Rev Dan, after dinner.

'Before you go Dakari. I saw some teenagers, lads, maybe young men. They didn't mention seeing who attacked me?'

'We only have, or now perhaps *had,* Ryan Piper staying with us. Sorry Nathan, I do not know who you saw.'

'Dakari, may I ask you another question? A real curveball. You may surmise why I ask this, and I hope you will keep my question to yourself.'

'We are good at keeping things in confidence, Nathan.'

'Why would someone feed a child ground wild animal bones, gold, silver, and platinum powder, and clay from a riverbed?'

Dakari swallowed hard as his eyes widened. 'Oh dear. Those poor boys.'

'Dakari?'

He gulped again. He forced a thin, sardonic smile.

'In my capacity representing all black people, Nathan?'

'Either you know, or you don't, Dakari.'

'Why did the police not reveal this at the press conference?'

'They reveal information to secure more information. They are less likely to detail facts of which they do not understand the significance.'

'Tell me, Nathan, what you know about Jashn-e-Baharaan, in Pakistan?'

'Why would I know about Pakistan?'

'And why would I know about things that sadly happen a similar distance south from my hometown as Pakistan is from here, Nathan? Africa is a big place.'

'Ok. So, you don't know?'

'I am no expert, Nathan, and I refuse to be quoted.' Dakari remained silent for a moment before continuing. 'You might look at Muti.'

'Is that a town?'

'It is a ... practice. Sometimes, rarely, they use body parts in medicines and witchcraft. Sometimes from children. The child is first *prepared*. They might make them swallow precious minerals, and animal or human bones.'

'Human sacrifices?'

'No. The body parts are components of the ritual. People who follow these beliefs often identify as Christians, although they can trace their witchcraft beliefs to long before Christianity washed up against our shores. There is plenty of human sacrificing mentioned in the Old Testament, although He was not best pleased with the practice.'

'Ah yes. And there is only one God, or so I hear.'

'Indeed, Nathan. I must go now. Thank you again for dinner. I will take an Uber.'

'No Dakari, I'll drop you back,' Amy offered. 'See you a bit later, Nath. I will have a quick scoot around; see if I can see Polly. I'll take your car.'

Nathan made an early start in the office, reviewing the input and analysis completed by Gill and Ann over the weekend. He took a moment to review the initial autopsy and scenes of crime reports on the decomposing body parts found on the Isle of Wight beach at Alum Bay. He clicked off the statements and onto google.

'Nath. A word, please?'

Nathan followed Vicky into the empty inspector's office.

'Well, Nath, another weekend of passion with Amy?'

'Not exactly.' Nathan held up his bandaged hand.

'If you need a trigger, just drop my name into the conversation. She will sulk for an hour, then spend the night riding you like a cowgirl. You're welcome.'

Nathan smiled, shaking his head. 'You really have the morals of an alley cat, Vicky. What do you want? I am busy.'

'I wouldn't mind a bit of what Amy is getting, actually. But I guess that is off the table. Remember that time on the conference room table …'

'Seriously Vicky. I am busy.'

'We are on the back foot Nath, to be honest. The inspector is giving a press update mid-morning. The *Portsmouth News* is whipping up the whole serial killer angle. They are suggesting the body on the Isle of Wight is the fourth murder by the same serial killer. Your Eve, Luke, Levi …'

'And John? You hold the donkey and I'll get on.'

'Wow, look at you, Nath! I get the cold shoulder when I try to keep the mood light. But you? You are just a regular comic grim reaper.'

'The Isle of Wight body is white and adult.'

'And that makes his life less important and open to ridicule? Anyway, I am not asking for your amateur detection. I just want you to look at preparing a report showing any connections, and crucially any disconnections, between the Isle of Wight *John* and the other three. Bearing in mind, we are still not officially connecting Levi and Luke with Eve.'

'Age and lack of voodoo gut contents, for a start.'

'John didn't have many guts left.'

'I'll ask Gill to prepare a report.'

'Hang on Nath. Do you know something?'

'As an amateur detective, a man, or a data analyst?'

'What do you know?'

'I *know* nothing. But I would like to *know* why you think my car has cropped up in places I wish it hadn't. As a detective, a woman, or a mistress.'

'*Ex*-mistress, Nath. Why has your white, mass-produced, same as everyone else's, mid-range BMW, cropped up as often as a Portsmouth football shirt on a Saturday afternoon? Ask Amy, as a wife.'

'I have already worked out Amy is involved, Vicky. Don't make this easy for me, will you?'

'You think Amy was involved in the murders?'

'Vicky! That isn't even the tiniest bit funny.'

'Ask her, why don't you?'

'Thanks for the advice.'

'That isn't my advice, Nath. My advice is to forget about your boy-racer, it's only a car. Forget about it unless you are absolutely positive you want to know the answer.'

Nathan straightened and walked to the door.

'Nath! The Isle of Wight body?'

He stopped to study Vicky's reddening and irritated expression.

'I will get that report to you.'

'Nath!'

He hesitated again. 'Have your DC Steve Mallick chat with the university oceanographer. Ask her about the Needles Spoil Ground. But don't bother searching as far as Newhaven in West Sussex, or Tynemouth in Northumberland.

'Also, closer to home, Vicky, pop along to see the youth minister Dakari Demarcus. Ask him about Muti. A type of voodoo. Tell him about the victim's stomach contents. Take someone along with you and check alibis. And I will give our inspector Teddy a warning if you like. Ted isn't ready to talk publicly about the Isle of Wight body. If he does, we will have a new inspector by the end of the week, which may not be a bad thing. Keep a safe distance from him. You're welcome.'

Nathan sat next to his empty hospital bed, tapping on his laptop with restricted access.

'Mr Hart.'

'Doctor doctor. Are you stalking me? And it is Nath, remember?'

'No, Mr … Nath. I am the brain doctor. You get your skull smashed with a bat, or you have wonky senses and headaches, then you get to see me. Lopez. Doctor Lopez. Or Cath.' The doctor's cheekbones pushed high into a smile, her face colouring slightly.

'I am pleased to be in your hands, Cath.'

'You are here for MRI and CT scans.'

'I was going to ask about that. Why the MRI?'

'Today is *BOG OF*. Buy one, get one free. Special offer.'

'Nothing better to do, Cath?'

'I am looking at your upper body with the MRI. Spine, neck, you know?'

'Yes. I am not medically inclined, but I know where the upper body is.'

The pair stood in silence for a moment.

'Nath, you have a visitor.'

'A visitor? I am an outpatient. And what, you are both a brain doctor and assistant ward nurse?'

Cath shrugged. 'It's a job. I was on the medical ward downstairs when I overheard someone asking for you. They hadn't realised we already discharged you.'

'Did they have a violin case?'

'I am well aware of the reason you were hospitalised, and we do have security protocols. But she is only young, small, and I don't think able to beat you up. She is also scruffy. And smells. I was going to have a nurse talk to her and maybe call Children's Services, but I could see she was ready to do a runner.'

'Name?'

'No. But I sat her in the corridor. Or she *was* sat in the corridor.'

'Can you bring her in?'

'We don't offer concierge, Nath. You can go out and see her.'

'The more doors we bring her through, the safer she will feel and the less likely to bolt.'

Cath sighed, glancing at her watch. 'Sure. I have nothing better to do. I was only going to take my first toilet break in seven hours.'

Cath returned with Polly, cowering behind her, and flicking nervous glances around the ward. Cath dragged over a plastic chair, sighed, glanced at her watch, and trudged away without speaking.

'Hey.'

'Nath.'

'You ok, Polly?'

'You ok, Nath?'

'We've missed you.'

Polly shrugged.

Nathan continued. 'No hurry, but shall I call social and let them know you are back from a sleepover?'

Polly raised her face, eyes wet. 'We thought you were dead. Then when you coughed-up blood, we thought you were dying.'

'Nope.' Nathan spread his arms to demonstrate his living.

'Where is Ryan?'

'London, innit.'

'What part?'

Polly shrugged.

'At some point, the police will want to talk with Ryan.'

'And me. I was there as well, innit.'

'Were you?' Nathan mimicked Polly's earlier shrug. 'Says who?'

'I will have to give my version. Otherwise, they won't believe Ryan.'

'Ok. That is a very mature approach. Who is Ryan with?'

'Some girl. I feel silly. I didn't want to give Ryan my V-card, at first. Turns out he didn't want it anyway. He says I am more like his little sister. He hasn't even got a little sister.'

'Sounds like he has now.'

'Yeah.'

'Is Ryan safe with the girl?'

'Yeah. She is dead straight and posh. Got her own bedsit, innit. Got proper tits and everything. Hangs out with trendy mushes and birds.'

'Got a name?'

'Course she has Nath. She is a woman, not a stray cat.'

Nathan managed to downplay his scoff to a smirk. 'What is her name, Polly?'

'Nye. It's a black's name.'

'Nyekachi?'

'Yeah. Do you know her? I fancy Ryan. He is dead sweet. But she is well out of his league. He is like her bit of honky-fun. I think Ryan knows, but she is dead pretty and hard to resist. Have you met her?'

'I met her friend, Ollie.'

'Ollie? Ollie is really Ryan's friend first. Ryan knows him from the church. He stayed in the hostel for a couple of nights. When Ollie moved to The Smoke, he met Nye. They are both Nigerian. Or like her dad is or something.'

'When did you last see Ollie?'

'Few weeks ago. I have only met him once. We met her at the same time. Not a party, but like hanging out.

None of them do drugs and nothing. Just like beer and pop, but they are all much, much older. Now Ryan can't stop talking about her, innit. Like totally hooked.'

'How much older?'

'At least 25. No other young kids; just me. I felt stupid. But they were all nice. Ollie talked to me about Portsmouth. He stayed somewhere near us in Drayton. Then in town, Copnor I think.'

Nathan grinned with pride now, as Polly referred to his house as *near us*.

The lunch cart clanked past the end of the ward as the auxiliary staff distributed the plates amongst the in-patients. The food smelt to Nathan like overcooked cabbage and wet dog. He suspected it was not a smell hallucination. Polly glanced at the cart and her stomach gave a deep rumble.

'That wasn't a fart and nothing!'

Nathan smiled back and winked. He waited until both staff members were distributing meals, before casually walking to the cart and collecting two covered plates and cutlery. Placing the plates on the empty bed tray, he pulled the curtain around and told Polly to *tuck in*. She was halfway through the second plate of food when a nurse walked in, glancing between the pair and the food.

'Are we feeding day-patient's family hot meals, Mr Hart?'

'Looks like it, nurse.'

'This isn't a canteen!'

'Good. If it is, I am in the wrong place.'

Polly continued to eat, fixing her eyes on the food.

Nathan spoke again. 'You can take it off her if you want, nurse. But she ate the last nurse who tried.'

The nurse raised her eyebrows and dragged her attention back to Nathan.

'We are ready for you now, Mr Hart. Please follow me.'

'Polly, please wait for me and look after my stuff. As in, don't break into the locked drawer, steal my cash, and do a runner. I won't be long, then we can go home.'

Polly nodded, still staring at her plate as she shovelled in the warm cottage pie.

'I'll bring you back a cuppa, love. Sugar and milk?' asked the nurse.

'Three.'

'Polly!'

Polly looked at Nathan, fork mid-way to her mouth. She glanced between the two, before rolling her eyes and adding, 'Milk and three sugars, please, nurse.'

'Nath, where are you?'

'I am at the hospital, serg. Some follow-up tests to the beating,' Nathan lied. 'I am leaving now. What's up?'

'Ted has postponed the press update. They are beating at his door. He wants to talk to you about the Isle of Wight body.'

'I have my young lady with me. I can meet in the Manor House Pub; I am not bringing her to the nick.'

'Can't Amy babysit?'

'Amy doesn't know I have her yet. Look, I am not explaining myself to you, Vicky. I can meet in the Manor.'

Nathan pulled into the evening traffic from the hospital and, driving past Cosham Police Station, continued to the Manor pub. He parked around the back – the pub sat directly opposite his house, and he wanted to avoid Amy seeing his car. Amy would be pleased and relieved to see Polly safe, but Nathan needed to contact Children's Services and take responsibility for smoothing the legals with the duty social worker. Polly was officially missing and no longer Nathan and Amy's legal placement.

Nathan sat Polly at a table along the empty bar and met Vicky, placing drink orders.

'And your young lady, Nath?'

'Large coke, no ice, crisps, and a sandwich, please. Tuna-mayo will do, one of her five-a-day.'

The bartender nodded. Vicky and Nathan took their seats with Ted.

'Thanks for meeting Bernie. It would be nice to see you in the office occasionally.'

'Yes Teddy, sorry about that. Being beaten half to death whilst working on your case has totally messed with my diary.'

'I am not aware there is any connection with any suspects on my case, Bernie.'

'True. Especially as you have no suspects on your case.'

Before the inspector could respond, the bartender appeared with the drinks and credit card machine.

'Twenty-eight-pounds-fifty, please.'

'How much?' The inspector held back his credit card.

'The lady in the corner added a large pinot, sir.'

The group turned to face Polly, who saluted across the bar with a large wine glass.

Both Nathan and Vicky smirked as they turned around to face the inspector.

'May I start?' Vicky held up her hand. The inspector nodded. 'Have you and PC Gill Walker followed up with Robert Kitty yet?'

Nathan let out a sigh. 'No serg. Been busy. And is that still a good idea? After what happened to me on Thursday?'

'Are you scared, Bernie?'

'I am scared it will contaminate your evidence if there is any connection found between Kitty and my attack.'

'Until we identify a connection, Bernie, I would like you to do as Vicky asks.'

'Ok, tomorrow evening. But I want this request entered into the investigation log. It is your decision to have a civilian worker, me, discuss a live investigation with a person of interest. I get blamed for most things, but I won't for this one.'

'I will do, Bernie. But this is just an admin follow-up, and he isn't a suspect.'

The group turned around to watch the fruit machine clatter as it dispensed winnings to Polly. Nathan automatically felt his now empty pocket for change. He shook his head as a pain shot up from his neck and through his jaw.

Vicky raised her hand again. 'John from the Isle of Wight? Thank you for your report, Nathan. There is nothing, other than the obvious, to connect the body to the murder of Luke and Levi.'

'Ok. Then the evidence suggests they aren't connected. Move on.'

'It doesn't work like that, Bernie. The Met missed Stephen Port's victims as serial killings. We can't say bodies washing up on our patch in the same week aren't connected!'

Nathan shrugged. 'Remember the Russian jet which crashed into the cemetery? Authorities recovered two thousand bodies before someone told them to stop digging.'

'Is that supposed to be funny, Bernie?'

With a deadpan expression, Nathan caught Vicky's eye, who immediately snorted into a laugh.

'Have you spoken with the oceanographer?'

'Yes,' answered Vicky. 'They could have dumped John anywhere in our quarter of the English Channel. But unlikely in the Solent, except perhaps at the very western end. He hasn't been bouncing around the

Solent and hasn't been bumping around the warm Southampton water, full of nuclear particles.'

'Southampton Water is full of warm water from Fawley Refinery and the oil-fired Power Station. Not nuclear,' Nathan added.

Vicky rolled her eyes. 'Whatever.'

'What has Scenes of Crime and the initial pathologist's report got to say?'

'You should read your own reports occasionally.' The inspector fired Nathan a sideways glance, and back down at his beer.

Vicky continued. 'Most organs and soft tissue are gone. Rotted, broken away or eaten by crabs.'

'We've all been there, love.' Nathan aimed his inappropriate joke at making Vicky giggle again, in front of the less than jovial inspector.

Vicky continued. 'One arm is missing. But at least parts of the other hand and feet remain, and much of the head.'

'An arm missing? And the hand?' Nathan continued, not waiting for a response. 'Fingerprints? DNA? Facial features? Age? Race? Foreskin?'

'No fingertips remain. Yes, we have DNA, but no match on the Police Database. We are asking the Met for some specialist support to come-up with a photo-fit from the remains of the face, but it will be amazing if accurate. Between twenty-eight and thirty-five years old. Nothing left to hold a foreskin. IC1, white European.'

Nathan closed his eyes in pain and concentrated through his worsening headache. 'Ex-military pensioned off. Navy or Marines. Suicide. Nothing to do with Levi, Luke, or Eve. Put your DNA results past the Home Office.'

'Ok Sherlock. I really need to know how you came by that deduction.'

Nathan pointedly checked out the doors around the pub, obvious to Vicky he was looking for a yellow door to continue his earlier joke. Unable to contain herself, she again giggled. The inspector stood, grabbing his empty glass.

'I am sick of you two and this cosy club. Get a room and leave all this outside the office; show some respect. And listen to me Bernie, this is not about your fucking Eve!'

Natham jumped to his feet and stood just inches away from the inspector, his fists and neck taught. 'You disrespect Eve again, and I'll knock you through that window.'

'Hey boys, enough. You are spraying testosterone around the bar.' Vicky had grabbed Nathan's right arm. 'We are all feeling this. If you sit down, sir, I will get you another drink.'

The inspector slammed his empty glass onto the table and shoulder barged Nathan. Without another word, he left the bar. Nathan took a deep breath as his shoulders relaxed. Vicky brought her lips to kiss his.

'Is that her husband, Nath? Innit.'

The pair jerked back from each other.

'No Polly. He is our boss. Finish your ... drink.'

Polly shrugged and headed back to the placemat she was colouring. 'I'm hungry, innit.'

Vicky watched through the window as the inspector drove out of the pub carpark.

'There goes my lift, then. And the expense account. If I follow your gut and dismiss John as being unconnected to the others, and you are wrong, I will be the one writing parking tickets.'

'Ok. Let him go to the press and say we are investigating another murder. We could do with a new *IC*.'

'Nath!'

'I want something back, Vicky.'

'Ok. Like what?'

'I want CCTV to see if, and with whom, Amy spent the day on the Isle of Wight; the day she parked my car in the hovercraft carpark. I want some tech-support to locate the IP address of someone who may, or may not, be my old foster kid, Neuro. He might be involved in this and might be in danger. If it isn't him, well, Neuro might even be Levi.'

'You are blackmailing me, love.'

Nathan shrugged. 'You don't need me to tell you about John. You will get there eventually.'

'After the inspector has publicly made a dick of himself?'

'Yep. Probably.'

'Ok. But you are going to have to trust me. I will do what I can, when I can. You first, Nath.'

Nathan looked at Vicky in silence. Vicky continued.

'Ok Nath. As a detective, a woman, and a mistress …'

'*Ex*-mistress.'

'Amy is seeing someone. My guess is Robert Kitty.'

'No! No way. Just because you cheat with married men.'

'He isn't married.'

'No, but she is. No way.'

Vicky shrugged. 'Ok.'

'Why use my car?'

'She uses her car when she can justify it being in a location. Church on Sunday, Eastney for PCiCN meetings, etc. But it is a grunter, with a removable lid, and painted with stripes. When she doesn't want to be noticed, she uses a white, popular, production car. Simples. Look, I am sorry Nath. Please don't overreact.'

'Did they do it in my car? God!'

'Probably. After the way you treated her.'

Vicky called over for more drinks, inadvertently allowing another wine for Polly.

'Sorry love. John?'

Nathan looked up at Vicky, confused for a moment.

'John? Yes, John. There are three places in the country you can have a burial at sea. Newhaven, Tynemouth and the Needles Spoil Ground. Our John has broken free from his weighted coffin and floated back to land. Why would a young man want to be buried at sea, in sight of the Royal Navy town of

Portsmouth? Because he served in the Navy or Marines. What is the biggest killer of young men who have retired young, or sick, from the services? Suicide. And I should know all about that risk.'

'Do you want me to take you home, Nath?'

'Yeah, right,' he snorted. 'Your best idea so far.'

'I meant take you home to Amy.'

'I know what you meant.'

'Shall I take Polly over to Amy?'

'No. Thanks. I will sort it.'

'Nath. You need to keep a lid on this.'

'I know Vicky. Thanks.'

'I really am sorry.'

'Yeah. Me too. What a fool, what a stupid bloody fool I have been. I need to get Polly home, while she can still walk straight.'

Chapter Eight

'Nath. Are you ok? Looks like you've seen a ghost.'
'Look who's here.'
'Polly! Oh my God. Are you ok?'
'Are you ok, Amy?'
'Where have you been?' Nathan gave the slightest shake of his head to Amy, from stood behind Polly. Amy continued. 'Anyway, that doesn't matter right now, love. Why don't you have a nice long bath and change? We can all have pizza tonight, yeah? We will have to make some calls.'

Nathan raised his hand. 'I'll call social and the police.'

'And we need to talk, Nath.'
'You can say that again, Amy.'
'I'm not with Ryan anymore, innit.'
'Did he hurt you?'
'No!' Polly spat back at Amy, then lowered her gaze to her feet. 'He's met someone his own age. No big deal, innit.'

'Oh, love.' Amy took Polly's shoulders, but she shook her off.

'It don't matter and nothing. At least she is pretty. It would be sad if he went with some slapper.'

Amy stepped forward to hug Polly, as Polly twisted to shake Amy away. Amy continued to embrace her, against her will and almost to the point of restraining her. Nathan extended his arm towards Amy.

'Back off Amy. Give her some …'

Before he could finish speaking, Polly howled out like a wounded animal, clutched hold of Amy, and sobbed into her chest. Amy pulled her tighter; Polly's legs buckled. Amy lowered with her to the floor as Polly continued to sob.

Nathan went through the proceedings of the day on autopilot. Only Vicky and Gill noticed his demeanour was a little more abrasive and shorter than usual. During the morning briefing, the inspector announced they were following a fresh path of inquiry, regarding the Isle of Wight body. The detectives sent to the island would liaise with the home office, who kept DNA samples of everyone buried at sea, and would likely return to the Cosham incident room later that day. The staff who sat in Nathan's section of the floor began a sweepstake on who would crack or receive dismissal first — the inspector or Nathan.

'Are you ok?'

'Don't start this again, Vicky.'

'Is Amy ok? Don't ignore me, Nath. Do I need to ask Gill to pay a welfare visit?'

'No, of course not. She is fine. We haven't spoken yet.'

'You actually don't have to, Nath. Let it ride for a few days until we break the back of this. Then woo her back.'

'Maybe.'

'Um. Look, I haven't told Ted why, but I said I don't want you to follow-up with Robert Kitty, obviously.'

'Yeah, makes sense, now.'

'I will talk to Mr Kitty again myself. How about you take Gill and speak with the ministers?'

'Why not send a detective?'

'We have interviewed them under general enquiries. I cannot justify sending detectives back without reason or until we have seen everyone on first pass. I can request a uniform visit, but you will get more from them. We can meet after, in the Maypole, for an ice-cream.'

'This is it, Vicky. Last time face-to-face with the public. I am not a detective resource-on-the-cheap.'

'You certainly aren't cheap, Nath. Also, it will be good for Gill to see my DC in action.'

'*Ex.*'

'Ex-DC? Or my ex?'

'I am not in the mood, Vicky.'

'Ok love. Sorry. Well done for not losing your rag. And remember, it was just a gut feeling. I have no evidence to suggest who, or if, Amy is … you know … seeing anyone.'

'You aren't helping.'

'See you in the Maypole.'

'Maybe.'

'Ann. Can you hold the fort, please? Gill, the sergeant has asked you and me to clear up a couple of points with some vicars. Fancy a trip out?'

'Sure Nathan. Cool. Should I change?'

'Change Gill? What, change out of a police uniform and dress up as a fire fighter?'

'No, I meant like plain …'

'Just get a move on, Gill.'

Nathan pulled into the church carpark. A shiver ran down his spine as he recalled the violent attack on his previous visit.

'Nathan look. Nath? That guy is waving. Is he who we are visiting?'

'Wait. He won't be able to see us through the tinted glass at this angle to the sun.'

Dakari walked to the driver's door with a big grin.

'Hey! Mr Hart, Nathan. I assumed you were Amy in this pretty little Beamer. We should allocate her a named parking space. She always parks over there, but her space is filled with our security lighting people.'

Nathan stepped from the car, shook hands, and introduced Gill.

'Sorting your lighting after the horse has bolted?' Without waiting for a response, Nathan continued. 'PC Gill Walker has a few questions to follow-up from our earlier visit regarding the murder of the boys.'

'Really? I had so little to offer.'

The three walked together towards the church and Dakari's office.

'We would like a quick word with Rev Dan, as well.'

'Unless you have an appointment with Dan, I suggest we speak first. He is halfway through a meeting.'

'That will be fine, sir,' responded Gill.

'I am just the officer's admin support,' added Nathan.

Gill ran through the original statement and then asked questions resulting from the additional information gathered from investigations. She was thorough and forensic. With everything else going on, Nathan was worried he might forget to put in a good report to Vicky regarding Gill's conduct, and so added a reminder to his phone.

'The boys are likely Christians from Sudan, sir. May I ask if you and other staff here are Sudanese? I am just wondering about any contact the boys and their associates may have had with the Church.'

'I am Sudanese, although I fled persecution from there, many, many years ago. Rev Dan is Nigerian, but lived in Pretoria, South Africa, I believe. He only joined the church as a minister once he emigrated from South Africa. The congregation is a mix of various African nations and a sizeable percentage of English – such as Amy.' Dakari gestured to Nathan with a smile. 'We are popular and have lots of fun. We even have a few Sudanese Muslims hang around during Sunday service to chat with fellow countrymen and play a little soccer on the field. I suppose Amy has told you all this, Nathan?'

Gill had closed her notebook and the three now talked informally, waiting for Rev Dan to finish his meeting.

'Probably. We don't talk ... I should say I don't listen as much as I should. I know she is gone most of the day on Sundays.'

'She is great with the kids. Do you know Jax Jade? Jax sometimes brings African asylum seekers to the church, including the Muslim boys, and your Amy organises games and helps them mingle with the congregation. And she helps with the kayaks and paddleboards.'

'Really? I should ask more. I thought she just came here to pray, and you know, clap.'

Dakari gave a long, howling laugh. 'I love your English deadpan humour. She takes our little tinny safety boat out. And I have seen her sailing with the guy from fostering – she is quite accomplished.'

'Robert Kitty?'

'Yes. He works with foster children, as do you, of course. I think sometimes they take foster children for a sail in his boat, I have seen them. Perhaps she is too modest to tell you of her good work.'

'Yes. Modest, maybe.' Nathan watched as Gill added to her notes – Robert Kitty and Amy Hart's names had cropped up again.

'Damn!' Gill mumbled and covered her mouth. 'Sorry sir. So sorry for my language.'

'I have heard worse, my dear, as I am sure has our Lord.'

'I forgot. I need to check your whereabouts on a couple of dates, if I may.'

'My whereabouts, officer? Are you sure you need that from me?'

'We use it for mapping, sir. If we need to speak to certain people who may have seen something in a certain place and at a certain time, we can see who was where. I cannot insist, of course, but we find people normally want to help.'

'Of course, officer. Fire away.'

'Sunday 17th September, when the boys were discovered.'

Dakari opened his diary on his laptop. 'What time?'

'Just generally, sir. Maybe some people are away on holiday, for instance. Just generally.'

'Let me see. I helped Rev Dan prepare for services and I took the early morning service at 08:30 and the late service at 6pm. I was right here all day. From getting up to going to bed.'

'Thursday 7th September, when the boys were likely put into the sea.'

Both Gill and Nathan saw a slight tremble in his hand as Dakari tapped open another page on his diary.

'Here again all day. My life is predictable.'

Nathan spoke. 'May we have a copy of that page, minister?'

'I can give you a screenshot, but with the names of people I met obscured. I am sure you understand.'

'Yes, please, sir. Thank you. Finally, Tuesday 5th September, when the boys likely died.'

'Ah yes. A busy day visiting parishioners. If we miss any regulars, especially the elderly and sick, on Sundays, then we follow-up on Tuesdays. We take it in turns to visit care homes and the hospital. Again, I can screenshot, but with any full addresses and names obscured.'

As Dakari spoke, pages printed behind him.

'Last one, Dakari, whilst we have you. Last Thursday when I was beaten to a pulp outside your window.'

Dakari cleared his throat. 'I was also here, Nathan. I saw you before your meeting at the Marina Bar next door. And I saw you with the paramedics afterwards.'

'Who were you and Dan speaking with in the carpark, earlier in the evening?'

Dakari pursed his lips, shaking his head.

'Taller than you. White, forty maybe.'

'Not that I recall, Nathan, sorry. We have all sorts stop to chat or ask for alms.'

Nathan nodded to Gill.

'Perfect sir. And that printout, please.'

Rev Dan called Nathan and Gill into his office and asked Dakari to arrange tea and coffee. Gill went through a similar list of questions and received mirrored responses. Rev Dan also printed sheets from his diary. She asked about the tall white man seen talking to him and Dakari on the night Nathan was assaulted. He gave an identical reply to Dakari's.

'You are not Sudanese, sir? But the church is the Sudanese Interior Baptist Church.'

'The Roman Pontiff is from Argentina, officer. But he is still a Roman Catholic.'

Gill smiled back at the minister but remained silent. Rev Dan continued.

'Am I under suspicion for something?'

'Not that we are aware of, sir.'

Rev Dan cleared his throat. 'I am Nigerian. I joined this church after arriving in the U.K. I suspect around the time you were born, my dear.'

Gill smiled back again. She held another silent pause before glancing at her notes. 'You came here from Nigeria?'

'Yes, I said that officer.'

Gill took a moment to make a couple of notes in her book before speaking again. 'Not South Africa?'

Rev Dan's eyes widened, and his nostrils flared. 'Yes, officer. I came here from Nigeria, via South Africa. Is this relevant?'

Gill pursed her lips. 'Nope. Just background, sir. Just establishing direct or cultural connections with the victims.'

'And do you see any, officer?'

'Where in South Africa?'

'Different places.'

'Specifically, sir?'

'Northwest.'

Gill pursed her lips again and raised her eyebrows.

'Johannesburg area, officer.'

'Pretoria, sir?'

'Yes. Look, if there is anything I can do to help, please call back. But I really …'

'Are you familiar with the practice called Muti, Dan?'

Rev Dan shot a glance at Nathan, then back to Gill.

'Can you answer Mr Hart, please, sir?'

'Yes. Sorry. It is a terrible word. Yes. It is a witchcraft practice. Terrible.'

'They sometimes mutilate children.'

'Yes Nathan, they do. But it is more complicated than just that.'

'You never thought to mention Muti to the police when you heard Luke and Levi were mutilated?'

'I … I didn't not approach the police, Nathan.'

'Sorry sir, you approached the police?'

'No. I mean, I did not consciously decide to not approach the police.'

'Sorry sir. You are losing me in double negatives.'

'It crossed my mind. But I have theories about many things I see in the news. I am not an expert on Muti, just because I am African.'

Gill let the excuse hang in silence for a long moment. Even Nathan felt uncomfortable.

'And from Pretoria, where the practice is common.'

'Sorry officer?'

'As a Christian minister in Pretoria, you must have been involved in educating, fighting, and … praying, against such practice.'

'Yes, officer.'

'As a minister?'

'As a Christian, officer.'

Gill flicked through her notebook at some length, finally settling on a page Nathan could see was blank. She studied it for some time.

'As a minister, sir?'

Rev Dan cleared his throat.

'No, officer.'

'As a …?'

'I was a mechanic. A car mechanic.'

'My word Gill. Well done. You have excellent *technique*.'

'Thanks Nath. But it is all twaddle when they aren't even suspects.'

'Interesting that Bertie Kitty and the church both own boats – right where the lads were dumped.'

'Obviously, I have noted that fact, Nath. But we are on the sunny south coast, home of English yachting. Everybody owns a boat.'

'I don't.'

'Neither do I, Nath. But you know what I mean. We can't arrest everyone who owns a boat.'

'Rush hour would be quieter. Fancy an ice-cream?'

'No. We need to get back to the office.'

'Orders. Serg is meeting us in the Maypole for a beer. Although you are in uniform, so ice-cream only.'

'I have never ridden the Hayling ferry. Do I need my passport?'

'I need to call the sergeant. Can you get me a beer, please?'

'No! I'm not going to the bar in uniform. I heard you were a shit copper.'

Gill immediately regretted making the comment until she detected the flicker of a smile on Nathan's lips as he concentrated on his phone. Nathan sat at a picnic table in the pub beer garden. Gill stood, half squatting against the table, trying not to look like she was settling in for a drinking session. Photos of uniformed police officers sitting in pubs risked appearing on social media and even newspapers, especially with bodies washing up weekly.

'Serg. Your beer is getting warm. PC Walker has lined up some songs for karaoke.'

'I am sat outside Mr Kitty's, Nath. His car is here, but no reply. I am sat with a uniform. If he is peeping around the curtains, he will brick it. If he has gone for a walk, I am sure his local neighbourhood watch representative will rush to tell him we were staking out his gaff. I will give it another ten-minutes and then see you in the beer garden. Tell Gill to try Raining Men.'

'*Staking-out his gaff*? Do police officers really talk like that? Don't be long. We are almost pissed already.'

Nathan ended the call and faced Gill.

'She won't be long.'

'I was just thinking, boss, we are getting more traffic from Amy's list than from any of the inspector's detectives. I like Amy. Not what I expected.'

'What were you expecting?'

Gill shrugged. 'I don't know. Someone less … likeable.'

'More like me?'

'If the hat fits, Nath. Talking about not being liked, the guy in the corner of the bar either doesn't like you, or police uniforms, or both.'

'Well, well, well. What 'ave we 'ere, then? The elusive Mr Kitty. Robert Kitty is on our list of interviewees.'

'No, he's not.'

'Well, he is now. Come on. I will give you a moment to flick through his page on your iPad. But, it is the same questions as for the creeping Jesuses.'

Nathan walked towards the open French doors, into the bar, and towards Kitty. At one point, it looked like he might stand to leave the bar. Nathan changed direction slightly to *head him off*. Kitty sat back again.

'Mr Kitty! We have been looking for you. This is PC Gill Walker.'

Gill smiled and nodded, without taking her eyes from the iPad.

'Nathan! Hi mate. I didn't notice you. How is … everyone? Everything?'

'Amy? Yes, she is fine, thank you for asking.'

'No. I was thinking of your placement. A young lady, I think you said.'

'Yep. She is also fine, thanks. All the women in my life are just fine.'

'Did you have any luck finding Baneuro?'

'Yep. Getting there. Thank you again for your input. My little extended family would be in a different place without you keeping an eye out for them.'

'Anything fostering Nathan. That's me. Anything fostering or foster kids related.'

'Yeah.'

'Sorry to hear you were attacked on Thursday. You are looking well, considering.'

Nathan suddenly brought his left arm up to show his wrist splint. The sudden movement made Kitty flinch.

'Yeah. Just sore ribs and wrist. Otherwise, not so bad.'

'Did they catch them?'

'They will.'

'Yes. Good.'

Gill watched the exchange before going back to reading Kitty's summary report. Nathan continued to speak.

'Shall we walk back to yours, Bert, or pop into the cosy for a quick chat?'

'Yes, here will be fine.'

'Safety in numbers?'

Kitty gave a nervous laugh, quickly scanning the empty Tuesday morning pub. Nathan continued.

'Lovely view from here. Same as from your garden. Oh look, you can see my car in the church carpark. And the lighting van, even clearer in that space. Drinking alone, Bert? Or expecting a guest?'

'Just out for a walk. Will this take long?'

'Nearly ready, sir. Sorry for the delay,' replied Gill.

'We have intel on everyone, pretty much Bert. George Orwell's 1984 and Big Brother is here at last, barely forty years late.'

'Shall we walk through, gentlemen?'

Gill led the way into an empty snug off the public bar, signalled *two-minutes* to the landlady, and slid closed the glass door.

'There, take a seat please Mr Kitty.' Gill signalled to an empty chair for Kitty and sat herself. Nathan remained standing and, Gill thought, *looming* over Kitty. 'We have established you are not aware if you knew, or ever had contact with, the two murdered boys?' Gill purposely avoided inflecting a question at the end of her sentence. She stared silently at Kitty for several seconds, watching him blush deeply as he tried to hold her gaze. 'Mr Kitty? Sorry, that was a question.'

'Yes, yes.' Kitty spluttered a response. 'I haven't been told a name for the boys, no. And I am not aware of any boys I know who are missing. Once you have names, I can think again.'

'Thank you, sir. Where were you on Thursday 7th September, please?'

'Oh goodness. May I check my calendar?'

'Of course, sir. This is not a closed book exam.'

Kitty laughed a little too shrilly for a man of his age. He opened his phone. 'I was mostly at home and around this area on the Thursday.'

Nathan spoke. 'And at the PCiCN meeting?'

'No. I mostly hold them on the third Thursday of the month.'

'Mostly?'

'Yes. Mostly.'

'A great day for sailing, sir?'

'I can't remember the weather.'

'Were you out sailing on Thursday 7th September, sir?'

'I am not sure, officer. It isn't in my diary, but I wouldn't normally put it in the diary. I keep the boat ready and just, you know, pop out.'

'Sunday 17th September?'

'Nothing in my diary.'

'It wasn't so long ago, sir. A week last Sunday. It may help if I remind you – it was the day we found the boys' bodies.'

'Yes. I remember. I hung around the church …'

'You *hung around the church*, sir? That sounds a bit… unsavoury.'

Kitty gave another quick burst of shrill laughter. 'Yes, it does rather. I am not a believer but, after Sunday services, the youth minister encourages youngsters, and their families, obviously, to play sports and games together. There are often Unaccompanied Asylum-Seeking Children there. I pop over to help, meet the kids and catch-up with any of my foster carers.'

'*Your* foster carers, Bert?'

'Any PCiCN Facebook members. You know. Not *mine* as such, Nathan. Just those I might know or get to know.'

'Cosy.'

'Yes, Nathan. We are all in it together.'

'And then, sir?'

'I don't remember.'

'Have a think, sir. Just a week last Sunday, after church.'

'Yes, I went for a walk.'

'Where sir? I am not trying to catch you out.'

'No. Of course not. I went for a walk along the Southsea seafront. We got as far as the pier, but it was police cordoned off. So, we walked back and caught the ferry home, to mine.'

'Alone, sir?'

'Yes. Absolutely. Alone.'

'You said *we,* Mr Kitty.'

'Did I? Goodness no. I should be so lucky.'

'You have been very helpful, sir. Thank you. I can see how this has upset you. We will catch the killers. Please be assured.'

'Sorry Bert. One more thing. Have a good think about if you took your boat out on Thursday 7th, please. Do you normally sail alone? Perhaps you could ask your sailing buddy. The police are keen to speak with people on the water that day, as I am sure you have heard.'

Kitty nodded.

'You interviewed Kitty, Nathan?'

'PC Walker here did the interviewing, serg.'

'Sorry serg. My fault. I just thought ...'

'Don't take the blame for his poor decisions, constable. It is a full-time vocation. Take my car back to the nick, please. I will go back with Mr Hart.'

'*Serg.*' The two uniforms answered together and headed for Vicky's car, parked in the pub carpark. Vicky and Nathan sat in silence, watching them leave.

'Well Nath, is it him?'

'Serial killer of four people, including a thirty-five-year-old marine?'

'No. Is he sleeping with Amy?'

'Yes. He is amazingly dexterous at not mentioning the only person we both know.'

'And you interviewed him, anyway?'

'No. Gill interviewed him. I don't yet *know* who, if anyone, is sleeping with Amy. And he isn't a suspect in the murders, as Ted reminded me.'

'Are you going to make me wait for Gill's statements and your analysis? Or are you going to talk about today?'

Nathan swiped open his iPhone and spent a minute tapping the screen before Vicky's phone pinged. Without looking at her phone, she responded.

'What's that?'

'WhatsApp, actually. Can you have tech chase down the IP addresses, please?'

'Your lad? I am not spying on Amy for you.'

'My lad, Neuro and another care leaver in need, Ryan Piper.'

'I will see what I can do. And?'

'All as guilty as sin.'

'Of two murders?'

'Maybe three.'

'Thanks Nath. Case closed.'

Nathan scoffed, tilting his head into the sun, to smile at Vicky.

'I hated all this when I served. Running around not getting scum off the streets. But I have loved being back.'

'You aren't back, love.'

Nathan looked ahead and nodded.

'Gill is seriously hot.'

'Yes, it's those enormous eyes, tiny waist, and firm tits.'

'I meant as a police officer. She will be your boss one day, Vicky.'

'Damn. Overtaken by a kid with enormous eyes, a tiny waist, and firm tits. Do you know how that makes me feel? How about the Eastney-three?'

'All hiding something.'

'Did they execute three Albanian gangsters?'

'Not helpful, Vicky. And they were Romanian.'

'I meant we are all hiding something.'

'I know what you meant. Have you got anything from elsewhere?'

'Nothing. Zilch. Amy, you, Ann, and Gill are giving Ted and me more to talk about than the whole of the rest of the team put together. Only Gill is a bloody police officer. What a clusterfuck.'

'They might not be child murderers, Vicky. But they all know something about something.'

'I agree. Shall I take that to the Crown Prosecution Service?'

Nathen scoffed again. 'Have a look at the two boats. The boys were taken out to sea and ... *dumped.*' The word caught in Nathan's throat. 'Dumped like rubbish. Talk to Gill about today, build a case and go to Ted. Drag in Dakari and Kitty, and forensic their boats.'

'Shall I have your wife's lover beaten in the cells at the same time?'

'Suit yourself. I am only trying to find a way forward.'

Vicky shifted closer to Nathan and gripped his bicep, hanging her weight from his arm.

'He is twice her age, Vicky. And boring as hell. What's the attraction?'

'He is twice her age and boring as hell, probably.'

Nathan let out a long sigh, his headache building for the first time that day.

'Here comes the ferry, love. Let's get back.'

'Hey. Is Polly ok?'

'Good evening, darling. I am fine, thank you. And you?'

'Sorry Amy. I didn't mean ... I can't get her sobbing out of my head.'

'She was fine today. She isn't the first girl to have her heart broken by a man. In fact, she isn't the first woman stood in this house now, to have her heart broken by a man. Jax Jade has a twelve-year-old girl fostered and has taken Polly along with them to see *Barbie* in Fareham Cinema. Polly is being all grown up, *mentoring* the girl who has only just come into care. You ok?'

'No, Amy. Not really.'

The couple sat at the kitchen table. Nathan leant his forearms on the table, his good right hand covering the splint on his left wrist. Amy lay both her hands over his.

'Work?'

'Not really.' They sat in silence for a minute before Nathan took a deep breath and sighed. 'Robert Kitty.'

'Bert? What about him?'

'He is seeing my wife.'

Amy gripped his hand a little tighter. 'Oh. Ok.' She dipped her head to stare at his hand, unable to look him in the eye. 'Are you ok?'

'Not really.'

'No. I am really sorry.'

'Sorry you are shagging another man? Or sorry I found out?'

'Both, I guess.'

'He is older than your father, Amy.'

'Not quite. But he is the same age as mum. It isn't about shagging. Not just about shagging. Sometimes we just hangout.'

'Hangout? You aren't high school kids.'

'You are so intense, Nath. When you finished work, sick, and I started working from home …'

'It's my fault?'

'No. I am not saying that. I am just saying I spent some time apart, away from the house. Just doing stuff.'

'What sort of stuff?'

'Foster kid activities …'

'With Bert?'

'Yeah. I did his garden – it lacked a female touch.'

'You did his gardening! What else?'

'Just stuff, Nath. I added a few scatter cushions and decoration. He taught me to sail.'

'You didn't realise you'd end up in bed?'

'No. I realised. Like you say, we aren't kids. Of course I realised.'

'And Vicky and I hooking up gave you a hall pass?'

'My personal life doesn't revolve around Vicky, Nath. This has nothing to do with Vicky. It was my decision.'

'Was?'

'Is.'

'So, you intend to carry on?'

'Seeing Bert? No, I guess not. I haven't thought about it.'

'Why did you use my car?'

Amy let out a sigh. She kept eye contact for a moment. 'Mine is a bit, you know, conspicuous.'

'You used yours when you had a bona fide reason to be parked-up near him, and mine when you were skulking in the shadows.'

'Yeah. And I knew you wouldn't be out and bump into us if I had your car.'

'Did you do it in my car?'

'Have sex? Yes. Only a couple of times. You know, a few times, maybe.' She looked back at their hands as she spoke.

Amy retrieved two of their best wine glasses and poured large measures into each. She sat again and took his injured hand.

'Glasses are a bit more grown-up than plastic beakers. Does it hurt to drink?'

Nathan raised his free hand to his stitched lip. 'Yeah, a bit.'

'What happens now, Nath?'

Nathan shrugged. Amy continued.

'You mustn't hurt him, Nath. Promise me.' She placed her palm against his cheek and stared him in the eye. 'Promise me, love.'

The front door slammed, and Polly skipped up the hallway, singing the theme song to the Barbie film.

'Hey! Who died, innit?'

'Everything's good Polly. The world is duller when you're not in the room.'

Polly laughed. She gave Amy a kiss on the top of her head, couldn't see a clean and uninjured area on Nathan's head to kiss, so shrugged. She grabbed his wine and downed it in one gulp before they could stop her. She skipped to her room.

'Nath, shall ...'

'Not with Polly in the house, Amy. She can hear a wine bottle unscrew from two-hundred yards. You have a think, I will have a think, and we will talk later.'

Amy squeezed his good hand. The doorbell sounded. Amy stood to answer it, finding the spot on Nathan's head to kiss, which had alluded Polly.

Amy walked back into the kitchen with two uniformed police offices, inviting them to sit at the table and filling the kettle. Nathan looked at the officers with a furrowed brow. A headache had started when confronting Amy, and he now felt shooting pains across the tops of his eyes.

'Mr Hart. Pc Rio Enzo and Pc Alex Bronte – you, um, remember us? From the hospital?'

'Sorry. Yes, of course. I was a bit out-of-it on Friday.' He stood to shake hands. 'Have you caught the little scrotes?'

'Not yet, sir. But we are a little closer. Inspector Ted Dunbar was asking after our progress. You are on his team?'

'Yes. The two lads found washed up under the pier.'

'You didn't mention that on Friday, sir. You said you were there for a fostering meeting.'

'Really? Yes, I was there for a fostering meeting, but I should have mentioned the case, sorry. I was spaced

– you pay good money for that feeling down the Pier Nightspot.'

The officers both smiled, glancing at each other and sharing a *look,* which was more about Nathan being five or ten years older than the nightclub's target clientele.

'We can run through that angle in a moment, sir. First, is Polly Preti here?'

Amy started to speak as Nathan spoke over her.

'Polly was an emergency foster placement of ours. She is a bit of an absconder and the placement ended Thursday.'

'Children's Services duty social worker said she was still here, placed back with you.'

Amy went to speak again, but Nathan continued to talk over her. A bedroom door slammed from upstairs, followed by someone peeing noisily, obviously having not closed the bathroom door.

'Amy, love, I have a splitting headache. Be a darling and go ask Tarquin to keep it down, will you? Social don't know their arse from their elbow, Rio. That probably means Polly is still missing. The notes will catch up once they find her and allocate a new home.'

'Not back to you?'

'Possibly, if they find her out of office hours. Or more likely a residential home, away from local distractions.'

'Do you know Ryan Piper?'

'Yes, we have met. I suspect he is one of Polly's *local distractions*. To give the lad some credit, I believe he sees Polly as too young to date, but she is smitten with him. What is this all about, please, Rio?'

'Your attack was called in by a nervous young woman. A nervous young woman and an agitated young man wearing a West Ham shirt, were on the scene covered in blood when the ambulance first arrived. The Reverend Dan says the descriptions are of Ryan and Polly. Both youngsters seem to have disappeared. Your wife Amy reported Polly missing. We assumed she had turned up again.'

Nathan shrugged.

'Polly, we need to talk. There is a bit of a net tightening around Ryan. My guess is, I am his best bet.'

Polly shrugged. 'Don't know what you are talking about, innit.'

Nathan let the answer hang, not responding. Eventually, Polly continued.

'It isn't what you think, Nath. He was helping you. Trying to help. Then he tried to stop the bleeding and told me to ring 999, innit. But from the church, not my mobile.'

'You saw the people who attacked me?'

Polly shook her head. 'No. I heard the fight and was going to stay in the church foyer, where I was waiting for Ryan. Then I heard Ryan's voice and ran out to see him ... helping you.'

'Good job you were both there. Thank you.' Polly shrugged a response. Nathan continued. 'Did you see a weapon? Maybe a baseball bat or a piece of wood? It seems to have gone awol with … whoever did it, perhaps.'

Polly shrugged again, concentrating on her bare feet. She shook her head slowly. 'A cricket bat from the hostel. It had Ryan's prints on it. He slung it in the harbour.'

'Not to worry. I have Ryan's IP address. My mates in the filth are running checks already. The Met will pick up Ryan. Polly, listen to me. It is a billion times better if Ryan comes back to Pompey and immediately hands himself in. I can't drive to London,' Nathan held up his injured arm, 'but I am more than happy to meet him at Portsmouth Harbour train station and go with him to the nick. I will make sure he has a solicitor.'

'He can't do that, Nath. They will kill him.'

'Who?'

Polly shrugged. 'I don't know, innit. Ryan said they will kill him. Ryan isn't scared of nobody and nothing. But he is shitting himself about these mushes.'

'If I can find Ham West, these mushes will be able to, as well.'

Polly's head shot up at Nathan using Ryan's nickname. 'These men probably know where he is already. They told him to go away and not come back. If he comes back, they will kill him.' Tears began trickling down her cheeks.

'Ok Polly. This is absolutely not your problem. I will sort it. I will keep Ryan safe. Don't you approach him for now, not until this is sorted. If, and only if, *he* contacts *you*, tell him he needs to trust me. But otherwise, keep away from him, please.'

'He's got this girlfriend now. But I'm still his baby sister, innit.'

'Absolutely, you are. And I will keep him safe. Promise.'

Polly folded her tiny body into a ball on the dining chair. Nathan resisted the urge to gather her into a hug, instead calling upstairs to Amy.

Chapter Nine

'Nath. A minute, please. And you Gill, please.'

Nathan and Gill followed Vicky into the inspector's office.

'Sit down, Bernie.'

'Thanks Ted. That's worrying.'

'We have had a chat with a few people under caution. I will brief the team tomorrow morning, but I have dispatched detectives, uniforms, and forensics.'

'Forensics? You are checking Kitty and Dakari's boats?'

'Yes. Vicky and I ran through the statements Gill took from Kitty and the youth minister Dakari. We don't see it as a hot lead, but worth a look. Thank you, Gill, and you Bernie, for your diligence. Also, Bernie, we finally had a response from the Home Office. Comparing DNA samples of John, we are now confident the body parts washed up at Alum Bay on the Isle of Wight are of an ex-marine buried at sea, having died of cancer at thirty-two years of age. His parents live on the island, and I will visit them shortly. The remains are sunk in weighted coffins, wrapped in steel mesh, but it is not unheard of to break free. Thank you for your input, Nathan. Hanging back from a full press conference was a good shout.'

'All part of the job, Ted.' Nathan moved to stand.

'Wait Bernie. There is something else.'

Vicky cleared her throat. 'Nathan, we understand from the statement Gill, and you, took from Dakari Demarcus, that Amy may have been in both boats. We suspect,' Vicky dropped her eyes to the floor, 'Amy may have been sailing with Kitty on occasions and may be a material witness if she was sailing with Kitty on the day the boys entered the sea.'

'What? You are joking!' Nathan reached for his phone.

'Wait a minute Nath.'

Nathan ignored Vicky, so Gill stepped forward, placing a restraining hand over Nathan's.

'Officers are on their way to bring Amy in for questioning under caution. Amy will come here to Cosham. Kitty will go to central nick in Portsmouth.'

'And the Reverend Dakari Demarcus gets to stay home for questioning because he wears his collar back to front!'

'Calm down Nath.'

Still holding Nathan's hand and phone, Gill rested her free hand firmly, reassuringly, on Nathan's back.

'Bernie, you will surrender your phone to Gill, log out of your workstation under her supervision, and sit in the messroom until Amy is downstairs in the interview room. You will then take the rest of today and tomorrow off work. Once we have cleared Amy of any connection, you will resume your duties.'

'Like fuck I will!'

'Or Bernie, I will arrest you for obstruction and interfering with a witness and hold you until I say you may go home, perhaps later today. If that happens, I will end your contract. You will be out of here. Understood?'

Nathan returned home mid-afternoon to find Jax Jade and her young foster child watching Disney Channel with Polly.

'What's going on, Nath? The pigs arrested Amy, innit. What has she done? I reckon murder.'

Nathan flopped down onto the sofa next to Jax, massaging his temples.

'She has done *nuffin wrong, innit*. There is a tiny possibility she may have seen something.'

'The pig said she was going to be interviewed under caution, Nath. I think she might be guilty, but they will never prove it, with you on her side.'

Nathan laughed. 'You are a card, Polly. They interview under caution if they think there is a possibility the statement might form evidence in court. She is guilty of nothing.'

'If she gets locked away, will your boss move in here? I don't fancy living with two pigs.'

Jax turned around to face Nathan, eyes widened.

'No Polly. Zip it!'

'Shall I take Polly home with me, Nathan?'

'Polly? You alright staying alone with me, until Amy gets back?'

'Course I am, innit. He looks like a paedo, Jax, don't he? But he isn't. He's cool.'

'Thanks, Jax. This is so appreciated.'

Nathan walked Jax and her young lady to the door.

'Did you track down Neuro, Nath?'

'Not yet Jax but getting close.'

Jax glanced at her young lady.

'You don't think …'

'Very unlikely he is one of the two boys, Jax. But I won't give up until I reconnect with him. Thanks again for keeping an eye on Polly. Just so you know, Amy really has done nothing wrong.'

'Of course she hasn't Nathan, I know that. Don't worry, if the PCiCN lot chatter, I will set them straight. I might get Robert Kitty on the case.'

'Mm. Good luck with that one, Jax. Tell me, just between us, what do you make of Bert Kitty?'

'I like him. Totally dependable, popular, loves the kids. Ask your Amy. She seems very fond of him.'

'Ah, right, is she? No worries, I will ask her.'

'Has he done anything wrong?'

Nathan laughed. 'I am sure he has done less wrong than I have.'

Polly restarted the Disney Film after making Nathan supper – undercooked oven chips and a tin of baked beans microwaved to destruction. He managed two convincing forks full until Polly left him alone, when he hid the meal at the bottom of the bin. He swiped open his phone, reading the email from Vicky's private address. Without explanation, there were two London addresses, starting with initials HW and OHK.

Nathan opened messenger under his African King account and sent a message to Ryan's *Ham West* account.

Ryan. Nathan Hart here, Polly's carer. How is Hammersmith? Thank you for helping the other night. Sorry you are involved. Call me straight back. It is better we have a chat before poor Nye is woken with a knock on her door by my colleagues from the yard. Call now, please.

Nathan sent a second message to Neuro's *Ollie Hart Kole* address.

Hey Ollie! Guess who? Uncle Nathan and Auntie Amy. How is Chiswick? Amy used to shop in Chiswick High Street when we were dating. We need to have a brief conversation. Facetime will do. I will explain. Nothing to worry about.

His phone rang almost immediately. Nathan swiped open Facetime.

'Wow, Neuro! Look at you all grown-up.'

'Mr Hart. Nice to talk. Sorry I haven't contacted you before.'

'Fluent English and a London accent. Impressive. How is, you know, everything?'

'Yep, I am legal. I have all the necessary paperwork. I have initial leave to stay for five-years. I am studying. Hopefully, I will successfully apply for

indefinite leave at the end of my five-years. How is Mrs Hart?'

'I was a bit worried about you … Ollie, to be honest. We had an unfortunate incident here.'

'Yes Mr Hart, I saw. Not me, thank God. But somebody's children.'

'When you say legal …?'

Neuro shrugged.

'I hope you are not in with the wrong people, Ollie.'

'I wish I wasn't. But you mustn't worry about me. I have a set fee to pay back, including interest. No worse than a student loan. I am dealing with a middleman, who I trust. I am cool.

'You have my number now, Ollie. Don't be a stranger.'

'Perhaps one day I will visit with my wife, 2.4 children, and a dog.'

'We would like that. Just generally, Ollie, how does the middleman situation work, please?'

Nathan watched Neuro's face frown with concentration, and then he dropped his gaze from the camera.

'Sorry Mr Hart. I had better not say.'

'Can you say if your friends are based in the U.K.? In Portsmouth?'

Neuro delayed answering again. Nathan continued.

'Do you remember Ryan Piper?'

'Yes, I do. I have seen him recently.'

'Does he know your middleman?'

'That isn't for me to say, sorry.'

'Is he … safe?'

'I gave him some advice recently, Mr Hart. I told him to keep his distance from certain people he is known to.'

'In Portsmouth?'

'That isn't for me to say. To answer your previous question, Mr Hart, I should say none of us are completely safe – certainly not Ryan.'

'Ollie …'

'Thank you for checking on me, Mr Hart.'

'Thank you for talking with me, Ollie. Good luck.'

Neuro rang off.

Nathan poured a large glass of wine and swallowed a fist full of paracetamol as his phone rang, number withheld.

'Nathan?'

'Ryan. Thank you for calling me.'

'I did nothing wrong.'

'The local police know you and Polly were there. They want a word.'

'They will never find me.'

'I did.'

The silence stretched, Nathan wondering if Ryan had rung off.

'Ryan?'

'What?'

'Why are you even thinking of running? You can't spend your life running just because you were a witness to a mugging. Or is there more? Do you know who attacked me?'

'Not exactly. But they know me.'

'Look. Come down to Portsmouth tomorrow. I will prime the police officer and have a chat with you, and your brief, before interview. You will be out before supper.'

'That's what worries me. Can I stay with you and Amy.'

'No. Polly is here. She is a child in care. We can't have men staying in the house. What about your room at the church?'

'No. Let me think. Maybe, if I am allowed to return to London straight away. But only if nobody else knows I am in Pompey. Just you, Polly, and the police.'

'I can argue that for you, Ryan. But whatever happens, the police will find you. So, you need to make this work.'

'You know I will get done for attacking you, Nathan? A kid from care, living in a temporary homeless hostel. No job. Seen covered in your blood. I know Nye won't have me back. Not because of this, she just isn't the settling down type. She said I can stay one more night.'

'Can you stay with Ollie?'

Another long silence followed.

'You know too much, Nathan. You are a liability. Let me think. I will text you tomorrow.'

Neither Nathan nor Polly heard the front door open above the screech of *Australian Married at First Sight* from the television.

Polly looked up. 'Amy! You escaped, innit?'

With Amy standing in the living room doorway, Nathan retrieved a cookery book from the shelf, handing it to Polly.

'Cooking for Students?'

'Take it to bed, Polly. Select a breakfast, a lunch, and a supper. Tomorrow you are cooking under my supervision. And you are learning to use a washing machine, a dishwasher, an iron, and a fridge.'

'No way! A fridge? I'm not stupid.'

'Good. Then it will be an easy day. Off to bed, please.'

'It's only eight o'clock innit!'

'Polly, bed please. And brush your teeth.'

'God! This is going in my report.' Polly gave Amy a brief hug on the way past.

'How'd it go, love? Do you want a drink?'

'You bastard! Is this revenge?' She snatched her phone from her hip pocket and stamped redial. 'I can't get hold of Bert! Is he arrested?'

'They are just checking to see if Robert's boat or the church tinny was used to put the boy's bodies into the water. What did they ask you?'

'Up yours Nath. You are pathetic!'

Nathan pulled her jacket off and sat her on the sofa, removing her ankle boots. He handed her his own wine glass.

'Are you bailed?'

Amy took a deep breath and closed her eyes.

'I was there voluntarily. Apparently. I'm just, you know. I'm just not there anymore.'

'You were in interview a long time.'

Amy drained the wine glass.

'They just kept asking the same things over and over.'

'About?'

'Bert, the church, the boats, the asylum seekers, foster kids. Over and over and bloody over. Vicky was twisting the knife.'

'Vicky was in the interview?'

'No, but I could smell her in the questions about Bert.'

'It is unlikely Vicky …'

'Don't you dare defend her, Nath! They said they were interviewing me about the boys being put into the sea. But they kept on about Bert. Nath, I know you don't want to hear this, but they asked about Thursday 7th September. I was, you know.'

'Go on Amy.'

'I was out with Bert on his boat. We cut it fine with the tide and didn't get back into Langston Harbour until late.'

'The day the boys' bodies were dumped?'

'Yeah. I did my best, but they wanted details.'

'Details?'

'Like my movements for the whole day. And exactly what I saw of Bert that day, and everything.'

'Go on.'

'I had spent most of the day with him. And, you know. Most of the night. I couldn't lie.'

Nathan let out a long sigh. Amy continued.

'He wouldn't hurt a kiddie, Nath. He honestly wouldn't. Something else. They kept on about the kids Bert has staying. I went round Bert's one day. You know, I just popped in.'

'Hang on. You would just rock-up uninvited?'

'This is so embarrassing. If I wanted to get away from, you know. If I wanted to get away from here for a bit, I would just go to his and do some gardening or sit in his garden. If he was there and we went inside, you know, it was like a bonus. Sorry.

'Anyway. One day, there was a young man sitting in the back garden. We both jumped. The conservatory door was open, but Bert was out. I mentioned it in interview. We had a break, then when we came back, they kept on about the young man.'

'Black lad?'

'Yes. You know that *look* the UASC kids have? He had that look. Scared, thin. You know? Like a shadow.'

'Did you mention him to Bert?'

'Yeah. He said he was just babysitting for the day until social collected him.'

'Like a Same Day Placement child.'

'Yeah. I guess.'

'And Bert left the lad unsupervised?'

'I didn't think, at the time.'

'Your mind was on other things?'

Amy stared at her hands. 'The lad looked ok. You know, as ok as they ever look. Can you find out about Bert?'

'No. The earliest I am back in the office is Friday.'

'Can't you call Vicky at home?'

Nathan scoffed. 'You need to rein it in, Amy. Stay away from Robert Kitty.

'I am not sure I can, Nathan.'

Chapter Ten

'Where are you going, Nath? Who was messaging you?'

'Go back to sleep. I have to go out. It is about the attack on me. I am going to Portsmouth Central Police Station. Please stay away from Robert Kitty. I will try to find out what is happening. Spend the day with Polly – she has only got a few weeks left to learn to fend for herself.'

'Have you time to come back to bed for a bit first?'

Nathan smiled.

'See you later.'

Nathan pulled into Portsmouth and Southsea railway station taxi rank as a nervous Ryan walked out into the early morning sunshine.

'Good lad. Right decision.'

'Will you visit me in prison, though?'

'Stay calm, tell the truth, be positive. You aren't going to prison.'

Nathan pulled into the Civic Hall carpark and walked with Ryan to the police station at one end of the law courts complex.

'Nathan Hart and Ryan Piper to see PC Rio Enzo, please. He is expecting us.'

Before they could take their seats in the waiting area, PC Rio Enzo opened the internal door and ushered the pair into an interview room.

'Mr Piper?'

'I did nothing wrong.'

'Your name, please?'

'Ryan Piper. I have done nothing wrong.'

'Ryan Piper, I am arresting you in connection with the assault of Mr Hart on Thursday 28th September.'

'I did nothing …'

'Listen to me, Mr Piper. You do not have to say anything. But it may harm your defence if you do not mention when questioned something which you later rely on in court. Anything you do say may be given in evidence.'

'I didn't …'

'Mr Piper. Mr Hart has already requested the duty solicitor attend on your behalf. I suggest you keep quiet until you have spoken with her. Then I am sure we will sort this out. Mr Hart has advised me you suggested coming in today. Very sensible. Now let's all stay calm and follow the procedures.'

The door knocked and PC Alex Bronte entered.

'Mr Piper's brief is here. Shall we get you booked in and settled, Mr Piper?'

Nathan held PC Rio back by the elbow, as the other two headed towards the custody desk.

'A favour, please, Rio?'

PC Rio laughed his reply. 'That will probably be a no, Mr Hart. But try me anyway.'

'Far more interesting than me getting a thick lip is the concentration of intel from around the Sudanese Interior Baptist Church in Eastney – where I also received my pasting. See if you can't have young Ryan chat about any strange goings-on, in connection with the church, the two ministers and a neighbour of the church called Robert Kitty.'

'We have cautioned Ryan Piper for an assault, Mr Hart, nothing else.'

'It may well be connected.'

'It may well not, Mr Hart.'

Nathan shrugged. 'Sure Rio, I understand. You just stick with volume crime.'

The two men squeezed back against the wall to allow a uniformed officer to escort a released prisoner to the outside door. The man recognised Nathan and stopped less than a foot away.

'Bert.'

'Nathan. I …'

'Amy is asking after you.'

'I, I am ok. I am released now. Bailed.'

'Have you transport home?'

Recognising Nathan from his previous service, the escorting officer spoke. 'I am taking him back to Hayling Ferry at Eastney, Nathan.'

'In a squad car? Do you want that, Bert? Sit in the reception waiting area for two minutes and I will be out. I will take you.'

'Thank you, Nathan. But I will …'

Nathan stepped forward, gripping Kitty's arm.

'I insist, Bert.'

Rio lay a restraining hand over Nathan's wrist, but Nathan did not release Kitty until he nodded back agreement. As the secure door to the reception area swung shut, Rio spoke.

'What was that about?'

'He is a friend of my wife. *The* Robert Kitty I want you to ask Ryan about.'

As Rio reopened the reception door for Nathan, Vicky appeared from the direction of the custody desk.

'Well, well. If it isn't Nathan Hart, who is supposed to be on gardening leave today.'

'I am here about my assault, Vicky. Do you have a moment?'

Vicky nodded to Rio and took Nathan back into the interview room.

'Is Kitty released?'

'Bailed.'

'For?'

'Conspiracy.'

'Come on, Vicky.'

'We found nothing on the boat. Amy's account confirms his version of events on Thursday 7th September, when the boys were dumped. The hardest part was getting him to admit Amy was on his boat.'

'Forensics?'

'Maybe. But it is scrubbed within an inch of its life.'

'By Kitty?'

'No. Guess again.'

'Amy? Fucking great.'

'He finally admitted she seems to like to clean it for him. And she confirmed how she finds it cathartic.'

'God, she will make someone a great wife one day. I do most of the cleaning at home. What about the young man he had at the house?'

'That is what we are bailing him on. Conspiracy to take away a child in care and to hold an illegal immigrant away from the legal process. We haven't identified the boy yet, so who knows, it might be perfectly legit.'

'Only it's not.'

'Exactly. He is not prepared to divulge any details. We will probably have a case of habeas corpus.'

'And the *corpus* couldn't be Luke or Levi?'

Vicky shrugged.

'Was Amy forthcoming with information?'

Vicky looked up at a camera set on the wall behind her, checking the red light was off. 'I am not talking about your wife's interview, Nathan. But I think she was helpful within the confines of her ongoing concern for Kitty. She will make a good character witness for him.

'Anything from God's crew?'

'Dakari kindly took us straight to the safety boat. It had sunk.'

'What?'

Vicky shrugged again. 'Apparently, it does that. They leave it tied to a short jetty in the marina, for free. They take the outboard off and a bag of gear, but sometimes it is overwhelmed by the swell and *floats* just under the water until Dakari and some of his guys drag it out and empty it. It really is tiny.'

'No forensics, then?'

Vicky squashed her lips together. 'Nah. I doubt it. Guess who was the last one to use the tinny and tie it off on the jetty?'

'Oh no, don't say it was Amy.'

Vicky nodded.

'Your house, or the ferry at Eastney?'

'Ferry please, Nathan. I need some fresh air.'

'It's no fun, is it?' Kitty shook his head, as Nathan continued. 'I am not happy you are dragging Amy in on this, Bert.'

Kitty dropped his gaze and nodded. 'Is she ok? I was worried …'

Nathan replied. 'She is ok. She was interviewed under caution, but not arrested. She was home last night, tucked up and snuggly in *our* bed. Listen carefully to me, Bert. You will not drag Amy any further into this mess. You will take a moment to get your thoughts straight and then contact sergeant Vicky with anything you know, or even suspect.' Kitty swallowed hard and nodded. Nathan continued. 'I have a temper, Bert, at the moment it is under control. I value my wife's opinion; she is an excellent judge of character. But you wouldn't want me to think you are one of the bad guys, you really wouldn't.'

Nathan guessed Amy must have mentioned, to some extent, Nathan's shootout with the Romanian gangsters, as Kitty trembled in the passenger seat. Nathan pulled into the church parking space, which he assumed Amy used as a signal when visiting Kitty.

'Ok Bert, ring Amy now to tell her you are safe and with me here as a witness to the conversation. Then stay clear of her until after this is over, understood?'

'The police have my phone and I only have Amy's phone number on a piece of paper. We never ring, rung, each other, just in case.'

'Just in case?' Nathan repeated. Kitty nodded. 'Before you catch the ferry, we just have time to talk about the Sudanese Interior Baptist Church.'

'What about it? I'm an atheist, same as …'

Nathan released another sigh, clamping his forehead with the heel of both hands, as pain shot through his head. 'But you know Dakari and Dan.'

'Yes. They are involved with some of the UASC foster kids and some kids leaving care, who are homeless. Dakari runs an emergency hostel. Kids can only stay for a few nights because Ofsted and Children's Services can't class it as a home for young people. It isn't properly staffed as a home. I understand Ryan, who knows your foster child, is *renting* a room for peppercorn - not staying free in the hostel.'

'You have had no reason for concern regarding the church and the vulnerable kids who seem to congregate there?'

'No, if I did, I'd have called it in, obviously. And I wouldn't let, sorry, I mean I would have warned Amy about going there. I called in about a man I saw hanging around once. But that came to nothing.'

'Did you tell Rev Dan?'

'Yes, I did Nathan. But he said he had seen no one. I phoned the police and gave a description; in case he is a known paedophile or something.'

'What did he look like?'

'Um, I can't remember exactly. A bit of a scally, too old to wear his hoodie. Younger than me, older than you. Taller than me. Swaggered around the grounds when the kids were playing football after church. I saw him a few times, but not recently.'

'Black?'

'No, white.'

'How do they make enough money to run a church and a hostel?'

'Honestly Nathan, I do not know. They are popular, but I know what you mean – most churches seem to struggle.'

'Yeah, like decent pubs. Bert, I want you to stay away from Amy. Understand?'

'Yes, of course Nathan.'

Nathan parked in his drive, next to GP Rachel Warr's car. Standing in the hall, he screwed shut his eyes against the pain in his head and cradled his wrist against the pain shooting up his arm.

'You look a mess, Nathan.'

'Thank you, doctor. You look lovely.'

Nathan kissed her cheek, and the pair walked together into the living room. Amy nodded a hello, her eyes red from crying. Polly half dragged her gaze from the Disney Channel.

'I've been cooking and working all day, Nath, innit. I'll have earned my wine tonight.'

'Good girl. What have you done?'

'I cooked breakfast. Cheese on toast.'

'Well done. My favourite.'

'And like, done washing and put it on the line. And made lunch. We had ham sandwiches; with bread you have to cut. And I did oven chips; they were dead lush. I'm doing you pasta tonight, but like making my own sauce, with Amy. But I've got to use vegetables and proper tomatoes.'

'Cool Polly. When you settle into your place, you can invite us over for a dinner party.'

'Yeah, I already said that to Amy, innit.'

'Rachel. It is always nice to see you. Is this a home visit?' Nathan sounded calm, but Rachel realised he loaded the question.

'No. I popped round to see Amy. Thursday is my day away from the surgery. Also, I thought I could help if Amy went with you for your results and consultation. I can stay with Polly, if you like.'

'Shit! I clean forgot.'

'What's going on, you two?'

'Nothing. Nothing, love. I had some tests after they whacked me on the head. They called me in for the results and to discharge me. I will change the appointment.'

Rachel responded. 'No, you won't Nathan! You are going. Amy said you are off work today. No time like the present. You can't mess the hospital around like you do me. Amy, why don't you go with Nathan? He can explain better in the car.' She glared at Nathan.

'I will go alone. You three have a girlie afternoon, down the shops or something.'

Amy curled up onto the sofa, looking like Polly's other bookend.

'You stay here, Amy, with Polly. I will go with Nathan to his appointment. He shouldn't be driving with a broken wrist. Anyway, it's ideal, with me being a doctor. You chill with Polly.'

Rachel drove as Nathan stared at the passing rows of houses.

'You haven't told Amy you came to see me.'

'Yeah.' Nathan scoffed. 'We famously don't keep secrets. I suppose you know about her bit-on-the-side. Have you known all along?'

'If I knew Nathan, I wouldn't tell you.'

'So, this is where the hospital tells me I have a brain tumour and a week to live?'

'And you were coming alone?'

Nathan shrugged. 'Amy would have an easier life without me.'

'Hey! Don't talk like that, pillock! You probably just have a migraine. Either way, you spill the beans to Amy today.'

Rachel pulled into the hospital and the pair negotiated the complexity of lifts and corridors. As soon as they entered the ward reception, Nathan was called through to Doctor Cath Lopez's office. Nathan made introductions; the two doctors having already spoken by phone.

'My wife is tied up with our foster child, so Rachel offered to drive me.' He held up his splinted wrist.

'Let's get straight to it.' Cath raised a sheaf of paper. 'I have a summary report, which I posted to your GP.' She gestured towards Rachel. 'Both scans are clear.'

'You aren't pregnant. I told you so,' added Rachel.

'Your bloods are clear, but we noted certain concentrations.'

'Of?' asked Nathan.

'Zolpidem, Xanax, and benzodiazepine.'

Nathan shrugged. Rachel spoke.

'Prescription drugs, love. Sleeping pills, anxiety meds and benzo depressants.'

Nathan kept eye contact with Cath. 'I am not here for a lifestyle lecture, doctor. I am here to stop the headaches and avoid dying of brain cancer. The meds help me cope. I have reduced my use of prescription drugs and other drugs. I'm doing *ok*.'

'You previously confirmed you take sildenafil. Why?'

Nathan looked at Rachel, who answered in a low voice, 'Viagra.'

Nathan looked back at Cath. 'Why do you think?'

'Erectile dysfunction?'

'Obviously.'

'You only take a tablet before sex?'

'Yeah. They help.'

'Not at other times, Nathan?'

'I explained this to my therapist. We have erections several times a day. It's like having phantom limb syndrome, when it just hangs there, limp.'

'How many do you take?'

Nathan shrugged. 'A couple in the morning.'

'That it?'

'And a couple at night.'

Rachel rested a hand on Nathan's arm. 'Tell the doctor exactly how many, Nath.'

'Four when I first wake. Four early evening. I am worried, or nervous,' Nathan hesitated, before continuing in a whisper, 'or scared, of not being able to perform when Amy wants to do it.'

'Every day? Dosage?'

'Yes. 100mg. I read the data sheet. Viagra is non-toxic and doesn't cause brain tumours.'

'It *opens the tubes.* It allows blood to flow more freely. Sildenfil can also cause cyanopsia. It can sensitise rod cells in your retina.'

'And give me blinding headaches?'

'Unlikely Nathan. But it can make things appear blue and make lights appear to blaze or colours, especially blues, more vibrant. I had a quick look in your mouth and massaged your neck when you were being patched up. The hospital dentist confirmed.'

'Confirmed what?'

'Your neck and jaw muscles are overly stressed and tense, and you grind your teeth, probably at nighttime. That is the probable cause of your headaches. The good news is, Nathan, you are relatively healthy, and you are not dying. But you need to ease back on your excesses. You need to learn to relax better and pop fewer pills. You don't have a brain tumour. Make an appointment with your GP to discuss.' Cath nodded towards Rachel again. 'I understand why and how you mistook the collective symptoms and signs, but they are separate symptoms of different conditions.'

Nathan and Rachel hardly spoke on the drive through town and back to Nathan's house. Rachel pulled up at the curb and cut the engine. Nathan saw both Amy and Polly standing at the window; he gave a wave.

'A good day then, Nath.'

'Yeah. Thank you for your help, Rachel.'

Rachel's smile broke into a giggle.

'What's so funny Rae?'

Through snorts of laughter, she managed, 'This is so funny, Nath. We thought you wouldn't make Christmas, but all you had was a stiff neck and overdosed on nob pills. You idiot. Have you any idea how much those tests cost?' She laughed again, so infectiously that Nathan had to smile back. 'You idiot, you absolute tosser! Thank God you are ok.' She wrapped both arms around his neck and pulled him into a hug. 'Thank God.'

Nathan watched Rachel drive away and gave a wave as she rounded the bend before walking to the front door where Amy and Polly stood.

'What was all that about, Nath?'

'No idea Amy. Perhaps she has hysterics and hugs all her patients.'

'Come on Nath. I'm doing pasta with sauce, peas, and everything.'

'Cool Polly, I'm starving.'

Amy stopped Nathan in the hall as Polly entered the kitchen. 'Well? What were the results?'

'Of the tests? Yeah, you know, fine. No problems, everything is normal, no big deal. Did you contact Bert?'

'No. I thought I'd talk to you first.'

'The police kept his phone. He is fine. I saw him earlier. They bailed him, but he is struggling to explain who the young man is, who you saw in his house. He asked after you and I told him you are home safe. I asked you to stay away from him for both your sakes, and I asked him to stay away from you, as well.'

Amy looked up into Nathan's face, smiled, and nodded. 'Thanks love.'

'Did you know he reported a suspicious man hanging around the kids?'

'Yes, but that was ages ago. Maybe two years.'

Chapter Eleven

Nathan walked towards Portsmouth Central Police Station feeling the early morning cold, as PC Rio Enzo and PC Alex Bronte were leaving the main entrance.

'Rio, Alex, good morning.'

The pair glanced at each other before Alex spoke. 'Mr Hart. Can we help?'

'Well, yes. I'd like to know how you got on with Ryan, please. When are you releasing him?'

Alex continued. 'We can say it was a productive interview, Mr Hart. Mr Piper gave a concise version of events. He won't say who his accomplice is, but we are fairly certain it is Polly Preti. We need a word with her.'

'Accomplice? Or do you mean witness and alibi?'

Alex shrugged, looking a little bored. 'We will decide that once we speak to her. Ryan, and to a lesser extent Polly, are still in the frame for your assault, Mr Hart.'

Nathan switched his attention to Rio. 'Did you ask about the church and Robert Kitty? Did he mention a guy in his early forties hanging around the kids?'

'He is extremely reluctant to discuss the church and the ministers. He said he knows Kitty, but had no opinion about him, other than *he wants to be liked*. I sent Sergeant Vicky Flemming an email, but I am not sure I should discuss one unrelated case with the victim of another.'

'Ok Rio. I will talk to Vicky. Thanks for following through. When are you releasing Ryan?'

'Again, Mr Hart,' responded Alex, 'there is only so much we can discuss. But I can tell you, we have already released Mr Piper on bail.'

'Already! When?'

Alex glanced at Rio, before continuing. 'One hour ago.'

'Shit. Where did he go?'

'We released him back to his last known address at the Sudanese Interior Baptist Church, Eastney.'

'Did you take him there?'

'No. He didn't want a lift.'

'Christ! What's up with you? The lad is scared for his life. Has he got his phone?'

'No. We kept it for a little looksie.'

Nathan turned and trotted back to his car, pulling his phone from his pocket.

'Amy. Has Polly heard from Ryan?'

'She is sound asleep. I'm sure I would have heard her talking on the phone.'

'I need to find him. I am going to the train station. Take Polly and drive around. Try the church and the beach. But don't tell anyone he is in Portsmouth, especially not your bit-on-the-side.'

Nathan drove to the train station and flashed the photo of Ryan, which he still had on his phone since the first night of meeting him. He showed the station staff near the turnstiles and again to the porters and staff on the two London bound platforms.

He then drove back to the Cosham incident room before checking in with Amy again.

'Anything, Amy?'

'Nothing, love. Except Polly here is going to include the fact I dragged her from bed, during a pleasant dream, in her report.'

'Switch to speaker phone. Polly? Ryan has given a full statement about what happened on the night they attacked me. The police are looking for you as a material witness. Stay calm and listen to me. I will ask the two officers to interview you at home, but it will be under caution. I will tell them you want Amy to sit in as an appropriate adult. When they arrive, you must ask them again for Amy to sit in. She won't be permitted to say anything. Don't big it up or try to paint Ryan in a better light. Just tell them what happened and answer their questions. Is that ok? What's for supper tonight?'

'I don't like the filth, Nath. Chicken and chips with peas, innit.'

'Lovely! My favourite.'

'Everything I cook is your favourite, Nath. What if I get him into more trouble?'

'Just stay calm, listen carefully to the questions, and answer truthfully.'

'Vicky, I need a word with you and Ted, please.'

Vicky stood and raised a hand. The inspector saw her through his office glass wall and beckoned them in. Nathan called to PC Gill Walker to join them.

'Ted, I think we have a problem. The young man who uniform was hunting in connection with my assault has been arrested and bailed. Now he's gone missing.'

'Done a runner?'

'I don't think so. He handed himself in for interview. If he was running, he would have run when I first talked to him.'

'Hang on Nathan! Is this one of the lads I authorised the IP address search for?'

'Yes Vicky. Ryan Piper.'

'Oh great. Thanks for dragging me into this.'

'He gave his bail address as his old address at the Eastney church. But I know he wouldn't go back there. He is a big lad, but he is genuinely terrified of going near the church. I think he was heading back to West London, but he didn't even make it to the train station. Uniform kept his phone for analysis.'

'Bernie, this lad is nothing to do with my case. I can't divert resource to look for random young men.'

'Vicky, PC Rio Enzo sent you an email regarding Ryan Piper commenting on members of the church, in relation to Luke and Levi.'

'How the hell do you know that, Nathan? There was nothing of interest in the email, other than Ryan Piper thinks Dakari Demarcus knows all the young people who hang around the church. I am actually a bit surprised the officer bothered to pass-on this non-information.'

'Look Ted, please. All I am saying is there is enough connection to our case, and a genuine concern that Ryan may be targeted by people unknown, possibly involved with the Levi and Luke murders, for you to talk to Rio Enzo's inspector and have them try to locate Ryan. If nothing else, he has given a false bail address. Please, Ted.'

'Ok Bernie. I will have a word on the QT.'

'No Ted. I strongly suggest you make an official request and include it in the investigation log. We are receiving more and more flags against this bloody church. I was right about the Isle of Wight body. Trust me, I am right about this.'

Vicky sat at the end of Gill's desk, facing Nathan.

'You need to strafe the Sudanese Interior Baptist Church, Vicky. Throw everything at it. Arrest the two ministers and Kitty. Beat out some information about a scally in his forties whom they know but won't talk about.'

'And Amy?'

'No! Ok, shit. Amy as well, if you must. You need to get dogs in there and search for Ryan.'

'You know we have no evidence to support a move like that. If we decide to arrest Amy at any point, you realise that is the end of your contract here. How are all your hospital appointments going, by the way? You seem a little … heightened.'

'Fine Vicky. Everything is fine. We can't allow Ryan to wash up on Southsea beach like the others. There are too many fingers pointing at the same place from different directions to be a coincidence.'

'Right Nathan, I want you to calm down. You are making me nervous. Are you sure you are well enough to be at work today? Why not take …'

'No, I am fine. Look, my doctor sent me for some tests. I have a series of symptoms, which appeared to suggest something worrying. It turns out I have a few totally unconnected ailments and the symptoms aren't connected. I am totally fighting fit.'

Gill raised her hand. 'Listen to yourself Nathan.'

'Don't you start Gill.'

'No Nathan, just listen to yourself. Everything pointed towards a single illness. But when the medics took a step back and looked at the bigger picture, they saw there were several unconnected things going on.'

Nathan shrugged. 'All's well that ends well, Gill. Thank you for your concern, but I have other things on my mind right now.'

'Not unusually Nathan, you are missing my point. What if all the evidence piling up around the church and Kitty are not related? What if Luke and Levi are separate from the lad seen at Kitty's? What if your assault is unrelated to one or even both events? What if the *unsavoury* hanging around the church is involved in a third activity? And Ryan in another? You tried to make all your symptoms fit one illness, but that was not the case. Now you are trying to have all the evidence fit one crime. Out of interest boss, what is the main illness you are suffering from, other than being smacked in the head?'

Nathan sat in silence, studying Gill, and slowly nodding. Eventually, he spoke. 'I have a stiff neck, Gill. That's it. A stiff neck.'

'Neuro, I am sorry to trouble you. I am not muscling in on your new life, I promise.'

'I would feel safer without contact, to be honest, Mr Hart.'

'I have lost Ryan Piper. I am worried and was wondering if you know where he might be.'

'I know his old girlfriend up here. But I heard they split after just a few days. I will check and let you know.'

'Do you know a friend of Dakari's and Rev Dan? Early forties, white, tall and … odd. Looks like a bit of a scally.'

'It sounds like Eamon Nica. A really nasty piece of work. Dakari knows him well. Please do not mention me to either of them.'

Nathan pulled into the church carpark and into Amy's normal spot. He sprinted to the ferry just as it pulled away from the dock.

'Sorry to disappoint you, Bert. It is only me, not Amy, this time.' Nathan pushed past Robert Kitty and stood in the centre of the tiny living room of the prefabricated bungalow. 'Is Ryan here?'

'Ryan who?'

Nathan pushed into the kitchen and then the conservatory. Retracing his steps, he continued into the second bedroom, which led directly off the living room. He pulled back the duvet to reveal fresh sheets. He knelt to glance under the bed. The chest of drawers was empty, except for a few items of underwear, tracksuits, and sweatshirts, presumably for Kitty's foster children.

'Amy's idea? She keeps the same emergency kit for our foster kids.'

Kitty followed closely behind. 'Don't you need a warrant or something?'

Nathan continued into the tiny square passageway and into the bathroom.

'Anyone else staying here?'

'No. I ...'

'So why two toothbrushes?'

Kitty swallowed hard and blushed.

'Does Amy keep stuff here?'

'Not really, Nathan.' Kitty flattened himself against the passage wall as Nathan barged past and into the main bedroom.

Nathan stopped in his tracks and inhaled deeply; certain his sense of smell was not deceiving him. He could smell Amy's perfume – he could smell Amy. Kitty stood in the doorway, watching the muscles tense on Nathan's forearms and neck. Nathan picked up a framed photograph from the bedside cabinet, of Amy pulling on the sheets of a small sailing yacht. Her hair blew across her face, her smile wide, mirrored sunglasses reflected the bow of the boat partly obscured by sea spray. In the cabinet drawer was a handful of creams and a hairbrush. Nathan picked up a set of pink fluffy handcuffs and a sex toy in a silk bag. He checked under the bed and glanced in the wardrobe, hesitating by a tallboy of drawers, deciding he did not want to know the contents.

'Who was the lad Amy saw here?'

'I don't recall, Nathan. It was probably a foster child, I guess.'

Kitty was taller and heavier than Nathan, and in better physical shape with Nathan's bruised ribs and fractured wrist. But fear and the speed of Nathan's attack disabled Kitty and prevented him from defending himself as Nathan forced him back against the wall. With his hand around Kitty's throat and his body squashing him against the wall, Kitty stared back at Nathan in wide-eyed fear.

'I'll tell you what Bert, stop guessing and start recalling.' Nathan tightened his grip until Kitty could not breathe, and pressure built behind his eyes. 'Now, who was the lad?' Nathan released the pressure on Kitty's throat a little, until he could talk.

'I don't know his name. Dakari asked me to let him stay for one night.'

'Then where did he go?'

'In the morning, another man collected him in a van, and I have not seen him since.'

'Did Amy see him go?'

'I don't think so. She was asleep.'

Nathan fought the urge to squeeze the life from Kitty. 'Were you paid by Dakari.'

'No. He offered me money, but I was happy to help for nothing. They were young men applying for asylum. They only stayed one night, or in one case, the weekend.'

'They? How many in total?'

'Just four, over the past four years. I wasn't told any of their names.'

'Always collected by the same man?'

'The others were collected, or left, when I was out. I don't know.'

'Does Amy know about the others?'

'No. She came around unexpectedly that day and saw the lad.'

'And he was the last one?'

'No, the third. The fourth lad was here for the first weekend in September.'

'Listen carefully, Bert. If you see or hear anything from Ryan, or you have any suspicions of where he may be, you call me immediately. Do you have a phone yet?'

Kitty shook his head. Nathan continued.

'Ok. You go down to the pub, ask to use a phone and call Sergeant Vicky Fleming. Have you still got her card?'

Kitty nodded.

'And you tell her everything you know about these lads. Got it?'

Nathan caught the return ferry to Portsmouth, hastening to the church and straight into Rev Dan's office. Dakari leant back against the rear wall of the office as the two men laughed with a young mixed heritage couple discussing their future wedding.

'Mr Hart, you can't …'

'I can and I am, Dan. One of you show me around the hostel. Now, please.'

'Mr Hart, you need to make an appointment. I can't just clear my desk of all work, just because …'

'What? Like this?' Nathan swiped his arm along Rev Dan's desk, sending documents, stationary, half a mug of coffee, and a desk lamp clattering to the floor. 'There, cleared.'

The young couple moved from their seats to the corner of the room, away from Nathan. Dakari lay a hand on Nathan's shoulder.

'Nathan, please. I will take you to the hostel. And while we are there, Rev Dan here will call your inspector and report your disgraceful conduct and threatening behaviour.'

Nathan left the office, followed by Dakari. The two men walked across the carpark to a converted outbuilding.

'This is the male dorm.' They walked into a large room with six cabin beds along two walls. 'The female dorm has four beds in a shared room. It is over by the manse.'

The beds were all stripped back to the mattresses. Nathan took a moment to check in each of the empty lockers attached to the beds. The bathroom had a private cubical with a large washbasin, a shower cubical, and two separate toilets. The room was clean and dry, having not been used recently.

Nathan tried the next door off the dormitory, which was locked.

'Open this, please.'

'I will have to fetch the key from my office.'

Nathan kicked open the door, sending a section of the doorframe spinning across the small bedroom. Inside contained belongings neatly stored away, and a poster of Danny Ings scoring against Nottingham Forest. Nathan opened the wardrobe and flicked through the clothes.

'Ryan's room?'

'Yes Nathan. Is Ryan in trouble?'

'Has he not contacted you to arrange collection of his gear?'

'No. We hope that is a sign he might want to return.'

'Why do you send young men to Robert Kitty?'

'I am sorry Nathan, I really can't …'

'Don't fucking push me, Dakari.' Nathan could see Dakari would not be easily intimidated. 'This is important. When I get back to the office, I will arrange for uniformed police to search every inch of this church and arrest anyone who obstructs us, or tampers with evidence. Or you can help me avoid having to do that.' As he spoke, he snapped on a pair of rubber gloves and rifled through Ryan's possessions. When was Ryan here last?'

'Last Thursday, when you were attacked. How about I tell you what I can, Nathan? But no names. Sometimes we have lads stay who cause trouble or we feel are too vulnerable to stay with the other lads. Occasionally, we ask someone we trust to look after them until we sort something out. We have asked Mr Kitty a few times. He is so good with the kids and because of the fostering, we know he has been DBS background checked. That is also why we appreciate Amy's help with the kids after church on Sundays. Like you, I am sure she is also DBS checked.'

'And who collects them?'

Dakari shrugged. We normally only offer a bed for one night or, if we have no other guests, then maybe longer. We don't check where they go, after us. We concentrate on youngsters, but although many seem young and vulnerable, they are legally adult.'

'You liar.'

'Sorry Nathan?'

'Those young men were collected. You handed them over to someone and you don't want the transaction to be associated with the church.'

'No Nathan. That is not the case, and I resent being called a liar. I suspect your sergeant will be here soon and I shall make it clear we will agree to no further contact with you. How dare you?'

Aware Vicky may arrive shortly, Nathan continued his search. He wanted to cover the girl's dorm, both manses, and the church. He realised he probably would not have enough time, unless he talked Vicky around with Kitty's revelation about the four young men.

The next closest building to search was the main church. As they walked past his office, Rev Dan joined the pair, locking closed his office door.

'I have complained to your sergeant Mr Hart, she will be here shortly. If you do not leave these premises now, right this moment, I shall also dial 999.'

'Eamon Nica?'

'Sorry Nathan?'

'Eamon Nica. You know him.'

The first door Nathan tried was to the cellar. Locked, he kicked at the door several times before returning to Dakari's office to retrieve a ring of keys from the open key safe. The first light switch did not turn on any lamps, but the next two turned on banks of lights to illuminate the extensive cellar. The ministers followed Nathan down the stairs.

Nathan saw no obvious signs of life. The cellar was largely empty, with only a bank of steel fire-resistant document cabinets and a few other storage crates packed with church vestments and religious paraphernalia and furnishings. A large wooden frieze depicting Jesus's baptism by John the Baptist hung securely, stored at one end of the room against the wall, hanging from a railing in the ceiling.

'Eamon Nica? You both know him. I saw him talking to you in the carpark, shortly before he kicked shit out of me!'

'Mr Hart, we are answering no more of your questions.'

'I am looking for a missing person, Dan, possibly in mortal danger. Why do you not want to help me? Which of the ten commandments states you are not to help?'

'Nathan!' Vicky powered down the stairs, followed by PC Gill Walker and a male officer Nathan recognised from the incident room.

'Sergeant Flemming. I …'

'Reverend Dan. I will take it from here. Can you leave us alone, please? I need to have a moment with my colleague. My civilian, contractor, colleague.

'Nathan, if half the complaint is true, you are in deep shit! What the hell are you thinking?'

'Kitty told me the lad Amy saw was an asylum seeker being moved around.'

'As in trafficked.'

'Yes, as in trafficked! If he is yet to be granted leave to stay, and is being moved around, then that is the very definition of *trafficked*.'

'What were you doing at Kitty's?'

'I am looking for Ryan. Which is more than anyone else is.'

'I've had a missed call and a message to contact Kitty, Nathan. Have you been interfering with a potential witness?'

'No! I just went round looking for Ryan, recognised Amy's toothbrush, then he spilled out information about Dakari's involvement with trafficked young men.'

'You idiot! You stupid bloody idiot. Did you hit him?'

'No! I barely touched him.'

'And you didn't ransack the minister's office in front of four witnesses?'

'Ransack? Hardly Vicky. Come on, give me a break.'

'Get in the car, Nathan. Now, before I arrest you. Christ!'

'We need to check the manse and the girl's dorm, Vicky. Ryan is in a lot of danger. If they dump him off the church tinny, or Loverboy's shag-boat, it will be down to you!'

'In the car!'

'Sergeant.' Gill raised a hand. 'I can speak with the ministers, explain a concern has been raised by a member of the public, and ask to look around the dorm and manse. It makes sense, skip.'

'Constable, you stay here with Mr Hart. If he tries to leave, or touches anything, cuff him, taser him, and beat shit out of him, in that order. Gill, come with me.'

Whilst waiting for Vicky to return, Nathan continued to walk around the cellar, closely supervised by the uniformed police constable. By the time Vicky returned, Nathan and the PC were back at the frieze.

'Well?'

'Well what, Nath? Rev Dan was more than happy, keen even, to help Gill search the manse and dorm. Perhaps if you had just asked nicely. I am taking you back to the office when Gill is finished. I shall then waste valuable time trying to smooth over this clusterfuck, and then guess what, Nath? No? No idea? I will waste more time having the buying department end your contract. A leopard never changes its spots. I can't believe I was stupid enough to ask for you to come back. All you have done is push this investigation backwards.'

'That isn't strictly true, Vicky, is it? Separate from the investigation, we need to find Ryan.'

'Ryan is probably the guy who battered you with a baseball bat!'

'It was a cricket bat, Vicky. And my money is on Eamon Nica.'

'Who? Who the hell is Eamon Nica?'

'I don't really know, Vicky. I will get Ann on the case …'

'You will do nothing! You are out of here, Nath. You have gone too far this time.'

They fell silent for a moment; the PC cleared his throat and shifted his weight self-consciously.

'At least I didn't shoot anyone this time.'

'Nath, there is nothing funny about this mess.'

'You need to talk Ted and the DCI around Vicky. I need to stay on the case until we find Ryan and we have Eve's killer.'

Vicky glared at Nathan.

'The lads. I meant the lads' killer, Vicky. You know what I meant.'

Vicky was in no mood to share the car back with Nathan. He rode in the back of the squad car with Gill, whilst Vicky drove her own car.

'Did you search properly, Gill?'

'Honestly Nathan, he is not there. I even tapped walls for hidden doors. I checked the garden sheds, every wardrobe, the back of wardrobes, everywhere. I promise.'

'You and Ann need to search for an Eamon Nica, his known associates, and any association with the ministers, the church, Kitty, and anyone else.'

Gill took out her notebook and wrote the sketchy information and description from Nathan. He continued.

'And you need to poke about in the church affairs. Who and how is it funded? Who are the backers and associates?'

'Not really our department ...'

'I know! I know that Gill. When I am gone, you need to raise it with Vicky, Ted, everyone who will listen and everyone who won't. Raise it at the briefings and raise it again in front of the DCI.'

'That will do my career the world of good, Nathan.'

'We need to find Ryan and move this investigation forward before we are picking out more body parts from under the pier.'

Gill let out a deep sigh and turned her gaze towards Hayling Island across Langston Harbour, glistening in the low autumn sunlight.

'Back on the naughty step, Nathan!' Vicky gestured to the messroom attached to the small kitchen as she peeled off to the inspector's office.

Gill followed Nathan into the messroom. Anneika joined them. She spoke.

'Is it true Nathan? You threatened two priests?'

'A bit of an exaggeration, Ann.'

'Did you arrest him, Gill?'

'No need. Vicky ushered him out before that was necessary.'

'I'd have arrested him. And cuffed him. Although he'd probably enjoy that.'

Nathan remembered Amy's handcuffs in her bedside drawer at Kitty's. He scoffed and shook his head.

'I think he fears Vicky. Actually, I think he fears all women. How's that stiff neck of yours, Nathan? Need taking to A and E, poor baby?' Anneika offered with sarcasm.

Without waiting for a reply, she slipped behind his chair and gently massaged his neck and shoulders. He released a groan and closed his eyes.

'You are wasted here Ann. You should be a masseur in one of those cheap whorehouses in Portsea.'

She pinched his ear, making him yelp. 'That is possibly the sweetest thing you have ever said to me, Nath. Gill let's have a cuppa while Nathan waits to hear about his lack of a future. The urn is cold. Use the kettle. I asked the floor secretary to order us a new urn. I reckon that one is all furred-up.'

Gill flicked on the kettle and switched the urn socket several times. 'Just a fuse blown, Ann. Probably under rated. I'll bring in a screwdriver and a spare fuse tomorrow.'

'And you are psychic, Gill? They used to burn women like you.'

'Science, actually Ann. I helped my mum rewire our house when I was a teenager. She is an electrician in the dockyard.'

'Your mum? Cool. I was not good at science class or technology. How can you tell?'

Gill flicked the urn switch several times to demonstrate. 'There is no load on the switch. There should be some resistance to turning it on, and less resistance to turn it off. Like this.' She now flicked the kettle socket, demonstrating the slight resistance turning it on, and a more positive click to turn it off. 'There is a load on the kettle switch, no load on the urn switch. Simples.'

'Hang on.' Nathan grabbed Ann's wrist to stop her massaging. 'If three light switches each turned on a bank of lights, they would have a similar resistance to being switched on? But if one wasn't connected to anything, it would switch differently?'

'And you really stopped my massage to talk light switches with Gill. No happy ending for you, son', pouted Ann.

Gill answered. 'Yes, basically. The more electrical load, the harder to switch. That is why you see massive, high-voltage, bar handled switchgear on disaster films about submarines.'

Vicky walked into the room. Gill straightened from her position resting against the back of a chair, and Ann took her hand from Nathan's neck and moved back. 'Ok Nath, the DCI wants a quick word.'

She walked Nathan to the inspector's office, where they could see the DCI and inspector waiting.

'This is it, Vicky. I'm gone?'

Vicky stopped and pulled Nathan to face her. 'Yes, Nathan, you're gone. What did you expect? Honestly Nath, I despair.'

'I believe time is running out for Ryan. Or has already run out.'

'And that makes it ok to interfere with a potential witness, or suspect, and terrorise two priests?'

Vicky pushed Nathan ahead and into the office.

'Nathan, thanks for popping in.'

'My pleasure, DCI.'

'Ted and Vicky were just telling me about the excellent work you have put in to help solve the Levi and Luke case. Well done.'

'Thank you, sir.'

'But I feel you are a little close …'

'Sir, I am very concerned for the safety of …'

Vicky shouted over Nathan. 'Let the DCI speak, Nathan!'

'Sorry, I …'

'The thing is, Nathan,' continued the DCI, 'Vicky has explained about your wife's involvement with a potential suspect. I also understand you went a little off-piste and questioned members of the public — way beyond your remit. Ted filled me in on the recent assault on you. I am also hearing you are suffering the effects of stress and tension. The thing is, Nathan, I am having your contract terminated. I am happy to keep you on our approved supplier list for future work. But I really don't think this case is doing you any favours.' He held up his hand for continued silence. 'Contracts are saying, contractually, we can continue to use your *system* in the capable hands of Ms Maneet and PC Walker, and they will reimburse you, accordingly. Nathan, thank you for your insight, and candour, to date. Good luck.'

The DCI extended his hand to shake. Nathan went to speak, but Vicky shook her head.

'Understood, sir, and thank you. It hasn't gone as I'd hoped. Sorry.'

Chapter Twelve

Nathan drove to the Portsbridge Pub and parked his BMW in the rear carpark. He drank the first two pints slowly, whilst phoning Neuro and Nyekachi in London – neither would admit to speaking with Ryan since he had left for Portsmouth. Nyekachi refused to admit she knew him, even when *African King* messaged her a photograph of the couple from her own Facebook page. By the time the investigation team drifted into the pub at six-thirty, Nathan was five pints down.

Gill came straight to the bar and hugged Nathan from behind, resting her head against his back.

'Sorry boss. I'm missing you already.'

Nathan patted her hand and ordered a round of drinks for Anneika, Gill, and himself. They watched Anneika beating a middle-aged BNP skinhead at pool, before Nathan spoke.

'Did you have chance …'

'I have done a couple of searches on the church. They are completely independent of The Baptist Union of Great Britain. Interestingly, they are not a charity. They are registered with Company House as a private limited company. Rev Dan and Rev Dakari are both directors, but the owner is a South African called Brandon Beyers.'

'Sounds like an Afrikaans name. Have you searched for him?'

'No Nath. I am not a detective. I have added the information to the inspector's report. Hopefully, he will pick up on it. And I have added Eamon Nica to the shortlist. I can't do more than that, Nath, sorry.'

As they spoke at the bar, Nathan saw the outside door open in the bar mirror. Vicky and Ted walked in and sat at their usual table. The pair talked for some time, glancing at Nathan throughout. Vicky came to the bar to order drinks.

'Office reunion? You only left a few hours ago. Glad you came for a pint, Nath. I know Ted wants to chat. No hard feelings, eh?'

Vicky gave Gill a wide smile until Gill made her excuses and moved to the pool table to play Anneika, the winner of the previous game.

'Ted, hi. Look, I know you can't say too much, but have you run up the flag about Ryan? I really think he is in danger.'

'I have Bernie. But we don't know where to look, or why.'

Nathan nodded, trying to squeeze the fug of alcohol from his head by pushing his hands through his hair. He flinched as he pushed against his healing wounds.

'I think we need to have another look in the church cellar.'

Vicky scoffed. 'You are not in the clear, Nath. Dakari is still pushing for threatening behaviour and aggravated trespass with criminal damage.'

'More important than that, Vics, is a young man's safety.'

'Evidence? A reason for yet another search? Other than because they believe in one more God than you do.'

'There's a spare light switch.'

'Sorry Bernie?'

'I'm not making sense. Sorry. I have been drowning my sorrows.'

'I agree with you there, Bernie. You are not making sense.'

'There are three light switches in the cellar. And they are all under load. But only two turns on any lights. There is something odd about the cellar.'

'Excellent Bernie. Case solved.'

'I know. Ok. I need to think.'

Vicky spoke. 'Another thing, Nath. Stop tapping-up Gill for information. She could lose her badge, especially with Kitty being so close to Amy. Don't drag Gill down with you.'

Nathan nodded and downed his beer. 'Same again?'

'No love, I will take you home. Then I am back in the office for an hour.'

'Why did Vicky bring you home, Nathan?'

'As you can tell, my darling, I am a little too tiddly to drive.'

'But why her? You could have walked home. Just.'

'Why do you keep pink handcuffs at Bert's?'

Amy swallowed hard and blushed a deep red. 'I'm not talking to you like this, Nathan. Are you working the weekend?'

'I am off the case.'

'Why? What happened?'

'Probably because my wife is fucking a suspect.'

'Suspect for what? This is all getting out of hand, Nath.'

'Where is Polly?'

'Keep your voice down. She is in her bedroom, listening to music and deciding what to cook you for Sunday lunch.'

'They took Ryan. I am worried for Polly as well. She was a witness to my attack. Did Rio and Alex interview her?'

'Yes. You are making me nervous, Nath.'

'We need to watch her closer. And I do not agree to her having more contact with the police. My encouraging Ryan to come forward was a bad call.'

Nathan woke with a start as Amy jumped from the bed. The thudding on the bedroom door continued.

'Polly! What's happened?'

'Nothing, innit. I done that pisshead some cheese on toast for breakfast, his favourite. Good for hangovers. I will give it to him.'

'No Polly. Give it here, please. That is very thoughtful. But we are not allowed in each other's rooms.'

'He was in my room, chasing spiders, innit. It's in my report.'

'Put the kettle on, love. We will be down in a minute.'

Back in bed, Amy took a big bite of Nathan's cheese on toast, before handing him the rest. Polly had made none for Amy.

'What is it with girls and women wanting to mother you?'

'I guess it's my cheeky boyish good looks and humble personality.'

'Yeah, or something else. We can always tell Polly we fell back to sleep because the breakfast was so filling.'

'That would go in her report. Maybe later, love, my head is full of Ryan and the murders. And, you know.'

Amy forced a thin smile, trying not to look disappointed.

'Sure. How are the headaches, vision, and smell hallucinations going?'

'Much better, thanks. It was nothing really – poor self-medicating. Rachel has given me something to calm everything down, without swinging it so far as to make me need uppers. I think I was trampoline medicating.'

'I realise this, with Bert, has piled more pressure on you, sorry. Are we going to survive this, Nath?'

Nathan shrugged, concentrating on his empty plate.

'I didn't get married to get a divorce.'

'That it?'

'What do you want me to say? I need to concentrate on Ryan. We will not sort out this mess in one sitting, over cheese on toast, and with a teenager running amok downstairs in the kitchen.'

'I need to talk with Bert, Nathan.'

'What do you *need* to talk about?'

'Ok, I *want* to talk with him.' Nathan let out a sigh. Amy continued. 'We were seeing each other for three years. We haven't even ... split, officially.'

'Christ Amy.'

'He was there for me, Nath.'

'When I wasn't?'

'That's not what I said.'

'But it is over with him, Amy. Isn't it?'

Amy dropped eye contact. 'That is what I am saying, Nathan. Bert and I need to talk.'

'Message him.'

'He still hasn't got a phone. Or if he bought a burner, then I don't have the number.'

'You have been trying to contact him, then?'

'This hasn't gone the way I planned.'

'You mean you didn't intend to get caught?'

'I meant this conversation is not going well.'

'Let me think for a bit, Amy. Come on, let's rescue the remains of the kitchen. You have created a cooking monster.' Nathan leant over and kissed the top of Amy's head.

Amy went through the contents of the cupboard under the sink, showing Polly how and where to use different cleaners and talking about the dangers of the different chemicals. She gave her a lesson on using the dishwasher, showed her how to clean mirrors using glass polish and newspaper, then set her the task of cleaning her bathroom, of which she had sole use. It never ceased to amaze Amy how little some young people in care knew of the practicalities of life, despite a maturity beyond their years - a combination of the absence of parenting, institutionalisation, and the availability of fast food.

Nathan spent the morning on his home laptop, surfing social media for any trace that Ryan had made it somewhere safe, or even somewhere dangerous. As part of his contract with Hampshire police, his secure work laptop remained in police keeping until the current investigation was complete. They would then revoke his username and password, removing his access to the Police National Computer database, until they awarded him any future contract.

He searched the owner of the Sudanese Interior Baptist Church, Brandon Beyers, before phoning Gill Walker.

'Are you working Saturday, Gill?'

'Looks like it, Nath. Good to hear from you.'

'I just called to ask you to check I logged out of my secure laptop.'

'I will check, Nath. Now we have established a legit reason for your call; how may I help?'

'I have been googling. There is a religious freak called Brandon Beyers, a member of the immoral Freedom Front. Also, formally of the Freedom of Religion South Africa and, if it is the same person, alleged founder of the prescribed terrorist organisation, Afrikaner Religious Resistance. If it is the same person, he owns property, logistics and a vehicle repair business, all in the Pretoria/Joburg corridor.'

'And he also owns the Sudanese Interior Baptist Church, here in Portsmouth? That is a big stone's throw from South Africa.'

'I am not saying it is him, Gill.'

'What are you saying?'

'I am saying highlight what you now know to Vicky and Inspector Ted and pester them until they allocate a DC to take a peek.'

'Sure, I will add it to the list of instructions you already gave me to pass-on.'

'No probs. If you can't, put Ann on please.'

'Hey! Easy tiger. I didn't say I wouldn't do it. I will either come out of this looking like a prize fighting bull, or as Nathan Hart's bitch.'

'Anything on Ryan?'

'Nobody is allocated to follow-up on your missing person, Nath, who apparently isn't even reported as missing. Try the officers who bailed him.'

'Eamon Nica?'

'Ann has been importing info and his bio from the database. He has previous with Irish republican groups, specifically the Real IRA. He has connections with Irish organised crime. The Irish Garda and Essex Police have warrants out for his arrest, but he has gone underground.'

'Arrest for what?'

'Thirty-nine Vietnamese found in the back of a lorry in Essex. They were close to suffocating. The tractor unit was from a Belgian company, but the sea container was rented by a haulage yard in Ireland, partly owned by Mr Nica. He isn't a nice person, Nath.'

'Can you email Eamon Nica's bio over to PC Rio Enzo, please?'

'Already done.'

'What about my mate, Kitty? Has he told you anything about the lads who stayed at his house?'

'He gave the sergeant some excellent descriptions, including photographs. He also gave times and dates.'

'Could any of them have been Levi or Luke?'

'Not Levi, they were all too short. Without DNA, fingerprints, or … you know, a face, it is difficult to exclude them. The most recent lad looks too well fed to be Luke, but who knows, maybe one of the previous lads. Including that lad Amy met, I suppose.'

'But nothing concrete?'

'You mean enough evidence to arrest Amy for conspiracy and re-arrest Kitty? No, I don't think so.'

'No connections with the church, ministers, Brandon Beyers, or Kitty?'

'Nothing showing. Eamon is Roman Catholic, if that is relevant.'

'Ok Gill, thanks. Don't forget to check I logged out. When this is over, I will invite you and Ann to ours, for cheese on toast and beer.'

'Cheese on toast? Ok. See you then. Stay safe, or at least safer.'

'You coming to church tomorrow, Nath?'

'No Polly, and neither are you.'

'Says who? We like it Amy, don't we? I'm not sure about the group chat with God thing; I have my own chats with him, innit. Not like bombard the poor guy with a chanting crowd and everything. But I like the singing. I might see Ryan if he is back.'

Amy spoke. 'He isn't back at the church, Polly. Nathan looked for him there yesterday. Nathan is right, let's not go this week. There is another church just around the corner from here. We can go there.'

'I need to see my mates. It is still sunny and not too cold. I think I'm over Ryan now. He can just be my brother if he wants. I will go to Southsea fairground instead and see who is there.'

'I think we should have a weekend together, Polly. Concentrate on your home economics.'

'No way! Weekends are for living, Amy, not for growing up.'

Nathan scoffed at her answer and smiled.

'Have you anything to add, Nathan? Or do you just load the bullets for me to fire?'

'Amy is right Polly. Ryan is missing, and I was attacked there. Let's keep our distance from Southsea and stick close together until we understand what happened.'

'Nothing personal, guys, but I am not spending all weekend with a couple of wrinklies.' Nathan laughed and Amy managed a smile. Polly continued. 'It is really nice of you guys to keep me on until I am eighteen. And I really like how you are getting me ready for having my own place and stuff. It is really sweet. But you are a bit, you know, boring sometimes.'

Amy and Nathan looked at each other. Both knew Polly was only with them on an emergency placement and children's services could place her elsewhere at a moment's notice. They both also realised social services would immediately remove Polly, if Amy is arrested in connection with Kitty, or if they arrested Nathan for threatening behaviour and criminal damage at the church. The couple did everything to make Polly feel safe and, temporarily, settled, but her chances of staying with them past the weekend were tenuous.

'Ok ladies, I have a suggestion. Let's all go to the African's church together, as a family. Polly can teach me when to sit, when to stand, when to clap and shout hallelujah! Whilst we are at the service, Amy can pop across to Hayling Island to see her friend. Then we can meet you in the Maypole Pub, Amy, for a pizza and ice-cream lunch. If the weather holds, we can walk along to Hayling Island fairground, together. Then home. Polly and I can cook Yorkshire Pudding and roast potatoes, to go with a beef joint-in-a-box. Deal?'

Amy complained at Nathan for undermining her again, but then stopped herself.

'Cool!' responded Polly. 'I've seen Hayling Island from Eastney, like a million times. But I have never been there, or on the ferry. It is a tiny boat. Is it safe, innit?'

Chapter Thirteen

Amy drove Nathan's BMW into her usual parking space in the corner of the church carpark.

'I'm just going to check Ryan isn't at the hostel.'

'Wait Polly, please. You must stay with Amy or me. It is really important. Look, I won't be welcome there, but maybe Amy will take you after the service and I'll wait outside. Deal?'

Polly nodded, following Amy and Nathan towards the ferry.

'Stay here in the queue, love. I'll get you a ticket.'

'It's ok Nath. I have a year's pass.'

'Yes. Of course you do.' Nathan shook his head.

'I am so proud of you, Nath. You are handling this so well. Thank you.'

Nathan scoffed and looked away. 'But you are coming back, Amy?'

'Sure I am. It's only a trip to Hayling Island.'

'Is that supposed to be funny?'

She took his bicep and squeezed it reassuringly. 'Come on, love. Chin up.'

'Ask Loverboy why he had the lads staying with him.'

'I'm sure he has done nothing wrong, Nath. I understand you don't trust him, but he really is a sweetie.'

'I think they might traffic the lads.'

'Don't be silly. Bert wouldn't traffic children. That is a terrible accusation.'

'Ask him. Say, *Nathan thinks the lads are trafficked.* Say, *Nathan will take a huge amount of pleasure in leading the police to your door and seeing you locked away, out of reach of his wife.* Say that and gauge his reaction. Also, love, and this is non-negotiable, tell him I dropped you here, I know where you are.'

'Nathan! Now you are just being melodramatic. He wouldn't hurt me. He is the gentlest ... um, chap ...'

'Lover? Swear you will tell him, Amy, or this meeting is off.'

Amy gazed over the narrow stretch of water to the row of beach houses, with the single bungalow, on the Hayling Island side.

'I am sure he knows already, Nath. Did you not see the big binoculars on a tripod, in his lean-to? But ok, I will tell him.'

Nathan and Polly joined the loose throng of congregation entering the Sudanese Interior Baptist Church. Rev Dan and Dakari stood on either side of the open double doors leading to the hall, shaking hands with the congregation. Nathan walked down the centre to avoid both men. As Dakari shook Polly's hand, he held her tightly, so Polly and then Nathan came to a halt.

'Polly, my dear. And Nathan. Good to see you on a Sunday and looking ... calm.'

Nathan nodded a response to Dakari, waiting for him to release Polly to continue into the hall.

As Rev Dan began a welcome and introduction to the service, Dakari slipped out of the main doors. Ten minutes later, as the instrumental ensemble prepared to play, Nathan lent close to Polly's ear.

'When did you last do as you were told, Polly?'

'When did anyone care enough to tell me to do something, Nath?'

'Right, listen. I am telling you this because I love you and I care. Stick that in your report. I will be back shortly. You stay here. You leave this room with nobody. Nobody except me or Amy, or at a push, a uniformed police officer. Understood? Nobody.'

'I'm not ten …'

'Nobody. Ok, see you in a few minutes.'

'Don't be long, Nath. Don't miss the singing.'

Nathan left the hall and tried the locked cellar door from the foyer. He marched purposefully to Dakari's office and flung open the door without knocking; the office was empty. Retrieving the ring of keys from the open key safe, he marched back to the cellar and let himself into the dark. He threw the *spare* light switch, which did not turn on the cellar lights, before edging down the stairs in the darkness.

Nathan stopped to listen intently to what he assumed was just an echo of his own steps. He continued down another three steps to stop and listen again, holding his breath to better hear the silence.

'Why do we keep stopping, innit?'

'Christ Polly! Are you trying to give me a fucking heart attack?' He spun around to face the silhouette of Polly against the light spilling from the opened cellar door. 'I told you to stay in the hall!'

'Actually, Nath, you said I could leave with you or Amy. So here I am. I left with you. And you aren't supposed to swear at children in care. I'm putting that in my report. What are we looking for?'

'Go back to the hall, Polly. Now!'

'What, on my own? What are we looking for?' Polly pushed past Nathan and made it to the bottom of the stairs as Nathan caught up.

'Right. You stay quiet and close to me. I'm looking for any chink of light or sound of a motor or anything which I may have switched on a moment ago.'

'Wouldn't it help to turn the lights on?'

'No. That is the whole point. The room lights might obscure …'

'Obscure what?'

'I don't know Polly. Obscure the light of whatever I just turned on. Look, stop talking and follow me. Eyes and ears peeled.'

'I bet you were a useless copper, Nath.'

'Polly!'

'Ok, ok.' Polly tucked her fingers into Nathan's belt and followed him as he moved along the row of steel cabinets.

Away from the narrow, opened door, the darkness was almost total. At the corner of each cabinet, he peered into the gloom, looking for any escaping light and listening for sounds.

'What's that smell, Nath? Smells like when your finger goes through the bog paper. This way.'

'No, Polly. We will continue searching this side first. Then the back wall.'

The pair continued to search between the cabinets until they walked into the concrete wall at the end of the cellar. Turning left, they made their way along the wall, Nathan looking down to where the floor joined the wall, and up to where the ceiling met the wall.

'There, Nath. Straight ahead.'

Nathan concentrated, but all he could see were squiggles and floaters in his own eyes. 'What?'

'God, you are so old, Nath! On the floor, like a strip of light. And I can smell that shit again.'

Nathan edged forward until he could feel the edge of the wooden frieze, hung against the wall. Kneeling and then sitting, he rested his forehead against the edge of the frieze and saw the faint strip of light disappearing behind the panel.

'Bingo Polly. Well done. I will use the torch on my phone and turn on the main lights.'

As he spoke, Nathan saw a shadow pass over the light seeping from the distant open door. The door slammed shut and locked.

'Fuck. Stay close to me Polly.'

Nathan swapped hands with his phone. Holding the phone away from him with his injured left hand, and ready to punch out with his good right hand. As he switched on the torch, he saw the figure swinging an object towards his head. Nathan shouted, ducked and brought up his left arm for protection. The object struck Nathan's wrist splint side on, knocking the phone from his hand. As the phone spun away, the torch flashed across the figure. Nathan twisted, still sat on the floor, and kicked out with both feet. His right foot contacted the assailant's knee. Polly pushed back against Nathan and launched into the darkness, past the attacker. Nathan continued to kick out in the darkness for a few moments before rolling away on the floor.

Polly screamed from the other end of the cellar, rattling the locked door. In the light of the discarded phone, Nathan saw the shadow move towards him. He launched at the shadow, hoping he would make contact below the weapon. The figure exhaled and groaned as Nathan head butted into his solar plexus.

The room lights blazed on, as Polly flicked the two light switches and continued to scream and kick at the door. Wrongfooted, Nathan spun around and landed back against the same cabinets as the assailant. Unbalanced, Nathan could not recover before the handle of a machete thudded into his chest. The attacker ripped off a pair of night vision goggles and swung around to hit Nathan in the temple. Grabbing hold of the machete handle with his good right hand, Nathan stumbled and fell, pulling the man on top of him. With the machete handle across Nathan's throat, the man used the night vision goggles to smash into Nathan's unprotected face.

For the second time in just a few days, Nathan saw Polly's face as a blur behind the man. This time he also saw Polly lift a fire-extinguisher above her own head, bringing it down on the head of the attacker.

Nathan lay back, gasping for air, the man fully prone on top of him. As Nathan struggled to push off the man, so Polly collapsed crossed legged next to Nathan.

'That is defo going in my report, innit.'

Staggering slightly, Nathan opened a toolbox sat on a bench, and found cable ties to secure the man's wrists behind his back, and to bind his feet.

'Shall I hit him again, Nath?'

'Probably unnecessary, Polly.'

Nathan walked gingerly to the cellar door and found a mobile phone signal, reluctant to unlock the door until help arrived. He heard the muted singing of the congregation. He dialled Vicky.

'Listen Vicky. Eamon Nica has attacked Polly and me, wielding a machete. We are in the church cellar. This is a major incident, Vicky. The cellar is a crime scene. We need uniform, CID, ambulance, and the fire brigade. Don't interrupt Vicky, I am serious.'

Nathan rung off and dialled Amy.

'Where are you?'

'Bert's house, still. What's happened?'

'Stay close to Bert. I will call again in a minute.'

'Is Polly ok?'
'Yes, we are both fine.'

Nathan tugged on the heavy wooden frieze, trying to pull it from the bracket. The whole frieze hinged around one end of the bracket, opening like a door. Behind the frieze was a steel door, painted the same shade of grey as the surrounding cement wall. Nathan removed a large screwdriver from the toolbox and worked on the narrow gap between the door and the steel frame.

'Nath! Here, look.'

Polly opened a small hatch in the door, six inches from the edge, to reveal a keyhole and draw handle. Nathan compared his keys to the keyhole and then found two keys in Nica's pocket, but none matched.

Nathan and Polly both jumped, startled, at the thudding on the cellar door. Nica groaned and pushed onto his back to face the pair. Taking the fire-extinguisher as a weapon, Nathan moved to the cellar door.

'Who's there?'

'The big bad wolf! Now unlock the door, you dick!'

Vicky and Gill entered the cellar together. Gill moved to Nica, carefully manoeuvring him onto his side and handcuffing him. Sirens wailed and flashing blues penetrated the foyer outside the cellar.

'What first Nathan? What on earth have you two been up to?'

'Ambulance and hospital for Nica, under arrest and accompanied by uniform. This whole church is a crime scene, including the manse, hostels, and the tinny boat. Arrest Dakari, Rev Dan, and better take Kitty in again. And impound his boat again in case it is connected. Behind that wall is a room.' Nathan pointed to where Polly stood. 'There may be one or more people trapped inside.'

'We will have to arrest Amy for conspiracy if we take Kitty. Whatever they were up to, they were doing it together.'

'I know.'

'Where is she?'

'With Kitty. At his house.'

Vicky raised an eyebrow.

Polly sat with a Community Police Officer as Vicky barked orders. Uniforms and detectives began work. The congregation filed out of the hall and could leave for home, having given names and contact details. Nathan now wore a hazmat suit, with blue plastic boot protectors and blue rubber gloves. The fire brigade used an electric hammer and hydraulic spreaders to remove the steel door.

Nathan moved into the room and knelt in front of Ryan, chained to rings on the wall.

'You ok, son?'

'I have been better, Mr Hart. I shit myself. They wouldn't let me use a toilet.'

'You certainly have, Ryan. Don't worry about it.'

The fire fighter cut the chains and eased Ryan onto the floor, stepping back to allow paramedics to fit an IV bag of saline and an oxygen mask. They stretchered him out of the cellar, followed by Nathan, and stopped to allow Polly to kiss his cheek.

Amy sat in the back of Vicky's car, the door open and her feet outside on the ground. Kitty stood to one side. Both were handcuffed. Vicky lent against the front door of the car, tapping her phone.

'May I Vicky?'

'No Nathan, you may not. They are both cautioned and under arrest. I am just waiting for separate squad cars to take them away.'

'I can't say anything to them now that I couldn't have said before church. What's the problem with a few words?'

Vicky stared at Nathan and then between her two prisoners. She stepped close to Nathan and leaned in, to whisper. 'You better tell me anything they divulge, Nath. Or I'll have you for obstruction.' Nathan scoffed. Vicky straightened. 'I said no. Now move away,' she added for the benefit of any eavesdroppers.

As she spoke, Vicky walked to a group of detectives, talking in a huddle, leaving the three alone, *not to talk*.

'Are you ok, love?'

Amy shrugged and nodded. 'Have you been fighting again, Nath? We saw the police lights and came over on the ferry. Where's Polly?'

Nathan touched his closed eye and broken nose. 'Well, Amy?'

'I honestly have nothing to tell the police, Nath. I was visiting Bert; I know nothing of this. I saw one lad at Bert's before, but we didn't really speak.'

Nathan swapped his stare to Kitty. 'Well?'

'I think it is better I say nothing, Nathan. Sorry.'

'That is not very moral of you, Bert, is it? Lads have disappeared, died, and been kidnapped.'

'That is nothing to do with me. I need a lawyer.'

'I agree with you there, Bert. He will tell you to go no comment, and justice for Luke and Levi will take a step backwards.'

'I never met Luke and Levi, Nathan. I am saying …'

'Tell him Bert. Please. Tell him, love. Tell him what you told me.'

'I can't do that, Amy. Please be quiet.'

'Tell him, Bert, or I will.'

Kitty dropped his head to stare at his feet. Amy spoke again.

'Nath, Bert told me …'

'Ok! Ok, this is nothing to do with you, Amy. Ok. There are young people being sent home to Africa, Syria, and Afghanistan. Asylum refused. Children being sent back to be abused, enslaved, and murdered. Just like your lad Neuro.'

'Neuro is living it large in Chiswick.'

'Neuro stayed with me for one night, before they took him away. They either gave him a new identity, or the reports, documents, and references, to dip under the radar and reappear having successfully applied for asylum.'

'And the other lads?'

'Each is different. I am not sure. But yes, they all get to stay in the U.K. They are all so vulnerable.'

'You are involved in trafficking children into the U.K.? For money?'

Amy spoke. 'Of course not for money. Bert only did what we all want to do. Keep these poor kids safe. And they were already in the U.K. They had all made it this far.'

'And you knew about this, Amy? You are involved? Who is your contact, Bert?'

'I am not saying, Nathan. I can't say. I just helped hide a few lads until they smuggled them away to safety.'

'And a life of debt and servitude?'

'I don't know about that; I just know they stand more chance here than back *home*.'

'Levi, Luke, and Eve might disagree.'

'That is very unfair Nath, leave him alone.'

Nathan glanced between his wife and her lover. 'You two deserve each other. You really do. Amy, if you really don't know anymore, you need to go no comment. I mean it, Amy, not a fucking word in this jerk's defence. I will talk to the brief I had when I was arrested. Keep your trap shut tight. You, Kitty, are a fucking disgrace.'

'I agree with Nathan, Amy. Please don't get more involved than … than I have already made you.'

'I don't need your support with talking to my wife, Bert.'

Vicky sauntered back to the three as a squad car pulled into the carpark, blues flashing.

'I told you not to speak with my prisoners, Nathan. Mrs Hart, your chariot awaits.'

Vicky helped Amy to stand, still cuffed, walking her towards the waiting squad car. As Amy faced away from the men, she mumbled.

'I am sorry. I do still love you, honest.'

Nathan and Bert glanced at each other and back to Amy, not sure who she aimed the declaration at, and if either should acknowledge it. Nathan turned to face Bert and moved to within a couple of inches of his face.

'You are in so much shit, Bert. So, much, shit. And screwing a member of the investigating team's wife has made your situation a whole lot worse.' Kitty nodded and Nathan continued. 'They have arrested Eamon Nica; he will not receive bail. Tell me your contact and let me set the wheels in motion, Bert. I don't care about you, but I want Amy home. Is your contact Eamon Nica?'

'No.'

'Then who?'

'Nathan! Move away from my prisoner now! Enough, or I will arrest you along with Amy.'

Nathan stood with Vicky, watching Kitty driven away by squad car. The carpark now filled with police and crime investigators. Detectives and uniforms searched the hostel dorms, manse, church, and outbuildings. Tow trucks removed the minister's cars.

'We have a search team at Kitty's house, and a team waiting at Amy's, sorry, I mean *your* house.'

'I swear Amy isn't involved. I would know if she was.'

'Really Nath? You don't even know who Amy is sleeping with. If we can pin trafficking on Kitty, Amy is also looking at trafficking, aiding and abetting, or conspiracy. Either way, she is going down.' Vicky nodded towards the inspector and DCI, leant against the DCI's Mercedes. 'We had our suspicions, thanks to you, Nath. And now we have our *corpus* in the form of the hidden room, and a kidnapped Ryan. We have a fugitive, in the form of Eamon Nica. All down to you.'

'But?'

'But, if Amy has committed a crime, we will charge her, without fear or favour.'

'My guess is she is infatuated with a fool trying to save the world. Kitty is no criminal mastermind. In fact, he is a bit of an idiot.'

'That is probably a conversation her brief needs to have with the court, at the point of sentencing. And I assume you aren't trying to defend Kitty. Or are you going soft in your old age?'

'The more serious the crime you charge Kitty with, the more serious the crime you charge Amy with abetting. What about Reverend Dumb and Reverend Dumber? Is the DCI going to have a chat over a sherry and open fire?'

'Both arrested, Nath. You found a kidnapped young man in a hidden room in their church. Even Chief Constable Olive Redney would struggle to justify not arresting them. Did you look around the room?'

'Glanced.'

'Sound proofed. All but airtight, except for soundproofed air-vents. And a ... *table* ... with restraints.'

'This is where the boys were killed.'

'It's looking likely Nath, yes. It is really macabre, more like a wooden slab, or even an altar, in the shape of a crucifix. There aren't any drains or water supply in the room – it must be swimming in forensics. How on earth did you find the room?'

'The third switch turned on lights somewhere, but I couldn't see where. Poor Ryan had no loo, and Polly could smell it, presumably through the vents. Polly's eyes, twenty years younger than mine, saw the miniscule strip of light from the hidden door behind the frieze.'

'We will take Polly into police protection, Nathan, sorry.'

'No way Vicky! Look what happened to Ryan on your watch.'

'Hardly *my* watch, Nath. And Polly has been involved twice with you receiving a beating. She could have killed Eamon Nica. How would that have messed her up?' The pair stood in silence for a couple of minutes as Nathan gathered his thoughts. Vicky then continued. 'Ann and Gill said you requested they search the hovercraft passenger CCTV footage, the day your car was parked overnight.'

'Amy was having dirty nights away with Kitty, Vicky. I think that is old news now.'

'Kitty wasn't on the hovercraft.'

'What? Just Amy alone? Perhaps they travelled separately to cover their tracks. Ask them if you still think it relevant.'

'Amy wasn't a passenger, either.'

Nathan paused again. His headaches had reduced following the medic's interventions, but he now felt the throb rising from his neck and shoulders.

'Have you spoken with the South African, Brandon Beyers, who owns the church?'

'We haven't tracked him down yet. Our guess is he is in Joburg, or one of his many other haunts. We don't believe he is in the U.K. at this very moment.'

'Hiding?'

'He seems to live his life in hiding. Or he is just a naturally private person.'

'Yeah. A shrinking violet, but with his own church. I don't think so.'

The police impounded Nathan's car following Amy's arrest. Refusing a visit to the hospital or a lift home, Nathan called an Uber.

Waiting at his house were a detective and a uniform, who searched the house and took away all devices except Nathan's phone. He bathed, patched-up his own wounds, and poured a beer and a whisky. He lit the wood burner to brighten the room. Having barely noticed or acknowledged Amy over the previous few years, he now desperately missed her. The door knocked. Nathan opened the door to two police officers and Polly. He stepped backwards and gestured to the living room.

'Are you ok, sir?'

'Absolutely, officer.'

'Um, we have been given this address for an emergency out of hours foster placement.'

'Yep, that's me.'

'Um, can I see your identity card, please, sir?'

Nathan produced his card. The officer studied the card and photographed it on her phone.

'Polly, are you happy for us to leave you here with Mr Hart?'

'Yeah! Duh! Obviously, innit.'

The officers gone, Polly walked around the living room, touching surfaces as if reuniting herself with a childhood home. She smelt Nathan's whisky, screwed up her nose, and gulped down his beer.

'So, how did you get me back, Nath?'

'I phoned the duty social worker, went back on *out of hours call*, told her what a pain in the arse you are, and offered to take you back, if you came back into care on police protection. Nobody seems to look at the bigger picture. So, one officer took you away from us on police protection, and another brought you back to us to look after. Goons.'

'Where's Amy?'

'The police kept her in for the night.'

'What? Why?'

'Her friend on Hayling Island might be involved with the room we found Ryan in. The police just need to check a few things.'

'Is he Amy's boyfriend?'

Nathan held Polly's eye. She did not appear embarrassed or judgemental.

'Yes, it's looking that way.'

'Did he kidnap Ryan?'

'I doubt it.'

'So, break her out of gaol, innit.'

Nathan laughed. 'If only it was that simple, Polly.'

'Don't laugh at me, Nath. I am not stupid.'

'I am not laughing at you, sorry. You found and rescued Ryan today. And you saved me. Well done. I am not laughing at you; I am laughing at the situation I have got myself into with Amy.'

'When the pigs took me tonight, I mean they were really nice and everything, not like the pigs on trains when you haven't got a ticket or when you get stuff from the shop without paying. Anyway, this pig at the nick said I mustn't worry. He said they will find a nice foster home for me if they can. I said I'm not bothered and everything, because I knew you would come and get me and bring me home.'

'All's well that ends well. Here you are.'

'But Amy's not here. I mean, I am going to tell the bitch off for having a boyfriend and everything and put it in my report, but first you will have to bring her home. Don't laugh again, innit. She is sat in the nick now, knowing you will come and get her, just like I knew you'd fetch me. Except I had to get a lift because your car isn't on the drive and you've been drinking again, innit. Bring her home, Nath. Bring her home.'

Chapter Fourteen

Nathan slept through the night until just before nine o'clock on Monday morning, before making phone calls. He dressed without showering or brushing his teeth; his injuries hurt too much. He gently rinsed with mouthwash and hot saltwater and headed out as the Uber arrived. At Cosham police station, he sat on the carpark wall.

A Porsche Cayenne pulled into the space reserved for the Police Commissioner. Arthur Finch, the criminal lawyer who had represented Nathan to the police enquiries following the shooting of the three Romanian gangsters, jumped out of the driver's seat, and grabbed Nathan's hand to shake.

'Shit mate! What happened to you?'

'Hey Art. Thanks for responding so quickly. I walked into a door.'

'The office said you are paying me directly as a private client. Wow, moneybags, let's see if we can't keep this to a half-day. I will discount the travel and expenses if you buy lunch.'

The two men entered the police station reception and Nathan asked to speak with Vicky. The three then continued the conversation in an adjacent quiet room.

'Vicky, you know I don't mess around. We need just five minutes with the inspector and DCI, or all your hard work will explode in your face in front of the national press.'

'That sounds like a threat, Nathan. Rein it in and I will ask. But no promises. Do you want a word with your client, Amy Hart, Mr Finch?'

Arthur glanced at his watch. 'Amy Hart? Mrs Hart isn't my client, sergeant. That would be a conflict of interests in this case. I would like a quick word with my client Robert Kitty, please.'

'Kitty is at Portsmouth Central police station, Mr Finch. And, um, since when is Kitty your client?'

'You haven't been informed yet, sergeant? Can't get the staff nowadays, honestly.' Arthur rolled his eyes for effect. 'May I have a quick telecon with Mr Kitty, please?'

Vicky dialled the phone fixed to the wall.

'In private with my client, sergeant, if that is ok with you, please.'

Vicky widened her eyes in indignation at Nathan, before leaving the room and leaning back against the glass half panel from outside.

'Mr Kitty? Are you alone? I am your solicitor, Arthur Finch. I have Nathan Hart sat with me. Sorry this initial consultation is by phone; I am at Cosham police station and hear you are in Southsea. Anyway, not to worry.'

'I thought they had given me a brief.'

'Obviously up to you, Mr Kitty. But I understand Amy and Nathan Hart are picking up my tab. But I represent you, in this matter. Mr Hart has briefed me of his understanding of the circumstances around your arrest, and I shall read the police report and charge sheet just as soon as I can get down there. Until then *no comment* please Mr Kitty, there's a good chap. Mr Kitty, I have Nathan Hart here, wanting to ask you a question. Are you ok with that? Mr Hart is anxious about the arrest of your friend, that is his wife, Amy Hart, you see. Then Mr Hart will leave the room to enable us to consult again in private. Seem like a good plan?'

'Nathan, what do you want? Is Amy ok? Is she still under arrest?'

'Yes Bert, Amy is still under arrest, so I guess she is far from ok. Depending on the shit you get done for, she is looking at a prison sentence, thanks to you.'

'There is no point in my apologising again, Nathan. But I really am desperately ...'

'Stop whining Bert and listen. You must give them the name of your contact for the child trafficking.'

'I know Nathan. This is such a mess.'

'So, you can tell me, or ...'

'Gentlemen! I am just popping to the loo. I will be two minutes. Please discuss nothing material. Good chaps.' Arthur left the room.

'Tell me the contact, now. If you do, I can get you out on bail today and you will face the absolute minimum charge which Arthur Finch can negotiate. Perhaps a charge of taking away and keeping a minor with their consent. We are looking at suspended sentence, or possibly even a caution, depending on what has now happened to the lads you had. And Amy will not be involved. Specialist interviewers will get it out of you anyway and they will use that information to throw the book at you and Amy. Child trafficking is a hugely serious crime, Bert. The specialist interviewers will eat you up and spit you out. Tell me the fucking name and what you know. Then shut up until Arthur Finch gets down to Southsea nick. Oh, and by the way, I can see Arthur has finished taking a *leg* and is stood in reception chatting to the sergeant who arrested you. You have seconds to spill the beans, Bert. Save yourself and Amy. Tell me what you know, now.'

'Sergeant, Inspector, and Detective Chief Inspector, it is most kind of you to find the time to see me and my friend Nathan Hart.'

'Not a problem, Mr Finch. But we are all busy with your client Mr Kitty and others. I am going to ask you to come straight to the point, please.'

'Of course, Chief Inspector. You already know how helpful Mr Hart has been to this investigation. Firstly, he shortlisted four suspects in his role as intelligence collator and data analyst. Then he located a kidnapped young man who, it turns out, is probably a victim of the same criminals you are seeking in connection with the murders of the two children washed-up under Southsea Pier.'

'Mr Finch, we are all aware of Mr Hart's contributions – both positive contributions and negative. I am sure we are here to discuss something else. Sergeant Vicky Flemming called this unusual meeting because she ... feared ... you may have concerns around the robustness of the arrests.'

'Indeed, that is the case, Chief Inspector. I was discussing the case with Mr Hart, who kindly brought me in to represent Mr Kitty. He pointed to anomalies, which will undermine the evidence used to arrest all five suspects. If you were to pursue charges against my client, and I imagine the other four defendants, I suspect the Crown Prosecution Service will reject your application.'

'Very public spirited of you, Mr Finch. But I suggest you leave the prosecution to us and concentrate on representing your client. Now, if there is nothing else?'

'Sir. I am sorry to interrupt. If Nathan Hart has anything to add, I strongly suggest we listen to him. He has a knack of ...'

'Being a troublemaker, sergeant?'

'Yes, sir.'

'Nathan, let's hear your concerns so we can all get back to work. We have a busy day ahead.'

Nathan walked to the window and stared down at the carpark. 'Yes sir. I would like that. I have an important meeting following this one, and the attendee has just arrived.'

Vicky joined Nathan at the window to see a woman lent back against her Mercedes, tapping on her phone.

Nathan's phone pinged, but he did not read the message.

Nathan continued. 'Philippa Ronki has driven all the way from ITV London to interview me about the situation in which I find myself. You will recognise Ms Ronki as the investigative journalist from the Eve story. She crucified the Metropolitan Police for their handling of the case. She made quite a name for herself. I can tell her a small amount of information within the acceptable limits of my role with Hampshire Police. Or I can whistle-blow and tell her how Sergeant Vicky Flemming and I had an affair a few years back. How Flemming then used her influence with Inspector Dunbar to bring me onto this case. Flemming realised my wife was also having an affair with another suspect, Robert Kitty. Using that knowledge, Inspector Dunbar approved my being sent to intimidate my wife's lover. The term Flemming used was *shake him up*. It worked – I interviewed and at one stage assaulted Mr Kitty, having found sex toys belonging to my wife, during an illegal search of Mr Kitty's home.

'Although I was assaulted on church property, Inspector Dunbar and Sergeant Flemming then sent me to interview the ministers of the church. I later returned to the church, intimidated the two ministers, and illegally searched the premises for a missing man then thought to be unrelated to this murder case. Flemming and Dunbar used their influence to avoid my arrest for those crimes, so I could return to the church yesterday and continue my illegal search.

'All this time I fed my wife intelligence to avoid arrest, which she subsequently passed to her lover, Mr Kitty.

'Ms Ronki will be as interested in these revelations as will the CPS, no doubt.'

'You shit, Nathan!'

Nathan turned to Vicky and shrugged.

'People! All calm down. Sergeant, that is an order.'

'Yes Chief. Sorry, sir.' She spat out the words.

'Mr Hart, I suspect you have a solution to this situation.'

'I do, sir. We all know Amy and Kitty are good people who care about the kids in their care. I know this, you know this, and I am sure Ms Ronki and her viewers will realise this. I suggest you de-arrest Amy, in the absence of any hard evidence that she colluded with Kitty. They are lovers, not a crime syndicate. I suggest you caution and interview Kitty for taking away a minor, with their consent, and taking away a child in care, also with their consent. You don't apply to extend questioning and you bail him pending further investigation.'

'This is bullshit, Bernie. We can't say if the lads were minors, or that he took them without duress. They may have included Luke and Levi, for all we know. We know one lad has the same build as Levi.'

'Then you need to find evidence to support that hypothesis, Ted. You can't arrest someone for murder just because you can't prove he didn't murder someone. And I can give you the tall lad who stayed with Kitty, who you suspect may be Levi.'

'You can *give us him.* What does that even mean, Nath?'

'As I said, Vicky. I can give you one lad who stayed with Kitty. At this stage I can arrange a Skype call, only. I can positively identify him, and confirm he was, is, a child in care who Kitty also hid. As can Amy confirm, Jax Jade his previous foster carer, and I am guessing DC Neil Morton from the Willow exploitation team. My guess is the lad will corroborate Kitty's version of events. If you talk to the CPS and home office and suggest it is not in the public interest to refuse him leave to stay indefinitely, or to deport him following his previous *abscondment*, I will bring the lad in for questioning under caution. Kitty will have a *victim* to corroborate his version of events, whilst you have nothing to rebut Kitty's and the lad's accounts. The lad will also confirm Amy was not present during his stay with Kitty. At the end of the day, sir, Kitty has only tried, foolishly, to help a few asylum seekers to stay safe.'

The DCI spoke again. 'Sorry Mr Hart; not enough. The best way for any innocents to be taken out of the frame is for our diligent enquiries to identify the actual perpetrators.'

'And how's that going sir? Ok, I can also give you the name of the traffickers and eyewitness accounts. I can't say they murdered the boys, but I can tell you who is trafficking the children.'

The police officers glanced at each other, the inspector and sergeant both nodded to the DCI.

'You can give us a reliable and corroborated account of those involved in the trafficking, which may have led to the murders? Ok Mr Hart. Following this line of enquiry, we de-arrest Mrs Hart and we bail Mr Kitty pending the thorough investigations of him taking away a child in care. If any of your … assistance … does not withstand scrutiny, we will be down on Kitty like a ton of bricks.'

'Be my guest, sir, so long as I have Amy home.'

Nathan recounted Kitty's version of the trafficking to Vicky, including identifying Rev Dakari as the key player in bringing the young men to Eamon Nica to process and *disappear* into society. Nathan assured her Kitty would now cooperate fully, if she confirms to him that Eamon Nica was under arrest for kidnapping, assault, and possible attempted murder. Nica was also still under investigation for the trafficking of Vietnamese nationals, by Kent police and Irish Garda. Nathan agreed a time he would arrange for Neuro to skype Vicky and the other professionals, for identification and for him to confirm Kitty's version of events, including Dakari and Eamon's involvement. Amy would be de-arrested early afternoon and they would bail Kitty.

'You threw me under the train in there, Nath. You bastard.'

'I gave you Kitty's testimony and his full and accurate confession for the part he played, which will be corroborated by Neuro. First-hand accounts. And now you have Ryan to testify against Eamon Nica for the first assault on me, and for assaulting Ryan and his subsequent imprisonment. If you do your job properly, Vicky, you will have Eamon for attempted murder as Ryan received no food or water when captive and because weapons were used to assault me. If Ryan confirms Eamon had access to the hidden room, then you have a direct link from Eamon to the murdered boys.'

'Why would Eamon kill the boys?'

'I didn't say he did. He is a career criminal and a people trafficker. Ryan can place him at my assault and possible attempted murder. Why he would kill and mutilate Luke and Levi is less obvious.'

'Why did he assault you in the first place?'

'I thought he was Ryan in the shadows. He thought I was chasing him. My guess is the other shadows were young men being trafficked. He panicked. He would have taken me to the cellar, dead or alive, and disposed of me later. Thankfully, Ryan saved the day. You need to bust this trafficking ring wide open and find those young men.'

'Eamon didn't build the hidden room.'

'No Vicky, he did not. Is forensics showing it as the murder scene?'

'Not yet, Nathan.'

'Once you have Kitty's account, go heavy on Dakari. Use the specialist interviewers. Accuse him of the murders. Beat the shit out of him in cells. You need to go for a confession.'

'You think Dakari killed Luke and Levi? It is an enormous leap from giving some lads a future, to mutilating and murdering them.'

'No, I don't. But you will get nothing from Eamon Nica. Dakari is all we have. Press for murder and see where he settles.'

'Not Rev Dan?'

'Well, he believes in a supernatural God and answers to that higher authority, not to lowly civil decency and humanity. But he is not alone with the whole above the law attitude. Look for a connection between Rev Dan and the hidden room, but we have nothing else to beat him with. Concentrate on Dakari.'

'You were wrong to do that to me back in the office, Nath. You may have ended my hopes of promotion.'

'So, you had better crack this case, then, Vicky.'

'Sorry to keep you waiting, Philippa. There have been a series of arrests around the *boys under the pier* murders.'

'My word, Nathan. What happened to your face?'

'All connected, Philippa.'

'What do you have for me, Nathan?'

'I have incitement to murder, conspiracy, and murder for you, Philippa, if you are interested. Drive me back to the pub opposite my house, please. I have a foster kiddie staying, so I'd rather chat away from home.'

Nathan drank his first pint as he stood at the bar, waiting for his second pint to pour and for the bartender to percolate Philippa's Americano.

'Is this anything to do with Eve, Nathan?'

'I don't know, Philippa. If it is, we might still not prove it.'

'But you are on this case as a civilian?'

Nathan sat back in his chair. 'Well, you know Phil, yes, they took me on as a civilian worker.'

Philippa laughed. 'You are so economical with the truth. You realise I nearly investigated the *Officer H* story?'

Nathan shrugged. 'They have just ended my civilian contract.'

'For?'

'Political correctness gone mad.'

Philippa laughed again.

'Inappropriate use of police resource, threatening two church ministers, threatening Amy's boyfriend, blackmailing a police officer …'

'Enough! Enough, already. Amy has a boyfriend?'

Nathan shrugged again.

'Has or had Nathan?'

'I wish I knew Phil.'

'Why are you telling *me* about these murderers and not telling the police?'

'One potential *perp* has slipped away already. I need to nail the other bastards before they also slip away.'

'What's my part in this?'

'Brandon Beyers. He owns the Sudanese Interior Baptist Church here in Portsmouth.'

'*Owns* a church. Who *owns* a church? Is that even a thing?'

'I will try to syphon off as much intel for you as I can. We need to find him and dig-the-dirt. My guess is, he is involved up to his neck.'

'Involved?'

'You don't have a sacrifice room built into your church without being involved in something.'

'Mm. Something smells nice, Polly. You have really got into this cooking lark.'

'Amy said you like egg fried rice, Nath. She is all arrested for having a boyfriend, so I made you some egg fried rice to cheer you up, innit.'

'She isn't arrested for having a boyfriend, Polly. Anyway, she will be home soon. We will have to save her some egg fried rice. She will be hungry.'

'I might make cheese on toast. This rice is shit.' Polly held up a burnt frying pan, with an inch of charred rice encrusted to the bottom. 'The rice was hard, so I kept cooking it. But it is still hard. So, I gave up.'

'Did you cook the rice first? Boil it?'

Polly shrugged. Nathan continued.

'Well, it smells nice, and that is important when cooking. What happened to the smoke detector?'

'It's broken, Nath. It kept going off when I was cooking the rice. I hit it with a rolling pin. It fixed it from making a noise, but perhaps you should buy a new one.'

Nathan smiled. 'It was getting old, anyway.'

Amy sat on the sofa next to Nathan, folded into his arms.

'You shouldn't have a boyfriend when you are married. And it sets a poor example to us foster kids, innit. I'm putting it in my report.'

'You are not wrong, love. How about you go to your room for an hour and watch your telly? Let me talk to Nathan? Then I will get Nathan to help you cook a nice Monday roast with proper Yorkshire pudding.

Polly rolled her eyes and tutted but left without argument.

'Is Polly safe, Nath? And you and me?'

'Eamon Nica seems to be the heavy. I will feel happier once they charge him. They are holding Nica and the two ministers for 96 hours under caution, for murder.'

'Vicky de-arrested me and drove me home. She is fuming with you. I guess you are no longer a team.'

'Yeah. Guess not.'

'Are they keeping Bert for 96 hours?'

'My understanding is, they will bail him this afternoon without charge, pending further investigation. At the end of the day, Amy, he shouldn't have had hidden Neuro and the lads. Regardless of his motivation. What were you both doing at the church on Sunday night? You were supposed to be safe across the water on Hayling Island.'

'We came over when we saw the blue lights. I was worried about you and Polly. You found Ryan then? Vicky said he was in a bad way.'

'Polly found him, really. Yes, he was dehydrated and peckish. My guess is, he will now testify against Nica for the attack on him and on me. I need to get Neuro onside now.'

'Neuro? Is that wise?'

'I need him to give evidence against Dakari and Nica for trafficking. I also need him to corroborate Kitty's story, to keep you safe from a significant conspiracy prosecution. I am still seriously pissed with you, Amy. It is bad enough you are having an affair, God only knows, but getting involved with children trafficking! Christ, Amy!'

She snuggled harder against his chest.

Amy slept while Polly cooked dinner, under Nathan's supervision. After eating, Nathan insisted the women stay at the table, as he stacked the dishes on the counter, pouring Amy a large white wine and himself a red.

'Ok ladies. You only get ice-cream if you give me your honest opinions. The press reports tell us that two teenage boys, probably malnourished Sudanese who had been in the U.K. or Europe for some time, were murdered, mutilated, and dumped in the Solent -

somewhere between Southsea Pier and Hayling Island. Almost certainly from a boat, not the beach.

'We know the two ministers, and a gangster called Nica, are still in custody in connection with the deaths and possible trafficking. We know Kitty is likely to have been involved at the relatively low end of the trafficking – with Amy to a lesser extent.

'Finally, we know the church, owned by one disappeared Brandon Beyers, has a rather macabre hidden room.

'The two women sat at this table know the three men arrested, to varying degrees. Discuss.'

'I think it is Amy, innit.'

'That is less than helpful, Polly.'

'She has a point, Amy. One nugget of intel the police have is you parked near the hovercraft, but you weren't a passenger.'

'They questioned me on that point. Your friend Vicky and presumably half the investigating team know what happened.'

'Which was?'

'I don't want to talk about it, Nath.'

'See, she has something to hide, Nath.'

'I parked the car there, got a bus to Hayling ferry, and sailed over to the Isle of Wight. And then caught the hovercraft back the next day.'

'Why do that? With your boyfriend? Like a dirty weekend and everything?'

'I am not discussing my sex life with you, Polly. And it wasn't a weekend.'

'See Nath. I said she was guilty. Just guilty of something else.'

'And the police are satisfied with your explanation, Amy?'

'Seemingly so, Nath. I told them the approximate time I caught the Hayling Ferry to meet with Bert, and the time of the hovercraft back the next day. I guess they can check CCTV.'

'Interesting what you said about being guilty of something else, Polly.' Amy sighed and raised her arms in despair. Nathan continued. 'My colleague Gill suggested the same thing. She said I was trying to get all the clues to fit a single crime, just like I had tried to get all my symptoms to fit one illness. If we take Kitty's and your strange behaviour as being caused by having an affair behind my back and under my nose, it leaves our other four suspects in the loop for the murders.'

'Right, that's it. I am not discussing any affairs or my sex life. Move on.'

'I don't trust Rev Dan, innit. Obviously, I don't trust the Eamon Nica guy. I should have caved his head in when I had the chance.'

'You did exactly the right amount of caving, Polly. Why Rev Dan?'

'You wouldn't have him babysit. His eyes are weird, like he thinks you are a lump of meat and everything.'

'That should hold up in court, Polly. But Dakari?'

'I think he is ok. A bit like you, Nath. You know, a bit of a wanker, but not a bad guy.'

'I have to agree with Polly, Nath. You are a bit of a wanker.' The couple managed a thin conspiratorial smile at each other. 'But I think Rev Dan is ok.'

'I have seen both talking to Nica. And I suspect Kitty knows Nica collected his lads. Why did they put up with him? He really is a nasty piece of work.'

'Amy, you are a middle-class woman with a house, a husband, and a boyfriend to protect you. I am a child in care with no one. Perhaps I can smell dangerous people, like I can smell pigs and everything.'

'Perhaps they don't have a choice with Nica. Perhaps they have instructions from above, Nath,' added Amy.

'You mean from their boss who lives in the clouds above Africa, Amy?'

'I was thinking more, the elusive Brandon Beyers who owns the church, provides the manse to live in, and pays their wages.'

'No way would they kill children to earn a bonus.'

'Or both bosses. Perhaps Brandon boss pays them to kill children, and God boss tells them it is ok to kill children. Like in the war, when both sides have a church telling them to kill people from the other church. Like World War One. Maybe also like World War Two and everything, except I stopped going to history lessons before we did World War Two,' added Polly.

The two women looked at Nathan for more questions. He shrugged and sent Polly for ice-cream. Holding both Amy's hands and lowering his voice, he spoke.

'I put in a huge amount of effort to have Kitty's charges reduced. I may have kept him out of prison.' Amy swallowed hard and nodded, not sure if she should thank him. Nathan spoke again. 'I want something in return.' Amy lowered her eyes to study their hands. 'No Amy, not dumping him. You must decide that in your own time. I want you to search your soul as a human being, not as Kitty's lover. How sure are you Kitty could not have killed those boys, trafficked them, or helped dispose of them? How sure are you Kitty knows nothing about their deaths, or how they got into the situation to be killed?'

Amy stared at their hands for a moment, processing the question, before answering.

'One-hundred percent Nathan. I trust him totally. I would trust him with Polly. If I had to choose the most likely person to be a murderer, Bert or you, I would say you.'

Chapter Fifteen

'Hi Gill. Can you invite Ann to a conference call, please?'

Nathan heard her long sigh, followed by a dialling tone.

'Ann? We have the venerable Nathan Hart on the line.'

'Thank you, ladies. I was just wondering if you have any updates, please?'

'Updates of a live investigation for a civilian who is no longer involved?'

Nathan allowed Gill's comment to hang. Eventually, Ann spoke.

'You realise we will have to note this conversation and, under the circumstances, report it to Vicky?'

'I am on the trail of Brandon Beyers. Any information will be helpful.'

'Nathan is like a one-man contract army.' Gill released another sigh. 'Ok. So, the boys were likely murdered in the hidden room. Someone used huge amounts of bleach to clean-up, but not quite enough, seemingly.'

'Any other forensics?'

'They took DNA and/or prints from three unidentified people. They also found matches for you, Ryan, Eamon Nica, Levi and Luke. And guess who else?'

'Our South African terrorist/come evangelical church owner, Brandon Beyers?'

'Yep. And one more.'

'Dakari?'

'Nope. Keep guessing, Nath.'

'Shit! Not Kitty or Amy?'

'Christ Nath! Of course not your own wife. What is up with you? No, Rev Dan.'

'How did he explain that away?'

'No comment.'

'Please Gill, this is important.'

'I mean, he has gone *no comment*. He was being just as cooperative as-you-like until they mentioned his prints and DNA in the room. Then shtum.'

'Can I see the transcripts of his interviews, please?'

'No!' Both women answered together

'Did either minister, or Kitty, mention or know anything about Brandon Beyers?'

Nathan heard Ann tapping on her keyboard before answering.

'Only your Amy admitted she has met him, and only the once. But only that. The ministers admitted they *would* have met him but could not recall any specific meetings. I am currently referencing Border Control and passport information with airline records and the minister's diaries.'

'Great. Are you actively looking for our Brandon Beyers?'

'Yes Nath. The inspector prioritised him at this morning's briefing. Unfortunately, South Africa is less cooperative when searching for their own citizens. Poor old Ted – the DCI has all but moved into Ted's office since your little intervention on Sunday.'

'Are they remanding the three suspects?'

Gill took over answering again. 'The plan is to charge Eamon Nica with the Vietnamese people smuggling incident and keep him on remand. Investigations for people trafficking and the murders of Luke and Levi are ongoing. We have shitloads of reasons to refuse bail. We will release the church ministers on bail, pending further investigations. They will be tagged, and passports confiscated.'

'Eamon Nica will never confess to anything, not even for a reduced sentence. His Irish cronies will negotiate for him to serve much of his sentence in Ireland, under the wing of his mates in the Real IRA. Ted needs to concentrate on the ministers.'

'Agreed Nath. That seems to be the inspector's thinking.'

'Look Gill, it is up to you. But I would ease off reporting this conversation back to Vicky just yet. If I get a breakthrough with Brandon Bryers, I will feed it through you first, so you can hide this conversation under bigger news. I also asked, or rather insisted, my lad Neuro makes contact with you, directly. Concentrate on confirming he was treated well by an altruistic Kitty and ask about Dakari's involvement. Ted and Vicky will be cautious of any information Neuro offers whilst still under my influence and until they can bring him in under caution.'

'Because of your efforts to get your wife's lover off the hook?'

'That is not exactly how I would word it. But yes, whatever.'

Philipa Ronki telephoned an hour later.

'Hey Nathan. My people have been researching your Brendon Beyers. ITV London is sending me and a producer out to South Africa to have a poke about.'

'Goodness Phil, that sounds promising. What has got your juices flowing?'

'He is a definite handful. They have investigated him for right-wing Christian terrorist activities in South Africa, Lesotho, and Botswana. They currently ban Mr Beyers from entering Botswana, even though he still holds business interests there. He has served time for money laundering and was banned from holding directorships in South African companies, although he is now currently legit in SA.'

'You always save the best for last, Phil.'

Philipa laughed. *'You should be a detective, Mr Hart! He served six months for promoting banned Muti practice. They prosecuted him in South Africa, for his Muti practices in both South Africa and Lesotho.'*

'Oh my God, Phil, we have our murderer. Have you made any connections or links with Eve?'

'We are nowhere close to making any connections with Luke, Levi, or Eve. We are yet to find any association with human component practices. His

crimes are around extortion associated with Muti. He took money to arrange Muti witchcraft spells against individuals, which is still a crime in both South Africa and, wait for it, here in the U.K. under witchcraft law. And he extorted money and business favours from individuals to have spells removed.'

'Isn't Muti, Traditional Medicine, and Witchcraft a black African thing? Our Brandon is a snow-white Afrikaner.'

'He is indeed Nath, to the point of white supremacy. But he grew up around Muti on his childhood Volkstaat homestead and embraced it along with evangelical Christianity.'

'Our white supremacist appears to employ two black ministers. How are we making that fit?'

'He has no problems with employing black people. Everybody should have one.'

'Philipa, is a black woman the right *type* of person to go looking for this sicko? What if you find him?'

'My producer is ex-special forces.'

'Even so Phil. Please be careful. Call me as soon as you land, and I will update you on anything that has happened here. Something is happening downstairs. I had better go.'

Nathan walked into the living room to be confronted by two uniformed police constables, Polly's social worker, a second woman, Amy, and Polly.

'Polly, put on your dressing gown.'

'Don't you start, Nath. Leave me alone.'

'I have already told her Nathan …'

Nathan held up a hand for silence.

'Polly, this is non-negotiable. Dressing gown or get dressed.'

Polly scowled at Nathan, calculating her next move. Eventually, she shrugged and smiled.

'Sure, whatever Nath.'

The group watched her leave the room. Amy introduced everyone to Nathan. The second woman spoke.

'I am Polly's appointed Personal Advisor.' She gestured between the social worker and herself. 'We are looking to move Polly into assisted living from soon after her eighteenth birthday. Polly is currently with you under police protection. Despite her colourful stay with you, we would like, and Polly insists, she stays with you until the move. Mrs Hart has already agreed.' Nathan nodded in agreement and the PA continued. 'Polly has another *requirement*. We have accommodation around the city, but she insists on staying in the facility close to you, on the Havant Road in Cosham. She wants to stay here at yours until a bedsit becomes available there, even if that takes a few weeks or months.'

Nathan glanced at Amy, who was nodding with a grin. Nathan answered.

'That makes sense. We can monitor her in the early days, and she can call in, should she feel lonely or overwhelmed.'

Amy grinned wider. 'Go on, tell him. I love to watch a grown man cry.'

The PA grinned back at Amy and continued. 'Polly wants to stay close to monitor you and Amy. She is worried about how you will cope when she leaves.'

Nathan threw back his head laughing, pushing his hands into his eyes to stem the tears. Amy hugged him tightly.

'Come here, you old softy.'

Polly walked back in, now dressed. 'What's up Nath, innit? Do I need to find a fire extinguisher and chase this lot out?'

Laughing again, Nathan drew a reluctant Polly into a three-way hug.

The rest of the day dragged for Nathan as thoughts spun around his head. They were on the home straight, but the finish line stayed worryingly out of sight. Nathan was halfway through his second bottle of wine before he eventually fell asleep in front of the television. Amy woke him as she headed for bed, leading him up the stairs.

'Shall I take your mind off it, Nath?'

Nathan smiled in the darkness, pulling Amy to his chest.

'Sorry love, rain check. I hear you met with the church owner, Brendon Beyers.'

'Is your tart Vicky relaying all this to you? Isn't there some sort of confidentiality around my interviews?' Nathan did not answer. Amy continued. 'I met him once. I did not meet *with* him. Rev Dan introduced him to the congregation during a service. We chatted outside for ten minutes whilst I waited for … waited to leave. He is quite a charismatic man.'

'Did Bert Kitty meet him?'

'Not that I am aware.'

'Was he involved with the homeless accommodation?'

'No idea, Nath.'

'It never ceases to amaze me how our foster kids are such perceptive judges of character.'

'They are Nath.'

'Polly really isn't impressed with Rev Dan, is she? She seems less creeped-out by Dakari.'

'I find Dakari quite confrontational, Nath. A bit like you. I probably get on better with Rev Dan. He is more … conciliatory.'

'More like Bert?'

'Stop it, love. Don't let it eat you up.' She hugged his chest closer.

'I'm going to take Polly's view.'

'There's a surprise. Please tell me you are not going near the ministers again, Nath.'

'Why not?'

'Are you even allowed? And so far, you have been beaten up twice at the church and narrowly avoided arrest for intimidation.'

'I am not on bail. I can go where I want.'

'What will you do? Trick them into a confession?'

'You know what, Amy? That sounds like a plan.'

Nathan phoned early on the Wednesday morning. 'Dakari, how are you enjoying your regained freedom?'

'Nathan Hart. Of all the *welcome homes* I may have received, I did not envisage one from yourself.'

'I am looking to pop round and speak with you, Dakari. I have a friend in South Africa who is tracking down your boss, Brendon Beyers. You might like an update.'

'Not really Nathan. A most kind offer, but I am a tad tired. Another time perhaps.'

'I would prefer today. Don't worry if you doze off – I will keep hammering on your door until you wake.'

The line fell silent for a moment before Dakari responded. 'Should I talk to my solicitor about harassment and a restraining order, do you think?'

'You can certainly try, Dakari, but I doubt you will have grounds. I am only checking up on you. You were at mine for dinner recently. I am not sure why you would want a restraining order against me.'

Another silence followed. 'Ok Nathan. But you need to keep it short. I really am exhausted.'

Dakari had aged. He wore tracksuit bottoms to cover his electronic tag.

'It is tiring and much more stressful than you might think.'

'It is Nathan. And knowing I am innocent of most of the charges is only slightly comforting. Whatever happens now, my career in the ministry is over.'

'Because of the child trafficking?'

'An ugly term, Nathan. You help young people who have nowhere else to turn, as do I. You put their needs above the law, as do I. You even break the law occasionally, as do I. We are not so different.'

'I do not traffic children into the hands of organised crime, and scum like Eamon Nica.'

Dakari closed his eyes and exhaled. 'And neither do I.'

Nathan waited for him to continue. When he remained silent, Nathan prompted him. 'So, what is your business model, Dakari? What is the godly way to traffic some of the world's most vulnerable young men?'

Dakari pulled himself out of his chair and retrieved a half empty bottle of whiskey from the cabinet under the television. He glugged a large slug into a tumbler before tilting the bottle towards Nathan.

'Thank you, Dakari. But nine o'clock in the morning is a little early for me.'

Dakari scoffed. 'Yes Nathan, me too. But it has been a busy couple of days.' He gulped down the neat whiskey, pouring another tumbler before retaking his seat. 'It isn't random, Nathan. We look hard at the young people's background. We consider the reasons U.K. authorities will not offer asylum. We are not looking to bring criminals into the country. If we think they are a deserving case, we contact our friend Eamon Nica. We pay him a set amount and maintain contact with the young people for as long as possible to ensure he does not pressure them for money or other *services*.'

'And who fronts the money?'

'The young people pledge to pay back the cost in the future, once they are settled, finished education, and can afford to. We are not into usury, Nathan.'

'And you have received such payments?'

'No. Not yet. They will come one day.'

'I asked who fronts the money, Dakari?'

'The church,' shrugged Dakari.

'Brendon Beyers?'

'I will not deny it to you, Nathan. But I will deny it to the police.'

'What is his motivation?'

'He can afford it, apparently.' Dakari studied Nathan's frown. 'His politics are not mine, Nathan, but he facilitates our work.'

'*We* and *our* being you and Rev Dan?'

'Goodness no.'

'Kitty?'

'You are making me uncomfortable, Nathan.'

The two men stared at each other for some time. 'Brendon practices Muti traditional medicine and witchcraft. We are on to him, Dakari.'

'If you say so, Nathan.'

'I do. And I say he uses spells requiring human components.'

Dakari held Nathan's gaze.

'I don't believe you can know that, Nathan.'

'Why do you think Luke and Levi washed up with heads and limbs missing?'

'I know what you are getting at, Nathan. But I am not speculating.'

'And where does Brendon Beyers find his victims?'

'I know nothing about Muti, Nathan. I need you to leave now, please.'

'My Polly thinks you are a decent chap, Dakari. Should I trust her instincts?'

'I might need a character witness, Nathan. I might ask for Polly.'

Collecting the bottle of whiskey, Dakari left the room and headed upstairs, leaving Nathan to let himself out.

Chapter Sixteen

The sky darkened, and the wind picked up in the time Nathan had spent in Dakari's manse. The forecast storm surged in from the Atlantic and even inland Langstone Harbour looked menacing. Nathan walked to the adjoining manse and rapped on Rev Dan's door. Rain fell against Nathan as he continued to knock, eventually heading for the Marina Lounge bar. Still too early for alcohol, Nathan ordered an Americano and a pastry. He sat looking out across the church carpark towards the manse, waiting for signs of Rev Dan.

Nathan watched a police car stop outside the manse. Officers first knocked at the front door, before walking around the outside and peering into windows. Nathan phoned Vicky.

'Hey Vic. What has happened to Rev Dan?'

'Christ, Nath, how do you do this shit? And sorry, love, none of your business.'

'Ok Vicky. Understood. You know about Brendon Beyers. A breakthrough, don't you think?'

'What? What about Brendon Beyers?'

'You haven't heard? Sorry, love, none of my business.'

'Don't be a prick, Nathan. What do you know?'

'About Rev Dan? Nothing. Nothing at all.'

Vicky waited for him to expand on Brendon Beyers. Nathan waited for her to expand on Rev Dan. Nathan slurped noisily on his coffee and took a bite on his pastry, chewing into the phone. Vicky sighed.

'Ok. You first.'

'I have people on the ground in South Africa and Lesotho.'

'People on the ground? What does that even mean?'

'Brendon Beyers has served time for Muti.'

'You are bloody kidding me. Why didn't the SA police tell us that?'

'Perhaps you didn't ask the right questions. There is something else, but you were going to tell me about Rev Dan. Has he been a naughty boy?'

'It looks like he has cut off his electronic ankle tag.'

'And buggered off?'

'Presumably so, Nath. Or maybe it is just on the blink.'

'Perhaps he is lying dead in a pool of his own blood.'

'Have you done something to him?'

Nathan laughed. 'You have an awfully low opinion of me, Vicky. I am just suggesting you have every reason to ask your uniforms to force the door or ask next door for a key. Just saying.'

The phone muted for a few moments. Nathan watched the officers talk into their radios and head for Dakari's adjacent house to ask for a spare key.

'What else have you?'

'Brendon Beyers is funding the trafficking of Dakari's young men.'

'And the significance of that?'

Nathan shrugged to himself. 'Perhaps he kept a couple back for his own purposes.' Nathan watched the officers gain entry to Rev Dan's manse. One officer left the manse holding a sealed evidence bag. 'And I have some more news for you. You owe me one, Vicky.'

'Go on.'

'Rev Dan removed his tag with bolt cutters and is awol.'

Nathan watched the officer talk into her radio.

'You smug shit, Nath. You need to get in here, now. I want a word.'

Nathan swiped open his Uber app before walking in a loop around the church, to the tinny boat, ferry slip, and back to the Marina Lounge just as his taxi arrived. Now soaking wet, wearing just a jumper over his T-shirt, he asked the driver to take him to Southsea Pier.

'Minister.'

'Mr Hart.'

Nathan sat next to Rev Dan on a bench facing out to sea, on the pierhead.

'You will catch your death, Mr Hart. Where's your coat?'

'This rain has caught me out, Dan. Please call me Nath.'

The pair watched teenage kite-surfers, dressed in wetsuits and minus the kites and boards, tomb-stoning into the angry sea to power back to shore and run the length of the pier, encouraging their friends to take the plunge.

'My people in South Africa have eyes on Brendon Beyers, Dan.'

Rev Dan nodded. 'Look at that, Nath. The youth. The energy. Would you bottle it, Nath, if you could? Would you bottle it?'

Nathan ignored the question, watching another teenager dive feet first into the swell below.

'Is that what you do, Dan? You take youth from the children to benefit others?'

'You are a non-believer, Nath; you wouldn't understand. And I am too tired to explain, right at this moment.'

'Brendon Beyers supplied you with Luke and Levi, to provide Muti body parts. Did Dakari know their fate?' Nathan moved his phone to a dryer T-shirt breast pocket, under his jumper.

'No Nath. He did not. He moved the boys to Eamon Nica. Nica presented them to me as per Brendon Beyers' instruction. Shackled in the cellar.'

'Who benefited?'

'From the Muti? Brendon Beyers benefited. He had hit rock bottom. With prayers for him every Sunday, including from your wife Amy, and the Muti as well, his fortunes are recovering.'

'*Were* recovering. And the recovery is because of prayers and Muti? Not just a coincidence, and other factors?'

'You are so cynical, Nath. You can see the benefits of faith around you, but even so, you cannot look.'

'And Eve?'

'Eve, Nath? Who is Eve?'

'The mutilated girl in the Thames ten years ago. What do you know about Eve?'

'Patrice Pomwosa is her name. You know this. I phoned Crimestoppers and told you. Her name is Patrice Pomwosa. A Muti practitioner named Queensley Aja from the Netherlands performed the Muti.'

'You told Crimestoppers? When?'

'I am not sure, Nath. Maybe five years ago. Brendan Beyers told me about the case. We all have moments of doubt, Nath. During one of my moments, I phoned Crimestoppers and gave them het name. Anonymously, of course. Brendon and Queensley are related to each other. Even with my unwavering faith, I still have urges to share my burden – as I am with you now.'

Nathan dropped his head to his chest. The rain now lashed down. The surfers moved to the shelter of a canopy over a closed ice-cream stall.

'Thank you for your candour but from where I am sitting, Dan, you look weak and pathetic. Who dumped the boys in the sea?

'The boys had already left their mortal husks, Nathan. You really are ignorant, aren't you? Nica released their bodies into the sea from our little tinny tender. I helped carry the remains to the boat, Minister Dakari was not involved.

'And Kitty?'

'Involved in the Muti? Of course not. He is a nonbeliever in everything he cannot touch. He is like you. You think I am pathetic? It is nonbelieving hedonists like you and Kitty who are pathetic. You understand only flesh and blood, nothing higher. The rumour is you both enjoy your wife's flesh. And you think you are better than me, Nath? You are little more that animals.'

'What is in the rucksack, Dan?'

'All I need for my journey. I wanted to apologise to Luke and Levi before I move on; pay my respects. I should have realised you would look here for me. But you won't stop me, Nathan; you are not great enough. I did what was necessary and I do not regret it, but I realise people suffered along the way. Shall we?'

Rev Dan produced two white lily flowers, now bruised and sagging from the downpour. The men stepped through the open railing gate, which the teenagers had used for access, and leant back against the railing in the wind. Rev Dan spoke again.

'Shall we pray, Nathan? Pray for Luke and Levi?'

'Go fuck yourself, Dan.'

'As you wish, Nath.'

Rev Dan mumbled a prayer into the wind and attempted to sing a verse of Eternal Father Strong to Save as the wind stole his breath. He took a step forward and released the lily flowers. As they tumbled and swirled towards the frothing sea, he took another step and disappeared over the edge of the pier.

Nathan shouted and grabbed at the empty space where Rev Dan had stood. Without a moment's hesitation and in the absence of a plan, Nathan dived feet first, following Rev Dan into the increasing swell and storm waves. Rev Dan's body twisted, weighed down by his rucksack, and back flopped into the sea, his legs jack-knifed. Nathan saw him disappear under the opaque waves moments before he entered the water at the same point as Rev Dan.

At a sharper angle and feet first, Nathan dived under the water and immediately collided with Rev Dan. Wrapping his legs around Rev Dan's legs, Nathan grabbed at the other's torso, gripping the rucksack straps. Nathan closed his eyes against the black seawater, his sinuses and ears exploding in pain with the pressure. Unable to release any carbon dioxide building in his lungs, he silently screamed, releasing a few bubbles. Seawater forced its way into his throat, nose, and down into his stomach and lungs.

The sea current ripped at Nathan's hold as he fought to keep grip; the pair anchored to the seabed by the weight of the rucksack. Nathan's legs pulled away from Rev Dan's. Now floating upside down and gripping the strap with his right hand, Nathan fought to loosen the buckle on the chest strap. A surge caught Nathan's body. He lost hold as he felt the buckle release and the chest strap loosen.

The sea carried Nathan, still upside down, slamming him into the pier structure, the barnacle encrusted and rusting ironwork ripping at his head and back. As the sea pulled him away, Nathan's body rightened, before slamming back against the structure, forcing out the last dregs of wet, salty air from his lungs. Even if Nathan knew where the surface was, he no longer had the capacity and strength to push towards it. He floated in neutral buoyancy for a moment, waiting for the next surge to slam him against the pier and squeeze out the remainder of his life.

One hand grabbed his hair and another under his chin, yanking his head above the surface and into the now raging storm.

'Breathe! Breathe you idiot!'

The male voice screamed into Nathan's ear above the wind and the waves crashing into the pier head. The arms dropped to around Nathan's chest and violently thrust in a Heimlich manoeuvre. As warm seawater and vomit flooded from Nathan's nose and mouth, so Nathan and his rescuer dipped under the surface. Bobbing back to the surface again, both took a deep and spluttering breath. Two more people grabbed at Nathan. A female screamed as all four washed against the pier again. With Nathan laying back against the first male, the other two pushed the human raft to the side of the pier as the next surge surfed them towards the beach. As Nathan struggled to turn over onto his stomach, the three continued to fight Nathan and the storm. The next surge toppled the four, Nathan landing face first under the water and smacking his face against a floor of pebbles.

He clawed at the pebbles, submerged, to prevent the sea from carrying him away. The sea retreated, leaving Nathan and the pebbles exposed to the air. Before the next surge hit them again, hands grabbed Nathan and pulled him up the shingle. Two more surges knocked them from their feet until they stumbled onto the beach and onlookers rushed to pull Nathan and his rescue party to safety.

Chapter Seventeen

Nathan lay in the back of the speeding ambulance, an IV bag fitted, and an oxygen mask clamped to his face. A paramedic worked on Dakari, who lay on a second trolley, shoehorned into the Ambulance. The paramedic shouted to the driver, who stopped the ambulance in the middle of the road to assist with Dakari. The back doors opened, and another paramedic climbed in to assist. A moment later, they took Dakari from the ambulance and into a second vehicle, which sped away under police escort.

The first paramedic climbed back into the ambulance, collapsing onto the floor with her head back against the side. With sirens blaring and blue lights flashing around the stationary ambulance, Vicky then climbed in, sitting on a seat by Nathan's head. The ambulance pulled away, blues flashing, but sirens silenced.

'Your friend is being taken ahead of us, Mr Hart. Once stabilised, they will transport him to Southampton by helicopter. He is in expert hands. Let's concentrate on getting you to the hospital now.'

Nathan nodded to the exhausted paramedic. Vicky spoke.

'You prize dick, Nathan.'

'I am fine Vic, thanks for asking. Are all the surfers safe?'

The driver called back. 'All the surfers who entered the water are being ferried to the QA Hospital to check them over and observe for secondary drowning. But no reports of anything critical. You and your friend are lucky, very lucky, that those brave kids were there, Mr Hart.'

'Yeah. I feel lucky,' croaked Nathan.

Polly and Amy were the first allowed into the hospital room once the medics had settled Nathan.

'Blimey Nath, you look like shit, innit.'

'Thanks Polly. That is very kind of you to say so. It's really kind of you to visit me Polly, but I do need five minutes alone with Amy, please.'

'Why? Because I'm not really family?'

'Of course you are family. It is not that, Polly.'

'Well then, I am staying. I can't let you out of my sight. If I leave you for five minutes, you will probably have Ghostface sneak in and kill you.'

Amy sat on Nathan's bed, crossing her legs.

'It looks sore, love.'

Nathan smiled a reply.

'They are worried about the seawater sloshing around in my lungs. I am on mega antibiotics. Otherwise, I am fine.'

'But you aren't love, are you? Your flesh is hanging in strips.'

'It is not as bad as it looks, Amy. Look, love, I have some information.'

'Information? You need information like I need air. And like I need a husband not trying to fight the world all the time.'

Polly yawned with boredom, pulling the television around to face the comfy patient's chair. She had brought Nathan a sandwich bag of cheese on toast, which she now ate. Vicky entered the room, leaning against the back wall. Nathan continued to talk with Amy.

'It's about Eve, love.'

'Eve? What about Eve?'

'Her name is Patrice Pomwosa.'

Nathan flinched as Amy hugged him around his neck. Tears streamed down both their faces. Gulping back sobs, Amy released her grip, wiping her wet face with the palms of her hands, and then gently dabbing a tissue to Nathan's torn, bruised, and tear-streaked cheeks.

'We can have her headstone finished, Nath, inscribed with her name.'

Nathan nodded a reply, not trusting his ability to stop sobbing if he tried to speak. Following a halting sigh, he changed the subject. 'Dakari has suggested Kitty may have been more involved than previously stated, but also confirmed he was not involved in the murders. I don't know how it will go for him.'

'Can I warn Bert to be … you know? Be on his guard.'

'Your conscience, Amy. Your friend. Your decision. Avoid perverting the course of justice. Maybe just tell him to find a good lawyer. Someone like Arthur Finch.'

'Can we help with the cost?'

Nathan snorted.

Vicky cleared her throat. Amy turned to glare at her, and then back at her husband. Nathan waved a hand to beckon over Vicky.

'Nathan. We will need a full statement.'

'We need to do it under caution, Vic. Keep Ted posted. I am a material witness to Rev Dan's confession. We have done this. The investigation is complete.'

'What happened? Did you threaten and then push Rev Dan into the sea?'

'Of course not, Vicky. He opened-up to me and confessed.'

'Confessed to what, exactly? I hope you haven't led or threatened a suspect, Nath.'

'Not at all. It all started with Gill telling me not to make the clues fit the crime. Like my headaches, smell hallucinations, and problems with my vision, all having more than one cause. There was more than one crime going on at the same time. They crossed over, admittedly, but different crimes by different perpetrators.

'Amy was aware Kitty had a boy staying without social services knowing. Equally, how was Amy to know he wasn't a young adult? Kitty thought he was helping Dakari keep young people from deportation to unsafe countries. If he didn't act so guilty in front of his lover's husband, he probably would have stayed under the radar.'

Amy lowered her eyes as Polly tutted loudly. Nathan continued.

'Dakari may have been well intentioned, but dispersing vulnerable young people around the country with the likes of Eamon Nica and Brendon Beyers was, at the very least, hugely reckless. If the police and social services cannot keep these youngsters safe, how on earth did Dakari think he could do it single-handed?

'We need to look at conspiracy for Dakari. If he intentionally handed vulnerable kids to Beyers and Nica, and two or more of those kids ended up murdered, then ignorance is no defence.

'Nica is absolutely in the frame for murder. He procured and imprisoned at least two teenagers so that they could be murdered. Beyers paid for those kids to be procured and imprisoned and then ordered those murders.

'And finally, we have Rev Dan. Regardless of his blind belief in the supernatural, he willingly murdered at least two children. His blind belief in an old book, a non-existent God, witchcraft and Muti, might get him in to heaven, but won't wash down here – on his new hell on earth. I hope his fellow prisoners kick the shit out of him daily for the rest of his pathetic existence.'

Amy laid a hand on Nathan's and gestured towards Polly, as Polly concentrated on his every word. Nathan continued.

'But the hero of this story is Polly. She saved me from worse than just a beating, twice. She found Ryan, and she was the only person who saw past Rev Dan's twisted dog collar.'

'But we only have one opinionated, slightly toxic, sacked twice, washed-up ex-copper as a main, and sole witness, to Rev Dan's confession.'

'Thank you, Vicky, for those kind words. First, he won't lie under oath, so you need to get him to court. Second,' Nathan gestured to the table of belongings, asking Polly to pass his phone, 'I recorded his confession. Pop the phone in a bag of rice and get it over to *tech*. Don't power-up, leave it to them.

'Philippa Ronki is all over our Brendon Beyers like a rash. Ted needs to direct a team of detectives to work with her and then liaise with the South Africans. You need to extract Luke and Levi's proper names from Rev Dan, and cross reference with Dakari and maybe Kitty. You need to visit their families.'

Polly rolled her eyes. 'And you two need to sort your shit. I can only keep an eye on you for a few more weeks, then I must move on with my life, innit.'

Printed in Great Britain
by Amazon